BOOKS BY

Carrie Carr

====================

Destiny's Bridge

Faith's Crossing

Hope's Path

Love's Journey

Strength of the Heart

The Way Things Should Be

To Hold Forever

Something to Be Thankful For

Diving Into the Turn

Piperton

Trust Our Tomorrows

Carrie Carr

Yellow Rose Books

Nederland, Texas

Copyright © 2012 by Carrie Carr

All rights reserved. No part of this publication may be reproduced, transmitted in any form or by any means, electronic or mechanical, including photocopy, recording, or any information storage and retrieval system, without permission in writing from the publisher. The characters, incidents and dialogue herein are fictional and any resemblance to actual events or persons, living or dead, is purely coincidental.

ISBN 978-1-61929-011-2

First Printing 2012

9 8 7 6 5 4 3 2 1

Cover design by Donna Pawlowski

Published by:

Regal Crest Enterprises, LLC
3520 Avenue H
Nederland, Texas 77627

Find us on the World Wide Web at
http://www.regalcrest.biz

Printed in the United States of America

Acknowledgements:

I have to thank my fantastic beta reader, Kelly, who helped make this book much better than I could ever have expected. Thank you to the cover artist extraordinaire, Donna, and last, but not least, Cathy, who took a chance so many years ago on a novice writer – thank you for allowing me to live my dreams.

Dedication

To my mom, who has always loved and supported me, no matter what I wanted to do. And of course, most of all, to my Jan—without her, I'd be lost and alone. Forever and always, my love.

Chapter One

THE ONE-STORY, brick house sat neglected on the tree-lined residential street. Lexington Walters parked in the driveway and got out of her green, Dodge quad cab pickup. Tall and slender, with shoulder-length brown hair, she stared at the overgrown lawn for a moment. Disgusted at its condition, Lex shook her head and navigated through the dry grass and weeds to get to the front door. She rang the bell. After a full minute, she rang it again. When there was still no answer, she pounded on the heavy oak door. "I know you're in there," she yelled. "And I'm not going away until I see you." She continued to beat on the door until it opened a crack.

A golden-brown eye peeked out. "Go away," the weak, feminine voice ordered.

Lex raised her sunglasses until they rested on the top of her head. Her dark blue eyes zeroed in on the woman. "Let me in, Ellie."

"No. Just leave me alone," Eleanor Gordon said quietly. "Please."

"I can't do that. You've hidden away in this old house long enough. It's time for you to rejoin the living."

The door opened wide enough to allow Lex to enter. Her nose wrinkled at the stale odor that permeated the home. She followed Ellie through the entry hall, which opened into the living room. What she saw broke her heart.

The sofa and loveseat were covered in mountains of discarded blankets, clothes and newspapers. Two end tables and a coffee table were laden with dirty dishes, most with barely-touched food on them. A dusty floor lamp was the only light source in the room, as it stood sentinel over a conspicuously empty recliner.

Ellie shoved a pile of junk from a corner of the sofa. She sat and covered herself with a ratty quilt, her bare feet peeking from underneath. "What do you want?"

Lex leaned her hip against the other end of the sofa. "I want you to quit hiding away from your family. Come back to the ranch with me."

"I." Ellie lowered her face until it was covered with her stringy, unkempt hair. The brown strands hung in greasy clumps past her shoulders, which were bony from malnutrition. "I can't."

"Damn it, Ellie! He's been gone for six months. We all miss him, but we've kept on living."

"Don't you think I've tried?" Ellie threw off the quilt. "But I have nothing left." She lowered her face to her hands and cried.

Travis Edwards was the one constant in Ellie's life. Ten years prior, Ellie arrived on his doorstep after finding a photo of her mother with her biological father. Travis welcomed her into his home, and his life, and gave her the love and security she never had with her mother. Grandfather to both her and Lex, he had given Ellie the confidence to complete nursing school not long after she moved in with him. Up until his untimely death from cancer, Ellie had worked as a nurse in the Somerville Assisted Living Center.

After he died, Ellie locked herself away in the house they shared, sending out for whatever she needed. She only left the house to walk to the curb and pick up the newspaper and mail. "Go home, Lex. You have a family to take care of."

Her temper got the best of her and Lex took handfuls of junk from the sofa and tossed it across the room, until it was completely clear. She sat next to her cousin. "You're a very big part of our family, Ellie. The girls keep asking about you."

Ellie raised her head and wiped her face with the back of one hand. "Why?"

"Good god, El. Because they love you, you jackass," Lex said. "We all do, whether you like it or not."

"I love them, too. We always had fun when I took them places." Ellie leaned against Lex and started to cry. "I just can't get past this."

Lex pulled Ellie into her arms and held her while she cried. "I know it's hard. I didn't feel like getting out of bed for weeks, but I somehow managed to do it." Lex felt Ellie's hands grip her shirt tightly. "Of course, the girls helped a lot. I rarely got a chance to be alone, which kept me from dwelling on things."

"It doesn't matter anymore," Ellie sniffled as she pulled away from Lex.

"Of course it does. What about your job?"

Ellie used a paper napkin from the nearby pizza joint to wipe her nose. "They called a month after Grandpa," her chin quivered, "you know, and fired me. Said they couldn't wait forever."

"But you told us you were on leave."

"I didn't want you to worry."

Lex sighed. "Are you sure you're not related to the Walters' side of the family? God knows you're stubborn enough."

"Am not."

"I'm not getting into this argument again," Lex said. She stood and pulled Ellie up with her. "Come on. You're going home with me."

Ellie tugged free and stepped back. "No. I can't." She crossed her arms over her body. "We have this conversation every single time you come by or call, but I'm not ready. Just give me a little more time. Please."

"You realize I'm going to be in big trouble with my wife, don't you?"

For the first time in a long time, Ellie smiled. "You've got Amanda wrapped around your little finger, and don't try telling me otherwise." She glanced around the room as if seeing it for the first time. "How did this happen?"

"I'm going to send one of the guys over to take care of the yard. Grandpa would kick both our asses for letting it get so out of hand." Lex rubbed the back of her neck in a nervous gesture. "I'm really sorry I haven't been paying much attention, El. But there's just so much going on at the ranch. And with this drought—"

"Don't worry about it. If the sprinkler system wasn't automatic, the yard would be nothing but dirt and rocks. As it is, I don't think it's been coming on all that often." Ellie put her hand on Lex's arm and led her toward the door. "I know you and Amanda mean well, but please. Let me get through this on my own."

Lex found herself standing on the front porch. "I'm going to keep bothering you until you come back with me, you know."

Ellie's answer was half-laugh, half-cry. "I know. And I love you for it." She closed the door and turned the deadbolt, effectively locking out the rest of the world, once again.

THE PRIVATE CEMETERY sat in a clearing, its wrought iron enclosure more for decorative use than security. A gentle breeze scattered leaves around the granite memorial stones as the screech of the gate's hinges silenced the afternoon birdsong. Lex's heavy boots crushed the dried grass, the sound carrying through the peaceful clearing. Her face was partially obscured by a black hat as she knelt by the most recently placed stone. The brittle grass crunched beneath the knee of her well-worn jeans. She used one hand to brush away Mother Nature's debris.

Lex removed her sunglasses and stared at the engraving. She sniffled and cleared her throat. "It's been half a year and I still miss you something fierce." Her vision blurred and she took a moment to regain her equilibrium. "We didn't have much time together, I know." She bent her head and closed her eyes, allowing the tears to fall. Scenes flashed through her mind as she remembered happier times. But even with the good memories, the grief threatened to overwhelm her.

She dropped onto her rear, pulled her knees up to her chest and wrapped her arms around her legs. "A little over ten lousy years. Doesn't seem fair, does it? I thought we'd have longer." Lex angrily brushed at her face. "The girls miss you. Lorrie asks about you almost every day."

The wind kicked up and blew Lex's hair into her face. She ignored it and continued to speak. "I sure could use your help right now. This drought has me at my wits end. I've had some water wells drilled, but we're still losing stock. At least I was smart enough to listen to you about one thing. Going back to cattle instead of horses made a huge difference. But even with that, things are looking rough. You were always so good about helping me figure out what to do." Her voice broke, and she climbed to her feet. "I know I should be thankful you're not in pain anymore." She tucked her hands into the pockets of the black duster she wore. "I wish I would have known, sooner."

Lex started to walk around, kicking at the leaves. "After you—" she had trouble finishing the thought. "After you were...gone, a few medical bills showed up. I called your doctor and he filled me in. You could have told me, you know." The knowledge that her grandfather had suffered silently for almost a year before he told his family of his condition hurt. Her heart ached at the loss, the pain as fresh as if it were yesterday. Taking a deep breath, Lex pulled herself together. "I probably won't be back for a while, okay? The kids are growing so fast, and they need me. I promised to take them to the Fall Festival at school tonight." She finally smiled. "Say a prayer for me, will you? I'm going to need all the help I can get." She kissed her fingertips and placed them on the stone. "I love you, Grandpa. Give Grandma Lanie a hug for me, okay?" Straightening her shoulders, Lex passed through the gate and closed it securely behind her.

AFTER PARKING HER truck beside the ranch house, Lex walked up the back steps and stepped inside. She hung her hat and coat on their usual pegs and checked the kitchen, finding it empty. Her curiosity piqued, she continued toward the front of the house. As she passed the stairs she heard Amanda's voice coming from the living room.

"I know you're excited about tonight, but that doesn't mean you can leave this room in shambles." Two younger voices apologized, but Amanda was only getting started.

Not wanting to interrupt, Lex waited out of sight in the hall. She could almost visualize Amanda's actions by her scolding voice and the sounds of toys noisily being put away.

"Neither of you were raised this way." A loud bang punctuated Amanda's words. "You know the rules. Clean up one thing before you get something else out. That's how it's always been." Another heavy thud followed. "My day is full enough without having to play maid."

Lex nodded to herself. She'd been trying for years to get another housekeeper after Martha and Charlie started traveling, without success. She also knew she was as guilty as the kids about not helping out more. But after being gone from sunup to sundown, the last thing Lex felt like doing was housework.

As Amanda's voice continued to rise, Lex decided she'd hid long enough. She stepped into the living room and watched as Amanda gathered toys, while Lorrie and Melanie stood guiltily by. Lex hoped she could charm her wife into calming down. "How're my favorite girls?"

"Momma!" Both children raced around the sofa to greet Lex. Each one wrapped herself around Lex, turning their sad faces up to look at her.

Amanda stopped what she was doing and put her hands on her hips. Her strawberry-blonde hair, cut short for easy care, was in disarray. "I'm glad you're home. Maybe you can get through to these two." She raised her arms and spread them wide. "Have you ever seen this room look this bad?"

"Hmm." Lex kept one hand on each girl's head, and made a point of turning slowly to take in the whole room. She understood why Amanda was so upset. There wasn't a clean spot anywhere. Games were strewn all over the floor, their pieces scattered everywhere. She glanced down at her children. "What in the hell was going on here?"

Ten-year old Lorrie, a miniature version of Lex, let go of Lex and stepped away. "We wanted to see how many games we could play." Her hands ended up on her hips, mimicking Amanda's earlier posture. "We were gonna clean up when we were done, I promise."

Hearing a sniffle, Lex scooped Melanie into her arms. "Is that right, sweetheart? Were you going to pick this mess up?"

"Uh-huh." The six-year old snuggled closer. "Mommy came in before we could."

Lex looked over Melanie's blonde head to meet Amanda's eyes. "Busted them, huh?"

Amanda was about to go off again about the state of the room, when she took a good look at Lex's face. The red and puffy eyes were a clear indication that something was wrong. She stepped closer and placed her hand on Lex's cheek. "Are you okay?"

"Yeah." Lex turned her head and kissed Amanda's palm. "I stopped by the cemetery."

"Ah." Amanda took Melanie from Lex's arms. "Go help your sister, sweetie. Lorrie, I want both of you to get this room clean or no Fall Festival tonight."

Both girls sighed. "Yes, ma'am," they replied in unison.

Amanda's attention returned to Lex. "Let's go upstairs."

"I'm okay."

"Then come help me calm down." Amanda took Lex's hand as they left the room.

ONCE UPSTAIRS, AMANDA closed their bedroom door and led Lex to the bed. She sat her down and removed her boots. "It's going to take the girls a while to clean up, so we might as well take advantage of it." With a gentle push, she made Lex lie back and snuggled up beside her. "Much better."

"As long as you're comfortable." Lex wrapped her arm around Amanda and kissed the top of her head. "You were right. This does feel good. Thanks."

"Anytime." Amanda unbuttoned Lex's denim shirt and began to lightly rub her stomach, the easiest way to get her to relax. "Now, want to tell me why you went to the cemetery?"

Lex sighed. "While I was in town, I stopped by to see Ellie."

"How's she doing?"

"Not too good. I tried to get her to come home with me, but she refused." Lex wiped one hand across her eyes. "She's just so damned stubborn."

Amanda had to laugh. "Family trait," she teased.

"Smartass." Lex shook her head. "Anyway, as I was driving home I realized I hadn't gone to the family plot for a while. I know he's buried next to my grandmother in Dallas, but I still feel closer to him out there." The private cemetery was located on the ranch, and was home to memorial stones as well as family gravesites.

"That's understandable. How are you doing now?"

"A lot better." Closing her eyes, Lex wrapped both arms around Amanda and tugged her as close as possible. "I love you."

Amanda kissed Lex's throat, and slowly moved upward until their lips met. "Love you, too." She felt warm hands slip under her shirt, making her hope their children took a long time to clean the living room.

LEX PARALLEL-PARKED her truck in front of the school playground and turned off the engine. She unbuckled her seatbelt and with a wry smile to her wife, turned to face the two excited children behind her. "Lorrie, do you remember the rules?"

Lorrie nodded vigorously, her gray eyes bright with excitement. "Yes, ma'am. Stay in the building and don't talk to strangers." She tugged her rubber zombie mask into place. "Do I have to take Melanie with me?"

Melanie's lower lip stuck out. "I don't want to go with you anyway," she said as her blue eyes filled with tears. "I'm old enough to go by myself."

Amanda bit her lip to keep from laughing. Their normally shy daughter was beginning to assert her independence, much to their amusement. "Melanie, I was hoping you'd go with us. We may run into your cousin Teddy."

"Oh. Okay." Melanie's tears immediately dried. "Teddy's s'pose to be dressed like a cowboy." She gave her sister a dirty look. "He's nice to me."

"Can I go now?" Lorrie asked. Her hand was poised on the door handle. "I bet Al's already inside."

"I guess—" Lex's words were lost on Lorrie, who hopped out of the truck and raced into the elementary school, "so." Lex climbed out of the vehicle, opened the back door and gave Melanie a kiss before she swung her daughter to the ground. "You look beautiful, sweetheart."

Melanie's blonde curls danced in the breeze. "Thanks, Momma."

She spun in a circle, causing her yellow costume skirt to whirl around her legs. "Snow White's my favorite." They rounded the front of the truck and joined Amanda, who held out her hand.

"She's my favorite, too," Amanda said. With Melanie between them, she and Lex swung their arms, causing her to giggle. "Let's go find your classroom."

As they passed through the front doors decorated with cutouts of pumpkins and a scarecrow, Lex muttered, "Fall Festival, my ass."

"What?" Amanda blinked as her eyes became accustomed to the bright fluorescent lights.

"I don't know why they can't call it the Halloween Carnival, like they did when I was in school," Lex said. "I mean, they've got the same decorations as they did then. And why on earth do they have it a blasted week before Halloween?"

Amanda laughed. "I'm sure they're just trying to keep from insulting anyone." She tightened her grip on Melanie's hand as they weaved through the crowded halls.

"I'm insulted by their stupid ideas," Lex said. "Next thing you'll know, they'll take away Christmas."

"Momma, look. There's my room," Melanie pointed out excitedly. "We're doing the cakewalk." She dragged them toward the room where loud music could be heard.

Lex looked questioningly at Amanda. "Cakewalk? Did we—"

"I brought a pie yesterday." Amanda cringed as they entered the room and the loud music assailed her senses. "Yippee."

NOT FAR AWAY, Lorrie roamed the familiar halls looking for her best friend, who she was supposed to meet by the cafeteria. As Lorrie rounded the corner, she saw a pudgy blonde girl dressed as an angel, surrounded by three loud boys. The ninja, fireman and soldier were all teasing her. "Hey!"

The angel turned at the voice and a smile lit up her face. "Lorrie!" She tried to push by the boy dressed all in black, but he stopped her.

"Wait," he ordered. The dark clothes clung tightly to his stocky frame, and his black pants were several inches too short, showing his white tube socks.

Lorrie joined the group and lifted her mask to the top of her head. "What's your problem, Jerry?"

The ninja-boy sneered through his black ski mask. "Nobody's talking to you. Go 'way." He flipped the mask off Lorrie's head and started to laugh. "Why didn't you dress like you usually do?"

"'Cause we're supposed to be in costumes, Jerry. Or do you always dress like a ninja?" Lorrie picked up her zombie mask and held it in one fist. "Al, let's go."

The angel, also known as Allison Skimmerly, jerked her arm free.

"Okay." She followed Lorrie away from the cafeteria, until Jerry's voice caused Lorrie to stop in her tracks.

"I figured you'd be a little cow-pie, like you are every day. Just like your mom." He constantly teased Lorrie about the boots and jeans she wore to school. Jerry's comment caused the two boys with him to start laughing.

Lorrie spun around and tossed her mask on the floor. "Take it back, Jerry."

"No." Jerry danced from foot to foot. "Your mom's a cow-pie. Cow-pie, cow-pie," he sang.

The former zombie rushed the ninja and pushed him to the ground. "Take it back, or I'll—" Lorrie's words stopped when she was grabbed by the back of her shirt and pulled away.

"Lorrie Walters, what's going on?" the middle aged woman asked. Dressed in denim bib overalls, flannel shirt and floppy hat, the pseudo-farmer separated the two feuding children.

Allison piped up. "It wasn't her fault, Mrs. Barrett. Jerry started it."

"Did not!" Jerry shouted. "I didn't do nothin'. Lorrie pushed me for no reason."

The fifth grade teacher took Jerry's arm in her free hand. "Let's go to the office to straighten this out." She gave the costumed fireman and soldier a stern look. "You boys have a choice, either find your parents or come with us."

"I—I—think I see my dad," the soldier said. He took off with the fireman close on his heels.

Mrs. Barrett looked at Allison. "How about you?"

Allison raised her chin defiantly. "I'm staying with Lorrie." She picked up Lorrie's mask and handed it to her.

"All right." The teacher escorted the trio down the hall. "Lorrie, are your parents here?"

"Yes, ma'am. They're with my little sister." Lorrie ignored Jerry's derisive snort.

"Cow-pie," he whispered.

"Shut up!" Lorrie yelled, twisting out of Mrs. Barrett's grasp. She would have knocked him down but the teacher's grip kept him upright.

Mrs. Barrett took a fistful of the back of Lorrie's shirt and yanked her away from Jerry. "Lorrie! That's enough!"

Allison pointed at the obnoxious boy as they walked into the office. "He's saying bad things, Mrs. Barrett."

With a heavy sigh, Mrs. Barrett separated the three, keeping at least two chairs between Jerry and Lorrie. "I don't want to hear another word out of any of you until your parents get here."

Lorrie crossed her arms over her chest and glared straight ahead.

IN THE FIRST grade room, Lex watched as Amanda and Melanie

walked around the perimeter to music. She couldn't get over how much their youngest looked like her wife. Although Amanda had started wearing her hair short years earlier, the two still favored each other. Melanie's hair was lighter and her head was covered with curls, but even their facial structure was similar.

The outer edges of the floor were taped off into squares, with numbers in some of the boxes. Amanda's sister Jeannie and her son Teddy were on the opposite side of the room, walking and laughing as well. When the music stopped, so did the walkers. Some of them ended up in numbered squares, while others were stuck in empty spaces. Lex laughed as Melanie danced around Amanda in a numbered box.

"We win, Mommy!" Melanie's clear voice floated across the room. "Number seven!"

Amanda clapped along with her. "Why don't you go get the prize and take it to your Momma?" She waited until Melanie skipped to the prize table before joining Lex. "Pretty cool, huh?"

"Yep. Hope it's the cream cheese covered brownies," Lex whispered. She watched Melanie claim a box of baked goods. "Damn. I think it's the peanut brittle."

"Yum." Amanda was about to say more when an announcement came over the loudspeaker.

"Would the parents of Jerry Sater, Allison Skimmerly, and Lorrie Walters please come to the office?"

Lex shook her head. "Great. I wonder what she's gotten into this time." She turned to her wife. "Do you want me to handle this?"

"No, let's both go." Amanda smiled at Melanie when she bounced forward with her prize. "Honey, would you mind staying with Aunt Jeannie for a little while?" She waved at her sister.

"Is Lorrie in trouble?" Melanie asked.

Lex scooped Melanie into her arms. "We don't know. But I promise we'll let you know as soon as we can, okay?"

Jeannie and Teddy joined the trio. "We're going to the kindergarten class and try the ring toss. Would you like to come, Melanie?" Jeannie nodded at Amanda's whispered thanks. She grinned when Melanie took her hand.

"We'll catch up to y'all as soon as we can," Lex called after them. Once Jeannie and the children were out of the room, she turned her attention to Amanda. "Want to take bets on what Lorrie has done?"

Amanda swatted Lex's arm. "Behave. She might surprise you."

"Uh-huh." Lex followed Amanda down the hall, her hands tucked into her back pockets in an effort to keep them to herself. She learned a long time ago that while the majority of people in Somerville left them alone, they didn't like to see two women holding hands.

Loud voices echoed from the office as they arrived. Lex was able to pick out Wanda Skimmerly's voice easily. She stepped into the room and saw Wanda and another woman going at it, nose to nose.

"Your kid is a bully!" Wanda shouted at the woman in front of her. "I'm sure he got at least a portion of what he deserved."

Mrs. Barrett stepped in between the two women. "Ladies, please." She turned her head when Lex and Amanda entered the room. "Lexington, Amanda. I'm glad you're here."

Lex glanced at Lorrie, who looked none the worse for wear. "What's going on here?"

"I caught Lorrie and Jerry fighting," Mrs. Barrett said.

Allison piped up. "Jerry started it."

Jerry's mother, Susan, a weather-beaten heavyset woman, snapped at Allison. "My boy didn't start anything." Years of alcohol abuse had aged her unkindly. Her puffy red face was slick with perspiration in the cool room. She gave Jerry a pointed look. "Did you?"

He raised his head until he met her face. "No, ma'am," he said quietly. His eyes tracked to the floor.

"See?" Susan whirled and pointed an accusing finger at Lex. "This is all your fault, Lexington Walters. You were no good in school, and—"

Amanda interrupted the woman's tirade. "Excuse me, we haven't met. I'm Amanda." She held out her hand.

Susan disregarded the offer and crossed her arms over her chest. "Walters, what are you going to do about your kid?"

Lex ignored Susan and knelt in front of Lorrie's chair. "Want to tell me what happened?"

Lorrie sniffled, trying not to cry. "I got mad." She lowered her gaze, focusing on Lex's knees.

"Did you hit Jerry?" Lex gently asked. "Tell the truth, sweetheart."

"No."

Lex shook her head and exhaled heavily. "Lorrie."

"I pushed him. But I didn't hit him." Big, heavy tears slid from Lorrie's eyes.

Amanda sat beside Lorrie and put her arm around her. "Why did you push him?"

Jerry jumped to his feet. "'Cause she's a big meanie!"

"No she's not." Allison said, "You're a jerk."

Susan took Jerry by the shoulder and shook him. "What have I told you about yelling?"

Mrs. Barrett held out her hands in an attempt to control the situation. "Ms. Sater, please."

Allison ran to her mother and wrapped her arms around Wanda's waist. "He called Lorrie a cow-pie, and said her mom was one, too."

"He said what?" Amanda looked at Lex to see how she took the news.

Lex clenched her teeth and made eye contact with her daughter. "Lorrie, is that why you pushed him?"

"Yes, ma'am." Lorrie blinked and wiped her tears on her sleeve.

"Remember what I told you about name-calling?" Lex quietly asked.

Lorrie nodded. "We're supposed to ignore people who have to use nasty words to make them feel better." Her big gray eyes stared into Lex's face. "I did okay until he talked about you. That's when I got so mad."

"I know, sweetheart." Lex put her arms around Lorrie and brought her close. "But words won't hurt me. It's okay." She kissed Lorrie's head and held her until she stopped crying.

"Oh, please," Susan snorted. She turned to Mrs. Barrett. "Are you going to let that little brat get away with this?"

Lex stood and turned. "Sue, I'd be careful what I said if I were you."

Susan would not be dissuaded. "You let your children run wild and then seem surprised when they get caught. Come on, Jerry. I'll take care of you when we get home." She yanked Jerry toward the door. "Keep your mongrel away from my kid, Lexington, or you'll be the one that's sorry."

Wanda tucked Allison close as well. "Well, isn't she the pleasant one?" She said, breaking the tension.

Amanda noticed Wanda was alone. "Where's Dirk?"

"He's with Penny. I think they were going to try the ring toss in her classroom." Penny was their other daughter who was one year behind Melanie.

Mrs. Barrett sounded truly regretful. "Lexington, Amanda, I'm afraid Lorrie will have to be suspended Monday and Tuesday. It's school policy."

"We understand." Amanda shook the teacher's hand. "Thank you for bringing the kids to the office, instead of handling it out in the hall." She followed Lex and Lorrie from the room.

Wanda wasn't as impressed, however. "What about Jerry? It was his fault to begin with."

"Mrs. Skimmerly, I can't do anything to Jerry because I didn't hear what he said. All I witnessed were Lorrie's actions."

"It's still ridiculous," Wanda said. "Come on, Allie. Let's go see what your sister is up to."

"Can we get a candied apple? I'm hungry," Allison trailed after her mother, her foil-covered wings bouncing behind her.

AT HOME LATER that evening, Lex sat on the edge of Lorrie's bed. Lorrie had to be punished for getting suspended from school, but Lex's heart wasn't in it. She remembered being in her daughter's shoes. "Do you understand what you did wrong?"

Lorrie, tucked under the bright blue covers, nodded solemnly. "Yes, ma'am. Fighting's bad, no matter what."

"Right." Lex looked around the room, seeing small pieces of herself in her oldest child's decorating. Posters of horses shared space with magazine pictures of sports figures. The full-sized, four-poster oak bed was a birthday gift made by Amanda's grandfather, Jacob, the previous year, with a matching dresser and nightstand. Books covered almost every available space, along with a softball glove and bat tossed in one corner. Lex realized how better rounded her children were than she was at their age, and knew it was due to her wife's influence. She cleared her throat. "Halloween is coming up next Saturday, and—"

"No! Please, Momma. I want to go trick-or-treating," Lorrie said. "I'll do better."

Lex sighed. "We already promised Melanie you could take her. So it wouldn't be fair to her if we kept you home." Lex decided on another punishment, one that would hurt her almost as bad. "No riding for the rest of the week."

"What? But Momma—"

"I'm sorry, Lorrie. But you have to realize that your actions have consequences. You still have to groom Mine every day, but no riding until Sunday. You'll just have to lead her around the corral for exercise."

Tears trickled down Lorrie's cheeks. "But me and you was going riding Friday after school."

"I know. I was hoping you could help me check the well on the west pasture, but now I'll have to go alone." Lex felt like crying herself. She enjoyed the time she was able to spend with Lorrie, just the two of them. At her daughter's sob, she brought Lorrie nearer and held her. "Sssh. We'll have other times, I promise."

Lorrie snuggled as close as she could. Although her feelings were hurt at the punishment, there was no safer place than in her mother's arms.

AMANDA LOOKED UP from the book she was reading when Lex came into the room. She could tell her wife's talk with their oldest had taken a toll on her. She closed the book and placed it on her nightstand, patting the bed beside her. "You look pretty ragged."

"Yeah." Lex sat on the edge of the bed and kicked off her boots, then stood and undressed, tossing her clothes on a nearby chair. Amanda had laid out her cotton nightshirt, so she draped it over her body before climbing into bed. "God, this feels good," she said, stretching out under the covers.

"Rough talk?" Amanda asked, crawling next to Lex and taking her usual position against her side.

Lex closed her eyes in an attempt to control her emotions. "I grounded her from riding until Sunday."

"Ouch." Amanda sneaked her hand beneath Lex's shirt, stroking the soft skin of her stomach. "Weren't you supposed to go riding together Friday?"

"Yep." Lex relaxed as the gentle touch continued. "It hurt me almost as much as it did her. But I don't know what else to do. She can't go around pushing other kids just because they say something she doesn't like."

Amanda kissed her wife's jaw. "I know. And for the record, I think you did the right thing." She played with the ends of Lex's hair. The dark strands were slowly losing the battle against the gray, especially around her temples. Lex had started wearing it shorter than when they first met, and now the ends barely grazed her shoulders.

"Thanks. I remember going through the same thing at her age. Town kids always picked on those of us who lived out on ranches and farms." Lex turned and propped her head on her hand, staring into Amanda's eyes. "Is it wrong to keep our girls so isolated out here?"

Mirroring Lex's posture, Amanda brushed her free hand along Lex's arm. "Honey, it doesn't matter where you live or what you do. Kids will always find something to pick on other kids about. I got teased because my dad's driver always dropped us off. One of my friends always got pushed around for wearing nothing but black."

"I guess you're right. I just don't want our kids to suffer because of how we live."

"I know." Amanda studied her face. "Not to change the subject, but I take it you and Susan Sater have a history?"

Lex shrugged. "We went to school together, that's all." When Amanda continued to look at her, she rolled her eyes. "Yeah. We've never gotten along. She was Rick's girlfriend back in the bad-old-days. She was just as mean as a kid." Rick Thompson had been an adversary of Lex's in school. Later, he managed the realty office that Amanda's grandmother, Anna Leigh, owned. He was fired for his animosity toward Amanda, and at Anna Leigh's request, Amanda now managed Sunflower Realty.

"Nice."

"She blamed me because she got suspended before homecoming, and didn't get a chance to be Homecoming Queen. Susan got caught cheating on a test, and she swore up and down that I turned her in."

Amanda frowned. "Did you?"

"Hell, no. But I think Rick told her I did, and that was good enough for her. After graduation she left town, but came back a few years later with a couple of kids and a hen-pecked husband. Last I heard, he left with the kids they had at the time. Guess it was before Jerry was born. No one knows who his father is. I haven't had much to do with her."

"Good." Amanda started to trace around the edge of Lex's ear. "I think we've talked enough, don't you?"

Lex shivered as Amanda's finger drew a line down her throat. "Um, yeah."

Amanda leaned closer and lightly touched her lips to Lex's. "I love you."

Threading her fingers through Amanda's hair, Lex rolled onto her back and brought her partner with her. "Love you, too." She had no trouble removing the nightgown Amanda wore, and somehow felt her own shirt disappear. The delicious skin-on-skin contact drove all other thoughts from her mind.

Chapter Two

WEDNESDAY MORNING LEX sat at her desk, enjoying the relative peace of an empty house. Amanda had taken the girls to school, and the silence was spooky. Amanda would spend the day at Sunflower Realty until their children were out of school. Lex took the opportunity to get caught up on her paperwork. She was scrolling through her emails when she came across one from a business contact in Houston. "Yes!"

Lex switched to her accounting program, searching for the listing of available cattle. "Perfect." She picked up the phone and dialed the number from the email. "Mr. Stewart? This is Lexington Walters. I just received your email." She listened for a moment. "Friday? Sure. What time's good for you? Thank you, Mr. Stewart." She hung up the phone and tapped a pen on the desk. Now came the hard part.

She picked up the phone and hit the speed dial. "Hi, this is Lex. Is Amanda available?"

A moment later, Amanda picked up. "Hi, honey. Miss me already?"

"Always," Lex answered honestly. "But I do have another reason for calling. Remember when I was trying to set up a chance to sell beef to that distributor in Houston?"

"I do. Wait, did it go through?" Amanda's voice bubbled with excitement.

"Yep. I have to be in Houston Friday morning to meet with the owner and go over all the particulars."

Amanda's excitement was short-lived. "Friday? But what about taking the kids trick-or-treating on Saturday? You promised them."

"Not a problem. I'll drive back Saturday morning and be home in plenty of time. There's no way I'll make you go through that alone."

"Thank god." Amanda exhaled. "Normally I wouldn't mind, but since we'd also agreed to take Ally and Penny, I don't think my nerves can handle four kids by myself."

Lex laughed. "I think Wanda and Dirk paid the church to have their retreat the same weekend as Halloween. How else could you explain the timing?"

"I wouldn't put it past them," Amanda said. "What are your plans for lunch?"

"Oh, I don't know. I thought I'd grab a sandwich or something, since Martha and Charlie aren't back from their trip. It's funny. I could never get her to step foot off the ranch after I took over. But ever since Charlie retired, they're rarely home."

Amanda giggled. "Are you pouting again?"

"No."

"Uh-huh. I bet you are."

"Nope." The smile widened on Lex's face. "Are you busy for lunch today? Or should I go up to the bunkhouse and beg for scraps?" It was a viable option. The food at the bunkhouse was always good.

Three years prior, their foreman, Roy, married a woman he'd secretly been seeing. As a wedding present, Lex and the hired hands built a small home not far from the bunkhouse. Roy's wife, Helen, was the cook for the men. She had come in to help their old cook, Lester, since he'd been having trouble getting around. He passed away in his sleep six months before Lex's grandfather, Travis.

Lex enjoyed Helen's cooking, although it tended toward the heavy side, and Amanda tried to get her wife to eat healthier, since Lex's last checkup showed her blood pressure was higher than it should be.

"No, I think I can squeeze you into my busy schedule," Amanda teased. "Give me an hour?"

"Sure, sweetheart." Lex shut down her computer. "But if you think I'm going to eat a damned salad today, you've got another thing coming."

"We'll see."

AMANDA STARED AT Lex's plate. "I knew I should have ordered for you."

"Why? It's not steak. I thought I did okay." Lex cut another slice from her meal and popped it into her mouth. "I ordered chicken."

Rolling her eyes, Amanda took a sip of her tea. "Fried chicken is not healthy, smartass."

Lex grinned. "Teach you to pick on me." She'd had every intention of finding something less greasy on the menu, until Amanda made an off-hand comment about her blood pressure. Not one to back down when challenged, Lex rebelled by ordering something deep fried and smothered in gravy. She had a feeling it would be the last good meal she'd get for a while, if Amanda had anything to say about it. "Hey, want to get some ice cream for dessert?"

"Ugh." Amanda pointed her fork at Lex. "You are in so much trouble, Lexington Walters. Just wait until we get home tonight."

"Promise?"

Amanda laughed. "Brat."

"What? Do I have something on my face?" Lex placed her napkin across her lap again and looked at her wife. The years had been good to Amanda, whose short hair always looked windblown. If she had any gray, it was well-hidden, much to Lex's chagrin. After the birth of Melanie, Amanda had been able to keep her trim figure. Other than her hairstyle, she hadn't changed much from the woman Lex pulled from the creek eleven years ago. "You are so beautiful."

Amanda blushed and ducked her head. "You're biased."

"Maybe." Lex leaned forward and lowered her voice. "But it's the truth. You are an extremely beautiful woman and I'm very lucky to share my life with you." Not caring if anyone noticed, Lex stretched her hand across the table and grasped Amanda's. "Thank you for finding me, Amanda. You've made my life worth living."

Squeezing Lex's hand, Amanda's smile widened. "Me, too."

LATER THAT DAY, Lex was in the barn when she heard the door open. She looked over the back of Rose, the small pony that had been purchased specifically for Melanie, and saw her oldest daughter carefully close the door behind her. "Hey there, Lorrie. How was school?"

Lorrie took off her jacket and draped it on a bale of hay next to Lex's, then climbed on the side of Rose's stall and sat on the top rail. "It was okay."

"Have any trouble?" Lex went back to brushing the pony.

"No, ma'am. And I apologized to Mrs. Barrett, like you told me to." Lorrie stretched so she could reach the pony's mane, and began to comb it with her fingers. "Momma?"

"Yeah?"

Lorrie took a minute to get her thoughts in order before voicing them. "Why is Jerry always so mean to me?"

"Honestly? I think he's jealous." Lex handed Lorrie a curry comb, pleased when she dropped to the floor and started gently working the pony's coat.

"Why?"

Lex started on Rose's tail, removing the tangles. "I figure he lives in a small house in town, with not much to do. Everyone knows you live on this ranch with all sorts of things going on. Not much chance of getting bored, is there?"

"No, I guess not." Lorrie peeked around Rose and noticed how Lex was dressed. Scuffed boots, faded jeans and the ever-present denim shirt was her mother's usual uniform. She looked at her own clothes, which were almost a carbon copy of Lex's. "Momma?"

"Yeah?"

"Next time we buy me new clothes, can I get something different?"

The plea broke Lex's heart. She remembered asking her own father that exact question, and hearing from him how there wasn't any sense in buying different clothes for school. She was determined to break the cycle. "Of course, sweetheart. Just because we dress in boots and jeans to work on the ranch, doesn't mean you have to dress like that for school. We'll go after school tomorrow and find you some different clothes, okay?"

Lorrie edged around Rose and wrapped her arms around Lex's waist. "Thanks, Momma." She giggled when Lex lifted her high and set her on Rose's back. She stretched so she could put her arms around

Lex's neck. "You're the best."

Lex felt like she'd done something right. "Come on, kiddo. Help me with the rest of the horses, and we'll go back to the house and pick on your Mom."

CONVERSATION ROLLED NON-stop around the dinner table. Melanie and Lorrie took turns telling about their day at school. Neither Lex nor Amanda was able to add much to the mix, as both girls chattered breathlessly.

Melanie related another playground story. "And then I told Teddy that just 'cause his daddy's a doctor, it didn't mean he knew more than me."

Amanda struggled to keep a smile from her face. "I'm sure he didn't mean anything by it, sweetie."

"I guess." Melanie speared her salad and took a bite, leaving more dressing on her face than in her mouth. "Is Teddy gonna come live with us?"

Lex almost spewed her iced tea across the table. She coughed and cleared her throat before answering. "What makes you say that?" A glance at Amanda showed that she was just as confused.

"He wants to be a cowboy when he grows up, but they can't have a horse in town," Melanie said. "It's against the rules."

Amanda patted Lex's hand where it rested on the table. "I'm sure he'll find a way to be a cowboy, if that's what he wants to do." They were both worried about the children learning Lorrie's true parentage in the wrong way. Teddy's mother, Jeannie, was Lorrie's biological mother. Her first husband, Frank, passed away shortly after Lorrie was born. Lorrie knew all about her father, but not the woman who gave birth to her. It never seemed to be the right time to bring up the circumstances in which Lorrie was adopted by Lex and Amanda.

"How can he be a cowboy if he's afraid of horses?" Lorrie asked. "He won't even pet Rose and she's just a pony."

"He says he's gonna use motorcycles." Melanie wrinkled her nose. "Teddy says that horses are old-timey and not any good."

"Teddy's dumb," Lorrie said, while she played with her spaghetti.

"Lorrie, that's not nice," Amanda said, giving her wife a glare when she didn't help. "Right, Lex?"

Lex was torn between being a good parent and being a proud rancher. "You shouldn't call people dumb just because they don't agree with you," she said. "But I think he's wrong. Horses can go through rougher terrain than bikes, and never run out of gas." She flinched as her shin received a well-placed kick. "Umm, but I've heard that some ranches get by with motorcycles instead of horses just fine," she added with a grimace.

"Jerry has a black eye," Lorrie said, changing the subject. "He says he fell down, but it looks like someone socked him a good one." Amanda's shocked expression caused her to hastily add, "I didn't do it, I swear."

"We believe you." Amanda gave Lex a worried look before turning back to Lorrie. "Did Mrs. Barrett do anything about it?"

"She sent him to the nurse's office this morning, but he came back all grumpy." Lorrie stuck a forkful of spaghetti into her mouth, noisily slurping the noodles. She wiped her face with the back of her hand, surprised when she didn't get into trouble. Her parents were looking at each other funny. A shuffling beneath the table reminded her that Freckles was waiting patiently for her share of dinner. As stealthily as possible, she broke off a piece of bread and dropped it on the floor. A warning glare at Melanie ensured her little sister's silence.

Amanda squeezed Lex's hand. "Lex, do you think—"

Lex shook her head. "Later." She saw a movement out of the corner of her eye. "Lorrie, are you sharing your dinner with Freckles?"

"Just some bread. She's been really good." A sharp bark from beneath the table punctuated her statement. The rat terrier was always ready for more tidbits.

"Are you done?" Lex asked, seeing the majority of the food missing from Lorrie's plate. Once she started feeding the dog, she was usually finished.

"Yes, ma'am. May I be excused?" At Amanda's nod, Lorrie took her plate to the sink. "Come on, Freckles. Let's go upstairs." Girl and dog raced from the room, accented by laughter and barks.

Melanie pushed her plate away. "May I be 'scused, too?"

"Only if you promise to wash your face before doing anything else." Amanda shared a fond smile with Lex as Melanie followed in her sister's footsteps. Once they were alone, her smile faded. "Are you thinking what I'm thinking about Jerry?"

"Yeah." Lex stood and helped clear the table. She loaded the dishwasher while Amanda put the food in airtight containers and placed them in the refrigerator. In the last few years since Amanda had taken over the majority of the household chores, Lex was finally able to purchase the dishwasher that Martha never wanted, although she was teased by Martha about it being totally unnecessary. "But it sounds like Mrs. Barrett is on top of things."

"Maybe. It just breaks my heart that someone could do that to a child." Amanda took a dishtowel and wiped down the table and chairs. "Is there anything we can do?"

Lex shook her head. "All we can do is keep our eyes and ears open. If we find out anything for sure, we can always notify Jeremy at the sheriff's department." Jeremy had taken over as sheriff after Charlie retired. Lex stepped behind Amanda and pulled her into an embrace. "Want to go to the den and make out?" she whispered in Amanda's ear.

Amanda turned in Lex's arms. "That's the best offer I've had all day." She tugged on Lex's belt, dragging her from the kitchen.

LORRIE WAS STRETCHED across her bed on her stomach, a book propped on her pillow, when her sister tapped on her door. Freckles, curled up next to Lorrie, raised her head, but lowered it when she saw Melanie.

"Lorrie? Can I come in?"

"Sure." Lorrie rolled over and sat up. Freckles stood, jumped off the bed, and decided to lie on the rug on the other side of the bed.

Melanie sat next to Lorrie, looking at her feet that hung off the edge. "We don't have a daddy, do we?"

"Nope." Lorrie started swinging her legs.

"How come?"

Lorrie lightly kicked at her sister's shoes, giggling when Melanie kicked back. "I dunno. Just 'cause. They told me a long time ago that my Daddy died when I was a baby. But I don't know about yours. Did you ask Momma?"

Melanie leaned into her sister, bumping shoulders. "No. They're in the den, kissing. I saw them go in there after I washed up, and I was gonna ask them. But they were too busy."

"Gross."

"I know." Melanie laughed when Lorrie almost shoved her off the bed. "Hey!"

"Sorry." Lorrie helped her sit up. "I think we're lucky. Will told me his daddy never does anything with him. And Al says her daddy sleeps on the couch when he comes home from work."

"Well, Mommy works while we're in school, but Momma doesn't go to work."

Lorrie hopped off her bed and put the book she'd been reading back in her bookcase. "She works here. We live at her work."

"How come?"

"I dunno." Lorrie picked up her glove and ball, and began to toss the ball into the air. "Want to play catch?"

Melanie shook her head. "Not in the house. We got in trouble for it the last time."

"Yeah, I guess you're right." Lorrie tossed the glove into the corner and rolled the ball toward it. "Want to play a game?"

"Chutes and Ladders?"

Lorrie rolled her eyes. "Sure. But you have to go downstairs to get it." The games were kept in a bookcase in the den.

Melanie shook her head. "Um, never mind. Can we read instead?"

EARLY THURSDAY MORNING, Lex packed her overnight bag with the essentials. Amanda sat on the bed, watching her fill the small duffel. When Lex stepped out of the closet, Amanda sighed. "I hate this."

"I'm not very fond of it either." Lex started to fold a shirt, but found it taken away from her. "Hey."

"Give me that." Amanda fussed over the gray oxford. She folded it neatly and handed it back to Lex, who placed it into the bag. "Did you say that you're supposed to meet the guy around eight-thirty in the morning?"

"Yeah. That's why I figured to go this afternoon and get a hotel room near his office. I don't want to try and find the place during rush hour traffic." Lex moved to the dresser and took out two pairs of socks and underwear. "If we get done in time, I may come in Friday night."

Amanda took the different items from Lex and added them to the bag. "Honey, as much as I'll miss you, I don't want you driving if it's late. Saturday morning is soon enough."

"But aren't Allison and Penny spending the night Friday?"

"Yes, but I think I can handle four little girls for one night." Amanda paused. "I hope." She laughed at the look on Lex's face. "Come on, Lex. Just how much trouble can they be?"

Lex laughed along with her. "Now you've jinxed yourself." She scooted the bag off the bed and gently pushed Amanda onto her back. "We've still got an hour before we have to get the girls up, right?"

Amanda ran her hands underneath Lex's sleep shirt. "At least." She pushed the garment off her wife's shoulders and grinned. "Whatever will we find to do for a whole hour?"

"I'm sure we'll think of something." Lex whipped Amanda's silky gown over her head.

LEX CAME IN from the barn and washed up in the downstairs bathroom off the kitchen. She joined her family at the breakfast table, surprised to see Lorrie in tears. "What's the matter?"

"Mommy said you're leaving this afternoon." Lorrie wiped her nose with the back of her hand.

"Right. I have a meeting in Houston tomorrow. But I'll be back in plenty of time to take you trick-or-treating."

"But you promised we'd go shopping for clothes after school today."

Damn. Thinking quickly, Lex made a decision she hoped wouldn't come back to haunt her. "That's right." She winked at her wife. "We'll still go shopping today. I'll see about moving the meeting back a little."

Amanda touched Lex's arm. "Honey, are you sure? I can—"

"Yep. I promised Lorrie. Right, kiddo?" Lex decided right then and there that if she had to, she'd leave either later this evening, or extra early in the morning. Her children were more important.

Although her lower lip still quivered, Lorrie nodded. "Yes, ma'am."

Melanie perked up at the thought of shopping. "Can I go too?"

Lex looked at Lorrie, who didn't seem bothered by the idea. "Sure. We'll pick you both up after school, hit Davenport's, and go out for dinner." She turned to Amanda. "How's that sound, sweetheart?"

"It's all right with me, if you're really certain." Amanda noticed the girls' empty plates. "Girls, would you please wash up and brush your teeth? We'll be leaving for school soon."

Excited about the impending shopping trip, both children carried their plates to the sink and hurried out of the room. Freckles came out from under the table and happily followed.

Amanda waited until they were out of earshot before speaking. "Lex—"

"Amanda, wait. I promised Lorrie yesterday that we'd go. It just slipped my mind." Lex scooped scrambled eggs onto her fork. "She's been getting a lot of flack at school, mainly by Jerry Sater and his buddies, about how she dresses."

"But she's never said word one about it to me." Amanda finished her juice and wiped her mouth with her napkin. "And what's wrong with how she dresses? Most kids wear jeans to school."

Lex nodded since her mouth was full. She chewed for a few seconds before swallowing. "I know. But I think it's because she wears western shirts and boots. She has tennis shoes at school for gym class, but doesn't wear them anywhere else."

"I'd like to teach that brat Jerry a few things," Amanda said, clearing her place from the table.

"Me too. But that would just make it worse for her and you know it." Lex finished her breakfast and joined Amanda at the sink. "Same thing happened to me when I was a kid. But my old man didn't see any need for separate school and work clothes." Old hurts came to the surface and Lex was grateful for the sudden loving embrace she found herself in. "I'll be damned if I let that to happen to our kids."

Amanda's arms tightened around her partner's waist and she buried her face in Lex's shirt. There were no words needed, just the promise of love and support freely given.

THE LONG DAY finally over, Amanda stretched out on the bed with a heartfelt moan. The shopping trip was a success, and both girls had a great time. As much as she adored her children, her favorite part of the day was bedtime. She rolled over onto her side and watched her nude partner step out of the bathroom. Most definitely her favorite time of day. Although Lex would be turning forty in a few weeks, to Amanda she still looked as athletic as she did when they first met. She sighed as Lex changed into boxer shorts and a tee shirt. *So much for the nice view.*

Lex came over and sat on the edge of the bed. "What's wrong?"

"Nothing." Amanda stretched and slipped her hand under Lex's shirt. "Mmm. Better."

"Oh yeah?" Lex rolled Amanda over and raised her gown. She blew a loud raspberry on her stomach, causing her wife to laugh.

"Stop it!" Amanda struggled, which only made Lex laugh and continue. "Aarrgghh!" Amanda stopped struggling when Lex moved lower. "Oooh." Her nightgown suddenly disappeared, as warm hands began a teasing dance over her body. She wrapped her legs around Lex's hips and twisted, putting her wife beneath her. "Hmm." Amanda straddled Lex's waist. "Now," she slowly divested Lex of her tee shirt. "How long can I torture you?"

Lex grinned. "Do your worst, woman. I can handle anything you can dish out."

"Sounds like a challenge." Amanda lightly ran her fingers along Lex's ribcage and over her chest. She enjoyed the reaction. "Cold?"

"N—" Lex had to clear her throat when Amanda's lips followed the same path. "No. Not cold at all." She jumped when Amanda nibbled a particularly sensitive spot. "Whoa."

SITTING AT HER office desk, Amanda glanced at her watch. It was a few minutes past one, and she sent a silent prayer to Lex, whom she hoped was having a good meeting. Lex had managed to reschedule for noon, allowing her to leave home at the same time as Amanda and the kids. With a heavy sigh, Amanda stared at her inbox. She picked up the top paper and was startled when her phone rang. "Yes?"

"Amanda, you have a call from Red Creek Elementary on line two," Margaret, the receptionist said.

"Thanks." Amanda tapped the flashing light on her phone. "This is Amanda Walters."

"Ms. Walters, this is Principal Nicks. I'm sorry to bother you at work, but I couldn't reach your, ah, partner."

Rolling her eyes at his unease, Amanda returned the paper to the inbox. "No, Lex had to run out of town. What can I do for you?"

The principal cleared his throat. "Ah, yes. Well, it's about your, ah, daughter? Lorraine?"

"Lorrie? What's wrong? Is she sick or hurt?" Amanda looked around the floor by her desk for her purse.

"No, no. Nothing like that. There's been an...incident...here at the school, and I'm afraid she's going to have to go home for the day."

Amanda hooked her right foot around the strap of her purse and tugged it out from under her desk. She stood and placed the bag on her chair. "What kind of incident? Is she all right?"

"She's fine, but she hit another child in the face with a dodge ball. I'm sure you understand that we can't condone that sort of behavior."

"Excuse me?" Amanda sat on the edge of her desk. "How do you know it was done on purpose?"

"The children all know that throwing at the head is not allowed. Poor Jerry Sater is still in the nurse's office. His nose may be broken."

Cringing, Amanda used her shoulder to hold the phone receiver while she put on her jacket. "I'll be right there, Mr. Nicks. Thank you for calling." Amanda hung up before she said something she would regret.

AMANDA WADED THROUGH a group of children who were returning from the playground. She tried to ignore the "wet kid" aroma that filled the hallway. Even as a mother of two active girls, she still had trouble stomaching the smell. She quickly stepped into the office and smiled at the school secretary. "Hi, Mrs. Clevens."

"Ms. Walters, hello." The matronly woman pointed toward the closed door behind her. "She's in there. Go right in."

"Thank you." Amanda tapped on the door.

"Come," the principal's gruff voice answered.

Taking a deep breath, Amanda stepped inside and closed the door behind her. She saw Lorrie sitting in a corner chair, head down, her new clothes covered with playground dirt. She immediately knelt next to Lorrie's chair. "Honey? What happened to your clothes?"

Lorrie raised her head. "Me and Al and Courtney was playing, and Jerry and Russ ran by and pushed us down. They made Al cry, Mommy." Lorrie lunged into Amanda, who caught her instinctively.

"Sssh. It's okay." Amanda tucked Lorrie's head against her shoulder and turned to the principal. "Mr. Nicks?"

"Well." He adjusted his tie. "I wasn't made aware of the other children's actions. But that still doesn't excuse your daughter from hitting Jerry in the face with the ball."

"Did you even bother to find out all the facts before you accused my daughter of something?"

Mr. Nicks frowned. "I take my job very seriously. You can't have bullies on the playground. And the only injury I was made aware of was Jerry Sater's."

It took all of Amanda's willpower not to yell at the pompous man. She decided to ignore him and brushed her hand through Lorrie's hair in an attempt to calm her. Amanda lowered her voice. "Want to tell me about throwing the ball?"

"Jerry pushed Al and made her cry. Her knee was bleeding and Jerry laughed." Lorrie wiped her teary face on Amanda's jacket. "I was mad and threw the ball, but Jerry turned around and it hit him in the face. I didn't mean to hurt him."

The principal interrupted. "It doesn't matter what the intent was, Lorraine. Your actions injured someone else."

"And what about what Jerry did? Is he exempt?" Amanda changed places with Lorrie so that her daughter was in her lap. "I have no problem with taking Lorrie out of school today for her part in the incident. But I do have issues with the instigator getting off scot free."

"Now see here, Ms. Walters—"

Amanda stood. "Lorrie, honey. Could you go out to the front office while I finish talking to Mr. Nicks?" She kissed Lorrie on the forehead before letting her go. Once the door closed again, Amanda turned toward the principal. Her eyes sparkled with rage. "I'm taking my daughter home and she'll be back in school on Monday. If you don't do something about Jerry Sater, I'll notify the authorities. Maybe they can help you handle one trouble-making little boy."

"Ms. Walters, please. I think we can come to some sort of understanding—"

"You're damned right we can. Either you handle the situation, or I will." She opened the door and held out her hand to Lorrie. "Come on, sweetie. You can help me at work until your sister gets out of class." Amanda stormed from the office before her temper totally got away from her.

SOFT MUSIC FROM a small radio filled Amanda's office. The door was closed in an attempt at privacy, as mother and daughter sat at the desk, intent on what they were doing.

Lorrie looked across the desk and watched her mother flip through a short stack of papers. "Mommy?"

"Yes?" Amanda stopped searching for an elusive contract and gave Lorrie her complete attention.

"When will Momma be home?"

"Probably around lunchtime tomorrow. Why?"

Focusing on the paper she had been writing on, Lorrie mumbled, "Is she going to be mad at me because I got sent home again?"

Amanda's answer was postponed by the buzzing of her phone. "Hold on, sweetie." She pushed the speaker button. "Yes?"

"I'm sorry, Amanda. But there's an extremely, um, agitated woman on line one for you."

Giving her daughter what she hoped was a comforting smile, Amanda nodded. "Thanks, Margaret." She picked up the handset and pushed the button. "This is Amanda Walters, how can I help you?"

"Walters? Seriously?" the woman said. "Whatever."

Amanda kept her voice steady, aware of the young ears not far away. She had legally changed her name before she became pregnant with Melanie, so everyone's last name would be the same. "Is there something I can do for you?"

"Damn right you can. I had to take Jerry to the emergency room."

"I'm sorry to hear that. But what—"

Susan's voice took on an even nastier tone. "You're going to pay for my son's medical bills."

Struggling to keep from upsetting Lorrie, Amanda cleared her throat. "Bills? Just what is wrong with him?"

"Well, the emergency room doctor couldn't tell me his nose was broken, so I'm taking Jerry to a specialist. And I expect you and Lexington to pay for it."

"I don't think so."

"You either pay, or I'll sue." Susan's voice grew in intensity until she was screaming. "Your little brat could have killed my boy!"

Amanda had heard enough. "Give me a break. I spoke to the nurse, and she told me it was just a bloody nose. And if your son wasn't such a bully, we wouldn't be having this conversation." Her anger got the better of her. "What happened today was an accident. And if you think for one damned minute you're getting as much as a penny out of us, you're deluded." She slammed the phone down, noticing too late the shocked look on Lorrie's face. "I'm sorry. I shouldn't have lost my temper like that."

Lorrie didn't say anything.

Amanda lifted her purse from the floor. "Why don't we pick up your sister and then get some ice cream? How's that sound?"

"Okay." Lorrie followed her out of the room, her head hung low out of guilt.

Chapter Three

INSIDE THE PICKET fence, the wooden swing set was strategically situated beneath huge shade trees. Lorrie kicked her legs forward to urge her swing higher. Her hair blew across her face and temporarily obscured her eyes. She tried to ignore the girl next to her, who attempted to catch up.

"How do you do that?" Ally huffed. Only a few days older than her best friend, she was several pounds heavier and a couple of inches shorter. She shook her head to move her curly blonde hair away from her mouth. Her own swing wasn't half as high in the air. No matter how hard she kicked, she never got far from the ground.

"I dunno. Just goes like I want it to." Lorrie grinned wildly when her toes touched the closest tree branch. "Yeah!" Her jubilance was short-lived when the back door of the house slammed and two younger girls hurried down the steps. "Crud."

Ally's sister, Penny, was the first to reach them. She was a year younger than Melanie, but they were as close as the older girls were to each other. "Hey, wanna know somethin'? We was playing dolls and I was a mommy."

"That's nice," Lorrie grumbled. She kept swinging, hoping they'd get the hint and leave her and Ally alone.

Melanie stood as close to the swings as was safe. Her small hands were on her hips and she looked eerily like Amanda. "Lorrie, we want to swing, too."

"We were first." Lorrie did her best to ignore her sister. "Come on, Al. Go higher."

"Mommy says you're supposed to share," Melanie said. Freckles sat beside her and she scratched the dog on the top of the head.

Penny jumped and swatted at her sister. "Ally, please? You're not swinging so high anyway."

"Stop it." Ally kicked and slid from the swing, hitting the ground flat on her back. She became completely still and her eyes were closed.

Lorrie waited until her swing came to a low point and nimbly jumped. She dropped to her knees beside her best friend. "Al?" She shook Ally's shoulder. "Hey, are you okay?"

"She's dead," Penny wailed.

"Hush." Lorrie carefully shook Ally again. "Come on, Al. You're scaring the little kids."

Ally's eyes and mouth opened, but she didn't make a sound. Her face took on a fearful grimace and her eyes grew wide.

"Hey." Lorrie lifted Ally into a sitting position and patted her back, causing the other girl to inhale deeply. She held her as Ally coughed and cried. "You're all right. Just got the breath knocked out of you. The same thing happened to me when I fell off Mine, once." Lex had helped her the way she helped Ally now.

Melanie still had tears in her eyes. "I'm gonna go get Mommy."

"No!" Lorrie was afraid they'd get into trouble, and she'd been in enough lately to last her a lifetime. "Everything's fine. Right, Al?"

"Y...yeah." Ally coughed a few more times and rubbed the tears from her face. "Ow."

Lorrie helped Ally to her feet and brushed off her clothes. "Maybe we should go inside and find something else to do."

"Like what?" Penny got on the other side of Ally and grasped her hand. Her spare hand ended up in her mouth and she began to nervously suck on her knuckles. "That was scary, Ally."

"Yeah, it was," Lorrie said. She tapped her leg and Freckles immediately jumped up on her. "You almost was a real angel, instead of just one for Halloween."

Hearing about Halloween perked up the younger girls. Penny especially got excited. "I'm a princess."

Ally rolled her eyes. "We know, Pen. And I'm an angel, Lorrie's a zombie, and Mel's Snow White."

"I know." Penny released her sister's hand and skipped over to Melanie. "I love Snow White. Your dress is so pretty, too."

"Uh-huh. Come on, let's go look at it." Melanie started running for the house, the rest of the girls hurrying to catch up.

FOUR EXCITABLE CHILDREN and one dog raced into the kitchen, which startled Amanda and caused her to drop the spoon she used to stir the pot of stew on the stove.

Melanie was the first to speak. "Mommy, can we wear our costumes? We'll be good."

Penny tugged on Amanda's blouse. "Hey, wanna know something? I'm going to be a princess."

"That's right." Amanda turned to look at the four children. "Lorrie, Ally, will you two help your sisters if they need it?"

Lorrie's smile grew. "Yes, ma'am." She tugged on her little sister's arm. "Come on, Mel. Let's go get dressed up." She led the little group from the room, breaking into a run as they hit the stairs. "Last one up's a rotten egg!" Freckles bounced along beside her, adding a bark every few steps.

"Wait for me," Penny cried, as she had trouble navigating. She was smaller than Melanie, but never let that deter her from following along.

Melanie waited for Penny, taking the younger girl's hand. "We can get dressed in my room." She led the way, moving slower in deference to Penny.

The two older girls had gone to the end of the hall to Lorrie's room and closed the door. She had shared a room with her sister until Melanie turned five. Lorrie had requested her own space and was given one of the guest rooms, which she was allowed to decorate as she desired.

Melanie's room was across the hall from her parent's, and she redecorated as well. The dominant color in her room was pink. Her white, full-sized canopy bed was draped in the bright color, and her white bedspread was covered with pink polka dots. She had posters of her favorite cartoon characters, mainly princesses. Where her sister's room had books to read and sports paraphernalia, Melanie had shelves of coloring books and art supplies. In one corner stood a sturdy easel that was covered with a large pad of paper. Her completed "artwork" covered an entire wall, taped there by her proud parents.

She went to her closet to get her costume, while Penny took her own out of the small suitcase on the bed. They chatted and giggled while changing, leaving their clothes scattered on the floor.

A knock on the door caused both girls to become silent. Melanie had finished dressing and was spinning in a circle. "Come in," she sang.

Lorrie and Ally joined the younger girls. Both were wearing their costumes. Ally was in her angel outfit, minus the wings and halo. Lorrie was dressed in torn, black clothing. Her zombie mask was still in her room. Freckles circled around Melanie, barking. "Mel, quit doing that."

"Hey, wanna know something?" Penny asked Lorrie. She held out the edge of her dress, which was a smaller version of a shimmering yellow ball gown. "I'm a princess."

"I know, Penny." Lorrie had heard the same refrain all afternoon.

Allison stared at Melanie, who had finally stopped spinning around the room. "Something doesn't look right with Mel, Lorrie."

"What?" Lorrie looked at her little sister. She was wearing the same costume as she had last weekend. The dress had a blue top with red sleeves and cape, and a yellow skirt. "She looks okay to me."

"Snow White had dark hair," Allison said. "Mel's hair is too light."

Lorrie turned her head to one side as she studied Melanie, then glanced at the poster over her bed. "You're right. We need to find something to make her hair look more like Snow White's."

"My mommy uses a creamy stuff for color," Penny said. "She's always keeping boxes of it in her bathroom."

"I don't think my moms use stuff like that." Lorrie scrunched her face in thought. "Wait. I got an idea." She left the room, coming back a minute later with Lex's boot shine kit.

AMANDA WAS SETTING the table for dinner when the sound of little feet pounding into the room caused her to look up. "Hi, Penny."

"Hey, wanna know something? Melly's looking just like Snow White."

"Yes, I know, sweetie." Amanda was about to go back to what she was doing when she noticed a dark smudge on Penny's dress. "Penny? What is that on your dress?"

The girl held the dress out. "I dunno." She danced in place. "Maybe it's from Melly's hair."

"What?" Amanda stopped what she was doing. "Penny, what happened to her hair?"

"I dunno."

Amanda sighed heavily. "Where are the other girls?"

"Upstairs in Melly's room." Penny took Amanda by the hand. "Come on, I'll show you."

Amanda allowed herself to be escorted upstairs. The door to Melanie's room was open and she could hear the children's voices coming from the attached bathroom.

"Hold still," Lorrie commanded.

Allison's voice piped up, "Careful. You're getting it in her ear."

Amanda stood in the doorway to the bathroom and was shocked speechless at the scene.

Melanie was seated on the closed toilet lid, a formerly-white towel around her shoulders and black streaks in her blonde hair. Lorrie and Allison were on either side of her, both with black shoeshine sponges in their hands. Freckles pranced between the girls, hoping for attention.

"What the hell is going on here?" Amanda asked, her voice bouncing off the walls.

Both Lorrie and Allison looked up with the same "oh shit" expression on their faces. Allison was the first one to speak. "We're making Mel more like Snow White." Her brilliant idea was quickly losing its luster, especially with the very angry adult standing so close by. "Um, my mommy puts colors on her hair, so we thought it would be okay."

Amanda closed her eyes and counted silently to ten. When she opened her eyes, she tried to keep her voice calm. "Allison, I want you and Penny to go downstairs to wash up, then sit in the den." After the two left, Amanda knelt beside Melanie. "Sweetie, keep the towel around your shoulders and go to the kitchen. We'll try to wash this stuff off in the sink." She stood and put her hands on her hips. "Lorrie, put your momma's shine kit back where you got it, then go to your room. I'll deal with you when I'm through with your sister."

"Yes, ma'am." Lorrie bowed her head and crept out of the bathroom, Freckles following close behind.

LEX CHECKED THE clock on the dash of the truck and grinned. Traffic had been light coming home, and as she pulled beside the house it wasn't yet five o'clock. She couldn't wait to see the look on her wife's face. After parking next to the picket fence, she whistled a tune as she grabbed her unused overnight bag from the back seat. She jogged up the steps and opened the back door. Hearing noise coming from the kitchen, Lex crossed the threshold with a huge smile on her face. "I'm home!"

Amanda looked up from what she was doing. She had Melanie stretched out along the kitchen counter, her head over the sink. "Good. That means you can go upstairs and talk to *your* daughter."

"What happened?" Lex crossed the room and stood next to Amanda. She looked down at Melanie. "What's that in her hair?"

"Boot polish," Amanda muttered. She poured more shampoo and started to scrub again.

The phone in the kitchen rang, halting Lex from asking any more questions. She picked up the handset. "Hello?"

"Hey, boss. Could you come up to the corral?" Roy, the ranch foreman asked. "Chet found an injured horse. I think you need to see it."

Never so relieved to be dragged from the house, Lex was more than happy to comply. "Sure, Roy. I'll be right there." She hung up the phone and turned to Amanda. "I'm sorry, sweetheart. Something's come up at the corral by the bunkhouse. It's going to be dark soon, so I shouldn't be long. I'll talk to Lorrie as soon as I get back, okay?" Lex kissed Amanda's cheek and left the house before the look she was getting could incinerate her.

LEX PARKED HER truck next to the bunkhouse corral and climbed out. She saw Roy and Chet looking over a gray gelding and walked over to join them. "Hey, fellas. What's up?"

Roy pointed to the horse's hindquarter. "Nothing good, that's for sure. See for yourself." He watched as Lex carefully examined the animal. Several deep gashes were bleeding sluggishly, and the horse kept stomping and dancing anytime someone came near.

"Damn." Lex turned to her foreman. "Did you call the vet?"

"Yeah. Dr. Hernandez should be here soon." He moved closer to Lex and lowered his voice. "Are you thinking what I'm thinking?"

Lex nodded. "Big cat of some kind. Probably hanging around one of the new wells." She turned to Chet. "Where did you find him?"

"That's the weird thing, Lex. Mac wasn't off in the brush somewhere. He was with the work horses down by the creek."

It wasn't what Lex wanted to hear. Having a predator so close to their home made her nervous. "I want everyone to keep a gun close by until we catch this cat. Roy, talk to the vet about setting up traps. Maybe we can work with the wildlife service and relocate this thing. It's probably come down from the hills looking for water."

Roy scratched his chin. "Sounds about right. This damned drought has thrown everything out of whack."

All three turned when the door of the bunkhouse opened. A

slender, middle-aged woman stepped out and brushed off her apron. She came over to the corral, but kept outside of it. "There you are. I came to tell you dinner's ready," she told the men. "Hello, Lex."

Lex ducked her head in greeting. "Hi, Helen. I see you're still putting up with Roy and the boys."

Helen laughed. "Someone has to. Are you staying for dinner?" She brushed one hand along her pinned up blonde hair. "It's fried chicken."

"No, I'm afraid I can't. I just came up to check out this horse." Lex joined Helen at the fence. "Besides, Amanda's got me on a diet. You're too good of a cook, and I'd end up weighing three hundred pounds if I stayed up here."

Roy ducked through the corral fence and put an arm around his wife. "Why do you think I walk to the main house?" He kissed her head. "Speaking of walking, I'd like you to stay close to home unless you're in a vehicle."

"Why?"

Lex crossed her arms and wished she'd have thought to wear her coat. "We've got a big cat somewhere nearby, Helen. Please be careful going to the bunkhouse. And take one of the trucks if you decide to come up to the main house. It's not safe for anyone to be out on foot right now."

LORRIE SAT ON her bed, sniffling to keep the tears at bay. Freckles jumped up beside her and started to lick her face. "Thanks, Freckles. At least you love me." She hugged the dog to her chest and closed her eyes. Lately she felt as if she could do nothing right. "It's not my fault," she muttered to the dog. "And I bet I'll get into more trouble when Momma comes home." She cried into the soft fur.

The sound of the back door slamming caused her to look up. When it slammed again, she shook her head. "Mommy doesn't want to even see me. All I do is cause trouble."

Freckles licked Lorrie's face again in an attempt to soothe her best friend.

"They'd be happier if I wasn't here, Freckles." Lorrie slipped off the bed and went to her closet. She took out a backpack and tossed it on the bed. "Maybe if I went and stayed with Gramma and Grandpa Jake, Jerry's mom would leave Mommy and Momma alone." She gathered a couple of books, a pair of socks, and her favorite pajamas and stuffed them in the pack.

After changing into her jeans and denim shirt, Lorrie put on her jacket. She took the emergency ladder out of her closet and opened her window. Having been coached by Lex on its use, Lorrie had no trouble attaching the ladder to the sill. Freckles danced around her, wanting to play. "You be good, Freckles." She kissed the dog on the head then put her backpack over her shoulders. With a last wistful glance at her room,

Lorrie climbed out the window and down the ladder.

Freckles barked at the open window. She stood on her hind legs and propped her front legs on the sill, trying to find a way to get down to Lorrie. Unable to bring Lorrie back, she ran to the closed bedroom door and barked. Not getting any attention, she started to scratch at the wood, and continued to bark.

LEX LOOKED ON as Dr. Hernandez and his assistant took care of the injured horse.

The vet watched his colleague carefully stitch the wound. Ronnie Bristol had recently returned from veterinary school. As he had interned with Dr. Hernandez, he had been thrilled by the prospect of joining the vet's already established farm animal practice.

Roy stood beside Lex. His wife had gone into the house, gently threatening him if he didn't follow soon. "He's turned into a fine young man," he remarked. "Hard to believe he's old enough to be doing that."

"I know what you mean. I still think of him as that kid who followed me all over the ranch. Being adopted by Martha and Charlie was the best thing in the world for him." The cell phone on Lex's belt vibrated, causing her to jump. "Damn." She glanced at the display before opening the phone. "Hi, sweetheart."

"Lex, it's about Lorrie." Amanda sounded frantic.

"Tell her I'll be there soon. We're just finishing up here, and—"

"She's missing."

"What? I thought you told me she was in her room."

"She was. But I heard Freckles going nuts, and I went upstairs to see what was going on. Lorrie used the emergency ladder and took off."

"Damn it!" Forgetting all about the injured horse, Lex jogged to her truck. "Roy, give me a call when the vet's done. Lorrie's left the house by herself," she yelled over one shoulder. She jumped into the truck and took off, still talking to Amanda on the phone. "I'm on my way. It's not quite dark yet, so I should be able to find her pretty quickly."

It took Lex less than three minutes to get to the house. The truck skidded to a stop next to the picket fence and Lex was out before the engine completely died. She leapt over the three foot fence and ran into the house.

Amanda met her in the hall. "I looked around outside, but couldn't tell which way she went." Her voice cracked as Lex put her arms around her. "It's my fault."

"No, sweetheart. She's ten. It's just something that kids do." Lex kissed Amanda on the forehead. "I'm going to run to the barn and saddle up. It'll be easier to find her if I'm on horseback. Call Roy and tell him I'll head toward the main road."

Amanda helped Lex with her duster. "You'll find her soon, right?"

"Yeah." Lex's hands shook as she tried to fasten the duster closed.

"Amanda, Roy called me earlier because a big cat attacked one of the horses."

"But we've never had any problems with them before. Why now?"

"I think the drought caused it to come down from the hills. Whatever you do, keep the kids inside. The horse was near the creek when it was attacked." Lex crammed her black Stetson on her head. She was about to leave when she remembered something. "Take the girls upstairs for a minute, will you? I want to get a gun out of the office."

Amanda's eyes widened. Lex was not fond of guns, and only brought them out when absolutely necessary. She took Lex by the hand and led her down the hall. "No, I think they need to know how serious this is."

Three quiet little girls sat on the sofa, staring at the television. Melanie was the first to see Lex and jumped to her feet. "Momma!" She intercepted Lex before she could get to the office. "Lorrie's runned away."

"I know, sweetheart. But I'm going to go out and find her, okay?" Lex pulled Melanie into her arms and held her close. "You be good for your mommy while I'm gone."

"'kay." Melanie kissed Lex on the cheek and giggled as she was spun down to the floor. Freckles danced along beside her, wanting in on the fun. They both returned to the sofa as the draw of the animated program was too strong for the little girl.

Lex opened the closet door in the office. She took the key that hung above the door and unlocked the gun safe inside. After she checked to make certain the gun was loaded, she felt a tug on her hip.

"Thought you'd want a radio, too." Amanda attached the handheld to Lex's belt.

"Thanks."

Amanda nodded. "I wish I were going with you." Over the years, Amanda had become an accomplished rider in her own right. "Please find her, Lex. I don't know what I'd do if anything happened to her."

"I will." Lex kissed her wife one last time before leaving the house.

After saddling Thunder, Lex stopped by the house again. She took a length of rope from her saddle and met Amanda at the front door. She had called ahead to have Freckles on a leash. "Thanks. I think Freckles can find Lorrie just about anywhere."

Amanda tied the rope to the end of the dog's leash. "I hope so. It's starting to get dark."

THE SUN WAS setting, and dark shadows covered most of the road. The wind was getting colder and stronger. Unaware of the drama at the house, Lorrie kicked at the rocks along the road. She was tired, and hadn't even made it to the bridge. "Wish I would have brought Freckles with me," she muttered. "I'm bored."

Her great adventure had quickly dulled, and she also wished she would have thought to bring along her horse. "Mine would like this. But I'm still grounded from riding," she sniffled. "Stupid Jerry."

The shadows unnerved Lorrie. Tired of walking, she spied an opening in the brush. "Maybe if I go through here I can get to Gramma's faster." She left the road, pulling her jacket up closer to her body as the chill settled in.

Small trees and heavy scrub made the faint trail hard to navigate. Within minutes, Lorrie stopped and looked around. Nothing looked familiar. With the sun barely above the horizon she couldn't see but a few feet in front of her. Tears welled up in her eyes when she realized she was lost.

FRECKLES DANCED ALONG the gravel road, enjoying the new adventure. Lex watched as the dog flitted from one side of the road to the other. "I sure hope you know where you're going, you crazy dog." She had tied the rope to her saddle horn and held up a battery-powered lantern to light the way.

Suddenly Freckles left the road and tried to go into the brush.

Lex stopped Thunder and groaned. "Damn. I was afraid of that." She raised the lantern and looked into the wooded area. "Thunder, I don't think you'll be able to get through there."

It only took Lex a few minutes to gather what she needed from the horse. She strapped the rifle across her back and tied the reins to the saddle. "Might as well head back to the barn. No sense in you hanging around here." She swatted his rear and watched as the horse trotted up the road. Lex took out her phone and called Amanda. "Hey."

"Did you find her?"

"Not yet. Freckles thinks she's left the road westward 'bout two hundred yards before the bridge. I've sent Thunder back to the house so if you could watch out for him, I'd appreciate it."

"All right." Amanda lowered her voice. "Any sign of anything else?"

Lex ducked to avoid a tree branch as she followed the dog into the brush. "Not that I can tell. Have Roy and the guys gotten there yet?"

"They're at the barn. Helen's here and is going to watch the kids, while I ride out with the guys. Ronnie's coming, too."

Knowing better than to tell her no, Lex kept silent. She was having trouble holding onto Freckles and the lantern with the same hand, so she pulled the dog close. "Amanda? I've got to hang up now. The damned dog is going nuts."

"Maybe Lorrie's close by. Call me as soon as you find her."

"I will." Lex put the phone back on her belt and squatted next to Freckles. "Since we're both on foot, I'm going to let you loose. Go find your buddy." Lex unhooked the leash and watched as Freckles took off down a small trail. "Sure, don't make it easy on me." She pulled her hat down tighter and struggled to follow.

THE SUN HAD set and the moonlight wasn't enough to break through the dense brush. Lorrie kept wading deeper into the trees, hopelessly lost.

She stumbled across a fallen branch and fell to her knees. She was cold, hungry and scared. Tired of walking, she huddled against a tree, wrapping her arms around her legs. She laid her head on her knees and started to cry. "I want to go home."

Wind blew through the trees, bringing a distinct chill. The dried branches rubbed together, making a frightful sound.

A twig breaking to her right caused Lorrie to raise her head and look around. "Momma?"

Through the darkness, the rustling sound came closer. Unable to see, Lorrie cried out as an animal broke through the dense brush.

"Momma!"

LEX GRUMBLED AS another tree branch scratched at her face. She was practically running to keep up with Freckles and more than once wished she'd kept the dog on her leash. "Damn it, dog. Would you slow down?"

Freckles came back to Lex and barked, loving the game. She bowed to Lex and wagged her stubby tail. Her sharp bark pierced the evening and she took off again.

"You crazy little beast," Lex growled, doing her best to follow along. She stumbled over a dead tree. Hearing a different noise, Lex stilled and listened. "Lorrie?" She hurried to her feet.

Twigs poked at her as Lex ran through the brush. Breathing heavily, she heard the sound again. "Lorrie!" She broke through to a small clearing and heard her child scream.

"Momma!" Lorrie saw the apparition come at her and squealed as an animal charged. "Help, Momma!"

Lex landed on her knees and spun the rifle around, but kept it pointed at the sky. She used one hand to wave the lantern toward the scream. She saw a white blur leap toward Lorrie. "Freckles, down!"

Lorrie's screams turned to giggles as her four-legged friend licked her face clean. She hugged the dog close. "I'm so glad to see you, Freckles."

Lex's relief made her weak. She checked to make certain the safety was on the rifle and propped it against the nearest tree before getting to her feet and crossing the clearing. She pulled Lorrie into her arms. "Lil' bit, don't you ever do this again."

"I'm sorry, Momma." Lorrie snuggled close. "But Mommy was

mad, and I got into trouble at school, and then we messed up Mel's hair, and—"

"Sssh." Without releasing her hold, Lex took the phone from her belt and hit the speed dial.

"Lex?" Amanda answered after half a ring.

"Yeah. I found her. She's fine."

A sob tore from Amanda's throat. "Oh, thank god." She muffled her phone and said something to the group she was with and then came back to the phone. "Where are you?"

Lex looked around the clearing. "Honestly? I have no idea. We left the road not far from the bridge and headed west. I think I can walk us back toward the road, but I'm not positive."

"We'll bring your horse back that way," Amanda said.

"Great. I'll keep the lantern aimed toward the road, so maybe y'all can see us before we get out of the damned trees."

Amanda's laugh came out as strangled. "I love you so much. Please be careful."

"Always. I love you too, sweetheart." Lex closed the phone and returned it to her belt. She slowly got to her feet, Lorrie still in her arms. "Come on, kiddo. Let's go home."

Suddenly Freckles turned and growled low in her throat. Her hackles rose and she stood in front of Lex and Lorrie, staring into the darkness.

"Freckles, stay." Lex heard another growl, then a high-pitched scream.

The scrub parted and an animal stepped into the clearing, its yellow eyes glowing in the light of the lantern. Not much bigger than Freckles, the bobcat's reddish brown fur blended in well with the dead leaves around it.

Lex placed Lorrie behind her. She looked across the clearing, where her gun still leaned against the tree. "Damn." She bent and grabbed the growling dog's collar. "Freckles, hush."

The cat's ears went back and it took another step forward. It focused on Freckles, apparently not noticing the humans with her.

"Lorrie, stay behind me." Lex started to edge slowly around the clearing in an attempt to reach the gun.

Growling, the animal turned its head and watched Lex closely. It took a step back as she came nearer.

Lex took that as a good sign. When Freckles struggled in her grasp, she lifted the dog and tucked it under her arm. She remembered something she had once read, and hoped it was true. The almanac article stated that bobcats were rarely harmful to humans, and could usually be run off with loud noises. "Hey! Get out of here," she yelled at the cat.

It snarled and crouched lower.

"Hyah, go on, you mangy beast!" Lex continued to yell nonsense at the bobcat while she moved closer to her gun.

The large, noisy creature coming toward the cat was more than it bargained for. The bobcat growled once more and took off deeper into the brush.

Lex took the extra steps and picked up the rifle. She hitched the strap over her shoulder and put her shaky hand on Lorrie's shoulder. "Ready to go home, kiddo?"

"Momma, what was that? It looked liked Terry's cat, but bigger." Lorrie tucked her hand into Lex's.

"That was a bobcat, Lorrie. They're wild animals and can be extremely dangerous. You did real good, sweetheart."

Lorrie snuggled close to Lex. "I was scared. But you made it run away."

"Yep. And until we can trap the cat and send it away, I want you and your sister to stay very close to the house, unless an adult is with you. All right?"

"Yes, ma'am."

Lex took the leash from her duster pocket and clipped it to Freckles collar. "Good girl." She ruffled the dog's fur before setting her down.

AMANDA LED THE way, while Roy led Lex's horse. She stopped and turned in her saddle to face him. "For the last time, I don't care."

"But, there's no sense in you being out here. Lorrie's safe with Lex, and—"

"And what?" Amanda turned her horse. "I'm not going home until my entire family is with me. You're more than welcome to go home, Roy."

He pushed his hat back and scratched his forehead. "You know better than that. I just thought—"

"I know, and I appreciate it." Amanda smiled at Roy. "Thanks for caring."

He ducked his head, embarrassed. "Um, do you want to split up so we can cover more of the road?" A bright light came out of the heavy underbrush to his right.

"Tired of being out here, Roy?" Lex asked, her voice weary.

Amanda dropped from her horse and jogged to Lex. She knelt in front of the ragged group and pulled Lorrie into her arms. "Don't you ever run away again, Lorraine Marie Walters. I was scared to death." She looked up into Lex's shadowed face. "Are you okay?"

"Yeah. Been a long day, though." Lex came close to dropping Freckles leash when Amanda stood and embraced her. She could feel her wife tremble. "It's all right, baby." She kissed Amanda lightly on the lips. "Let's go home." She let Amanda take the lantern from her.

Lorrie looked up at her hero. "Can I ride Thunder with you, Momma?"

"Sure thing, kiddo." She lifted Freckles and handed the squirming dog to Roy. "Mind handling this one?"

He held the animal against his chest. "She take you right to Lorrie?"

"Yep." Lex scratched Freckle's head before taking control of her horse. "Thanks for coming out here tonight with Amanda."

"Anytime." He tipped his hat and turned his horse toward the barn.

Lex put Lorrie into her saddle. She hooked the backpack over the saddle horn and climbed up behind her. "You want to drive?"

"Can I?" Lorrie took the reins as Lex put an arm around her waist. "Let's go, Thunder." Lorrie directed the horse to follow Roy, grinning at Amanda when she rode up beside them. "I'm handling Thunder," she said.

Amanda laughed at the joy on her daughter's face. She could tell by Lex's expression that something shook her wife, and was almost afraid to find out what had happened.

ONCE ALL FOUR girls were tucked into bed, Lex and Amanda returned to their own room and closed the door. Lex sat on the edge of the bed and removed her boots, sighing as she felt the long day catch up with her.

Amanda heard the sigh and joined her on the bed. "Are you all right?" She put her arm around Lex's shoulders and leaned into her.

"Yeah." Lex kissed Amanda's head. "Cut it close tonight," she muttered, talking about finding Lorrie shortly before the bobcat came along. She had filled in Amanda on the entire ordeal earlier, after Lorrie couldn't stop talking about it.

"I know. I can't believe you yelled to make it run away."

Lex's arm snaked around Amanda and pulled her even closer. "I'd read it in a magazine once. Just hoped it would work. They're usually afraid of things bigger than them, that's why I was so worried when we found a horse scratched up. But Mac more than likely startled it at a watering tank."

"Whatever the reason, I'm glad you were there." Amanda started to unbutton Lex's shirt. "I think we could both use a nice, hot shower. I don't know about you, but eau-de-horse isn't my favorite fragrance." Her hand tracked down the smooth stomach, getting the expected laugh.

"Best idea I've heard all day." Lex stood and brought Amanda with her.

Chapter Four

THE SILENCE OF the empty house was beginning to get to Eleanor Gordon. She'd spent the last six months hidden away from the outside world, only going out when the cupboards and refrigerator were bare. She sat in the shadowed living room, curled up in one corner of the sofa. She hadn't bothered to turn on the heat. Instead, she wrapped herself in one of her grandfather's suit jackets and stared at the darkened television. Her eyes tracked to the set of photos strewn across the fireplace mantle. "I wish you were here," she whispered.

Last week's visit from Lex was Ellie's undoing. She thought she was doing better until Lex arrived and tried to get her to step outside of the house. "How can I make her understand?" Ellie hadn't just lost a grandfather, but the one person she had come to count on in the world. Within days of his passing, she'd shut everyone out.

She'd sent Nancy, Travis' housekeeper of many years, away not long after the funeral. The older woman was too much of a reminder of what Ellie had lost. Nancy had been excited by the prospect of living closer to her own grandchildren. Her return to Dallas was both a relief and another painful loss for Ellie.

The phone rang, breaking Ellie out of her bout of self-pity. She tried to ignore the sound, but it continued to ring for several minutes. "Damn it!" She flung the jacket off her shoulders and stalked across the room. "What?" The gentle voice on the other end caused her to tear up again. "No, I'm doing okay."

Ellie took the cordless phone with her and sat on the sofa. "No. I'm not really dressed for company." She released a heavy sigh at the caller's persistence. "Really, you don't have to." The voice became adamant and Ellie relented. "Fine. I'll see you in a little while." She disconnected the call and tossed the handset onto the coffee table. "Damn."

She frowned when she noticed what a mess the house had become. Empty glasses and dirty dishes covered every available space in the living room and she knew she didn't have time to do much about it. Ellie stood and tried to comb her fingers through her brown hair. Limp and filthy, the stringy mess was so knotted with tangles she wasn't sure if she'd be able to brush them all out. With another resigned sigh, she headed for the bathroom to take a shower.

Fifteen minutes later, Ellie emerged from her bedroom feeling much more human. The medical scrubs she wore hung off her frame, but they were the only clean clothes she could find.

She was still hauling dirty dishes out of the living room when the doorbell rang. "Hold on." Taking the handful she had into the kitchen, she hustled to the front door and opened it. "Hi."

Amanda stood on the porch with her arms crossed. "You keep ignoring my invitations."

"Yeah, well." Ellie shrugged and held the door open wider. "You know how it is. Come on in."

"Thanks."

Ellie led her to the living room and had the good grace to blush. "Sorry about the mess. I wasn't expecting company."

"I'm not company, Ellie. I'm family." Amanda scooted old newspapers off the couch and sat at one end. Even through her coat she felt the chill in the room and suppressed a shudder. "It's freezing in here."

Curling up on the opposite side, Ellie put her feet on the cushion and wrapped her arms around her legs. She rested her chin on her knees. "I hadn't really noticed."

"Honey, you can't keep living like this. We all miss Travis, but he wouldn't want you doing this to yourself." Amanda scooted closer and put her hand on Ellie's arm. "When are you going back to work?"

"I'm not. At least not at the nursing home. They let me go about a month after Grandpa, uh, passed." Blinking away the tears, Ellie sniffled. "There's nothing left for me here."

Amanda wrapped her arm around Ellie. "You're wrong. You've got a family who loves you." She kissed the grieving woman's head. "Gather your things. You're coming home with me."

Ellie shook her head and tried to push Amanda away. "No, I can't."

"Why not?" Amanda stretched her other arm out wide. "Afraid to leave all this? Sorry, that's not going to work. Pack up some clothes." She flicked the edge of Ellie's shirt. "On second thought, just put on your shoes. We'll stop by Davenport's and get you some things that fit."

Allowing herself to be pulled to her feet, Ellie tried one last time. "I don't want to sound ungrateful, but this isn't really necessary. I was already working on the house when you called."

"Uh-huh. And that's why it looks so nice?" Amanda lightly yanked on the ends of Ellie's hair. "And your hair's wet because?"

"I just got out of the shower." Ellie tried to hide newspapers under the sofa with the tip of her foot. From the look on Amanda's face, she wasn't successful. Even after all these years, Amanda was still the one woman she couldn't say no to. "Um, okay. Wait here. I'll be right back."

Amanda laughed at Ellie's actions. "Just grab your shoes and toothbrush," she yelled to the retreating woman. "We'll come back next weekend and clean up together."

THE LONG DINING table was not quite half full, yet the few who shared the space were boisterous enough for an entire crew. Lex groaned and pushed her plate away. "Helen, that was fantastic." She glanced at the remains of the roast and potatoes that littered her dish. "I'm going to have to take up jogging or something to combat your cooking."

"That's very sweet of you to say. But I don't think you have anything to worry about." Helen stood and started to clear the table but was stopped by the two hired hands.

"We'll handle it, Mrs. Wilson," Jack said. He gathered several plates while Chet picked up a couple of serving dishes.

Lex shared a smile with Roy. "Looks like she's got them trained. Especially Jack. I think he's got a little crush on your wife."

Roy leaned back in his chair. "Can't really blame him, can you?"

"Nope. She's a wonderful woman, my friend. And a hell of a cook." Lex lowered her voice. "I know it's slow right now, but are Chet and Jack enough? We can always bring in a few more guys."

"The three of us can handle things, Boss. And I've got a few guys in town I can call if we need them. Hell, you do more than your share." Hearing the two men arguing over who would wash and who would rinse the dishes, he raised his voice. "No wonder the boys are turning into housewives."

"Hey!" Chet yelled good-naturedly. It didn't stop him from running Helen out of the kitchen.

Helen returned to her place at the table and smiled her appreciation to Roy, who had poured her a cup of coffee. "I swear, those two men won't let me do the cleanup after meals anymore. I think you need to find more for them to do, since they have so much energy."

"I'm sure something can be arranged." Roy edged his chair closer and put his arm around Helen's shoulders. "Lex, if you'll take the north well, the guys and I will divvy up the rest."

Lex nodded as she sipped her coffee. "Sounds good to me. I promised Lorrie a chance to spend the day in the saddle so that will be perfect."

"You're not taking the truck?"

"Nah. I know it's a ways off from everything, but if we ride slowly we can make it last all day. Lorrie's been having some trouble at school, and I think a day out will help."

Helen played with the hand on her shoulder. "That's a shame. Is there anything we can do? She's such a sweet girl."

Leaning back in her chair, Lex released a heavy sigh. "It's the same as it's always been. Just a couple of rotten kids spoiling it for everyone. I went through the exact thing at her age." She was about to say more when her cell phone rang. "Sorry, folks." Lex stood and flipped open the phone as she walked into the living room. "Lex Walters." She listened for a moment and checked her watch. "That's right. Sure. Okay, then. Do you need directions? No? All right. See you in a few." She closed her phone and returned to the dining room.

"Everything all right, Boss?" Roy asked.

"Yep. Got a buyer coming out to look at Coco's colt. Said they saw the flyer I placed at the feed store." Clipping her cell to her belt, Lex leaned against the doorframe.

"Thunder's latest, right?"

Lex nodded. "I was hoping to place him before Christmas. If this buyer looks good, that'll be one less we have to worry about this winter." She crossed the room and took her coat from the back of her chair. She slipped it on and gave Helen a nod. "Guess I'd better get up to the house. Thanks again for a great lunch."

AMANDA PARKED THE Xterra in her usual spot in front of the playground. It was where the girls knew to look for her and she always arrived early enough to secure the location. She stole a glance at her passenger, who had been silent since they left the clothing store.

The shopping trip had worn Ellie out. Her energy levels were practically non-existent since she spent the majority of her time locked up in the house she had shared with Travis. After traipsing through the clothing store for an hour, her entire body felt like jelly. She rested her head against the window, her eyes closed.

Concerned, Amanda touched Ellie's shoulder. "Hey."

"Hmm?" Ellie opened her eyes and faced Amanda. "Sorry."

"You don't have to apologize. I was only going to ask if you're about ready to be invaded by the girls. They should be out in a few minutes."

Ellie's face slowly creased into a smile. "I've missed them."

"They've missed their 'El', too." Amanda squeezed Ellie's arm. "We all have. That's one of the reasons I kidnapped you today."

"Just one?"

Amanda studied the crease in her jeans intently. "Lex and I have been going 'round and 'round about bringing someone in to help with the house and the girls."

"And my cousin has been her usual stubborn self about it?" Ellie asked.

"Not exactly." Amanda turned in her seat so she could face Ellie. "Don't tell Lex, but I've pretty much come over to her side of the argument. I just don't want her to think she's going to win every time."

Ellie laughed. "Don't worry. Your secret is safe with me. Over the last few years, I've become quite fond of that bull-headed wife of yours. But I agree it's best to keep her on her toes."

"Thanks."

"So, you also took me hostage because you needed someone on your side against Lex?"

Amanda shook her head. "Actually, I want to surprise her by hiring a new housekeeper, and I'd like another opinion when I start interviewing."

The sound of the school bell could barely be heard over the engine of the SUV. Within minutes, the first group of happy children poured through the front doors. First out was the kindergarten class. Escorted by their teacher, the youngest members of the school milled around in little groups close to the door.

Ellie, who had never seen school let out, was completely fascinated. "Even at that age, they've already developed their little cliques."

"Scary, isn't it? Here come the first and second graders. Watch how they totally ignore the younger ones, as if they are that more mature."

Less orderly than their predecessors, the next wave came tearing through the doors. They brushed by the kindergarteners just as Amanda had said.

"Unbelievable." Ellie watched as the final set of children came out. She easily spotted Lorrie, who somehow found her little sister in the melee and solicitously escorted her toward the SUV. "Is it like this every day?"

"Pretty much."

"Wow. Elementary school teachers have got to be some of the bravest people on the face of the earth," Ellie mused. She turned around to face the back seat as the door opened. "Hey, girls."

Melanie was the first inside and she scooted across the seat to her usual spot. "El," she squealed. "Are you not sick no more?"

Ellie glanced at Amanda, who shrugged. "Yeah. I'm feeling a lot better now, thanks to your mom."

Lorrie climbed in beside her sister and closed the car door. "Hi, El. Whatcha doin' here?"

"Lorrie! That's not polite. But for your information, Ellie is going to be staying with us for a while."

Both girls cheered, causing Ellie to blush. The love that surrounded her eased the ache that had been in her chest for the last half year. She looked forward to being a part of an active family again.

BACK AT THE ranch, Lex paced in the living room as she waited for the buyer to arrive. She was about to return to her office when she heard the sound of tires rolling across the graveled driveway. She fought the urge to peek through the living room blinds and instead slowly made her way to the front door. She opened it as her guest stepped up the stairs to the porch. "Welcome to the Rocking W. Come on in out of the cold." After closing the door behind her guest, Lex held out her hand. "I'm Lex Walters. Let me take your coat."

The smaller figure removed their hat and coat to reveal a woman close to Lex's age. "Pleased to meet you. I'm Shelby Fisher."

Lex accepted the woman's coat and hung it on a spare hook by the door. You from around here?"

"Yeah. We bought a small place on the other side of Somerville a few years ago. Nothing like your spread, but I'm enjoying it."

Pleased to meet another businesswoman, Lex gestured for Shelby to enter the living room. "Come on in, I've got some coffee in my office."

Freckles, who had been asleep in her bed by the fireplace, raised her head at the newcomer. When she decided Shelby posed no threat, she lowered her head and closed her eyes again.

"Coffee sounds great." Shelby looked around the spacious living room as they headed for the office door in the far corner. "Nice place you've got here."

"Thanks." Waiting until her guest was seated, Lex poured two mugs of coffee from the carafe on her desk. "Take anything?"

Shelby shook her head as she accepted the cup. "No thanks." She leaned back in her chair and studied the woman across the desk. "I really appreciate you meeting me on such short notice. When I saw your flyer at the feed store, it took all I had not to race out here."

"Not a problem. To tell you the truth, I wasn't sure if anyone was going to be interested. Not many folks are buying right now."

"True. I've been looking for a good stud, but haven't been able to find one in my price range that wasn't broken down. When I saw your ad, I thought I'd take a chance."

Lex nodded. "Good idea. Are you in the horse trade?"

"No, not really. We've got a paint mare, and I picked up a nice sorrel mare a year or so ago. Right now we mainly board other people's stock. But I'd like to start up a training facility or a riding school." Shelby sipped her coffee. "The old guys at the feed store have good things to say about you."

"They're a fun bunch," Lex said. "Since you're on the other side of town, have you done any business with Lockneer? He's got some real good horses."

Shelby choked on her coffee and wiped her chin. "Uh, no. He doesn't care much for me, or my partner."

Lex caught the subtle hint. "Don't feel bad." Lex handed Shelby a tissue. "He hates me, too. Homophobic bastard." She put her cup on the desk. "Want to go see the colt?"

"Sure." Shelby set her mug down also and followed Lex from the office.

In less than five minutes, the pair stepped inside the barn closest to the house. Shelby glanced around and whistled. "Impressive."

"Thanks." Lex led her to a stall near the rear of the barn. Inside was a small bay colt. His face had a white streak down the center that went all the way to his nose. Lex opened the stall and gently grasped the animal's halter. "Come on, fella."

Shelby studied the colt as Lex walked him around the barn. "He's a handsome one, that's for sure."

"Yep. Good stock." Lex pointed to the other side of the barn. "Sire's over there. Dam's up at the other barn. We can drive up and take a look at her if you want." She handed the colt to Shelby. "Why don't you two get acquainted?"

With an almost reverence, Shelby brushed her hands over the animal's coat. She carefully inspected every inch of him before looking at Lex. "He's magnificent. Why on earth do you want to sell him?"

Lex smiled, pleased with the other woman's obvious knowledge of horses. "He's too good an animal to geld, and I've already got a nice stud. No sense in him competing with his sire."

"I guess not. I'm almost afraid to ask how much you want for him." Shelby's eyes widened at the figure Lex quoted. "Kinda low, isn't it?"

"Maybe." Lex stepped to the opposite side of the colt and began running her hand across his back in a soothing motion. "This drought has made things rough for us. One less mouth to feed will easily offset what I could get for him next spring. Besides, I'm hoping this could be the start of a good business relationship. Having an ally is never a bad thing."

Shelby held out her hand. "You've got a deal. I've got my checkbook with me, but I'll have to run back to the house for my trailer."

"Actually, I need to pick up a few things in town and was going to take a trailer. I can follow you and do my errands afterward, if that's okay with you."

"That would be more than okay. Thanks."

AS SHELBY'S TRUCK left the highway onto a small dirt road, Lex took in the surroundings. They passed a small frame house, the well-kept flowerbeds around it attesting to its care. Not far behind the house was a barn and corral. Several horses milled freely in the enclosure, heads turning as Shelby's truck parked nearby.

Lex pulled past Shelby then backed the trailer up to the corral. She got out and met Shelby by the gate. "I like how you've got the corral sectioned off. How many horses do you stable here?"

"Five in all. Three boarders and our two. I'm about to add another set of stables this winter. We tore down the old barn a couple of years ago when business picked up. My partner and I built this one ourselves." Shelby opened the trailer and climbed in beside the colt. She slowly backed him out. "Easy there."

The slam from the back door of the house caused both women to turn. Hurrying down the steps was a voluptuous redhead. She buttoned her blue quilted jacket as she jogged toward the corral. Her blue eyes lit up when she spied the colt. "He's adorable!"

Shelby grinned. "Rebecca, I'd like you to meet Lex Walters. Lex, this is my partner, Rebecca Starrett."

Rebecca shook hands with Lex. "Hi, Lex. I've seen you at Carson's with your family." Rebecca had recently been promoted to assistant manager at the western-wear store. It was the only one of its kind in the county, and most of Somerville shopped there.

"I thought you looked familiar. It's nice to see you again." Lex stepped back and allowed Rebecca to get closer to the colt. She grinned as the younger woman began to stroke the animal's coat.

"Oooh, Shelby. What's his name?" Rebecca asked.

Shelby looked over at Lex, who shrugged. "I guess that's up to you, darlin'. We've got Patches and Dutchess. What do you think this little fella looks like?"

Rebecca looked into the colt's eyes. "How about Morgan?" She gently rubbed his nose. "You like that, don't you?" She continued to coo at Morgan, while the other two women looked on in amusement.

"I have a feeling I've lost my new horse," Shelby joked. "Lex, you want to come up to the house for some coffee? I think Morgan's in good hands."

"Coffee sounds great. I'm getting too old to stand out in the cold wind nowadays." Lex glanced over her shoulder before she stepped into the house. The joy on Rebecca's face solidified in her mind that she'd made the right decision on selling the colt.

Shelby laughed as they headed for the house. She held the door open for Lex, exhaling heavily as they stepped into the warm kitchen. "Tell me about it. My old aches from the rodeo get worse every year. Take your coat off and get comfortable. I'm sure Rebecca will get Morgan settled and be in shortly."

Lex grinned. The more she was around Shelby, the more she enjoyed the other woman's company. She decided to talk to Amanda, and see about inviting the couple out for dinner in the future.

Chapter Five

AMANDA PACED THE bedroom as Lex watched from the bed. The house was quiet, as the sun was only now peeking through the blinds. The children were fast asleep, which allowed their parents the privacy early morning brought. "I don't know, Lex. Keeping Lorrie out all day, especially with a cold front expected, doesn't sound like a very good idea."

"We'll be back by lunch." Lex pulled her boots on, stood and stamped her feet. "The cold front's supposed to hit tonight. I'll have her home sipping hot chocolate long before then." She held out her arms and waited until Amanda snuggled close. "We've been out plenty of times. Why are you so worried?"

"You'll think I'm being silly," Amanda muttered into Lex's shirt. She felt lips lightly touch her head.

"Never."

Amanda raised her head and looked up. Lex's eyes sparkled with tenderness and Amanda felt her heart speed up and overflow with love. "How did I ever get this lucky?"

Lex's lips curled into a familiar smile. "I'd have to say we're both very lucky, sweetheart." She lowered her face and kissed Amanda. When they finally separated, her grin widened. "Now what was it you were going to say?"

"Like I can remember anything after being kissed like that," Amanda grumbled good-naturedly. She adjusted Lex's shirt collar. "I have a weird feeling about today. I wish you and Lorrie would stay closer to the house."

"We're only going to the northern pasture and checking the pump on the tank. It's about a forty-five minute ride out there. If the weather even seems the least little bit chancy, I promise we'll head right back."

Knowing she was fighting a losing battle, Amanda gave up. "All right. I know Lorrie's been looking forward to this. The extra week of grounding nearly killed her."

"Wasn't easy for me, either. But she had to understand that using the emergency ladder had consequences. She'll think twice before doing it again." Lex lifted Amanda off the floor and slowly spun her around. "Are you sure you don't want to come with us? I bet Ellie wouldn't mind watching Melanie for us." Even after being given her own pony, their youngest wasn't as fond of horseback riding, and would rather spend her time in more artistic pursuits.

During the past week, Melanie had become Ellie's shadow. She had even talked her into playing dolls, something that the other members of the family had little time, or inclination, to do.

Amanda laughed. "I have enough trouble separating them as it is. Poor Ellie's going to get sick of Melanie at this rate."

Lex thought about the changes in her cousin during the past week. Day by day, Ellie's face relaxed, and she was returning to the woman they had all come to love. "I doubt that. If anything, I think Mel's been good for her." Lex put Amanda down and gave her another quick kiss. "I'm going to go wake Lorrie so we can get started early. Why don't you head back to bed?"

"No, I think I'll take advantage of the quiet and get some things done downstairs." Amanda picked up an item from the dresser. "Don't forget your phone."

"Yes, ma'am." Lex clipped it to her belt, resting the leather holster on her right hip. She started to leave the room, but was stopped by Amanda's grip on her back pocket. "What?"

Amanda stepped into Lex's arms and kissed her again. "Be careful."

Lex started to joke, but saw the real worry in her wife's eyes. "I promise. What we have is too precious to me."

THE SUN PIERCED through the barren trees, the glare causing Lex to wish she had remembered to wear her sunglasses. She squinted at Lorrie, who rode alongside her on Mine. Her daughter's face showed all the wonder of being alive on a beautiful day. Lex dipped the brim of her hat to block the worst of the blinding light. "You doing all right, lil' bit?"

Lorrie turned and gave Lex a huge smile. "Yep." The grin took on a decidedly wicked turn. "Wanna race?" Mine sidestepped as Lorrie tightened her grip on the reins.

"Sure." Lex pointed to a dead tree a few hundred yards ahead. "Last one there has to brush down both horses when we get back."

"And give Freckles a bath," Lorrie added.

The little dog wasn't happy being left behind, but Lex didn't want her out that far with the weather being chancy. And giving her a bath usually meant that the bather would need one afterward. "All right."

Lorrie kicked her horse and whooped, taking off and leaving Lex behind.

"You little—" Lex urged Mac forward. His wounds had healed nicely, but she knew they'd have a difficult time catching the younger quarter horse in a short distance race. "Come on," Lex yelled. "You're not going to let a little mare win, are you?" She leaned over Mac's neck. They got within a length of Mine when Mac stumbled. Lex pulled up on the reins and finally brought him to a stop. "Damn."

"Yay!" Lorrie cheered and brought Mine to a halt, turning to look for Lex. She saw her standing beside Mac. "Momma?"

Lex bent over to look at Mac's leg. She raised his hoof and found a small stick wedged beneath his shoe. Using her pocketknife, Lex gently removed the stick and brushed her finger across the frog, testing for tenderness. Mac didn't flinch, so she stood and patted his shoulder. "We'll get her next time."

Lorrie rode back to where Lex stood. "Is he okay?"

"I think so. Just a stick in his shoe." Lex climbed into the saddle. "Looks like I'm going to be busy this afternoon, aren't I?"

"Yep. Unless you want to race again."

Lex laughed. "Nope, I think you had us beat before Mac came up lame. Next time, I'm riding Thunder. No way you'd outrun him."

They soon came upon the clearing where the stock tank was located. Normally forty feet wide, the muddy pond would hold enough water to take care of the stock in the north pasture. Since the drought, Lex had a water well dug with the pump running off solar power.

The pump was supposed to keep the tank filled, yet Lex could see that it hadn't. Only a small amount of water remained in the very center of the tank. Something had broken through the fence that protected the pump. It knocked the solar panels off and left them lying in the dirt. In the middle of the tank stood a cow, apparently stuck.

"Damn." Lex could tell by the demeanor of the heifer that it had been stranded for quite some time. She urged Mac into a gallop. "Lorrie, keep Mine away from the tank. I don't want her getting in the mud, okay?"

"Yes, ma'am." Lorrie followed behind Lex and pulled up short when they arrived at the tank. "Where's the water?"

Lex brought Mac to a stop and climbed from the saddle. "Dried up. Looks like the pump lost power." She glanced at the pump. "We'll have to get someone out to fix it. Damn it all to hell!" She picked up a twig and broke it in half, throwing the pieces away in her anger.

Lorrie prudently kept silent. She rode over to Lex, being especially careful to stay away from the muddy tank. "What are we going to do about the cow?"

"Haul her out." Lex stood with her hands on her hips while she considered the challenge. "Lorrie, give me your rope. We'll have to use both horses."

"Yes, ma'am." Lorrie detached the rope from her saddle. She watched in awe as Lex worked the loop and tossed it over the mud to land around the heifer's neck.

"Here you go. Tie that off, will you?" Lex handed the rest of the rope to Lorrie, who quickly tied it to her saddle horn. "Keep the slack out of it, until I can get my rope on her."

Having done similar things with her mother before, Lorrie had no trouble following instructions. She guided Mine back slightly, keeping the rope taut.

Lex nodded and retrieved the rope from her own saddle. "Good job, Lorrie." She threw another perfect strike and got a good grip on the rope. "Back up a little. Let's see what happens."

Lorrie did as she was told, well versed in the action.

The cow didn't budge, and Lex called on Lorrie to stop. "Looks like she's good and stuck." Dropping her rope to the ground, Lex removed her duster and draped it across her horse. She rooted around in her saddlebag until she found a small, folded shovel. "You're in charge of the horses, all right? Once I get out there, I'll take my rope off. All you need to do is keep the horses calm."

"Yes, ma'am." Lorrie accepted Mac's reins. "You're walking out in the mud? Mommy's gonna get mad if you come home dirty."

"Yeah, I know. But it can't be helped." Lex winked and squeezed Lorrie's leg, then started to wade into the tank. The farther she walked, the gooier the mud. By the time she reached the cow, she had to crawl across the mud on her knees. "Lorrie's right. Amanda's going to kick my ass for this mess." She laughed at herself. "Martha always said I could find mud in a drought. Never thought I'd prove her right."

Lex patted the cow on the neck. She could see it was buried up to its belly in the mud, and its eyes were dimming. "We got here too late, didn't we?" Lex took her rope off the animal and tossed it nearby. "I'm sorry. Hang in there, okay?" She took the shovel and started to dig carefully around the cow's legs.

Lorrie watched her mother work, but sitting still in the warm sunshine made her sleepy. She yawned and tried to keep her eyes open.

Not far away, the cry of a bobcat caused Mine and Mac to both dance wildly. Lorrie was unable to hang on to Mac, who took off into the trees. "Momma!" As Mine struggled under Lorrie's control, she reared. Lorrie did a good job of handling the frightened horse, but couldn't keep her from backing several feet.

Unable to help, Lex watched as Lorrie fought to stay astride. She was about to holler encouragement when the tight rope caused the cow to bellow and fall toward Lex. With her knees buried in the mud, Lex couldn't move, and found herself trapped on her back beneath the dying animal.

"Momma!" Lorrie saw Lex fall under the cow. She untied the rope from her saddle and was finally able to bring Mine under control. Terrified, she jumped down and started out into the mud.

Stunned from the weight, Lex struggled to breathe. She was grateful the mud cushioned her, but the burning pain in her bent knees and lower back made it difficult to think. She was surprised when Lorrie appeared above her. "Lorrie?"

"It's okay, Momma." Lorrie started frantically trying to dig Lex out with her hands.

"Shhh." Lex tried to comfort her. "I'm okay, just stuck," she wheezed. She felt the heifer exhale one final breath, then stilled. "Damn. Lorrie?"

"Yeah?"

"The cow's dead. I'm going to need you to go back to Mine, and try to drag her off of me, okay? We can't hurt her anymore."

Lorrie sniffled and nodded. "Okay. Should I try to catch Mac? I couldn't hold him, Momma. I'm sorry."

Lex awkwardly stretched her arm out and patted Lorrie on the arm. "You did perfect, sweetheart. Letting Mac go so you could control Mine was the right thing to do."

"Okay." Lorrie wiped a muddy hand under her nose, trying not to cry. "I didn't fall off, either."

"You're a good rider." Lex coughed as she tried to take a deep breath. "I need you to help me get out from under this heifer, okay? So be real careful going back to Mine. When you get there, I want you to pull from that other side, so the cow will roll off me."

Lorrie nodded. "'kay." She crab-walked across the mud and was soon back in the saddle. It took a little maneuvering, but she got Mine into position. "Ready, Momma?"

"Yep," Lex yelled as loud as she could. She braced her hands on the cow. As Mine started to pull, Lex pushed with all her might.

The carcass slowly rocked until it flipped over onto its other side.

Lorrie stopped Mine as soon as she saw Lex was free. She leapt from the saddle and raced out into the mud once again. "Momma? Are you okay?"

"I'm fine, sweetheart. You did real good." Lex hadn't moved, but at least she was able to breathe freely once again. "Untie the rope from the cow and hand it to me, okay? I don't think I can walk out of the mud just yet."

"Okay." Lorrie quickly did as she was asked, even going so far as to help tie the rope around her mother. "Are your legs broke?"

Lex tried to keep from scaring her. "No, they're just stiff from how I was sitting. And it'll be a lot easier to pull me out than to try and help me walk."

"Oh." Lorrie made certain the rope was fitted properly under Lex's arms. "Is this right?"

"Yep." Lex gave her what she hoped was a reassuring smile. "I want you to have Mine pull real slow. Don't stop until I'm out of the tank, no matter what, all right?"

"Yes, ma'am." Lorrie hugged Lex and hustled back to her horse once again. "Ready?"

Lex wrapped her hands around the rope and nodded. As the horse backed up, Lex was pulled forward. She bit her bottom lip to keep from screaming as her body unfolded. Rotating onto her side, Lex closed her eyes as she was dragged from the mud.

Lorrie stopped Mine once Lex was free of the tank. She untied the rope from her saddle and got down to check on her mother. Dropping to her knees, she brushed her hand across Lex's face, which was damp with sweat and tears. "Momma?"

Although it hurt, Lex rolled into a sitting position and pulled Lorrie forward. "It's okay, sweetheart. You did perfect." She held the crying girl close, shedding a few more tears herself.

Once they both settled down, Lex gave Lorrie a hug. "I'm so proud of you."

"Thanks, Momma." Lorrie put her hand on Lex's cheek. "Your mouth is bleeding."

"I'll be okay." Lex kissed Lorrie on the forehead. "But I think I'm going to need some help getting back to the house." She pulled her cell phone off her belt, grimacing at the caked-on mud. "Hope the case protected it." After several shaky tries, Lex finally gave up getting the phone free from the holster and handed it to Lorrie. "Why don't you call the house for us?"

Lorrie took the phone out of the leather holder and hit the proper speed dial. The phone rang several times before being picked up.

"Rocking W Ranch, Amanda speaking."

"Mommy," Lorrie started to cry again at the sound of Amanda's voice.

Lex gently took the phone away from her. "Amanda?"

"Lex, what's going on? Is Lorrie okay?"

"She's fine. We ran into a little trouble out here—"

Amanda cut her off. "I knew it! What happened? Are you all right? Is Lorrie all right?"

"Sssh. Give me a second, and I'll tell you everything. But before I get too far into it, do you think you could come get us?"

AMANDA PEERED INTO the rearview mirror, checking on her wife and daughter. Lex was sprawled out across the bed of the truck. She had refused to sit inside, saying it would be more comfortable to lie down. Lorrie wasn't about to leave her mother's side, so she was curled up next to Lex. Amanda drove slow in deference to Lorrie's horse, which trotted behind the vehicle. "One of these days, Lex, I'm going to wake up and have totally white hair," she muttered.

They arrived at the house and were met by Roy. He untied Mine. "I'll take care of her for you, Lorrie." He tipped his hat to Lex. "Mac showed up here about half an hour ago. He's fine."

"Good." Lex slowly sat up, trying to keep from crying out at her stiffened joints. "Get someone out to the northern tank as soon as possible to remove the dead heifer and fix the pump. No other animals are going to go near the place until then."

Roy nodded. He'd been able to get things organized, thanks to Amanda calling him before bringing Lex and Lorrie back to the house. "Already sent the boys out with the trailer. I told them to have it running before they left, or don't bother coming back to the bunkhouse."

Lex laughed. "You're sounding more like me every day." She allowed Amanda and Roy to help her from the back of the truck. "Thanks." Lex started to stand, but her knees buckled. She would have fallen if not for Roy's firm grip. "Damn. I guess I'm going to need a little help getting to the house, too."

"No problem, Boss." Roy tied the horse to the truck. He put Lex's arm over his shoulder. "Lean on me and we'll get you inside."

Amanda took position on the other side of Lex. "It's going to take a week to get all the mud off," she teased, trying to keep her thoughts light.

"I told Momma you were gonna be mad that she got so dirty," Lorrie said, following behind the trio. Her clothes were caked with mud, too. "She said it couldn't be helped."

"I bet she did," Amanda said. She kept a tight grip on Lex's belt. Lowering her voice, she asked, "Are you sure you don't want to go to the hospital?"

Lex kept her voice equally soft. "I'll be fine. My knees are sore and I probably pulled a muscle in my back. But I promise if it's not better tomorrow, we'll go see Rodney." Dr. Rodney Crews was married to Amanda's sister, Jeannie. He took over the local practice after his partner, Dr. Anderson, retired.

Amanda patted Lex's stomach. "I'll hold you to that." In a louder voice, she asked, "Lorrie, would you please open the back door for us? And make sure the downstairs bathroom is clear."

"Yes, ma'am." Lorrie raced ahead to do as she was asked. She clomped into the house, forgetting to take her boots off at the back door. A trail of mud followed her.

"She's definitely your daughter," Amanda said.

As they reached the door, Lex paused. "Maybe I should just strip out here and save you the extra trouble."

"Too late now." Amanda poked her. "Besides, I think that's more of you than Roy wants to see."

Roy shook his head as he grinned. "I appreciate the thought, Amanda. But I remember seeing her race half-naked across the back lawn when she wasn't any bigger than Melanie."

Lex groaned. "Do we have to talk about that right now? I'm dying, here."

"Serves you right." Amanda laughed at her discomfort. "All right, I'll be good. I can get stories from Roy later."

They were going to put Lex in the downstairs bathroom, but Amanda decided that they might as well get her upstairs, where she could take a shower. She wasn't strong enough to help Lex from the tub, and even though Roy joked about it, Amanda knew that neither he nor Lex would be comfortable otherwise.

Halfway up the stairs they were met by Ellie, Melanie and a very excited Freckles.

"Momma, you're all dirty," Melanie said.

Lorrie hugged Freckles, who had made a beeline for her. "We were trying to save a cow."

Ellie put her hands on Melanie's shoulders, to keep her away from Lex. "What can I do to help?"

Amanda was about to brush off the offer when she felt Lex's weight shift more toward Roy. "Could you get the shower started?"

Ellie nodded. "Come on, Mel. You can help me."

"Lorrie, could you go clean up in your bathroom?" Amanda knew that Lex wouldn't want her children to see her in such a weakened state. "I'll have your sister come help you in just a minute."

"Okay." Lorrie trudged toward her room. "Let's go, Freckles." The rat terrier pranced happily beside her.

Lex sighed as the trio continued up the stairs. "Thanks," she whispered. "The crowd was starting to get to me."

"No problem, love." Amanda guided them into the bedroom. "Roy, if you'll help me get her to the bathroom, I think Ellie and I can take it from there."

"Sure thing."

Barely through the doorway of the bathroom, Lex's legs started to go out from under her.

Roy got a tighter grip around her waist. "Hang on, Boss. Almost there." He helped her lean against the double sink, while Amanda bent to remove her boots.

Ellie came over to relieve Roy. "Mel, why don't you go check on Lorrie? I bet she has a great story to tell you."

"'kay." Melanie started to leave the room, but stopped to look at Lex. "Momma, are you sick?"

Lex tried to stand up straighter. "I'll be fine, sweetheart. After I get in bed, do you want to come read me a story?"

"Sure!" Melanie bobbed her head up and down. "I got a new book that El gave me. We can read that."

"Sounds great."

Amanda stopped what she was doing and gave her youngest a kiss. "Make sure your sister puts her dirty clothes in the laundry room and her boots on the back porch." If Melanie was put in charge of such an important detail, they'd have more than enough time to take care of Lex.

"I will," Melanie promised as she raced out of the room.

Roy laughed at her exuberance. "Glad I'm not Lorrie." He gave up his position to Ellie. "If you folks have things handled, I'll finish with the horses and run on to the house."

"Thanks for everything, Roy." Lex closed her eyes as Amanda tugged on her socks.

"Anytime, Boss." He leaned close to Amanda so as not to be overheard. "Let me know if you need help getting her to the doc, or anything else."

Amanda squeezed his arm. "I will, thanks." She waited until he was on his way down the stairs before she started on Lex's jeans.

Lex swatted at her hands. "I'm not an invalid."

"I know. Just stay still." Amanda unbuttoned the muddy pants and slid them down Lex's legs. She paused halfway down, concerned. "Your knees are pretty swollen."

"Yeah. Got bent backward when the cow fell over on me. It hurts," Lex said quietly.

Ellie stood silently by, lending her physical support. Although Lex was leaning against the sink, she still needed help standing upright while Amanda undressed her. "You know, Lex. I think I'm going to have to buy you a rabbit's foot or something. You get into the damndest messes I've ever seen."

The comment got its desired effect, as Amanda laughed. "If you do that, I'll make her wear it around her neck." She started to unbutton Lex's shirt, when Lex grabbed her hand. She looked into the sheepish eyes and sighed. "Ellie, would you mind waiting in the bedroom? Miss Prude is getting all shy."

"Come on, Lex. I'm a nurse." Ellie leaned closer to whisper in Lex's ear. "Do you really want to put the extra stress on Amanda?"

"No," Lex grumbled. She released Amanda's hand. "I get to bathe myself, don't I?"

Amanda kissed Lex on the cheek. "Only if you want to take away my fun." She turned to Ellie. "Could you check on the girls for us? I'll holler if I need help."

"As long as you're sure." Ellie slowly stepped away from Lex, who seemed to be standing fine on her own. "I'll close the bedroom door to give you some privacy."

"Thanks, Ellie." Lex gave her a weary smile. "Maybe if I'm really lucky I can talk Amanda into joining me."

Ellie comically covered her eyes. "TMI, Lex." She laughed as she left the room.

Amanda poked her wife in the stomach. "You're evil."

"But hopeful?"

With a martyred sigh, Amanda started to unbutton her own shirt. "It would be easier to get you clean," she theorized.

Lex's only answer was a pleased grin.

Chapter Six

AMANDA STARED AT the poster on the wall, wrinkling her nose at the detail. "I really didn't need to see the inside of a stomach," she muttered. She was doing whatever she could to keep her mind off the group of people huddled in the tiny examination room. With her, Lex, Dr. Rodney Crews and his nurse Laura scattered about, there wasn't enough room to turn around.

Rodney patted his annoyed patient on the leg. "It's only a precaution, Lex. A second opinion."

"I don't care." Lex crossed her arms over her chest and glared at her brother-in-law. "No one's coming near me with a scalpel."

Rodney sighed. "I'm not saying he will. But I'd feel a lot better if the orthopedic surgeon looked at your knee." He turned to Amanda. "Will you please try to reason with her?"

Amanda was torn between siding with Lex or doing what was best for her. "Can't we wait and see how she's doing in a week or so? Lex should know better than anyone how much pain or discomfort she's in. She can't cause any more damage to her knee if she waits, can she?"

"No, not unless she does something new to it. But I'd still advise a consultation with Dr. Needham." Rodney pointed his pen at Lex. "One week. And you have to use the crutches. Keep as much weight off your leg as possible."

Lex grinned. "Sure." She started to climb off the exam table when Rodney stopped her.

"I mean it, Lex. Use the crutches. Or else."

With her feet on the floor, Lex towered over him by several inches. She looked down into his face as she tucked a crutch beneath each arm. "And exactly what will you do?"

Rodney winked at Amanda before staring into Lex's eyes. "I'll sic Martha on you."

The smirk on Lex's face disappeared. "You wouldn't dare."

"Watch me. After all, I'll see her on Thanksgiving." Rodney tucked Lex's chart under his arm and adjusted his glasses, trying to ignore Amanda and Laura's laughter. "In all seriousness, the crutches will help. Maybe even enough to put off a trip to Dr. Needham. But I honestly think the consult would be in your best interest." He gave Amanda a hug. "Give Jeannie a call. We've missed seeing you both."

Amanda kissed his cheek. "I will. Thank you." She took the prescription from a chuckling Laura. "Come on, honey. We'll get this filled before we pick up the girls from school."

Lex paused at the door. "Thanks, Rodney. We'll see you in a couple of weeks." She followed Amanda out of the office and down the hall.

"I'll kick his ass if he—" The slap on her stomach silenced her. "What?"

"I swear, Lex. You're worse than the kids." Amanda tried to keep the smile off her face, but wasn't very successful.

"I thought that's why you married me." Lex waited for Amanda to hold the door open for her as they left. "Hey, can we get the prescription filled at the store? I want to get some ice cream for the girls."

"Yes, we can, my oldest child." Amanda sighed, secretly pleased that Lex seemed to be content to follow Rodney's advice, at least for the time being.

"MILD SPRAIN, MY ass." Lex stretched while she stood next to Amanda, who was studying the different flavors of ice cream. Her back had stiffened up due to the use of the crutches and she was more uncomfortable than ever.

"You could have waited in the truck," Amanda chided, not bothering to look at her. Less than half an hour after they'd left Rodney's office, Lex was already complaining. It actually made Amanda feel better because she knew Lex wouldn't gripe if she was feeling too bad.

"I hate waiting in the truck." Lex pointed at one of the cartons closer to Amanda. "One of those, please." She adjusted the crutches beneath her arms.

"Big baby." Amanda placed Lex's choice in the cart and added one of her own. "We'd be done already if you had, you know."

"But then I couldn't help you," Lex teased, as she dropped another container of ice cream in the shopping cart. "I think we need more hot fudge, too."

Amanda laughed. "How about sprinkles?"

"Ooh, yeah. Almost forgot about those."

On the next aisle, the cry of a child caused both women to become silent.

Amanda looked at Lex. "I'll be right back." She left Lex with the cart and disappeared around the corner. She felt her heart begin to pound when she saw Jerry Sater lying on the floor with his hands covering his head.

Jerry's mother stood over him. "Quit your whining and get your ass up," Susan said. She grabbed him by the arm and jerked him to his feet.

"Mommy, please. I'll be better." Jerry tried to break free of her grasp.

"Stop it!" Susan slapped his head with her open hand. He cried even louder. "I said shut up!"

Amanda pulled Jerry away from his mother and stood between them. "Have you lost your mind?"

"Get away from him. It's none of your damned business what I do with my son." Susan reached for Jerry.

"I don't care who you are, you can't hit a child," Lex interrupted. She stood next to Amanda, presenting a united front. "And shouldn't he be in school?"

Susan's face scrunched into a nasty scowl. "You two dykes have no room to talk. At least I'm not ruining my kid by being a pervert." She snapped her fingers low, as if calling a dog. "Jerry, over here. Now."

Still crying, Jerry stepped around Lex and Amanda. He wiped his runny nose on the back of his hand and kept his eyes on the ground.

"Stop that sniveling, or I'll give you something to cry about." Susan turned her attention to the couple a few feet away. "If you come near me again, I'm calling the cops. Come on." She roughly twisted her hand in Jerry's shirt and led him away.

Lex stopped Amanda from following. "Hold on, sweetheart. You can't do anything."

"I'd like to give her a taste of her own medicine." Amanda clinched her fists at her side. "We can't let her get away with that, Lex."

"I know. Let's go put the ice cream back. We'll run by the sheriff's department and talk to Jeremy."

Amanda sighed but agreed. "That's a good idea. I saw her hit him in the head. If we're lucky they'll arrest her and throw away the key."

"Maybe so." Lex followed Amanda to the ice cream aisle to clear out the shopping cart they had started to fill. They could return after their visit with the sheriff.

ALTHOUGH SHE'D SPENT a lot of her youth visiting the sheriff's department, Lex felt uncomfortable stepping into the building. She hadn't had a reason to return after Charlie retired, and things felt, "...different."

"Hmm?" Amanda turned to look at Lex. "What's different?"

"Everything."

Amanda looked around. The waiting area was dingy but clean, with institutional tan walls and scuffed furniture. "Looks the same to me."

Lex shook her head. "I used to come here all the time when I was growing up. I think I spent as much time here as I did at the ranch. It was like a second home to me. But now, it feels really weird."

"Is this the first time you've been here since Charlie retired?"

"Yeah."

Amanda patted Lex's arm. "I'm sorry, love."

"No, I'm okay. It's just that—"

Jeremy stepped into the reception area. "It's good to see you." He shook hands with Amanda, then Lex. "I don't know how Charlie kept from losing his mind all those years. I spend more time behind the desk writing reports and fielding calls from politicians than I do handling police work. Anyway, enough of my complaining. What can I do for you?"

"We need to report a case of child abuse." Amanda stood. "Can we talk in your office?"

"Sure." Jeremy waited until Lex got to her feet and tucked her crutches under her arms. "Geez, Lex. What did you do to yourself this time?"

Lex followed Amanda. "Went swimming in a mud tank with a dying cow." She grinned. She loved messing with Jeremy.

He stepped ahead of them and held open his office door. "Why do I even bother to ask?"

"Hey, it's the truth." Lex sat in the chair Amanda steadied for her. "Thanks."

Once both women were comfortably seated, Jeremy sat in the rolling leather chair behind his desk. He slid a legal sized notepad close and picked up a pen. "All right. Why don't you start at the beginning?"

Half an hour later, Jeremy pushed the notepad away and exhaled heavily. "I hate cases involving kids. All right. I'll contact Child Protective Services and go from there."

"Lorrie told us that Jerry came to school with a black eye, so you might pass that along as well," Amanda said. "Is that all we can do?"

Jeremy tapped his pen on the desk. "For now. You did the right thing. I'll make sure the case is a high priority, and offer our assistance to CPS." He dropped the pen on his desk and stood. "Don't worry. I'll keep my eye on things."

"Thanks, Jeremy. Let us know if there's anything else we can do." Lex slowly got to her feet, fighting the crutches. "Stupid things."

Amanda helped her and shared a grin with Jeremy. "Come on, tough stuff. It's almost time to pick up the girls. Thanks again, Jeremy."

"Anytime." Before they left, he picked up his phone. "Lydia, could you get me Child Protective Services, please?"

AMANDA TAPPED ON the steering wheel and stared at the front of the school. The meeting at the sheriff's department had taken longer than expected and she wasn't able to get her usual parking space. She turned her head when a strong hand covered hers, effectively stopping the nervous habit. "What?"

"I was going to ask you the same thing." Lex squirmed in the seat. "I think you need a bigger vehicle."

"It's not that much smaller than your truck." Amanda released the steering wheel, but didn't let go of Lex's hand. "Although it can be a beast to control when the wind gets up."

Lex stretched the best she could, bracing her hands against the top of the Xterra. "I've always worried about how top-heavy the damned thing is." She groaned as her back protested the movement. "There's not enough legroom, either."

"There is for normal people," Amanda teased. She stretched out her own legs quite easily. "I think I'll go wait by the door to the school. The girls aren't used to looking for me over here and I don't want to miss them."

"Lorrie's smart enough to find us. What's the real reason you're so antsy?"

Amanda twisted around in her seat so she was looking directly at Lex. "I'm worried that we didn't do enough today to help Jerry. What if she did something else to him when they got home? It breaks my heart to think that she could do god-knows-what and there wasn't anything we could do about it."

"Have faith in Jeremy, sweetheart. He knows we're not jumping to conclusions. I wouldn't be surprised if he had a deputy go with CPS. He's very good at his job."

The loud ring of the school bell caused them both to turn and look at the front door to the school.

"Almost time." Lex grinned as she kept her eyesight glued to the front of the school. "Want to get pizza tonight?"

Amanda laughed. "I suppose you want to go back to the store and get some ice cream, too?"

Lex turned and her grin widened. "That's a great idea. Why didn't I think of that? Besides, I have to pick up my prescription."

"You are such a brat."

"Here they come." Lex turned toward the back seat as the back door opened. "Hey, girls."

Melanie, the first in, squealed. "Momma! You never come to get us."

Lorrie tossed her backpack into the floorboard and crawled in after her sister. "Momma? Is something wrong?"

"No, everything's fine." Lex turned to Amanda. "Is it so weird for me to be here?"

Melanie piped up innocently, "You're always working. We don't see you most of the time until dinner."

At the stricken look on Lex's face, Lorrie added, "At least on school days. We see you lots on weekends."

Amanda tried to repair the hurt in Lex's eyes. "Honey, we all understand that the ranch isn't an eight to five job."

"That's the one thing I didn't want to do," Lex whispered. "My father put the ranch and everything else, before his family."

"It's not the same," Amanda said. She put her hand on Lex's arm. "You've had to work very hard during this drought to keep helpless animals alive. No one blames you for that."

Lex shook her head. "I do." She turned toward the backseat. "I'm sorry, girls. We're going to have some changes around the house, starting right now."

"Lex—" Amanda's words were stopped by Lex's fingers on her lips. She didn't want Lex to put the ranch on the back burner. She knew how much their home meant to her wife.

Melanie started bouncing in her seat. "Ice cream parties after school?"

"No, silly. Momma means she's not gonna work all the time." Lorrie leaned over Lex's seat and put her chin on Lex's shoulder. "Right, Momma?"

Giving Amanda a reassuring smile, Lex kissed Lorrie on the forehead. "That's right." She winked at Melanie. "Although an ice cream party sounds pretty good to me, too."

Amanda sighed. "All right. I can take a hint. Buckle up, girls. Let's go get some ice cream." She laughed at the chorus of cheers, which included her wife. "Overgrown kid," she mumbled.

Since they were taking a different route to the store, they came upon a new office building under construction. Amanda pointed it out to Lex. "I wonder what's going there?"

Lex checked out the structure as they passed. "Hard to tell. Maybe if we're lucky, it's an ice cream parlor." She laughed at the frown on her wife's face. "Aw, come on. You know you'd like it."

"You are such a troublemaker." Amanda shook her head but couldn't help but smile.

AMANDA PULLED THE Xterra into its usual place behind the house and turned off the engine. Her cheeks were sore from laughing and smiling. Lex definitely added a different dimension to the drive home. She kept both girls happy and energized with her ongoing commentary.

A familiar SUV was parked in front of the small cottage that Martha and Charlie called home. The silver 2006 Jeep Grand Cherokee had been a compromise between the couple after Charlie retired. He wanted something they could take on long trips and be comfortable. Martha wanted something shiny. They both enjoyed driving the Jeep, which withstood the rough country roads.

"Mada's home!" Lorrie yelled, opening her door and leaping from the vehicle.

"Yay! Hey, wait for me," Melanie cried. She quickly followed her.

Knowing it was useless to call the girls back, Amanda got out at a more sedate pace. She removed their bag of groceries from the back, and came around the passenger's side in time to see Lex ease herself out as well. "Aren't you forgetting something?"

Lex slowly stretched, her crutches still leaning against her seat. "Umm, do you need help with that bag?"

"No, smartass." Amanda pointed to the inside of the SUV. "Long, shiny things, remember?"

"Hurts more when I use the damned things," Lex grumbled. She took them out of the vehicle and tucked one beneath each arm. "Satisfied?"

Amanda ignored her and continued toward the house. "Guess I'll just have to eat all this ice cream myself." She'd compromised and allowed the ice cream, but told her family they'd be having sandwiches instead of pizza. It helped retain her mom-status, at least in her own mind.

"Hold on there, woman. You're not touching my chocolate chip cookie dough." Lex muttered several other things under her breath, much to Amanda's amusement.

"Keep it up and I'll wash your mouth out with soap." Amanda left the back door open and took the groceries into the kitchen. An excited Freckles romped into the room, dancing around her feet. "Calm down. Your favorite people will be inside in a minute." Amanda unpacked the bag and put the cold items in the freezer.

Lex came up behind Amanda and kissed her on the neck. She struggled to keep the crutches from falling to the floor when Amanda turned and tugged her close.

Amanda's arms automatically went around Lex's neck so she could pull her head down for a kiss.

"I swear, it doesn't matter how long I'm gone, the second I come back I catch you two all over each other," Martha said from the doorway. She had a child on each side of her, each keeping a firm grip on one of her hands.

Freckles barked and joined the girls, happy to have her playmates home.

Amanda released her hold and patted Lex on the stomach. "Later," she whispered. She edged around her wife and met Martha halfway. "Welcome home." The older woman's embrace was warm and familiar.

"It's good to be back." Martha looked past Amanda to Lex, who had a wide grin on her face. "I've been gone over a month but it looks like nothing's changed."

"What's that supposed to mean?" Lex asked, moving toward the group. She leaned the crutches against the edge of the table and held out her arms. "Where's my hug?"

Martha made a tsking sound, but enveloped Lex anyway. "You're nothing but skin and bones, Lexie."

"Ha! Blame my wife. She's the one that's got me on a blasted diet all the time." Lex kissed Martha's cheek and pulled back to look at her. "And why do you keep looking younger? Did y'all find the fountain of youth on your trip?"

Martha brushed the hair away from her face and blushed. Gone was the bun she kept her hair rolled in for decades, and in its place was a short, naturally-colored style that took years off her face. "Lexie, you're so full of bull pucky. I don't know how Amanda puts up with you." She swatted Lex lightly across the stomach. "Are you going to enlighten me on what you did to yourself this time?"

"Ow." Lex rubbed her belly. "I figured Ellie would have filled you in on everything."

"Ellie? She's here?"

"She's staying with us for a while." Amanda walked around Lex and picked up the crutches. She handed them to Lex. "Here. You forgot something. Again." She gave the children a loving smile. "Who's up for some ice cream?" The sandwiches could wait.

Both girls cheered, while Freckles barked.

Amanda laughed at their exuberance. "All right. Run and wash your hands."

Lorrie stopped on her way to the bathroom across the hall. "Yes, ma'am. Come on, Mel." She tugged her little sister along, wanting to hurry back before the adults changed their minds.

As soon as the children had left, Amanda turned to her wife. "If you'll sit down, I'll get you a bowl."

Lex started to argue, but the look on Amanda's face stopped her. "Yes, ma'am." She kissed Amanda on the cheek, and with a smug look toward Martha, took her place at the table.

"She's up to something," Martha whispered to Amanda.

"Probably. It'll be fun to see how long she behaves," Amanda said just as quietly. "Where's Charlie?"

Martha gathered the bowls and spoons, while Amanda took the different ice cream containers out of the freezer. "He's probably sacked out in front of the TV. Ornery old man wouldn't let me do any of the driving home." They'd spent the last month in a rented cabin in Colorado. It was Charlie's turn to choose the vacation spot, and Martha swore he picked camping to get back at her for the cruise they'd taken last year.

"You drive like a little old lady," Lex teased. "If you'd been behind the wheel, y'all would probably still be on the road."

"Hush, you." Martha balled up a dish towel and tossed it at Lex. "At least we'd get here in one piece. Charlie drives the Jeep like it was a police car."

Lex caught the towel and tucked in into the top of her shirt for a bib. "Thanks, Martha."

"Rotten brat."

Amanda laughed. "I call her that all the time." She took a bowl of ice cream to Lex, just as the girls raced into the kitchen.

"We're all clean, Mommy." Melanie held out her hands for inspection. "Lorrie made me wash two times."

Lorrie took her place next to Lex. "That's 'cause she didn't use soap the first time."

"Did too!"

"Did not!"

Melanie stomped her foot, which caused a waiting Freckles to bark. "Yes I did!"

"Girls," Lex said. It was all she had to say, as both turned silent.

Mumbling under her breath, Melanie pulled out her chair and crawled into it. "Did so use soap."

When the girls took their places, Freckles hid under the table to wait for scraps from them.

Lex held up her index finger and looked Melanie in the eye. "Last warning."

"Yes, ma'am."

Martha chuckled. "I'll swear both of those girls have Lexie's attitude." She placed a bowl in front of each child, getting a quiet "thank you" from both.

"And Amanda's temper," Lex added. She gave her wife an innocent smile. "Isn't that right, love?"

Glaring at Lex, Amanda prudently refused to answer. "Martha, do you remember saying that Lex could find mud in a drought?"

"I surely do."

Lex tried to cut her off. "Amanda—"

"You were right. That's how she hurt her back and her knee." Amanda blew her wife a kiss. "Playing in the mud."

Lex set her spoon in her bowl. "I was not playing."

Lorrie piped up. "We tried to save a cow that was stuck in a tank." Her face fell. "It died."

Martha's eyes widened. "You were there, sweetie?"

"Yes, ma'am. Me and Momma was checking the pump and found the cow. The pump was broke, but the cow died before we could get it out. Momma tried to dig the cow's legs out of the mud, and it fell on her when the big cat made a noise." Proud that she finished her story, Lorrie returned her attention to her ice cream.

"Lexie?"

Lex sighed. "We've got a bobcat running loose and haven't been able to catch it. We've got some traps set, so we can let it loose in the hills, but we haven't had much luck so far. So you might want to be extra careful walking up to the house, just in case."

"I certainly will. But what's this about mud?"

"The pump had quit working and the tank dried up. The cow was in the middle of what was left of the tank, and I tried to dig it out. I had Lorrie holding a rope that I'd thrown around the heifer, and when the cat hollered, her horse jumped. The rope tightened and the cow fell over on top of me."

Martha gasped. "Oh, my." She turned to Lorrie. "I bet that was scary for you, sweetie."

Lorrie used her napkin to wipe the ice cream from her face. "Yes, ma'am. But Momma made it okay."

Melanie giggled. "And when they got home, Momma was really

dirty. And smelly." She sat up straighter. "I got to help Lorrie get clean. She was kinda dirty, too."

"It was necessary," Lorrie said. "That's what Momma said."

"She would," Martha added with a wink. "Your Momma has always thought that getting dirty was necessary."

Lex blushed. "Aw, come on, Martha."

Martha finished her ice cream and stood. "Now, if you'll excuse me, I'm going to go check on my husband. If he naps too much now, he'll never get to sleep tonight." She kissed each child on the head. "You sweet girls be good, and we'll see you at dinner."

Amanda gave her a quizzical look. "Dinner?"

"I've got a roast in the oven and I'll bring it over about six." She left the room before either woman could argue with her.

"How in the hell does she do that?" Amanda asked. "She just got home. There's no way she could have cooked a roast."

"I dunno. I gave up trying to figure it out a long time ago." Lex scooped out the last of her ice cream and licked the spoon clean.

A GRAY, CHEVROLET pickup, bearing the logo of the Rocking W ranch on the doors, pulled to the curb on the tree-lined street.

Ellie stepped out of the truck. "I really appreciate it, Roy."

"Anytime. It was nice having the company on the drive in. Do you need me to pick you up when I'm through with my errands?"

"No, that's okay. I've got a car here. But thanks." Ellie closed the passenger door and gave him a little wave.

Roy returned the gesture and slowly drove away.

As the truck disappeared from view, Ellie turned and headed up the walk to her home. The knee-high, dead lawn had been neatly mowed, and all the weeds were gone from the barren flower beds. "Something else to thank my cousin for, I guess." She opened the door and stepped inside, feeling the heavy weight of loss rest once more upon her shoulders.

Her eyes tracked to the item left on the arm of the sofa. She crossed the room and lifted the men's suit jacket to her chest. She raised it to her face and inhaled, trying to catch even the slightest hint of her grandfather. Unable to detect anything, she felt tears burn her eyes.

"He's gone." Ellie blinked the moisture from her eyes and took a deep, cleansing breath. She knew in her heart that Travis wouldn't have wanted her to continue mourning his passing. "I'm sorry, Grandpa."

With a new resolve, Ellie gently folded the jacket and started for the master bedroom. She had a lot of things to go through and pack.

Travis had made Ellie promise that she'd donate everything of his that she couldn't use. She had tearfully agreed, and felt a deep shame at the thought that she'd let him down.

She opened the master bedroom door and peered inside. A layer of dust covered everything. Ellie walked in and rubbed her itchy nose. After Travis died, she'd cleaned the room one last time and closed the door.

She ran her hand along the handmade quilt that covered the queen-sized bed. "I bet Lex would like this," she mused. Travis had told Ellie years ago that it was the last thing her grandmother had finished before her passing, and he'd only allow it off his bed long enough to have it cleaned.

After she stripped the bed and got over a sneezing fit, Ellie opened the window. The cool air felt good on her dusty and overheated skin. She turned and surveyed the room. "The sooner I get started, the sooner I get finished." Brushing her hands together to remove the dust, she focused on her task.

EARLY THE FOLLOWING morning, Lex awoke to the gentlest of kisses. She opened her eyes and saw Amanda's face. "'Mornin'."

"Happy birthday, honey." Amanda kissed her again, this time making the contact last longer. "I wanted to give you a chance to wake up before the girls came barreling in here."

"Thanks." Lex threaded her fingers in Amanda's hair and brought her close again. "I think I need more awakening," she said, right before Amanda bent down and took her breath away.

They were able to spend almost an hour "waking up" before a series of knocks thumped on the bedroom door.

Amanda adjusted her nightgown and sat up. "Come in."

"Happy birthday, Momma," both girls sang, right before they jumped onto the bed.

"Careful, girls. Your Momma's still hurting," Amanda warned.

Melanie waved a folded piece of red construction paper. "I made you a card. Lorrie helped me with some of the hard words." She handed it to Lex, who showed the proper respect for the artwork.

"It's beautiful, Mel. Thank you." Lex held out her arm and waited until Melanie was tucked against her. "I love you, sweetheart."

"Love you too, Momma."

Lorrie was more cautious as she crawled to the other side of Lex. "We stayed up late working on our presents." She fought off a yawn. "I made you a coupon. It's for one boot polishing, and then I'll clean your saddle, too."

"Wow." Lex looked at the handmade coupon and grinned. "This is great, Lorrie. Thank you." She tugged Lorrie close and kissed the top of her head. "I love you."

"Thanks, Momma. Love you."

Amanda watched as the children closed their eyes. "I'll give you my present, later," she whispered.

"I thought you already did that." Lex winked at her. "Don't worry about it. This is better than any present."

"They've grown so fast, haven't they?" Amanda lightly played with Melanie's hair. "How upset would you be if I said I wanted another one?"

Lex's eyes opened wide. "Another girl?" She quickly looked at her wife's flat stomach. "Is there something you want to tell me?"

Amanda poked her. "No, silly. It's just," she grinned as Lorrie snuggled closer to Lex. "I miss having a little one around." A light tap caused both women to look at the open door. "Can we talk about this more, later?" At Lex's nod, she raised her voice just enough to be heard. "Hey, Ellie." Amanda waved her in. "We didn't wake you, did we?"

Ellie shook her head as she stepped into the room, carrying a plastic-wrapped bundle. "I heard the girls, and figured it was safe to come in."

"For now," Lex said. "What do you have there?"

"Uh, well," Ellie stammered. "This seemed like a good idea at the time, but." She placed the bundle on the foot of the bed and removed the protective plastic. "I was clearing out the house yesterday, and came across this." She lifted the quilt and opened it up.

The morning light brought out the vibrant colors of the quilt, causing both women on the bed to hum in appreciation. Lex was the first one to speak. "That's beautiful."

Ellie smiled bashfully. "It was on Grandpa's bed. He told me Grandma made it, and he never slept without it. I took it to the cleaners yesterday morning and had them freshen it up." She placed the quilt over Lex's legs. "I thought you might want to have it. Happy birthday."

Lex blinked several times and finally had to clear her throat. "That's, ah, damn, Ellie. Thank you. Are you sure?"

"Yeah, I'm sure. She was more your grandmother than mine, since I'd never met her. I figure it would mean more to you."

"What means more to me is that you thought about it. Thank you." Lex looked down at the sleeping children sprawled across her. "Expect a hug when I'm not covered in kids."

Ellie laughed and nodded. "Sure thing. Well, since the sun isn't up yet, I'm going to go on back to bed for a while. See y'all later."

After Ellie left, Amanda pulled the quilt up and studied the craftsmanship. "This is amazing. I can't believe how great of shape it's in."

"Yeah. Guess Grandpa took good care of it." Lex touched the quilt with one finger. "I really miss him."

Amanda clasped Lex's hand and kissed the knuckles. "I know, love. So do I." She rolled onto her side and tucked their joined hands beneath her chin. "Get some sleep, birthday girl. We've got a fun day planned."

Chapter Seven

AMANDA TWIRLED HER pen in one hand, staring at her silent phone. Her inbox was empty. With her office door open, she usually had to struggle to think over the din of women's chatter. Today, however, all was quiet. She dropped the pen to the desk and sighed. "This is ridiculous."

Business had trickled to a crawl at Sunflower Realty. Amanda had tried everything imaginable to drum up business. In the slow economy, very few people were in the market for a house, especially in a town the size of Somerville. When she first started working at the realty office, they were staffed with six realtors, not including Amanda. Over the last year that number had dwindled to three.

She heard the bell on the front door ring and looked up from her desk to see Peggy and Wanda hustle inside. Curious, Amanda stood and met them in the front of the office. "I thought you two were at lunch."

"We were." Wanda perched atop the receptionist's desk. "I mean, we were on our way. But Peggy wanted to walk, since it's not that far and then we saw the sign, and had to go look and see what was going on. But we couldn't see much until we got really close and—"

Amanda held up her hand to stop Wanda's story. "Take a breath." Turning to Peggy, she asked, "Would you mind?"

"Oh. Sure." Peggy grabbed a chair and pulled it close. "Sorry. My feet are killing me. These heels aren't made for walking fast." At Amanda's glare, Peggy continued. "As Wanda said, we decided to walk to the café. The weather's not too bad, and I was tired of being cooped—"

"For god's sake, would one of you please get on with it?" Margaret, the receptionist said.

Peggy gave her a hurt look. "All right, fine. We were almost to the café when Wanda noticed a new building going up down on Steward."

"Lex and I saw it the other day, too," Amanda added. "Oops. Sorry, go ahead."

"Anyway," Peggy drew out the word slowly, to make sure she wouldn't be interrupted again. "Wanda took off down the street to see what was going on. When we got there, we saw the sign." She paused for dramatic effect, much to everyone's annoyance.

"What?" Amanda and Margaret yelled, simultaneously.

Wanda took over the story again. "Horn Realty." The new business was a national chain real estate firm, specializing in fast turnover. "Can you believe it?"

Amanda dropped into a nearby chair. "Damn. I was afraid of something like that."

"What do you mean?" Peggy asked. "Did you know about this?"

"Of course she didn't." Wanda put her hand on Amanda's shoulder. "You didn't, right?"

Amanda shook her head. "Not exactly. But I had a sneaking suspicion that something was off." She wiped her face with both hands before standing. "I need to take a look at a few things." She returned to her office, feeling the eyes of the other women upon her.

Once at her desk, Amanda opened the bookkeeping program on her computer and looked at the figures for the second time that day. They would be hard-pressed to break even this month. She had stopped taking a salary several months prior, hoping to weather the fiscal storm. It had only delayed the inevitable. She rubbed her eyes and picked up the phone.

The phone rang twice and was picked up. "Hello?" Anna Leigh Cauble answered.

Amanda swallowed the lump in her throat. Her grandmother had opened Sunflower Realty over forty years ago. "Gramma? Are you busy right now?"

"Not at all, dearest. Is everything all right?"

"Um, well. Would it be okay if I came over for lunch?"

The sound of the television, which had been in the background, shut off. "Why don't you come over now? I've got a stew simmering on the stove. We can make it brunch." Anna Leigh's gentle voice was tinged with concern.

"That's even better. I'll be there in a few minutes. Bye." Amanda hung up the phone and looked around her office. Photographs of her family dotted the credenza opposite her desk and also along the shelves of the nearby bookcase. When she became the office manager she'd seen no sense in changing the furniture. The solid wood pieces had been made by Jacob Cauble for his wife, and Amanda felt a deep sentimentality for the set.

Amanda took her purse from beneath the desk, stood, and pushed in the leather chair. She walked out of the office and turned the light out behind her.

Near the front of the office, Wanda and Peggy still hovered around the receptionist's desk. The three women turned as Amanda approached.

Wanda scooted off the edge of the desk. "Are you okay?"

"Not really. But since you seem to have everything under control, I thought I'd go see my grandmother." Amanda hitched her purse strap over her shoulder. "Unless you'd rather I stayed here and kept the three of you company."

Margaret laughed. "We could always use a fourth for canasta. But if you're too good to play with us, then I guess we'll let you go. But you'll miss the pizza we ordered."

Amanda stepped by the trio. "That's all right. If you get too bored, just lock up and go home. I doubt anyone will notice." She walked out the door and tried to ignore the whispers behind her.

LEX GRUNTED IN pain as she swung herself up into the saddle. It had been a week since her injuries, yet she was still hurting. Thunder danced sideways but she had no trouble settling him down.

"Should you be riding?" Ellie asked from her perch on Amanda's paint pony, Stormy. "Can't one of the guys go?"

Lex leaned down and used her hand to put her right foot in the stirrup. The brace she wore on her knee was too bulky to allow much movement. "I've only got three guys working right now, and they're doing other things. It's a short ride to check one of the cat traps. If you don't want to go, that's fine."

Ellie shifted in the saddle. She'd been riding before, but wasn't as comfortable as Lex and Amanda on horseback. "There's no way I'd let you go alone. Besides, I like riding."

"Uh-huh." Lex took in Ellie's rigid posture. "I can see how relaxed you are," she said. "But thanks for coming along. I'd take the jeep, but the terrain's too rough."

"You couldn't drive, anyway. And I completely suck at driving a stick." Ellie coaxed her horse forward. "Come on. Let's get this over with. I swear it's getting colder."

Thunder shook his head as Lex tapped his flank. "She's a wimp, isn't she boy?" She patted his neck and laughed at the look Ellie gave her. "Are you sure you're up to this?"

Tugging her leather gloves, Ellie laughed. "I am if you are, cuz."

"Smartass." Lex led the way, trying not to show how achy she felt. They hadn't even left sight of the barn and her back was already stiffening up.

They rode for a while in silence, both seemingly content to enjoy the brisk morning. The trees had lost their leaves, giving them an eerie, skeletal look. The only sound was the rhythmic thump of the horse's hooves through the deadfall. When a cool gust of wind blew through Ellie's coat, she tightened the material around her and suppressed a shiver.

Lex noticed the action. "Are you doing all right?"

"Yeah. Kind of spooky out here, isn't it?"

"It can be, at times. This damned drought has made it worse." Lex edged Thunder closer to Stormy. "How are you doing, otherwise?"

Ellie turned to face Lex. "What do you mean?"

"I know our kids can be a handful. I guess I just want to make sure they're not driving you crazy."

"Actually, they've been great. It's hard to stay down for long when you've got those two around." Ellie's smile reflected the recent healing of her heart. "I owe you and Amanda a lot."

"Nah. You're family. Nothing to owe." Lex decided the conversation was getting too serious. She grinned. "You're looking pretty settled on Stormy."

It took Ellie a moment, but she finally recognized the look on Lex's face. "Uh, yeah. I guess I am. Why?"

"Let's have some fun." Lex whooped and gave Thunder's reins some slack, causing the big horse to rear. "Heeyah!"

"Oh, shit." Ellie was barely able to stay on as Stormy took off after Thunder. "I'm going to kill you," she yelled at Lex, who laughed in response.

AMANDA SAW FEW cars on the way to her grandparents' house. Due to the light traffic, it took her less than five minutes to get through town. Everywhere she looked, she noticed the decline of the area. Businesses boarded up and overgrown yards showed the lack of attention. As she passed the newly constructed Horn Realty, she fought off the urge to stop and throw a rock through their brightly-decorated picture window. She turned onto a residential street and was soon at her destination.

The Cauble's residence, a two-story Colonial, was located in one of the oldest neighborhoods of Somerville. The house was surrounded by mature oak and pecan trees and had been Anna Leigh and Jacob's home for over forty years.

Amanda pulled into the driveway and looked at the place where she had spent much of her youth. She hoped that the news she brought wouldn't change how her grandparents lived. Taking a deep breath, she turned off the car and climbed out.

The front door opened and Anna Leigh stepped onto the porch. Of average height, her powder blue slacks and navy blouse complimented her slender frame. The breeze caused a lock of silver hair to blow into her face, and she used one hand to brush it back into the short style she wore. She waved as Amanda neared. "This is certainly a pleasant surprise."

"Hi, Gramma." Amanda gave her a hug before following her into the house. "I hope you feel the same way after we talk."

"Of course I will. Nothing you could say would change my feelings." Anna Leigh looped her arm around Amanda's waist and escorted her to the kitchen. "Your grandfather's going to be upset that he missed you."

Amanda took her usual place at the kitchen table and inhaled deeply. "Lunch smells wonderful. Where is Grandpa?"

Anna Leigh filled two glasses with iced tea and placed one in front of Amanda. "He's gone to Austin to pick up some special lumber. He's planning on making a new dining table for Michael and Lois' anniversary. We were at their home for dinner the other night and Jacob couldn't stand their old table. Lois told us she'd had the same piece for over twenty years, and even then she'd bought it second-hand."

"That sounds like Grandpa, all right." Amanda added a packet of sugar substitute to her tea. She stared into the glass as if to find all the answers there. The light touch of her grandmother's hand on hers caused Amanda to raise her head. "I've ruined Sunflower Realty," she said quietly. "It's not even making enough money to pay the utilities."

"Oh, my darling, no." Anna Leigh patted Amanda's hand. "You've kept it going much longer than I ever expected it to be. I opened it on a whim, so many years ago." She intertwined their fingers. "Growing up I'd never had a job. My father didn't think a proper young lady should do such a thing. Once Michael was in school, I felt the need to do something constructive. I'd bought Sunflower Realty for an investment, but soon became interested in doing more than just collecting dividends."

Amanda raised her head. Her hopeful face encouraged Anna Leigh to continue.

"Before I knew it, your father had grown, married and had his own family. I'd become so engrossed in running my business that I didn't know where the time had gone. I hired a manager and was able to cut my hours significantly." Anna Leigh got up and spooned out two helpings of stew. She brought the bowls to the table and finished her story. "I allowed the details of the office to slip away and was on the verge of closing it for good when you moved here. When Jacob had that horrible accident, nothing else mattered to me."

In between bites of stew, Amanda paused. "And I just rushed right in and took over."

"Not in the least. You showed such an aptitude for business that it actually gave me a new appreciation for it. I was very happy to turn Sunflower Realty over to your capable hands."

Amanda sighed. "But I haven't been able to keep it going. Maybe Rick was the right person for the job."

"Nonsense. That man couldn't manage a cesspool."

"Gramma!" Amanda nearly choked on her stew.

Anna Leigh looked very pleased with herself. "You're right. I'm sure he would have found a way to mess that up, too. Although he'd have been right at home." She raised her spoon to her lips and blew a demure puff of air over it. "Are you still looking for a housekeeper?"

"Yes, and no. Lex wants to, and I admit we could use the help. But I'm not sure I want a stranger in our home. I know she's right; I don't have the time to work in town and at home. I was going to start interviewing women in the next week or so." Amanda nibbled on a tender chunk of beef. "Mmm. I can never get my stew this good. What's your secret?"

"I cut up a roast instead of using stew meat. Makes all the difference in the world." Anna Leigh put her spoon down and covered

Amanda's hand with hers. "The office has run its course, Amanda. I think it's time to shut it down."

Amanda blinked the unexpected tears away. "But what about Wanda, Peggy and Margaret? What will they do?"

"Wanda will probably be more than happy to stay at home and raise her daughters. She's often hinted around at wanting to do so, but I believe stayed because she didn't want to leave you in a bind."

"She's never said a thing to me," Amanda said. "But Peggy is single. I'd hate for her to be out of work, especially in times like these."

Anna Leigh laughed. "And she's been commuting back and forth from Austin, because of her new boyfriend. Honestly, Amanda. Do you not know the goings-on at your own office?"

"Obviously not." Amanda put her elbow on the table and propped her chin in her hand. "And I suppose you know something about Margaret, too?"

"Possibly." Anna Leigh returned her attention to her meal.

"Well?"

Ignoring the outburst, Anna Leigh took a sip of her tea. She daintily wiped the corner of her mouth with her napkin. "Margaret's mother has been after her for years to move to Dallas and stay with her. She's used her job as an excuse, although I believe she's become quite agreeable to the idea."

Amanda sighed heavily and dropped her spoon into her bowl. "Why is it that I go to work every day and don't know any of this? But you come in to 'visit' once or twice a month and know everything?"

"I believe it's because you're too close to the situation."

"Maybe."

Finishing her stew, Anna Leigh nudged her bowl aside. "Answer me this. What is the main reason you're dragging your feet over this? Do you and Lexington need the money you were bringing in?"

"Not exactly." Amanda started to push the last of her vegetables around in her bowl. "I haven't been drawing a check for several months."

"Excuse me?"

Amanda shook her head. "I didn't feel right. We weren't making any money and I didn't want to take away from the business."

"What am I going to do with you?" Her words weren't said with any heat, but Anna Leigh still frowned at her. "What does Lexington say about that?"

"Uh." Amanda suddenly found something on the tablecloth interesting.

"You didn't tell her?"

"She's been busy with trying to keep the cattle alive on the ranch. The last thing she needed was me whining about my work."

Anna Leigh gathered their dirty dishes and put them in the sink. She stared out the window, as if weighing her words. "Are you two having trouble? You used to share everything with each other."

Joining her grandmother at the sink, Amanda put her arm around her. "We've never been better, Gramma. I thought I could fix things at the office before she found out." She lowered her head until it rested against Anna Leigh's shoulder. "I don't want her to know I'm a failure."

"Oh, dearest." Anna Leigh turned and held Amanda's face in her hands. "The only way you could fail is if you stopped being yourself. We are all very proud of what you've accomplished." She kissed Amanda's forehead. "I was ready to close the office down years ago. You brought new life to Sunflower Realty. But I think it's time you focused on your family, don't you?"

Unable to speak, Amanda could only nod.

WITH A HEAVY heart, Amanda returned to the office. As she stepped through the door, all three women stood to greet her. Amanda's emotions must have shown on her face, because Wanda immediately enveloped her in a warm embrace. Clinging to her as if her life depended on it, Amanda choked out, "Did my grandmother call you?"

"She didn't have to." Peggy moved to one side of Amanda, while Margaret silently took the other. "We've all wondered how long it would take you to see the writing on the wall."

Surrounded by their compassion, Amanda greedily absorbed all they had to offer. "I've been worried about the three of you."

"And we were more concerned with how you would handle things." Margaret snagged the box of tissue off her desk and passed it around. "My mother will be thrilled when I move in with her."

Wanda laughed, although there were a few tears mixed in as well. "Dirk has been begging me for years to stay at home with the girls. I think they've about worn him out."

Turning to Peggy, Amanda asked, "What about you?"

Peggy left the group and took her purse from her desk. She removed a small jewelry box and opened it. Nestled inside was a small diamond solitaire. She took the ring from the box and slipped it on her left hand. "Steven gave this to me a couple of weeks ago. I told him I needed to think about it for a while." She held out her hand and grinned as the light sparkled off the ring. "I've given it a lot of thought and can't think of any reason to say no. I was going to give my notice this Friday." She was quickly surrounded by the three women, all of them speaking at once.

"Why didn't you say anything?" Wanda asked.

"It's about time," Margaret gushed.

Amanda felt a weight lift from her shoulders. "We have to give you a party."

Wanda and Margaret squealed together. "Party!"

THE BARN WAS a welcome relief from the cold as Ellie led her horse inside. She took Stormy to her stall, while Lex did the same with Thunder. "That was fun," Ellie said, as she removed the saddle. She watched as Lex struggled with the larger horse's tack. "Do you need any help?"

"Nope." Lex gritted her teeth while she stretched to lift the bridle from Thunder. "Been doing this my whole life."

Ellie started to brush Stormy's coat. "I know that, smartass. But I also know that you've got to be hurting by now, and thought I'd offer to give you a break."

"I'm fine." The grunt that came from Lex when she stretched to brush the top of the horse belied her comment.

"No, what you are, is stubborn." Ellie left Stormy to stand in front of Thunder's stall. "It's past lunch time. Why don't you head to the house, and I'll finish up here? It'll take me less time to do both horses than it would for you to do one."

Lex turned to argue the point, when her knee gave out. She caught herself on the side of the stall, barely able to stand. "Damn it."

Ellie tapped the top of the stall with one hand. "*Now* do you need my help?" She ignored Lex's growl and carefully eased her cousin's arm around her shoulder and led her from the stall. "You have a choice," she said, as she bore the brunt of Lex's weight. "You can sit on a bale of hay and watch me work, or I can call Martha and Charlie to come get you."

"Stay," Lex said. She groaned in relief as Ellie lowered her to the bale. "Thanks."

"You're welcome." Ellie patted Lex's cheek and winked. "Now sit there and be a good girl while I finish the horses." She laughed at the muttered curse she received.

THE TELEVISION WAS on low as Lex flicked through the channels on the satellite dish. She was tucked in one end of the couch, her legs stretched across the leather. The ice pack on her knee helped, but she still hated being treated like an invalid.

Ellie came into the den carrying a tray. She set it on the coffee table and handed Lex one of the plates, as well as a canned soda. "How's the leg?"

"Better." Lex lifted one corner of the bread on her plate. "Mmm. Roast sandwich. My favorite."

"I thought so." Ellie sat at the end of the sofa and popped the top on her soft drink. "Hope you like barbeque chips. That's all I can find."

Lex took a bite of the sandwich and nodded. She chewed and swallowed before answering. "Those are my favorites, too. Thanks for making lunch."

"No problem." Ellie started on her sandwich. "What are you watching?"

"There's not much choice. Either soaps, talk shows, or cooking." Lex finally landed on a classic sports station. "Ah. Much better."

Ellie rolled her eyes but kept quiet.

The sound of tires on the gravel drive caused both women to turn toward the front windows. Lex was about to put her plate on the side table when Ellie stood. "Don't even think about it," Ellie said. "I'll see who it is."

Lex grumbled but kept her place on the sofa. She watched as Ellie peeked through the window. "Well?"

"They must have driven around back. I'll go check." Ellie crossed the den and headed down the hallway. She was almost to the back door when it opened, and Amanda stepped inside. "Oh, hey."

Amanda hung her coat up on one of the hooks by the door and set her purse on the bench below. "Hi, Ellie. Do you know where Lex is?"

Ellie used her thumb to point back over her shoulder. "She's in the den. Is everything okay?"

"I think it will be." Amanda stepped by Ellie. "Come on. You might as well hear this, too."

"All right."

When Amanda stepped into the den, all thoughts left her as she noticed her wife's posture. "What happened to you?"

Lex turned and looked over the top of the sofa. "Amanda? What are you doing home so early?"

"I asked you first." Amanda sat beside Lex and gently removed the ice pack. "Did you hurt yourself again?"

"No, it's just a little swollen, so Nurse Ellie fixed me up." Lex took in Amanda's red-rimmed eyes and gently cupped her cheek. "What's wrong?"

Amanda leaned into the touch and closed her eyes. "Nothing, now."

"Sweetheart, talk to me."

Opening her eyes, Amanda kissed the hand against her cheek. "Remember when we talked about getting someone to help out with the house because neither one of us had time to do everything?"

"Yeah?"

"Well, I don't think that's going to be a problem anymore. We've shut down Sunflower Realty."

Lex sat up straighter. "What? Why? But I thought—" Her mouth was covered with Amanda's fingers to stop her stammering.

"We haven't had any clients in a couple of months, honey. I talked to Gramma about it, and she agreed that it was time." The grim look Amanda wore eased into a gentle smile. "Besides, it's been getting harder and harder to leave the house and go into work every day. I'm tired of it." She removed her fingers, her smile widening when they were caught and kissed.

"Are you sure?"

Amanda nodded. "More now than ever." She turned to Ellie, who'd been quietly sitting in the nearby chair. "Looks like you'll have more company around here."

Ellie sat up straighter. "Actually, I may have a lead on a job. Don't know if it'll pan out or anything, but I'm waiting to hear back from the hospital in Parkdale."

"Really? You didn't mention it when we were out riding," Lex questioned.

Amanda's head turned back around so quickly it would have been funny, if not for the completely pissed off look on her face. "Riding?"

"Um." Lex's countenance took on the spitting image of Lorrie when she was in trouble. "We just rode over to the edge of the creek to check on a live trap." She turned to Ellie for help. "We weren't out very long, were we?"

Laughing, Ellie stood. "I think I'll go see what Martha and Charlie are up to." She left the room, obviously enjoying her cousin's plight.

"Lex, do you have any sense? I can't believe you would do something as irresponsible as going out for a ride when you can barely walk! What if something else had happened? Do you—" Amanda was effectively silenced when Lex's mouth covered hers. She melted into the kiss.

Feeling Amanda's arms lock around her neck, Lex slowly leaned back until Amanda was straddling her lap. She worked her hands under the soft sweater. The tiny yelp as she unhooked Amanda's bra made her smile. "I love you."

Amanda unbuttoned Lex's shirt. "I love you, too." She closed her eyes as Lex's hands left warm trails across her skin. "Don't think this will get you out of trouble." As Lex hit a particularly sensitive spot, she moaned.

"I like trouble," Lex murmured, falling back and sliding Amanda's sweater off.

Chapter Eight

COLD DRY AIR whipped through Ronnie's scrubs as he hurried across the graveled lot toward the back of the veterinary office. He stripped off his disposable gloves and tossed them in the trash can inside the rear door. At the sink, the warm water felt good against his hands as he scrubbed them. He looked up when an interior door opened, and nodded to Dr. Hernandez. "Hi, Ben."

"Afternoon, Ronnie. How's everyone looking out there?"

Ronnie turned off the water and dried his hands. "Pretty good. I think we'll have a couple of vacancies in the next day or two. Tracy's finishing up the paperwork now."

"Excellent." Ben leaned against the stainless steel counter and crossed his arms over his chest. "What about the Bower's heifer?"

The paper towel Ronnie had used to dry his hands hit the rim of the trash can, before bouncing in. "The stitches can come out—"

"Dr. Hernandez," the intercom buzzed with their receptionist's voice. "I have Sheriff Richards on line two for you."

Ben winked at Ronnie before he picked up the phone. "What did you do this time?"

"Hey, I'm innocent."

"This is Dr. Hernandez. What can I do for you, Sheriff?" Ben listened for several minutes. "We'd be glad to help, of course. But I don't think we have a space available at the moment." He nodded as the sheriff continued to speak. "Uh-huh. Would you mind giving my assistant directions? Excellent." He handed the phone to Ronnie. "Time for a house call. Since I've done my share, why don't you take this one?"

Ronnie grinned as he accepted the phone. "Hey, Jeremy. What's up?"

LORRIE CLIMBED TO the top of the monkey bars and hooked her legs over a pipe. In the shape of a dome, the metal bars interconnected and were popular with the children. Six other kids were draped in various poses, chattering away. She bent backward and looked at the playground upside down. "Everybody's on their head," she laughed.

"Nuh-uh," a younger voice piped up from below her. Teddy sat cautiously on a lower rung. "You're upside down."

"Duh." Lorrie reached for him. "Come on up here, Teddy-bear. It's fun."

He shook his head and held on tightly to the bar in front of him. "No way. You're gonna fall on your head and splat, and then my daddy will have to fix you."

Tired of the view, Lorrie raised her head and changed positions. Now she hung by one leg, while the other reached for a different bar. "Don't be such a scaredy-cat. The ground's soft." She gestured down at the rubberized padding. "My Momma said it's made of old tires, so I'd probably bounce."

"No way!" Teddy looked at the ground.

"Yep." Lorrie tapped the straw cowboy hat he wore. "You wanna come riding on Saturday?"

Teddy's eyes grew larger at the thought of horses. "I dunno. By myself?"

"No, you can ride with me, if you want. Or maybe Momma will take you." She grinned. "If you're scared."

"I'm not scared! I just don't wanna ride some stinky ol' horse, that's all." He climbed from the equipment and stood on the ground. "When I have my own ranch, I'm not gonna have any dumb old horses."

Lorrie dropped down beside him and dusted off her hands. She looked around the playground until she spotted her sister, who was sitting under a tree with two other girls. Satisfied that Melanie was okay, she turned her attention back to her cousin. "You can't have a ranch without horses, silly. How do you 'spect to get around everywhere?"

He held out his hands as if holding handle bars. "With motorcycles. Vroom-vroom."

"Momma says motorcycles aren't no good in the mud, or in rough 'train. You need a horse for that."

"I don't care. Horses are gross. And my ranch won't have no trains."

When the bell rang, Lorrie tipped the back of Teddy's hat forward, making it fall over his eyes. "That's not what I meant, goofy." She laughed at him. "Come on. Let's go inside. Maybe when you grow up you won't be afraid of horses."

Teddy adjusted his hat and followed her. He glared at her back. "I'm not afraid. I just don't like them."

RONNIE CRINGED AS his truck bounced over another deep pothole on the dirt road. He glanced at the directions he had written on a piece of paper. "There should be a gate somewhere. Ah. There it is." He tossed the paper onto the seat beside him and drove over the rusted cattle guard. "I'm going to charge Jeremy extra if I have to get my shocks replaced after this," he grumbled.

The road led to a clearing, where a corral and collapsed wooden barn sat amongst the dead, knee-high weeds. Ronnie parked in between two sheriff's cars and got out of the truck. He saw two deputies and an animal control officer racing around the broken corral, chasing an emaciated horse. The deputies each had a blanket, and the woman with animal control carried a coiled length of rope. Ronnie stopped outside the corral and watched the show.

"Glad you're here." Jeremy stepped next to Ronnie as the horse shook its head and raced away from one of his men. "Maybe you'll have better luck catching the blasted thing."

From where they were standing, Ronnie could see open wounds on the animal. "What happened to it?"

Jeremy sighed. "We think it was in the barn when it fell. I can't believe it's still alive. Animal control got an anonymous call about an abandoned horse, and when she got here, she called us for help." He saw the horse rear. "You guys, watch out," he yelled.

"They're never going to get anywhere like that," Ronnie said. He crawled through the slats of the corral and walked to where the control officer stood. "Can I borrow your rope?"

She handed him the coiled rope. "Be my guest. I don't get paid enough to do this kind of crap."

In a low voice, Ronnie replied, "That's okay. I've been around enough horses, so maybe I'll have more luck." He moved closer to the panicked animal. "Guys, could you back away, slowly? He's spooked enough as it is."

Oscar patted Ronnie on the shoulder. "No problem, kid. I wasn't lookin' to get stomped today. Come on, Jay. Let's leave it to the expert." He tugged on his partner's arm to lead him away from the horse.

"Sweet." Jay dropped the blanket he had been holding. "Damned beasts scare the hell out of me. Do you think the vet will be safe?"

Ronnie couldn't help but grin when he heard Oscar's response.

"Well, if you had a big sister like Lex Walters, you'd have 'em following you around like a pied piper. I don't think Ronnie's got a thing to worry about."

When Ronnie stepped closer to the gelding, it reared and angrily snorted. "Easy, there." He slowly held out his arms while he murmured gentle words of encouragement. "It's all right, big guy. No one wants to hurt you."

THE OVERSIZED DIESEL pickup truck idled roughly as rust-colored leaves blew across the empty schoolyard. Lex tried to keep the grin off her face as she studied her wife's smaller frame in the driver's seat. Amanda had her left leg tucked beneath her, so she could see over the steering wheel.

Amanda didn't even bother to look at Lex. "What's so amusing?"

"Nothing."

"Liar." Amanda shifted in the seat in order to keep her left foot from falling asleep.

"You'd be a lot more comfortable if you'd use the cushion I bought for you," Lex drawled. "Or you could let me drive." She always got a kick out of watching Amanda try to see over the steering wheel of the Dodge.

Amanda turned her head. "I don't need a booster seat to drive."

"I never said you did."

"And there's no way in hell I'm going to let you drive when you can barely walk."

Lex crossed her arms over her chest. "I can walk just fine."

"Lex—" The school bell rang, and both women looked anxiously at the front of the building. Amanda tapped the steering wheel. "I still wish you'd talk to Rodney again."

"All he'd tell me is to keep using the stupid crutches, which I hate." Lex sighed when she realized how she sounded. She held out her hand, which Amanda automatically took. "I'm sorry, sweetheart. I feel completely useless right now, and I don't mean to take it out on you."

"You're anything but useless, Lex. Don't feel bad because you have to allow your body to heal. You're only human."

Lex kissed Amanda's hand. "Thanks." The opening of the back door of the truck caused them both to turn around.

Melanie slowly crawled into the truck and across to her place behind Amanda. She took an unusually long time to buckle her seat belt, while Lorrie hopped in and closed the door.

"Mrs. Barrett says Jerry don't go to our school no more," Lorrie excitedly announced.

Amanda exchanged looks with Lex. "Jerry doesn't go to our school anymore," Amanda corrected. "Did Mrs. Barrett tell you why?"

"No, but my friend Shelly lives across the street from Jerry. He always throws rocks at her cat, but when her daddy told Jerry's mommy about it, they got into a fight and then she told me on the playground today that she saw a moving truck at Jerry's house the other day." She finally stopped long enough to breathe. "Do you think Jerry moved away?"

It took Lex a moment to follow Lorrie's non-stop chatter. "Wait a minute. There was a moving truck at Jerry's house? When?"

"I dunno. The other day." Lorrie bounced in her seat. "Are we still going to Gramma and Grandpa's? You promised that if we were good we could go see them today after school. I've been good." She turned to her little sister. "You've been good too, haven't you?"

Melanie shrugged her shoulders but didn't say anything.

Lex held up her hand to stop Lorrie before she could get going again. "Melanie? Are you okay?"

"I don't feel good," Melanie mumbled.

Amanda unbuckled her seatbelt so she could turn all the way around. "What's wrong, sweetie?"

"My tummy hurts."

Leaning over the seat, Amanda touched Melanie's forehead. "You're a little warm. When did you start to feel bad?"

"I dunno." Melanie wrapped her arms around her body. "A while ago."

"Maybe we should go on home," Lex said.

"No," Melanie and Lorrie said together. Melanie sniffled. "I wanna see Gramma."

Amanda looked at Lex. "What do you think?"

"We could always take her temperature when we get to your grandparents', and then figure out what to do. And if we need to go to the doctor, it's closer than the ranch."

"That's true." Amanda brushed the hair away from Melanie's eyes. "Think you'll be okay until we get to Gramma's? I bet she'll know exactly what to do for your tummy."

"'kay."

Amanda turned around and buckled up. "All right, girls. On to Gramma's."

Lex kept her voice low, so the children wouldn't hear. "Do you think we should call the pediatrician?"

"Why don't we wait until we can find out a little more? I'd hate to bother him if it's something as simple as constipation, or a stomach bug."

Within a few minutes, Amanda pulled the truck into the Cauble's front drive. "All right, gang. We're here."

Melanie started to cry. "Mommy, I don't feel good."

Amanda turned off the truck, climbed out and opened Melanie's door. "Is your tummy still hurting?"

"Uh-huh." Melanie waited until Amanda removed her seatbelt. "Will you hold me, Mommy?"

"Of course I will, honey." Amanda hefted the child into her arms. "Come on. Let's get you inside." They were halfway to the house when Melanie cried out and vomited, covering both her and Amanda.

Amanda coughed at the rancid smell. Strong odors had always been hard for her, and she struggled to keep from joining her daughter.

"Ooh, gross. She got you good, Mommy." Lorrie kept her distance and stood partially behind Lex.

"Hush, Lorrie." Lex playfully swatted their oldest on the rear. "Could you go to the house and get a towel from Gramma?" She limped toward Amanda to see if she could help.

"Yes, ma'am."

When she heard Amanda gag, Lex gingerly took Melanie away from her. A rancid fish odor emanated from the crying child. Lex used one hand to strip the soiled top off of her, effectively removing the majority of the mess. "Sssh. You're going to be okay, sweetheart." She tucked Melanie close to her and headed for the front porch.

"Lex—" Amanda stopped, knowing that Lex would ignore her anyway. "Stubborn old thing."

Anna Leigh followed Lorrie out of the house. "Lorrie told me what happened. What can I do?"

"Mind if we borrow your bathtub?" Lex covered Melanie with the towel that Lorrie handed her. "Thanks, kiddo. You're a great help."

"I'll start the water for you, Lexington." Anna Leigh moved ahead of the group.

Lorrie wrinkled her nose as Amanda walked past her. "Want me to get you a towel, too, Mommy?"

Amanda held her filthy blouse away from her body and hurried into the house. "I'll be all right." She focused all her energy on not throwing up, and followed Lex to the guest bathroom upstairs. "Let me carry her, Lex. You shouldn't be straining your knee like that."

"I've got her," Lex argued. She ignored the dueling pains in her knee and back as she trudged up the stairs. At the sound of running water, Lex kissed the top of Melanie's head. "We'll have you cleaned up in no time, sweetheart. You're going to be all right."

Melanie sniffled and buried her face into Lex's shirt.

"That was so gross, Momma. I didn't know anyone could throw up like that. She spewed like a water gun, or something," Lorrie chattered. "And, wow. What a nasty smell."

Anna Leigh stepped away from the filling tub. "Lorrie, why don't you go out to the workshop and see your grandfather? I'm sure he'd love to have your help on the table he's making."

"Awesome." Lorrie rubbed her nose. "I bet it doesn't stink out there." She turned and headed down the stairs at a trot.

"Thanks, Gramma." Amanda whipped her blouse off and tested the water. "Perfect."

Lex stripped Melanie of the remainder of her clothes and carefully set her in the water. "There you go, sweetheart. Getting clean should help." She watched as Anna Leigh gathered the dirty clothes in a towel. "Let me take those to the laundry room. You shouldn't have to."

"No need, dearest. But perhaps you should check the guest room dresser for spare clothing. I believe we have some pajamas that will fit Melanie." Anna Leigh left the trio alone.

"All right." Lex bent and kissed Melanie on top of the head. "Guess I'll leave you two to get clean."

Amanda already had her shoes and socks off, and was unbuckling her belt. "Thanks. Would you mind seeing if I left anything here the last time we stayed over? I can't remember if I did or not."

"Sure thing." Lex washed her hands at the sink, and doubled-checked her reflection in the mirror. Not seeing anything amiss, she dried her hands and gave Amanda a quick kiss. "Holler if you need me."

"We'll be fine," Amanda said, slowly sinking into the water. "Oooh. Nice."

Lex stepped into the hall and met Anna Leigh. "Thanks for letting us invade you like this."

"It's never an invasion." Anna Leigh tucked her arm around Lex's waist as they headed for the nearest guest room. "I believe we have several pairs of Mandy's sweats in the top drawer of the dresser." She gently guided Lex to the bed. "Why don't you take off your boots and stretch out, while I get what the girls need?"

"Have you been taking sneaky lessons from my wife?" Lex removed her boots and sat back against the headboard. "Or maybe you're where she gets it from."

Anna Leigh ignored her grumbling. She rifled through the dresser until she was satisfied with the clothing choices. "After I get these to Mandy, I think I'll have Jacob run to the store for some Pedialyte. That's usually the best thing for a sick little girl."

"I can do that," Lex argued, swinging her legs off the bed. One look from Anna Leigh caused her to roll her eyes and resume her earlier position.

"I knew you would see it my way, Lexington." Anna Leigh gathered the clothes into one arm and kissed Lex on the cheek. "Be a good girl, and maybe Jacob will bring back some ice cream, too."

The ringing of her cell phone kept Lex from making a parting comment. She took the flip phone from her belt. "Lex Walters."

"Lex? This is Ronnie."

She gingerly stretched her legs out. "Hey, Ronnie. What's up?"

"I've got a bit of a dilemma, and I was hoping you'd be able to help me." He cleared his throat. "You know anything about an abandoned farm out west of highway twenty-one?"

Lex started to pick at a thread that stood out on her jeans. "Not right offhand, I don't. Are you looking to buy it?"

"No, no. Nothing like that. But the sheriff's department came across an injured gelding that's going to need a lot of rehabilitation. And we don't have any empty stalls right now. So, I was wondering—"

"If I'd mind you keeping him at the ranch, right?"

Ronnie laughed at her tone. "Yeah. But, Lex? He's a real mess."

"What kind of mess?"

"I had to suture so many cuts on him, I lost count." Before Lex could ask, he explained. "We think he was inside a barn when it collapsed, which explains why we couldn't get him into a covered trailer. And, I think he was attacked more than once by a wild dog, because his legs are covered solid with infected bites. We had to cover his head with a blanket so I could get close enough to administer a sedative. Otherwise, we'd have never been able to get him out of the corral."

Lex closed her eyes as he spoke. She had a bleak picture in her mind of the condition of the horse, and it made her sick to her stomach. "Take him out to the ranch and put him in the corral closest to the house. I'll help you any way I can."

"Thanks, Lex. I really appreciate it. I'll talk to you later."

After clipping her phone onto her belt, Lex sighed. "Never a dull moment, that's for damned sure."

AFTER DRYING OFF and changing into the sweats that Anna Leigh had given her, Amanda helped Melanie from the tub. Before she could finish patting her dry, Melanie doubled over and threw up again, this time on the rug by the bathtub. "Oh, sweetie." Amanda tried to calm her daughter, who had begun to dry heave. "Lex!"

Moments later, Lex limped into the room. She took one look at Amanda's pallor, and quickly rolled up the rug to get it out of the way. She picked up Melanie and used the damp washcloth to wipe her face. "Sssh, baby. It's going to be okay."

"Momma, my tummy hurts," Melanie gasped, lying her head on Lex's shoulder. She coughed, but didn't throw up.

Lex held her close and whispered to Amanda, "She's still running a fever. I think we'd better call Dr. Weisner."

Anna Leigh appeared in the doorway. "Don't bother. I've got Rodney coming over."

"Gramma," Amanda started to argue.

"What's the use in having a doctor in the family if he doesn't make house calls?" Anna Leigh brushed her hand across Melanie's hair. "Don't you worry, little one. Lexington, bring her into the first guest room. Neither one of you can be very comfortable in here."

Amanda reached for Melanie. "Let me take her, honey."

Lex thought about denying her, but one look at Amanda's face changed her mind. "Sure. I'll finish cleaning up in here, then I'll join you." She kissed Melanie's forehead and gently passed her to Amanda.

By the time Lex had rinsed the rug and cleaned the tub, she could hear Rodney's voice coming from the nearest guest room. She washed her hands and turned off the bathroom light, before joining the rest of the family.

"Hey," Amanda murmured, leaning into Lex, who had automatically put her arm around Amanda's body.

"How's it going?" Lex whispered into Amanda's ear. She kissed the side of her face when Amanda sniffled.

Rodney carefully palpitated Melanie's abdomen. When she cried out, he shared a concerned look with her parents. "It could be one of several things. I may need to take her to the hospital for more tests."

"Appendicitis?" Anna Leigh quietly asked.

"Definitely a chance of it, I'm afraid." He looked back at Melanie. "What did you have to eat today, Mel?"

"I dunno."

"She had a peanut butter and jelly sandwich, a sliced apple, chips and a bottle of juice," Amanda said. "At least that's what I packed in her lunch bag this morning."

Rodney turned back to his patient. "Is that right?"

"Uh-huh." Melanie cut her eyes at Amanda for a moment, and then back to Rodney. "I didn't trade."

Lex turned to Amanda. "Peanut butter and jelly? Are you sure?"

"Why?"

Crossing to the bed, Lex sat next to Melanie and gave her a no-nonsense look. "Because someone smelled a lot like tuna when she got sick."

Melanie's eyes grew wide, as she was torn between telling the truth, and getting into trouble.

"Sweetheart," Lex leaned closer to Melanie and lowered her voice, "please tell us what you ate. I promise we won't get mad."

"But, Mommy said—"

"Sssh. How can Uncle Rodney make you all better, if he doesn't know why you're sick?" Lex brushed Melanie's hair away from her face. "Did you trade lunches today?"

Melanie shook her head. "No."

"Mel."

"I didn't, Momma."

Lex sighed and rubbed her eyes with one hand. "Did you share anyone else's lunch today?"

"Uh-huh." Melanie started to cry. "It was after recess. I was in line next to Bryan, and we was hungry. So Bryan gaved me some of his lunch sandwich that he didn't eat."

Rodney bit back a laugh. "Warm tuna salad. Sounds like a mild case of food poisoning." He flipped through his bag. "Melanie, from now on you need to stick with what your Mom sends to school with you, okay? No more sharing."

"Okay." Melanie started to cry when she saw Rodney remove a hypodermic needle and a vial. "Do I have to get a shot?"

"It'll make you feel better a lot quicker," he said. "Does anyone have a contact number for Bryan?"

Amanda stood behind Lex and put her hand on her shoulder. "I have a list of phone numbers for all her classmates in my purse. Would you like me to call his parents and see how he's feeling?"

"That's a good idea. If he's sick, tell them I can drop by on my way home." Rodney put away his equipment and ruffled Melanie's hair. "I'll see you next week on Thanksgiving, okay? Be a good girl for your moms."

Melanie blinked the tears from her eyes and nodded. "Okay." She yawned and rolled onto her side, curling her hand around Lex's wrist. "I'm sleepy, Momma." Her eyes closed and she dozed off before Rodney could stand.

Lex smiled down at her daughter. "Whatever you gave her, I'll pay you a million dollars for a ten-year supply. Bedtime tends to be a fight at our house."

He stood and stretched. "She was so worn out from the nausea and cramping, it didn't take much to help her rest. She should be fine in a day or so, but give me a call if she gets worse."

"Thanks, Rodney." Amanda gave him a hug. "If you'll follow me downstairs, I'll make that phone call, so you'll know if you need to stop by Bryan's house." When Lex made a move to get up, she pointed her finger. "And you sit right there." She glanced at Lex's feet. "As a matter of fact, since your boots are already off, why don't you lie down next to Mel for a while?"

Lex didn't feel like arguing, since she was hurting more than she wanted to admit. "That's a good idea. I'd like to stay close in case she needs anything." She winked at Amanda. "Don't think you've won this one, though. I'm only doing it for Mel."

"Uh-huh." Amanda kissed the top of Lex's head. "You believe what you want, honey."

A FEW DAYS later, Amanda opened the front door and smiled a warm welcome to the couple standing on the front porch. "I'm so glad you could make it. I'm Amanda. Please, come in. Let me take your coats." After placing her guests' coats on separate hooks by the door, she led them into the living room. "I know we've spoken on the phone, but it's so great to finally meet face to face."

Rebecca Starrett rubbed her hands together to warm them. "Thank you so much for inviting us. It's nice to have a chance to visit with another couple, isn't it, Shelby?"

"Yep." Shelby followed Amanda's lead and moved to sit on the loveseat opposite the sofa. "Hey there, Lex."

"Shelby. Good to see you again." Lex began to stand, but a not-so-subtle glare from Amanda kept her seated. "How's that colt doing, Rebecca?"

After she sat beside Shelby, Rebecca appeared to bounce in place. "He's wonderful. I've already gotten him used to a halter."

"That's great." Once Amanda sat next to her, Lex stretched her arm across the top of the sofa behind her. "I've got a wild gelding I'm working on right now. Maybe I should turn him over to you."

Rebecca blushed. "I don't know how good of an idea that would be. Training a colt is easy, but a grown horse is another matter."

Amanda lightly swatted Lex on the leg. "Behave. Rebecca, Lex told me that you're a barrel racer."

"That's true. Although I'm teaching more than I'm competing these days. My horse is getting older, and I just don't have the heart to ride another one in competition."

"I can certainly understand that. I don't know what I'll do when my stallion, Thunder, gets too old." Lex sighed at the thought.

"Don't worry, honey," Amanda leaned closer. "When it's time, I'll make sure to put you out to the same pasture."

Shelby laughed at Lex's expression. "She's got your number."

The sound of laughter and barking came trailing down the hall, before the guilty trio arrived in the den. "Mommy," Melanie squealed. "Lorrie's chasing me!"

Freckles followed her happily, barking and snapping at her heels.

"Come back here, Mel! I'm gonna thump you!" Lorrie stopped when she saw the two extra adults in the den. "Oh. Hi. Mommy, did you see what Mel did?"

Amanda stood and gave both girls what Lex described as her "mommy glare." She was almost knocked over when Melanie raced over and wrapped her arms around her legs. "What on earth is going on?" When Freckles continued to jump around frantically, Amanda snapped her fingers and pointed to the dog bed by the fireplace.

Immediately chastised, Freckles went to her bed and lay down.

"She—" Lorrie started.

"I was just—" Melanie countered at the same moment.

Amanda pointed to the office. "Both of you. In there. Now." She gave their guests a 'what can you do' look. "If you'll excuse me, I've got to referee."

Lex waited until the office door closed before chuckling. "And that, I'm afraid, was the wrecking crew. Also known as our daughters, Lorrie and Melanie."

"They're adorable, Lex." When Shelby stiffened beside her, Rebecca took her hand and gave it a squeeze. "As much as I love children, I'm afraid I would never have the patience to be a parent."

"Well, it's taken some getting used to, but I wouldn't trade the experience for anything in the world."

The office door opened, and two penitent children came out, followed by Amanda.

Lorrie held her sister's hand and stood in front of Rebecca and Shelby. "Hi. I'm sorry for being rude." She looked at Amanda, who nodded. "My name's Lorraine Walters, but you can call me Lorrie." She tugged on Melanie's hand.

"I'm Melanie Walters, and I'm sorry too. We wasn't raised to be wild heathens." Melanie's big blue eyes were filled with remorseful tears.

Rebecca leaned forward. "It's nice to meet you both. I'm Rebecca, and this is Shelby."

Lorrie's eyes grew big. "You're the rodeo riders!"

Shelby blushed and shook her head. "I used to ride, but Rebecca here is a barrel racer."

"Wow." Lorrie sat on the coffee table in front of them. "Is it fun?"

"It can be. But it's a lot of hard work, too. Do you ride?" Rebecca asked.

Lorrie nodded, then remembered her manners. "Yes, ma'am. I have a horse called Mine, but she doesn't go around barrels or anything. Maybe after dinner, I could show you?"

Melanie, already bored of the conversation, crawled into Lex's lap. When Amanda sat beside them, she moved to sit between her parents.

"Sure, Lorrie. That would be fun." Rebecca smiled at the girl. "I was about your age when I started getting interested in horses. But if you want to know something really exciting, you should ask Shelby about riding bulls."

"Wow," Lorrie mused, looking at Shelby with new respect. "You rode bulls?"

Shelby gave her partner a dirty look, but answered Lorrie. "I did, for a few years, until I retired."

"Were you scared?"

"It could be scary at times." When Lorrie's face shone with hero worship, Shelby continued, "It's also extremely dangerous, and if I had to do it all over again, I wouldn't do it." She saw Freckles come over and nudge Lorrie's knee. "Um, has your dog always had pink stripes?"

Melanie slipped off the couch and started to carefully sneak away.

Lex snapped her fingers. "Freckles, come." When the excited dog hopped into her lap, Lex started to laugh. "Pink marker. Looks like someone was playing connect the dots. Thank god we only have washable markers around here."

"I tried to tell you," Lorrie said.

Amanda closed her eyes and silently counted to five. "Melanie Leigh Walters! Get back here!"

Chapter Nine

THE BLACK LIMOUSINE drove slowly past the park, its smoky windows blocking out the noise of children playing. One of the occupants, a middle-aged woman, sighed and stared longingly at the playground.

"What's your problem, Veronica?" her husband asked. He chewed on the unlit cigar that hung from his mouth and shifted so he could look through her window. "Well?"

She dabbed at her eyes with a handkerchief. "Nothing, Harrison."

"It must be something for you to carry on like that."

Reluctantly turning away from the view, Veronica Rivers gave her husband her full attention. "I can't help but think what might have been."

Harrison jerked the cigar from his mouth. "For god's sake, woman. Our son has been dead for ten years. Why on earth are you crying about it now? You can't keep dwelling on the past."

"I know. But, still, it's so difficult, listening to our friends talk about their grandchildren. They always have photographs, videos, plays and ballgames. Every year, it gets harder and harder, knowing that somewhere in Texas we have a grandchild. It's even worse now, since we're not traveling as much as we did before. Why haven't we talked to Jeannie about seeing Frank's daughter?" She turned toward the window once again. "I always liked Jeannie. She made our son so happy."

"We never saw her because they hauled Jeannie and our granddaughter to some god-forsaken place." Harrison tossed the soggy cigar onto a tray and took a fresh one from his breast pocket. He used a gold cigar cutter and snipped away the end. Within moments, a thick cloud of smoke hovered above them. "I don't know how Cauble stands it, his own daughter turning out that way."

Veronica casually covered her nose and mouth with her handkerchief. "They seemed nice enough to me."

He spit a tiny piece of tobacco onto the floor. "Bullshit. They're nothing but deviants, and they influenced Cauble to allow them to take our daughter-in-law and granddaughter halfway across the damned country. For all we know, they placed Jeannie in some sort of institution and spent all her money. God knows Frank left her well-off."

"I don't think—"

"Enough! Whining about the past won't bring Frank back," Harrison said. His expression softened when he saw the total look of defeat on his wife's face. "But perhaps I can hire someone to look into where our granddaughter is, and go from there."

She laid her hand on his leg. "Thank you, Harrison. Maybe she can come visit us for summer vacation. She's old enough."

Harrison covered his wife's hand with his own. For all his bluster and bravado, he truly loved her. "She certainly is. I'll call my investigator when we get home."

THE COLD NOVEMBER wind brought tears to Lex's eyes, as she cautiously moved closer to the spooked horse. She blinked to clear her vision, not wanting to make any sudden moves. "Easy, now," she murmured, holding her hands out away from her sides. She had a lead rope dangling from her left shoulder in the hopes of catching the gelding.

Lorrie sat quietly on the top of the corral. Her legs jiggled impatiently, but she knew better than to disturb Lex while she was working. She held a bag that contained gauze pads and ointment, for whenever her mother caught the horse. Her legs stilled as it reared, causing Lex to take a step back. "Momma!"

Lex turned her head and winked at her. "It's okay, Lorrie." She turned her attention back to the horse, confident in her abilities.

The restless animal huffed at her. It shook its head and kicked its rear legs into the air in an attempt to warn her away.

"Sssh." Lex got close enough to grab the halter, but didn't move. She stared the horse down, waiting until it calmed before reaching out and scratching the gelding's damp neck. "Easy." She grinned as the horse leaned into her touch. "That's it. Good fella."

Not far away, the back door of the house slammed, as Melanie raced across the yard. She was unable to open the gate on the fence, so she climbed over. It didn't take her long to get to the corral. "Lorrie, help me up." When her sister ignored her, she stomped her foot. "Lorrie!"

The high-pitched voice startled the horse. It reared and unintentionally knocked Lex over with its front hooves. She landed hard on her back, stunned.

"Momma!" Lorrie started to jump into the corral, until she saw her mother roll out of the way of the horse.

"Stay back," Lex ordered. She climbed to her feet and gingerly walked to where her daughters were. Rubbing her chest with one hand, she took off her hat and wiped her forehead. "Melanie, what have I told you about yelling around the animals?"

"I'm sorry, Momma. I just wanted to get up like Lorrie." Melanie's lower lip quivered and tears welled up in her eyes. "I never get to sit up high."

"Are you okay?" Lorrie said. "That looked like it hurt."

Lex climbed through the slats of the corral. "Nah. Scared me more than hurt me," she said. "Why don't you two go see what Mada's up to?

She's been back from church long enough to bake some cookies." Lex never felt bad about sending the kids to Martha's. Sunday after church service was one of the best times to get something tasty. She knew there were always fresh goodies available.

"But who's gonna help you with the horse?" Lorrie asked, while she climbed off the corral. "You said you needed someone to hold the medicine."

Lex removed her gloves and put her hand on Lorrie's shoulder. "How about you help me once you're out of school next week? Maybe by then I'll have him settled down enough." She stopped and knelt in front of both girls. "I want you two to be very careful around that horse, okay? I need your help to make sure no one gets in there and gets hurt."

Both girls solemnly nodded. "Yes, ma'am," they echoed together. Giggles broke out when Lex tickled their stomachs.

"Good." She took the bag of medical supplies from Lorrie and gave them each a kiss. "Now hurry over to Mada's, before your Grandpa Charlie eats all the good stuff."

With more laughter, two sets of feet took off toward the cozy cottage that Martha and Charlie called home.

Lex slowly stood and rubbed her chest. "Amanda's going to kill me if I come home with any more bruises." She headed for the house, trying not to limp.

The back door opened before Lex made it up the steps. Amanda stood in the threshold with her hands on her hips. "What did you do?"

"What makes you think I did anything?" Lex asked. She stopped in front of Amanda and kissed her on the nose.

"Let's see. Could it be the fact that you're covered in dirt? Or maybe the way you're walking like an old woman." Amanda lightly touched Lex's pale, blue shirt. "Or maybe it's the hoof prints on your chest that are a dead giveaway."

Lex lowered her head and glanced at where Amanda's hands rested. "Hoof prints?" she couldn't help but grin when those same hands began to unbutton her shirt. "Uh, sweetheart?"

"Hmm?"

"As much as I'm enjoying the attention, do you think we could take this inside? I'm starting to feel a bit of a draft."

Amanda gently ran her fingers over the upside-down, u-shaped blemishes. Red and scraped, they would most likely be ugly bruises by morning. "Let's go upstairs and get you into the tub. You can tell me what happened while you soak." She peeked around Lex. "Where are the girls?"

"Martha's." A diabolical grin covered Lex's face. "Probably having a nice, long snack."

"Oooh." Amanda wore a matching smile. "They usually fall asleep after one of Martha's snacks, don't they?" Cake, cookies or pie and a large glass of milk were almost always guaranteed to bring on the need for a nap.

"Yep."

Amanda tugged on Lex's open shirt. "Good. We'll get you cleaned up, and then have a nap of our own."

WITH AN EXHAUSTED sigh, Michael Cauble loaded the last of his equipment into the back of the black Ford Explorer. He checked his watch, relieved to see he'd get home at a reasonable hour. The wedding he had photographed hadn't taken as long as he'd expected, so he was glad he'd get to see his wife before dark. A glance in the rearview mirror reflected his weariness. His reddish-brown hair was mussed, and there were dark circles beneath his hazel eyes.

The drive home seemed to drag on forever, and by the time he pulled into his driveway, he could barely keep his eyes open. Michael hit the remote for the garage door and drove inside, so he wouldn't have to unload his gear. Before he could get out of the SUV, the inner door to the house opened.

A dark brown head poked out, and Lois watched from the doorway as her husband sat silently in the SUV, unmoving. When he didn't get out of the Explorer, she came and tapped on the window. "Honey? Are you okay?"

Michael raised his head and gave her what he hoped was a decent smile. He got out and kissed Lois on the lips. "Hey, beautiful."

She brushed her fingers across his cheek. "Are you all right?"

"It's been a long day," he said, putting his arm around her waist as they walked into the house. "I've never seen so many bratty kids in my life."

"Poor baby. Are you hungry?"

He sighed. "I don't think I have the energy to eat anything. Maybe I'll just take a shower and go to bed."

Lois touched his forehead. "Are you coming down with something? I could call Rodney. I'm sure he wouldn't mind—"

"I'm just tired, Lois. A shower should perk me right up." He shuffled toward the bedroom, leaving his worried wife behind.

SHE WAITED UNTIL he was in the bedroom, before she went to the living room and picked up the phone. "Hello, Anna Leigh? This is Lois."

"Well, good evening, dearest. It's so nice to hear from you. How is everything?"

Lois bit her lip while she considered her answer. "To tell you the truth, I'm worried about Michael. He hasn't been himself, lately."

"So, you've noticed, as well? Jacob mentioned something at dinner this evening. I was going to call you tomorrow. He said that Michael looked pale this morning, when he stopped by on his way to his studio."

"He still is," Lois said. "Pale, I mean. And he's been so tired. Tonight, he refused dinner." She shook her head. "I just don't know, Anna Leigh. Even after a good night's sleep, he looks completely worn out."

Anna Leigh sighed. "He needs to go see Rodney."

"Good luck with that one," Lois muttered. "He about bit my head off when I suggested it."

"He did, did he? Well, we'll just see about that. I'll call Rodney right now. I'm sure he'll—"

"No, wait. As much as I'd love to have him checked out, I don't think he'd appreciate being bothered tonight." Lois paused and listened to see if Michael had left the shower, but there was still no sound coming from the bedroom. "I'll call you in the morning, and we can go from there."

"That's fine, Lois. But, please, let me know if you need anything, no matter what time it is. Try and have a good evening, dearest. I'm sure everything will work out fine."

"I hope so. Goodnight." Lois put the phone away and went to the bedroom. "Oh, Michael."

Michael was stretched out across the bed on his stomach, still in his clothes. He had one shoe off and one shoe on.

Lois touched his shoulder. "Honey, wake up."

He groaned and rolled onto his back. "Hmm?"

"You need to get undressed," Lois gently chided. She removed his remaining shoe, while Michael fumbled with his tie.

"Stupid thing," he growled, unable to undo the knot.

Lois pushed his hands away. "Quit fussing and let me help."

"I can do it."

She kissed his forehead. "I know you can. But I can do it," she pulled the tie away from his collar, "much faster."

"Showoff." His smile belied the gruff tone. "Thanks."

Within a few minutes, Lois had Michael undressed and under the bedcovers. Before she could turn out the light on her nightstand, he was snoring softly. "Goodnight, my darling." She kissed his cheek and soon joined him in slumber.

THE LIGHTS IN the bedroom were dim as Lex stepped out of the bathroom. She towel-dried her hair with one hand while she searched through a dresser drawer with the other. After she found the sleep shirt she was looking for, she turned and noticed what her wife was doing.

Amanda was propped on her side of the bed, a laptop balanced on her legs. Her fingers typed away furiously and she was so engrossed in what she was doing she didn't notice Lex until she sat on the bed. "Oh, hi, honey."

"Hi. Whatcha doin'?"

"Updating my blog." Amanda squinted at the screen, frowned, and went back to typing.

Lex stretched across the bed until she could see what Amanda was working on. "Your what?"

"Blog."

"Oh. Thought you said you were plating a frog." Lex grinned. "Didn't know exactly why you'd need a laptop to play with a frog, though."

Her head tilted, Amanda didn't pay any attention to what Lex was saying. "Mmm-hmm."

With a sigh, Lex got comfortable. "So, what exactly is your blog about?" When she didn't get an answer, she started touching the edge of Amanda's ear, which always got a response. "A blog about a dog, wrestling a frog, in a bog. Maybe they took a break on a log, because of the fog," she teased.

Amanda stopped what she was typing and turned to look at Lex. "What did you say?"

"Um, don't ask me to repeat it, because I don't think I can."

"Nut. That's what you get for reading Melanie's Dr. Seuss books." Amanda brushed her fingertips along Lex's cheek. "Give me another minute or two to finish this up, okay?"

Lex kissed the fingers. "Sure." She quietly watched Amanda type, secretly enjoying the look of intense concentration.

Less than five minutes had passed when Amanda shut down her laptop. "There. All finished." She packed it into its case and slid it under the bed. "Sorry about that. I thought I'd be finished before you got out of the tub."

"Not a problem, sweetheart." Lex turned onto her side so that she was facing her. "Can you tell me what you blog about? Or is it private?"

Amanda laughed. "Blogging is anything but private, honey. But it's something I've just started to do. As a bit of therapy, I guess."

"Therapy? What's wrong?"

"Nothing's wrong. But I've been a little restless since the office closed, and Gramma suggested I try my hand at writing. And since I'm not going to write the Great American Novel any time soon, I thought I'd try something a little less strenuous."

"What do you blog about?" Lex was charmed by the blush on Amanda's face. "Oooh. Is it dirty?"

Amanda slapped Lex's arm. "No! I can't even read erotica without being embarrassed. It's the last thing I'd ever write about, you know that."

"I know. But it's always fun to tease you about it." Lex tried to roll out of the way when Amanda pounced on her. "Hey, watch it!"

"Teach you to pick on me." Amanda tickled Lex's ribs. "Actually, I blog about us. Or more to the point, about things that happen around here."

Lex pulled her closer. "Like day to day stuff, huh? Considering our kids, you certainly get enough material. What do you call it? I'd like to check it out sometime."

"They're not the only ones, you know. And, it's called RockingWMom. Perfect, don't you think?" Amanda squirmed until she was comfortably resting across Lex. "I forgot about your chest. I'm not hurting you, am I?"

"Not a bit." Lex wrapped her arms around the body across hers and nuzzled Amanda's hair. "What were we talking about?"

Amanda nibbled on Lex's throat at the same time warm hands slipped under her nightgown. "I haven't a clue."

THE TICKING OF the clock on the kitchen wall was drowned out by Amanda's pacing. Freckles skipped along behind her, wagging her stubby tail. Amanda glanced at her watch, then the clock, and finally at Lex, who had an amused look on her face. "What?"

"You're going to wear a hole in the floor, sweetheart."

Amanda glared at her. "I don't see how you can sit there so calmly." She stomped to the refrigerator and opened it, peering inside. With a disgusted snort, she slammed the door shut and resumed her pacing.

Lex stood and stretched. When Amanda passed her, she wrapped her arms around her and held her close. "You know, I rode the school bus my entire life, and I think I turned out okay."

"I know. It's just—"

"They're our babies, and you're not used to handing responsibility over to anyone else," Lex finished for her.

Amanda turned in Lex's arms, so that her cheek rested against Lex's chest. "I'm going to lose my mind before lunch, at this rate."

"Nah." Lex kissed the top of her head. "I need to run out and check the live traps on the northern side. Want to go with me?"

"Are we riding, or driving?"

Lex's breath caught as Amanda's lips touched her throat. "You keep that up, and I won't be able to do either. But, let's ride. We haven't been out together in quite a while." She laughed when those same lips blew a raspberry on her neck.

Amanda stepped back. "All right. Let's saddle the horses before I decide to drag you upstairs."

"Not much of a threat, if you ask me. Maybe we can come back to the house for an early lunch." Lex helped Amanda into her coat, before donning her own heavy duster. When the dog barked, Lex shook a finger at her. "Sorry, girl. You're going to have to stay home."

After a side trip to the office for a rifle, they left the house. As they walked toward the barn, Amanda watched Lex. "Are you up to a ride? You're still limping."

Lex held the barn door open for her. "Yeah, I'm just stiff. This cold air makes everything ache." She left the rifle and scabbard on a bale of hay, away from the horses.

"You probably wouldn't tell me anyway," Amanda mumbled.

"Sweetheart, I'd never talk about anything else if I told you every time something hurt." Lex carried out Amanda's saddle and blanket and placed it on the floor by Stormy's stall. "But I promise, if it gets too bad, I'll let you know."

Amanda kissed her on the cheek. "I'll hold you to that, Slim." She nudged Lex out of the way. "I can saddle my own horse, honey."

"I know. But I like doing it for you." Lex backed away slowly when Amanda playfully curled her fingers into claws, threatening to tickle her. "But, I think I'll let you handle it yourself, this time."

"Chicken." Amanda laughed at the exaggerated squawk that Lex gave out, as she ducked into the tack room. She stepped into Stormy's stall and patted the paint pony's neck. "Are you ready for a ride today?"

Lex came out of the tack room carrying her own saddle and blanket, as well as having both bridles draped over one shoulder. She hung Stormy's bridle across the top of the stall for Amanda. "What are you going to do if she says no?" she said, opening Thunder's stall. "Hey, fella."

"Probably the same thing you'd do if Thunder ever answered you."

"Smartass."

Amanda laughed and quickly saddled Stormy. "Takes one to know one."

"That's real mature, Amanda. No wonder our kids are such smartasses. They come by it naturally." Lex finished with Thunder and led him from his stall.

Amanda opened Stormy's stall and led the horse out. She lightly poked Lex in the shoulder. "Considering you're the Queen of the Smartass Remark, I'd say our girls were doomed." Before Lex could retaliate, she put her horse between them.

Lex laughed. "You've got a point, sweetheart." She attached the scabbard to her saddle, double-checking to make certain it was secure. Once they were outside, both climbed on their horses. "Wanna race?"

"Real funny, gimpy. I don't think so." Amanda shifted in the saddle until she was comfortable. "Let's take it easy and enjoy the ride, okay?"

"Spoilsport." Lex stretched in the saddle and inhaled the cool air. "God, it feels good to be out here." She nudged Thunder until he was beside Stormy. "I've missed our rides together."

Amanda looked at Lex. The winter's sun painted her in an almost ethereal glow and the sight took her breath away. "Me, too." She loved how the light brought out the strands of silver in Lex's brown hair.

They rode along silently for the first ten minutes, each lost in their own thoughts. After Lex sighed for the third time, Amanda asked, "What's the matter?"

"Nothing." Lex caught the look she was given and shrugged her shoulders. "Okay, nothing serious, I suppose."

Amanda cleared her throat, but didn't say anything.

"I got a letter last week from Great Aunt Loretta. Did you know she's ninety-two?"

"Wow. I had no idea."

Lex nodded. "Yeah. Anyway, she's been after me to go to the family reunion next year."

Nodding, Amanda moved Stormy closer to Thunder, so she could touch Lex on the leg. "And? Where is it?"

"West Texas."

"Okay, so go. I mean, it's not like you've been in a while, right? At least since we've been together."

Lex took Amanda's hand and squeezed. "No, I haven't been since I was about twenty-five, or so. They only come along every five years, and Melanie was too little during the last one."

"When is it, exactly?"

"The second weekend in January. They learned the hard way not to have them during the summer." Lex grinned. "There's nothing out there for miles, except cotton fields and sand. The last time I went, they had it in June."

Amanda cringed. "Oh, god. I can just imagine."

"Yep. And to top it all off, the community center air conditioner wasn't very good. Aunt Loretta told them if they wanted to keep the 'old timers' around, they'd better come up with a different solution, or she'd book a cruise to Alaska every five years, instead."

Laughing, Amanda squeezed Lex's hand. "I'd love to meet her."

"Really?"

"Of course. I know you write to her all the time and send her photos of the girls, but wouldn't it be nice to introduce them in person?"

Lex kissed Amanda's hand before releasing it. "Yeah, it would. Thanks, sweetheart." She pointed up ahead. "It's not far to the first trap. We placed it up there, on the other side of our little pond."

"It's gotten that close?"

"It's a water source, so I figured better safe, than sorry." Lex unsnapped the end of the scabbard, but didn't remove the rifle.

Amanda watched nervously. "Are you expecting trouble?"

Giving her a wink, Lex grinned. "Considering both you and I are magnets for trouble, I didn't want to take any chances."

They cautiously skirted the pond, which was half the size it used to be. Even though it was fed by an underground spring, the extended drought had hurt it. When they got close enough to the live trap, the scream of the bobcat startled both horses.

"Whoa!" Lex got Thunder under control with no problem, and watched helplessly as Amanda's mount bucked beneath her.

With one hand on the saddle horn and the other holding the reins, Amanda tightened her knees around Stormy. "Damn it, Stormy, calm down!" Once her horse was under control, she gave Lex a shaky grin. "That was fun."

"Not." Lex dismounted and stepped over to where Amanda held her horse. "Are you okay?"

"I'm fine. But I think we have a bigger problem."

Lex hadn't taken her eyes off Amanda. "What?"

"How are we going to get that creature back to the house?" Amanda pointed to the trap, which held a live, and very pissed off, bobcat.

"Umm." Lex tipped her cowboy hat back and scratched her forehead. "I guess I can always tie it on the back of my horse. I don't think it can get its claws through the cage."

Amanda's eyes grew wide and she shook her head. "Like hell you are! I don't want that thing anywhere near you!"

Lex patted her leg. "Okay." She tilted her head and studied the cage, then took her cell phone off her hip. Hitting a number from memory, she blew Amanda a kiss. "Hey, Roy. We're out by the pond near the north pasture, and found a little friend." She laughed at whatever her foreman said. "Yeah, I didn't think that far ahead. Would you mind bringing out a truck? Thanks." Lex snapped the phone closed and returned it to her holster. "How's that?"

"Better, thanks." Amanda got off her horse and ran her hands along Lex's arms. "So, now what do we do?"

Lex's hands gravitated toward Amanda's hips. "I've got a few ideas." She tugged her closer, and grinned when Amanda linked her hands behind her head. Following the unspoken request, Lex lowered her head and kissed her.

Chapter Ten

NOT QUITE EIGHT o'clock in the morning, great smells were beginning to come out of the kitchen. Amanda stood at the counter, chopping onions and trying not to wipe at her tearing eyes.

Martha peeked over her shoulder. "Honey, you keep whacking at those things, there ain't going to be anything left of them."

"I wanted to make sure they're cut up small enough so that Lex doesn't notice them."

"Good idea. She definitely turns up her nose at any kind of onion."

Melanie raced into the kitchen. "Mommy! Save me," she yelled. She wrapped her arms around Amanda's waist, just as Lorrie and Freckles crossed the doorway.

Lorrie's shirt was wet and water dripped from her hair. "There you are!" She started for Melanie, who squealed and tried to climb Amanda.

Freckles barked and jumped around Lorrie, who kept trying to catch Melanie.

"Come here, Mel. I'm gonna—"

"Mommy!"

Amanda put her knife down and lifted Melanie into her arms. She turned and noticed Lorrie's wet hair and shirt. "What's going on around here?"

"I didn't do nothin', Mommy," Melanie said.

"Liar!" Lorrie reached for Melanie's leg.

Melanie kicked at her, almost hitting Lorrie in the face. "Am not!"

"Are too!" Freckles' bark accentuated Lorrie's case.

Martha put her hand on Lorrie's shoulder and moved away from Melanie and Amanda. "Hold it right there, young 'un. You're going to get a knot on your head if you're not careful." She touched Melanie on the nose. "And you, little miss, better behave yourself, or you won't get any dessert today."

"I didn't—"

Amanda popped Melanie on the rear end. "You'd better not be telling us a story, Melanie Leigh Walters." She put her face up to her daughter's, so close their noses almost touched. "Now tell me the truth. What did you do to your sister?"

"She dumped a glass of water on me for no reason," Lorrie said.

"Nuh-uh! You did too do somethin'!" Melanie kicked at Lorrie again, then cried out when Amanda popped her gently on the rear again. "Mommy!"

After setting Melanie down, Amanda put her hands on her shoulders. "Why did you dump a glass of water on your sister?"

"'cause she's a baby!"

Martha stopped wiping Lorrie's hair with a towel and waggled her finger at her. "Lorrie, that's not nice."

Lorrie's lower lip jutted out. "Well, she is."

"Am not!"

"Are too!"

Amanda felt like screaming, too. "Girls, enough!" She pointed at Lorrie. "You! Go out to the barn and see what your momma is up to."

"But I didn't do anything wrong," Lorrie whined.

"You're not in trouble." Amanda ruffled Lorrie's hair. "Yet," she added, playfully. "Go on, now."

Lorrie slowly marched out of the kitchen, mumbling under her breath. Freckles followed, even though she wouldn't be allowed out of the yard.

Melanie had a very pleased look on her face, until her mother tapped her on the head. "I want you to go upstairs to your room and think about what you did today."

"But, mommy—"

"I don't know why you did what you did, but it's going to stop. The rest of the family will be here soon, and I don't want you and your sister going at it all day. I'll come up and get you when I think you've been up there long enough."

Melanie started to cry as she left the kitchen. "Lorrie started it."

Once the room was quiet again, Amanda sighed. "I don't think this house will survive their teen years."

"Oh, honey. It's going to get a lot worse, before it gets better," Martha sagely advised. "Especially since Lorrie is so much like Lexie."

Amanda rolled her eyes. "God help us all, then."

Martha laughed right along with her. "Welcome to my life."

SLOW AND PURPOSEFUL, the rented Town Car cruised the residential streets of Somerville. Harrison Rivers glanced at the papers he held before he laid them on the seat. "I believe it's that one, with the yellow flower pots by the steps."

"It's lovely. Most of the houses here are, though," his wife said.

Once the car was parked, Harrison checked his image in the rearview mirror. He started to open his door, when Veronica put her hand on his arm.

"Maybe we should wait until after the holiday. I'd hate to disturb their family."

"We are part of the family, damn it." He got out of the car. "Are you coming?"

Veronica tucked her purse beneath her arm and joined her husband on the front stairs of the house. She tried to peer into a window. "It doesn't look like anyone's home."

"You don't know that." Harrison rang the bell. Not even fifteen seconds passed before he started pounding on the door. "Goddamn it! Where the hell would they be on Thanksgiving?"

"They could be at Michael's home." Veronica followed him to the car and waited until they were inside to continue. "Didn't the report also say he lived here?"

Harrison took a cigar from the case inside his suit pocket and snipped off the end. He crammed it into his mouth, but didn't light it. "The whole damned bunch of them live in this rotten dump of a town."

"I know you're frustrated, dear. But since the report only has their addresses and very little else, perhaps it would be a good idea to return to our hotel suite in Austin until after the holiday. There's no telling where they could be today."

He checked his notes for Michael Cauble's address. "No, we're already here. There's not that many places they can be. I'll be damned if we don't get to see our granddaughter today."

THE SOUND OF car tires on the graveled driveway caused Lex and Lorrie to make a detour. They stepped around the edge of the porch and saw two cars pulling up alongside the house.

Lorrie took off toward the parked vehicles at a dead run. "Gramma! Grandpa!"

"Hello, there," Jacob Cauble embraced the child who was wrapped around his body. "What have you been up to?"

"Helping me at the barn," Lex said, as she took a bag from Anna Leigh. "Does Amanda know you're bringing half your kitchen?"

Anna Leigh laughed as she placed her arm around Lex. "Of course she does, dearest. It's really not much, just some of the girls' favorites."

"Fruit salad?" Lorrie asked, gladly getting between her grandparents and getting a hand from each of them.

The other car door opened and Jeannie, her husband Rodney and their son Teddy joined the group. "I see how we rate," Jeannie teased, pecking Lex on the cheek.

"If you had goodies, we'd have helped you, too." Lex grinned at her nephew, who was dressed in his usual cowboy outfit. "You ready to take over the ranch, Teddy?"

Teddy took Lex's hand. "Do you still have horses?"

"Yep." Lex released his hand and opened the back door for everyone. She took a deep breath and enjoyed the mingling scents of a holiday dinner being prepared. "I believe Amanda and Martha are already at it in the kitchen, if you ladies care to join them."

Jeannie took the bag from Lex's hand. "I'll take this to them, Slim. I'm sure you and the guys have better things to do."

"She has a point," Rodney said, slapping Lex on the back. "Let's go turn on your beautiful big-screen TV and get some football hype."

"Sounds like a great idea." Jacob kissed his wife on the cheek. "Let me know if you need any help in there," he gallantly offered.

Anna Leigh patted his side. "I'm sure we'll manage, dearest. But thank you." She followed her granddaughter into the kitchen, while the rest continued down the hall.

Teddy gave Lorrie a bashful smile. "Can we go to the barn? I like the way the hay smells."

"Um, Momma?" Lorrie didn't seem enthused about being his tour guide.

"Go ahead, Lorrie. But you're responsible for Teddy, remember?"

Lorrie nodded. "Come on, Teddy. We'll make forts out of the hay bales."

He happily followed. "Cool!"

HARRISON TOSSED WHAT was left of his unlit cigar out of the car window. "Damn it all to hell! Cauble's not home, and his parent's house is deserted, too. Where the hell are they?"

"Now can we go back to Austin? It's obvious everyone's together today." Veronica dabbed at her lips with a lace handkerchief. "All this cold air is really not good for my asthma."

He flipped through the folder with a vengeance. "No! They've got to be around here, somewhere. I think I remember one other place," his voice drifted off as he read. "Damn! They wouldn't be there, would they?" His face reddened as he tossed the report on the seat between them.

"Where, dear?"

"That god-forsaken ranch," He muttered. "All right then. It can't be that hard to find." He made a sharp U-turn .

"Do you think that is a very good idea, Harrison? After all—"

"Enough!" he bellowed. "If they think they can have Frank's daughter anywhere near those, those, *women*, they've got another thing coming." He took out another cigar, this time lighting it.

Veronica delicately waved her handkerchief under her nose. "But, Harrison, Amanda is part of their family. I'm sure—"

He held up his hand to silence her. "If Cauble wants to have a perverted daughter, that's his business. But if Jeannie thinks we'll sit by idly while her sister and that other thing corrupt our son's only child, she's in for a rude awakening."

NO LONGER EXILED, Melanie sat at the kitchen table filling in a picture from her favorite coloring book. She had tearfully apologized to her mother, and would have to do the same to her sister, once Lorrie returned from outside.

Amanda watched as Jeannie gazed fondly at Melanie. She took in her sister's attire, which consisted of a colorful flowing top and black stretch leggings. Suddenly, something occurred to her. "Jeannie?"

"Hmm?"

"How are you feeling?"

Jeannie raised her head and met Amanda's eyes. Her mouth turned up into a playful grin. "Not too bad. I'm not nauseous at all."

Anna Leigh and Martha looked at each other, then at Jeannie. They both clapped and cheered at the same time. "Are you—" Anna Leigh asked, hopefully.

"I am!" Jeannie stood and met the others in the middle of the kitchen, where they shared a group hug. "I wanted to wait until we were all together to make the announcement."

"That's wonderful," Amanda gushed, holding onto Jeannie and rocking from side to side.

Jeannie giggled. "We're so excited, Mandy. Rodney's been almost beside himself for the last few days, ever since we found out."

"What does Teddy think of becoming a big brother?" Anna Leigh asked, once they had all calmed down.

"He doesn't know, yet." Jeannie glanced at Melanie, who was studiously coloring, unaware of the ruckus around her. "We wanted it to be a secret, and you know how kids are."

Amanda sighed. "All too well." Her smile returned in full force. "I can't wait to host the baby shower."

Martha nudged Anna Leigh. "Any excuse for a party, with these girls."

"Isn't that the truth?" Anna Leigh agreed.

"THAT'S GOT TO be the turn, up ahead," Harrison flipped on the turn signal and took the car off the main road. The car passed beneath an ornate metal gate, proclaiming the Rocking W Ranch.

"Harrison, please. We've been driving around for hours. Let's return to Austin and find a nice restaurant for lunch." Just the thought of the dirt from the road they were traveling on caused Veronica to cough. "This is barbaric."

He gave her a nasty look. "I can't help that the damned woman lives out in the middle of god-damned nowhere!"

Veronica bit off a retort as they came to a covered, wooden bridge. Her outlook changed as they drove closer, and her eyes were drawn to the seasoned structure. "Oh, how lovely. It's almost like something out of a magazine."

"It's a wonder the blasted thing doesn't collapse," Harrison grumbled. He bumped his head on the side window when the car hit a rock. "For god's sake, this road is a mess!"

It wasn't long before the road ended in front of a two-story house. The lower half was covered in brick, and the first floor was surrounded by a wrap-around porch. On the second story, French doors opened out onto a balcony. Veronica tore her eyes away from the impressive sight. "It appears we may have found them," she said, indicating the multiple vehicles parked beside the house.

"It's about damned time." Harrison parked behind the other vehicles. "Come on, Veronica. Let's see about Lorraine."

WITH ONE EYE on the road, Lois glanced over at her husband, who had been quiet for the entire drive. "Michael, are you sure you're up to this? It's probably going to be a madhouse at the ranch today."

Michael held back the sharp remark that was on the tip of his tongue. "Of course I am. Just because I didn't sleep very well is no reason to skip a holiday dinner. I'll be fine."

Feeling chastised by his tone, Lois sighed and turned her attention back to the road.

"I'm sorry, sweetheart. I shouldn't have snapped at you." Michael rubbed her back. "I hate to see you worry."

Lois smiled at him. "Does that mean you'll go see Rodney next week? Because you know I'll keep worrying until you do."

His laughter was a balm to her heart. "I think I've just been set up."

"I'll make the call on Monday," Lois offered.

LEX HANDED THE television remote to Jacob. "Don't let Rodney change the channel to some goofy documentary while I'm getting us some coffee." She stood and laughed at the indignant sound coming from her brother-in-law.

"Hey, I like football, too. But I can't stand those morons on the pre-game show." Rodney playfully reached for the remote, which Jacob held over his head.

Charlie, who had been sitting quietly, joined in the laughter.

"Oh no you don't," Jacob teased. He tossed it to Charlie. "Here, you take it."

Rodney laughed. "You guys are nuts."

"Yeah? What was your first clue?" Lex made it around the couch when there was a knock on the front door. "That must be Michael and Lois. Be right back, guys." She was still smiling when she opened the door. "What have I told you about knocking? The door was—" Her voice trailed off when she saw the vaguely familiar couple standing in front of her. "Uh, hello."

Harrison pushed by Lex and forced himself into the house. "Is Jeannie here?"

"Who?" Lex noticed the quiet woman still standing on the porch. "You might as well come in, ma'am."

"Thank you. Miss Walters, isn't it?" Veronica held out her hand. "I'm not sure you remember me. I'm Veronica Rivers."

Lex shook the older woman's hand automatically. "Rivers?" Suddenly she remembered where she had seen the couple before. "Frank's parents?"

Veronica nodded. "That's right."

Harrison barged into the living room. "Where's Jeannie?" he asked the men, who had all turned quiet.

"Mr. Rivers, I don't know what you're doing here, but why don't you sit down and I'll get us all some coffee?" Lex offered.

He turned and glared at her. "I don't want any damned coffee, I want to see my granddaughter!"

Amanda stood in the doorway with Jeannie, Anna Leigh and Martha right behind her. "What's going on in here? We could hear you all the way in the kitchen."

Lex turned and shrugged her shoulders. "I'm not sure."

Footsteps could be heard coming up the front steps, as Michael and Lois arrived. Michael edged around Lex, took one look around and his face started to redden. "Harrison Rivers? What are you doing here?"

"Looking for my granddaughter, that's what. Where is she?"

Jeannie came into the room. "Harrison, Veronica. It's good to see you." She held out her hands, which Veronica took.

"You look wonderful, dear. The last we had heard, you were still recuperating from your illness."

"Thank you. I've tried to contact you, but all I was able to do was leave a message with Harrison's secretary. I've been recovered for years." Jeannie nodded toward her husband. "All thanks to the great care I received from my doctor. Honey? Could you come over here?"

Rodney stood and brushed the wrinkles off his slacks before he joined his wife. "Mr. and Mrs. Rivers? I'm Rodney Crews."

Harrison pushed Rodney's hand away. "Whatever. We've come to see our granddaughter."

"Why now?" Michael asked.

"What?"

Jeannie drew strength from her husband's arm around her waist. "You've never tried to reach me before, Harrison. Why now, after all this time?"

With her husband's mouth moving silently, Veronica was the one who answered. "I've never stopped thinking about her, Jeannie. Neither of us have. But, it's just been in the last year, since we retired, that we thought we'd finally be able to see Lorraine and spend some quality time with her." She dabbed at her eyes. "She's the only link we have with Frank. I'm sure you've raised her well, but, we just can't help but wonder how she's turned out."

Everyone in the room was silent.

"Well? Where is your daughter, Lorraine?" Harrison asked Jeannie.

"Mommy?" Melanie peeked around the corner of the living room doorway. "Momma?"

Amanda and Lex both turned at the sound of their daughter's voice. Lex was the first to get her wits about her. "Hey, kiddo. Come here." She held out her arms and Melanie quickly jumped into them. "Where have you been?"

"In the kitchen. But nobody was there no more, so I got lonely." Melanie snuggled against Lex's shoulder.

"I'm sorry, sweetheart. I'll go back there with you, how's that?" Lex kissed her cheek.

Harrison had heard enough. "For god's sake, who gives a damn? I want to see our granddaughter, Lorraine!"

Melanie turned toward the loud man. "My sister's named Lorraine, too. Where's your granddaughter? Can she come play with us?"

Before Harrison could say anything else, Michael stepped forward and pointed a warning finger at him. "Not another word."

"What? Why not?" Harrison softened his voice and grabbed Lex's arm to keep her from leaving the room. "Are you Jeannie's daughter, too?"

"That's enough." Amanda got between Lex and Harrison. "Everyone sit down, please, while we try to sort this out." She gently pushed her wife toward the door. "Please take her to the kitchen, Lex."

"Sure. But holler if you need me, okay?"

Melanie's eyes were wide as she peered over Lex's shoulder, on their way out of the room.

Once her daughter was safely away, Amanda joined the group on the other side of the living room. She sat on the arm of the sofa, next to Jeannie. "Mr. and Mrs. Rivers, things are a little complicated."

"Is our granddaughter here, or not?" Harrison bellowed, then paused. "Wait." He turned to Jeannie. "Was that little girl yours, too? What did she call that woman?"

"That woman," Amanda hissed, on the verge of standing and tearing into Harrison, "is my wife. And Melanie is our daughter." Only Jeannie's hand on her leg held in her place.

Harrison frowned. "Yours? But, she said—"

Jeannie jumped in. "Harrison, please. As you recall, I was not fit to raise a child after Lorrie, um, Lorraine, was born. Amanda and Lex were here for me, and for her, when we needed them."

"That still doesn't explain," Harrison argued.

"For god's sake, Harrison, would you please shut up and let my daughter finish?" Michael yelled, his face almost purple. He jumped to his feet. "You couldn't be bothered at the time, so our family took care of Jeannie and Lorrie."

Veronica held up her hand. "Excuse me, Michael, but I don't understand what you're trying to say. Your family took them away. We never got a chance to help."

Michael looked at Harrison. "You didn't tell her?"

"Tell me what?" Veronica touched Harrison's arm. "Dear? What is he talking about?"

"I personally asked Harrison if he'd like to help us decide on Jeannie and the baby's care. But he made some excuse about a business venture he was working on." Michael used a shaky hand to wipe the sweat out of his eyes. "I believe his exact words were, 'she's your problem, not ours.' Wasn't it, Harrison?"

"Well, I may have," Harrison stammered. He faced Veronica, whose disappointment was evident. "Veronica, you remember. It was that deal in Sidney. We left the country almost immediately after Lorraine was born."

She turned away from him. "And you kept us there, and all over the world, for almost nine years, Harrison. Yes, I remember quite well." She shook her head. "So much time, wasted. Please continue, Jeannie."

Jeannie exchanged looks with Amanda, who nodded. "It took me almost three years to recuperate from the stroke. By that time, Amanda and Lex were the only family Lorrie had known. As much as I loved her, I knew that she was happy, here with them." She held out her hand to Rodney, who took it automatically. "I signed over all my parental rights to them, close to her third birthday. As far as she knows, they *are* her parents."

"You gave up our granddaughter to them? But they're..." Harrison fished for a word that he could use, and not get pummeled over. "...Queer," he finished in a whisper.

Lex returned to the room, alone. "Don't worry, we're not contagious."

"Where's Melanie?" Amanda asked.

"She's gone out to play with the other kids." Lex purposely avoided the children's names. She put her arm around Amanda, much to Harrison's dismay. "Mr. Rivers, Lorrie knows all about her father. We told her years ago about the great man Frank was."

Veronica's eyes misted over at the mention of her son. "Thank you," she whispered, lowering her eyes.

Harrison jumped to his feet. "I want to see her."

Michael stepped in front of him. "That's for her parents to decide. For god's sake, man. You can't just barge in here and start making demands. This is a child we're talking about." He frowned and rubbed at his chest. "I—" His knees buckled, and he would have hit the floor, if not for Lex catching him.

LORRIE BRUSHED THE hay off of Teddy's back as they left the barn. "Hold still. You've still got some back here."

"Ow," Teddy whined. "That's too hard." He dodged out of her way.

"Come back here." Lorrie chased after him, laughing when Teddy jumped away from her again. "Don't go in the house with hay on you.

My mom hates to sweep."

They rounded the corner of the corral, when Lorrie saw Melanie climbing over the picket fence by the house. "Mel! You're gonna get in trouble for doing that," she yelled. No matter how many times she tried to show her how to operate the gate latch, Melanie would much rather climb over the fence.

Melanie landed on her feet and ran to them, while Freckles stayed on the other side of the gate, whining. "Whatcha been doin'?"

"Making play forts in the hay barn," Teddy said. He held his hand over his head. "Mine was this tall."

"Cool." Melanie tugged on Lorrie's arm. "Will you push me in the swing?"

Teddy's lower lip stuck out. "We was going to go to the tick tack room. I was going to get to sit on a real saddle."

"Tack room," Lorrie corrected. "And you can still do that, Teddster." She took him by the hand. "Come on. I'll help you on the saddle, then I'll push Mel on the swing. Okay?"

His face quickly brightened. "'kay."

Melanie stomped her foot. "Me first."

"Company first, Mel. You know the rules." Lorrie led their little band toward the main barn. "Is everybody here, yet? I'm getting hungry."

"Uh-huh. But there was some grumpy people here, too. They were all yelling in the living room."

Lorrie stopped at the barn door and turned around. "What kind of yelling?"

"I dunno. Something about their granddaughter. She has your name."

"Her name's Lorrie? Cool." Lorrie opened the door. "Remember, Teddy. Stay away from the tools, and the horses."

He ran ahead of her. "Okay."

"No running in the barn," Lorrie reminded him.

"Sorry."

Melanie walked behind them. "No, the grumpy man said her name was Lorraine. That's your long name, right?"

"Uh-huh." Lorrie followed a jubilant Teddy into the tack room. "That's cool, 'cause I'm the only Lorraine in our school. Do you think she's going to come here?"

"I dunno." Melanie climbed onto her saddle, which was draped over a small barrel. "But everybody was getting mad."

Lorrie helped Teddy onto Lex's saddle. "Hang on, cowboy."

"Yeehaw," he yelled, rocking back and forth.

"Will you push me now?" Melanie asked. "Please?" She slid off her saddle and hopped from one foot to the other.

Lorrie bit her lip while she thought. "Teddy? Do you promise not to wander off?"

"Uh-huh." Teddy continued to rock, then pointed his finger at the wall. "Pow, pow! I'm a real cowboy, Lorrie!"

"Yep. You sure are." Lorrie started to leave the room, with Melanie following behind.

Melanie laughed at her cousin. "He won't never be a real cowboy, 'cause he's scared of horses and cows."

"Hush, Mel." Lorrie took her hand and led her from the room. Neither of them noticed the tears that fell from Teddy's eyes.

AS SOON AS Michael collapsed, the living room erupted into bedlam. Rodney immediately took control and directed Lex to lay Michael on the sofa. "Everyone, please calm down." He touched Michael's neck, which caused the older man's eyes to open. "Michael? Can you hear me?"

"Of course I can." Michael tried to sit up, but was stopped when Rodney put a hand on his chest.

"Rest easy, Mike. Do you remember what happened?"

Michael frowned. "Why are you asking me all these stupid questions? So, I got a little dizzy. I'm fine."

Lois sat on the footstool next to the sofa and took her husband's hand. "Honey, tell Rodney how you've been feeling."

On the verge of denying it, Michael was stopped by the concern not only on Lois' face, but his parents, as well. "I guess I've been a little tired, lately."

"And?" Lois prompted.

Michael sighed.

Seeing that his patient was reluctant to speak with a room full of people around, Rodney turned to Lex. "Would you mind going to our car and getting my bag? I think it's in the back seat."

"Sure." Lex patted Michael on the shoulder. "Hang in there, Dad." She walked quickly down the hallway, toward the back door.

Rodney tipped his head toward Jeannie, who nodded. She took Amanda's hand. "Mandy and I will bring coffee to the dining room, if everyone will head across the hall. Right, Mandy?"

"Sure."

One by one, the group cleared out, leaving Rodney, Lois and Michael. Even Harrison was respectfully silent. Once they were alone, Rodney tapped Michael on the chest. "Now, tell me the truth, and don't leave anything out."

LEX HURRIED TO Jeannie and Rodney's car, and easily found his medical bag. "I didn't know anyone actually carried one of these anymore," she mused, as she headed back to the house. She was almost to the kitchen door when she heard Melanie's squeal of delight.

"Higher, Lorrie," Melanie demanded, kicking her feet in the air as she swung forward. She was careful not to kick Freckles, who would dart back and forth in front of her.

Seeing her two girls, Lex wondered where Teddy had gone. "Lorrie? Where's your cousin?" She yelled from the porch.

Lorrie pointed toward the barn. "He wanted to play cowboy, so I let him stay in the barn."

"You know you kids aren't supposed to play in there." Lex stood on the edge of the porch. She saw the new horse race around the corral in a panic. "Damn it." She started running toward the corral. "Lorrie, take this bag to the den and give it to Uncle Rodney right away."

Lorrie took the bag and held it against her chest. "Momma?"

"Do as I asked, Lorrie. I don't have time to explain." Lex hurdled the short picket fence, stumbled then awkwardly ran.

Melanie dragged her feet until she came to a stop. "Are we in trouble, again?"

"Probably." Lorrie looked at the house, then back toward the direction her mother took. "Can you take this to Uncle Rodney? I'm going to go help Momma."

"Okay." Melanie skipped to the house, swinging the black bag.

Once she was certain her sister took the bag inside, Lorrie opened the gate and hurried through it. She closed it in Freckles' face. "I'm sorry, Freckles. You know you're not allowed by the barn unless Momma says it's okay. 'Specially with that new horse. He's really scared of you."

Lex stopped outside the corral, where the horse continued to pace restlessly. Teddy stood in the middle, holding a lead rope in his hand. "Teddy? You need to stay really still, okay?"

"I'm not afraid," he blustered loudly, startling the horse even more.

Lowering her voice, Lex started to walk slowly toward her nephew. "I know you're not. But you also need to be very quiet, to keep from scaring the horse. Can you do that?"

Teddy nodded.

Lex took very deliberate steps, keeping her eyes on the horse. When she was within a few feet, the animal shook its head and started running in frantic circles, getting closer and closer to Teddy. "Easy." She only hoped she could get to him before the horse did.

Lorrie stood at the outside of the corral, watching as Lex tried to get Teddy out of harm's way.

Teddy had been brave as long as he could. With the horse getting closer, he began to cry. "Aunt Lex, I'm scared." His breathing became heavy as he started to hyperventilate.

"Damn." Lex hurried as quickly as she dared. "It's going to be okay, Teddy. The horse doesn't really want to hurt you, but he's scared. Just stay very still, okay?" She was within five feet of him when the horse started to snort and wildly sling its head. In a sudden burst, Lex lunged forward and wrapped her arms around Teddy, twisting so his body was away from the horse. She threw Teddy as far as she could. "Run, Teddy!" she yelled, just as a heavy hoof hit her in the back. Unable to breathe, Lex crumbled to the ground.

IN THE KITCHEN, Amanda heard the back door slam, and saw Melanie come inside. "Melanie, come here, sweetie."

Melanie swung the black bag. "Lorrie told me to give this to Uncle Rodney."

"I'll take it to him, honey. Thank you." Jeannie took the bag and left the kitchen.

"Where's your momma?" Amanda asked.

Shrugging her shoulders, Melanie climbed into a chair and picked up a crayon. "I dunno. She jumped over the fence and was running to the barn."

Amanda knelt by her chair. "What happened in the barn?"

"I dunno. But Teddy was playing there, while Lorrie swinged me."

"Oh, god." Amanda quickly stood. "You stay here and color, okay? I'll be right back."

"Okay." Melanie opened up her coloring book, already lost in her art.

Torn between waiting to see how her father was, and needing to know what was going on with Lex, Amanda went through the back door and jogged toward the barn. She had just closed the gate behind her when she heard Lorrie scream for Lex. Not needing any more incentive, Amanda broke into a full run.

Lorrie pulled Teddy through the fencing of the corral, and was about to climb inside to help Lex when Amanda arrived. "Mommy, the horse kicked Momma," she cried, unable to control her tears.

"It's okay, baby. I'll take care of your momma. You two run to the house, and go inside." Once the children were safely away, Amanda unlocked the corral gate and opened it wide. Lex had fenced off the barns years ago, so the horse was in no danger of getting near the main road, but it would be hell to catch. She headed for Lex, who lay on her stomach, unmoving. When the horse started to get too close, Amanda waved her arms and started to yell. "Hyah!"

Snorting, the horse raced around the corral until it saw the open gate. It kicked its heels and galloped away.

Amanda dropped to her knees beside Lex. Her hand shaking, she brushed the hair away from Lex's face. "Honey, can you hear me?"

With a groan, Lex clinched her fists. "Amanda? What are you doing here?"

"Saving your ass," Amanda snapped.

"It's not safe," Lex gasped. "Horse."

Looking around the corral and surrounding area, Amanda shook her head. "That horse is probably halfway to the north pasture, by now."

Lex opened her eye to look at her wife. "It got out?"

"I let the damned thing out." Amanda wiped dirt off of Lex's cheek. "Are you okay?"

"I think so." Lex cautiously stretched, grimacing at the pain in her back. "Ugh. Help me up?"

Amanda didn't bother to argue with her. "You let me know if it gets to be too much. We've got a houseful of people—"

"Damn. What about your dad? How is he?" With Amanda's help, Lex rolled into a sitting position.

"As far as I know, he's okay. After you left, he woke up, and told Rodney he had gotten dizzy. How about your legs? Are they tingling or anything?"

Lex stretched them out and wiggled her feet. "No, I think they're okay. Why?"

Amanda pulled Lex's shirt away from her back. "Because you've got a bloody spot on your back, where it looks like you were stepped on, or kicked."

"Kicked, I think." Lex tried to look over her shoulder. "How bad is it?"

"Ruined your shirt."

Once Amanda stood, Lex allowed herself to be tugged to her feet. "Ugh. That stung." She put her arm around Amanda's waist. "Thanks for coming to my rescue. I was having the damndest time catching my breath."

"I bet." Leading them toward the house, Amanda sighed. "Is Ronnie coming out today?"

Lex shook her head. "Not until this evening. He's having lunch with his girlfriend's family."

"Good."

"Why?"

Amanda kicked a pebble. "Because if he were here right now, I'd probably whack him on the head with something for bringing that horse out here." She opened the gate. "Wait a minute. Girlfriend?"

"Yep."

"Why didn't you tell me he has a girlfriend?"

Lex grinned. "Because you didn't ask?" She flinched as her stomach was poked. "Hey, watch it."

"Teach you to keep secrets from me."

"I didn't mean to. It slipped my mind." Lex grunted as they slowly took the stairs. "Hey, Amanda?"

"Hmm?"

"Ronnie has a girlfriend. Ouch!" Lex rubbed her stomach where she'd been pinched. "Think we can sneak in without anyone noticing?"

The back door opened. "Momma! You're okay," Lorrie yelled.

"Probably not," Amanda said, as they stepped into the house.

Chapter Eleven

DRESSED IN A pair of clean sweats, Lex was lying on her stomach across the bed. She flinched as Rodney finished his ministrations and lowered her shirt.

"That's a very nasty laceration and contusion, Lex. You don't need any stitches, but I'd like you to meet me at my office tomorrow for x-rays."

Lex struggled to a sitting position. "Come on, Rodney. I've been kicked more times than I can remember. It's fine."

He shook his head and wiped his hands on a towel, before turning to Amanda, who sat on the bed behind her. "It's near her spine, and I don't want to take any chances. Watch for unusual swelling, tingling, or numbness in her extremities. And try to get her to take it easy for a few days." He shook his finger. "I mean it."

Jeannie came into the bedroom and sat next to Lex. She brushed a hand along Lex's leg in a light caress. "Thank you for what you did today, Slim."

"How's Teddy? I didn't really think, just tossed him as far away as I could." When Jeannie's fingers twined with hers, Lex gave a sad look. "I'm so sorry about that damned horse."

"It's not your fault. Teddy knows better. When we get home, he's going to be losing some privileges." Jeannie leaned into Lex. "I asked him why he climbed in the corral like that. He said he was tired of being teased about his fear of horses."

Amanda walked on her knees across the bed and rubbed Jeannie's back. "Our girls are going to learn the consequences of teasing, trust me. But first, we've got another problem to think about."

"Frank's parents," Jeannie added. "I know." She exhaled heavily. "What should we do? We can't expect Gramma and Grandpa to keep them occupied forever."

Rodney stood. "I know it's not really my place to say, but I think you should tell Lorrie the truth. She's very smart, and probably has some of it figured out."

"You're a part of the family, so of course you have a say." Jeannie stood and went to him. "I just don't want her to think that I'm a horrible person because of all of this. It almost broke my heart to give her up. I don't think I could handle her hating me, too."

He kissed her lightly on the lips. "I'm going to check on Mike. Do you want me to find Lorrie and send her in?" They had coerced Michael into lying down in the guest room down the hall, hoping to lower his stress. Lois was also there, keeping an eye on him.

Lex hated having these types of talks. "We might as well get it over with, I guess. She's most likely in her room, listening to music."

"Good luck." Rodney kissed his wife again before leaving.

A few moments later, Lorrie stepped slowly into the room. "I'm sorry."

Amanda slid off the bed and came toward her, while Jeannie sat next to Lex. "Why are you sorry?"

"'Cause I was s'posed to watch Teddy, and I didn't." She stood in front of Lex and stared at the floor.

Lex lifted Lorrie's chin with her fingers so she could look her in the eye. "And why didn't you?"

Lorrie fought back the tears that threatened to fall at the disappointed tone in her mother's voice. "Mel was wanting me to push her in the swing, and Teddy wanted to play cowboy on the saddles. But Mel kept whining, so I told Teddy to stay in the tack room, while I got Mel started on the swing. But I was gonna go right back. He must have followed us out of the barn, 'cause Mel had just started to swing when Momma saw Teddy in the corral."

"Did you tease him about being afraid?" Lex asked.

"Nuh-uh, I didn't." When Lex's eyes narrowed, Lorrie rushed out, "I swear! He's just a little kid. I wouldn't make fun of him, honest."

Amanda knelt next to Lorrie. "We believe you, honey. But something made him decide to go into the corral. Do you know what it could have been?"

Lorrie was silent for a moment. Tattling usually carried a worse punishment than the original deed, but her parents were expecting an answer. "Mel kinda said something when we were leaving the tack room, but I didn't know Teddy heard."

"All right. We'll talk to Melanie in a little while," Lex promised. "Come here, sweetheart." She held out her arms, ignoring Amanda's glare. The discomfort was worth holding her daughter. Once Lorrie was comfortably ensconced on her lap, Lex cleared her throat. "You know we have company downstairs, besides family, don't you?"

"Yep. Melanie told me they have a granddaughter with my name."

Amanda sat on the other side of Lex. "I should have known," she mumbled. In a louder voice, she added, "That's what we wanted to talk to you about. Do you remember when we told you about your father, Frank?"

"Sorta. You said he died when I was a little baby." Lorrie noticed the tears in Jeannie's eyes. "Why are you sad, Aunt Jeannie? Did you know him?"

Lex shifted so she could put her arm around her sister-in-law in silent support.

"Um," Jeannie tried to think of a good way to start. She took a deep breath. "Yes, I did. Frank was my first husband." At the confusion on Lorrie's face, she began to rub the little girl's leg. "You see, when you were born, there were complications. I became very ill, and couldn't take care of myself, move or even talk."

Lorrie frowned. "You were my mommy? But, how come," she

looked up into Lex's face. "I don't understand."

Amanda stood and once again knelt in front of Lorrie. "Jeannie was so sick, we didn't even know if she was going to be all right. Frank was driving you home from the hospital, and there was an accident. You weren't hurt, but your daddy," here her voice broke, "died."

"But, why are you my mommy, if Aunt Jeannie was?" Lorrie looked at Jeannie and started to cry. "Didn't you want me?"

"Oh, baby. Of course I did." Jeannie was surprised when Lorrie climbed into her lap. She held her close. "I wasn't able to do anything for myself, for so long. Amanda and Lex took care of both of us, until I decided to move into a rehabilitation center so I could get well. It took almost three years before I was healthy again."

Lorrie's eyes widened. "Three years? That's forever."

The adults laughed, and Jeannie brushed the hair out of Lorrie's face. "It certainly seemed like it." She sobered. "But, when I came back, you didn't know me. Your moms were the only parents you knew. And, as much as it hurt me to do so, I signed papers that made you their little girl." Jeannie shook her head and started to cry again. "It was the hardest thing in the world to do, you have to believe me. But, you were so happy here."

Quiet for a moment, Lorrie considered everything that she had been told. "Do I have to come and live with you, now?"

Amanda looked at Lex, who appeared to be on the verge of panicking. "Do you want to live with Jeannie?"

Lorrie shook her head. "No. I like it here." She hurriedly added, "That's okay, isn't it? I don't want you to cry no more, Aunt Jeannie."

Jeannie squeezed her tightly. "I'm glad you're happy, honey. And it's very okay with me. I'm your aunt, now. Lex and Amanda are your moms, okay?" She kissed Lorrie on the head and allowed her to slip into Amanda's arms. With her heart breaking, she watched as her daughter once again became her niece. She wiped at her eyes. "I need to take a little break, okay?" She went into the adjoining bathroom and closed the door.

"Are you all right, lil' bit?" Lex asked her daughter.

"Uh-huh." Lorrie snuggled closer into Amanda's embrace. "You're still my mommy?" she asked quietly.

With Lorrie in her arms, Amanda stood so she could sit next to Lex. "We'll always be your parents, honey."

"Momma?"

"Yes?"

"You promise you won't give me away?"

Lex had to clench her teeth together to keep from crying at the plaintive question. "Never, sweetheart. I will fight to my last breath for you, always." She wrapped her arms around Amanda and Lorrie, and tucked her head next to theirs. "I swear it."

DOWNSTAIRS IN THE den, Harrison was fit to be tied. He took out a cigar and stuffed it into his mouth, chewing on the end. "I don't see why it's so hard for you people to understand. We came all the way from Los Angeles to see our granddaughter. Why are you putting us off?"

Anna Leigh set her coffee cup down on the table in front of her. "Mr. Rivers, please. There are dynamics at work that even I don't fully comprehend." She looked to her husband for help. She and Jacob were left with the task of keeping the Rivers' placated, while Martha and Charlie took over cooking the meal.

Jacob had his hand on Anna Leigh's shoulder. "My wife's right. I can see where you're coming from, but—"

"No, you can't," Harrison snarled. "You've never been denied the right to see your grandchildren, have you?" He stood and paced toward the fireplace. Across the mantle were family photos, and he picked up a group shot of Lex, Amanda, and the girls. "This is her, isn't it?" He took the framed print to Veronica, who touched the glass with a shaky finger.

"Yes. Michael took it a few months ago." Anna Leigh's voice was soft.

Veronica shook her head. "If I didn't know any better, I'd swear she was Miss Walter's daughter. Although her hair looks a lot like Frank's."

"She is, in so many ways," Jacob said. "When we brought Jeannie home, none of us knew if she'd ever be able to take care of herself, much less a newborn. And when she realized that she needed more help than any of us could give, Jeannie did the only thing she could, and that was sign over Lorrie's care to her godparents."

Harrison sat beside his wife, looking over her shoulder at the picture. "What idiot gave them that title?"

"Your son," Anna Leigh said, a little too gleefully. "Along with our granddaughter, of course."

"But Frank had plenty of friends, *normal* friends, which could have held that honor." Harrison was truly confused. "Why on earth would he allow his own flesh and blood to be anywhere near people like that?"

Jacob felt Anna Leigh tense beside him. He had to squeeze her arm to keep her from going off on the man. "Did you know Frank at all?" he asked. "Do you have any idea how close he was to not only Amanda, but Lex, too? He loved Amanda like a sister, you know."

"I'd heard him mention her," Veronica said quietly. She raised her head to look at the other couple. "I remember not long after they met. He talked about her so much, I just knew he'd bring her home to meet us, one day."

Anna Leigh laughed. "We thought the same thing. All Mandy ever talked about was 'Frank this,' and 'Frank did that,' when she'd call or visit. I was completely surprised when Jeannie announced her engagement to him. We were afraid she had stolen him from Mandy, and were quite concerned about the consequences."

"Not long after that, Amanda came for a visit. She was certainly not the heartbroken girl we had been expecting," Jacob continued. "I think I said something like, 'Aren't you upset at losing Frank?' She told me that she was looking forward to having him as a brother."

Harrison sagely nodded. "So, it was losing my son to her sister that made her that way. I see."

"You're an idiot," Anna Leigh said, her temper flaring. "Did you know that your son was the first person that Amanda came out to? Not us, not her sister, but Frank. He'd always been a brother to her."

"Now, see here," Harrison blustered. "You have no right—"

Anna Leigh had heard enough. "I have more right than you, mister. I'm sick and tired of listening to your bigotry. Either grow up, or shut up."

The room became quiet as Anna Leigh seethed and Harrison regrouped.

Veronica was the first one to break the ice. "Could you tell us about Lorraine? We've missed so much time."

"She's always been quite a handful, but not in a bad way," Anna Leigh said. "Just very rambunctious."

"Sounds a lot like Frank, as a child." Veronica turned to her husband. "Wouldn't you agree, dear?"

He grumbled something, but didn't elaborate.

Jeannie came into the den. "Hi, everyone. Sorry it's taken so long." She sat next to Jacob, who immediately put his arm around her.

"How are you doing, pumpkin?" he asked. In a lower voice, he added, "Are you all right?"

She leaned into him. "It was rough, but we got through it."

Harrison perked up at seeing Jeannie. "Does this mean we'll actually get to see our granddaughter?"

"Damn it, man. Can't you see Jeannie's been through a rough time? Give it a rest," Jacob said.

"It's okay, Grandpa." Jeannie sat up and ran her hand through her hair. "Lex and Amanda will be bringing her down in a few minutes."

Anna Leigh turned to her. "How is Lexington?"

"I'm fine," Lex answered from the doorway, where Lorrie stood in front of her. Beside her was Amanda, who had her arm around Lex's waist.

"That's up for debate." Amanda allowed Lex to go in front of her. But the look on her face wasn't a pleasant one. It was obvious they had disagreed on Lex coming downstairs.

For once, Harrison Rivers was speechless, as he saw his granddaughter for the first time. His eyes never left her as Lex led Lorrie around the sofa, finally taking a seat on the second loveseat.

In an unusual bout of shyness, Lorrie climbed into Lex's lap and tucked her head against Lex's shoulder.

Veronica leaned forward, and in a soft voice, said, "Lorraine?" When she didn't get any response, she tried again. "Lorrie?"

Lorrie turned around and faced the two strangers. "Hi." She looked at the well-dressed older couple. "Are you here for Thanksgiving?"

"Actually," Harrison finally found his voice, "we're here to see you."

Unaware of the tension in the room, Lorrie slid from Lex's lap and moved to sit closer to them. She sat on the oak coffee table, not far from Veronica. "Really? Where do you live?"

"We have a house in Los Angeles. Have you ever been there?" Veronica's voice shook and she clinched her fingers together to keep from grabbing the little girl.

"I don't think so." Lorrie turned back to Lex. "Have I, Momma?"

Lex shook her head. "Not since you were born."

Seeing that things were under control, Anna Leigh took Jacob by the hand. "I think we'll go see about helping Martha and Charlie in the kitchen."

Lorrie scooted closer to Veronica and Harrison. "You're really my grandma and grandpa?"

"We are." Harrison took the soggy cigar from his mouth and tucked it into his jacket pocket.

"How come I've never seen you before?" Lorrie was still trying to wrap her mind around everything. "Didn't you want me?"

Veronica could no longer stop herself from taking Lorrie's hands. "That's not it at all, darling. We want you very much."

"Then, how come you're just now here?"

Harrison took over. "It's quite complicated, young lady. My work took us out of the country for many years, until recently." Now that he was faced with the reality of Lorrie, he wasn't certain how to interact with her. "You do understand the concept of work, don't you?"

"Yep. Momma works here at the ranch, and Mommy used to work in town." Lorrie turned to her parents. "Right?"

"Very well." Harrison straightened his tie. "My work was much more complex, but I'm glad you get the idea."

Lorrie frowned at his words. "Do you not work anymore?"

"No, I've retired."

"Does that mean you're going to come here to live? My Grandpa Travis moved here after he retired." Lorrie's face saddened. "He died."

Veronica rubbed Lorrie's hands. "We're sorry to hear that, honey. But we can't live here, because we have a home in Los Angeles. Would you like to come and visit, sometime?"

"I dunno." Lorrie turned to her parents. "Can I?"

Amanda squeezed Lex's hand before answering. "We'll see, sweetie."

"Perhaps you all would like to come," Veronica offered. She ignored the sudden gasp from her husband. "Jeannie, that means you and your family, as well."

Jeannie gave her a sad smile. "I think we'd like that, Veronica."

Everyone turned toward the doorway when they heard Charlie announce, "Come on, folks. Lunch is ready."

Lorrie gave Veronica a hug. "Come on. Mada's the best cook, ever!" She smiled at Harrison, and hurried across the room to take Charlie's hand. "Right, Grandpa?"

"You betcha," Charlie agreed, leading her across the hall to the dining room.

Veronica watched her leave. "She's a lovely girl," she said to Lex and Amanda.

Lex slowly got to her feet, trying not to groan at the aches. "Thank you, Mrs. Rivers. We're very proud of her."

"Please, call me Veronica." She stood and held out her hand. "After all, we're family, aren't we?"

Harrison had heard enough. "Now, hold on. I don't think—"

Veronica turned to him. "Hush. I'm not going to let you ruin this." Her smile was genuine as she shook Lex's hand. "Right, Lexington?"

"Yes, ma'am." Lex saw a glint of Frank in his mother's eyes. She held out her arm. "Ready for lunch?"

"I am, thank you." Veronica took Lex's arm, leaving her husband behind.

Amanda grinned at Harrison. "Guess that leaves you and me, doesn't it?"

His panicked look said it all, as Amanda took one arm and Jeannie took the other. "I, ah, well—"

"Might as well give up, Harrison," Jeannie said. "I think you're outnumbered."

AFTER LUNCH, LORRIE was given permission to show her new grandparents around the ranch. She took Veronica by the hand and led them through the back door. "This is where we play most of the time," she told them, sounding like a seasoned tour-guide. "Over there's the sandbox where I used to play when I was a little kid. My sister still plays in it, sometimes, with my Momma and Mommy."

Harrison looked around the fenced-in yard. Besides the sandbox, there was an expansive swing set, all surrounded by a three-foot white picket fence. "Do you like it here, Lorraine?"

"Sure." She seemed confused by the question. "Don't you like it?"

"Well, um, of course. It's very, ah, nice."

Lorrie opened the gate. "You've got to hurry. If Freckles sees us leave, she'll want to come." Once they were all through, she closed and latched it. "She's not allowed, because the horses don't like her very much."

Almost as if hearing Lorrie, Freckles suddenly bounded out of the pet door and into the yard. She stopped at the gate and barked.

"Hush, Freckles. We'll be back in a little while." Lorrie stuck her hand through the fence and brushed the rat terrier's head. "Be a good girl and go back in the house."

The dog barked again, then sat by the gate.

Lorrie looked up at the adults. "She'll get tired of waiting and go back inside in a little while. She always does." Once again she took Veronica's hand. "Can I call you Grandma?"

"I think I'd like that a lot, darling." Veronica allowed herself to be led toward an impressive looking barn. "Goodness, that's large."

"Momma says the horses have it better than she did when she was a little kid," Lorrie said, as she opened the barn door. "Mommy says she's full of bull."

Even Harrison snorted at that comment. When they stepped inside, he nodded his head. "Very nicely done," he said under his breath. "How many horses do you have, Lorraine?"

She turned to look at him. "You can call me Lorrie, if you want. I only get called Lorraine when I get into trouble."

"Very well. And you may call me grandfather, if you'd like."

"Okay." Lorrie tugged on Veronica's hand until they were in front of one of the stalls. "This is Mine." She climbed the wooden slats of the gate and rubbed the horse's nose.

Veronica took a step back. "What's its name?"

"Mine." When Lorrie noticed the confusion on Veronica's face, she laughed. "Momma says when I was little, I thought everything was mine, so I sorta named her." Lorrie sat on the top rung of the stall and faced her grandparents. "Do you have horses where you live?"

Harrison laughed. "Of course not. We live in a city with millions of people."

"Oh." Lorrie seriously considered his answer. "Do you like it?"

"Of course, we do." Harrison turned to his wife. "Don't we, Veronica?"

Veronica stepped closer to the stall and cautiously glanced at Mine. "It has its perks, I suppose. We haven't stayed there long enough for me to know. I'm sure you'd enjoy it. With your parents, of course."

"Hrumph. Parents, indeed," Harrison grumbled.

"Not another word, Harrison." Veronica glared at him.

He cleared his throat. "Are we about finished, Lorraine? We really should be getting back to our hotel."

"Sure, Grandpa, I mean, Grandfather." Lorrie jumped from the top of the stall. "Will you be back tomorrow?"

"We'll see," he hedged. Now that he had gotten his wish to see his granddaughter, Harrison was ready to move on. "We have things to attend to at home, I'm sure."

Veronica ignored him. "I'm sure we'll see you again real soon, Lorrie." She gave her husband another dirty look. "At least one of us will."

RODNEY FOLDED THE blood pressure cuff and placed it in his bag. He gave Michael and Lois a reassuring smile. "You seem to be doing better, Mike. Your blood pressure is down. But I'd still feel a lot better if we'd take a trip to the office for a more thorough checkup."

"What do you think caused it?" Lois asked.

"I really can't say, without more tests."

Michael sat up and rubbed his jaw with one hand. "It's my heart, isn't it?"

"That's one possibility," Rodney said. "Perhaps a blocked artery. If that's what we have, we may be able to treat it with medication. But, I'll have to run some tests to be certain."

Lois stood. "Then that's what we'll do. Should we go to the hospital?"

"I can do most of them at my office. Let me go tell Jeannie, and we'll leave soon."

Michael started to argue, but the look on Lois' face kept him quiet. "Thank you, Rodney. Looks like we'll owe you one."

"You can pay me back by getting better." Rodney put his stethoscope in the bag. "And maybe a night of babysitting."

"It's a deal." Lois hugged him and kissed his cheek. Once Rodney left the room, she lightly slapped her husband on the shoulder. "Next time, maybe you'll listen to me."

Michael pulled her into his arms. "Where's the fun in that?" He cupped her face with his hands. "I'm sorry I worried you, Lois. I promise to do better."

"See that you do," she said, before kissing him. "We've got grandkids to spoil, and I don't want to do it alone."

"You won't, I promise." Michael kissed her again, enjoying the feel of her in his arms.

AMANDA CLOSED THE front door and let out a heavy breath. She looked at Lex, who was casually leaning on the doorway to the den. "Why do we always have holidays like this?"

"Like what, sweetheart?" When Amanda came even with her, Lex put her arm around her waist.

"Non-stop chaos."

Lex laughed. "It was pretty wild, wasn't it?" She bit off a groan when Amanda's arm came too close to her injured back.

"I'm sorry. Did I hurt you?" Amanda asked, leading the way toward the stairs.

"Nah."

"Liar."

As they trudged up toward their bedroom, they could hear the sound of their children's laughter. "I wonder which room they're destroying," Amanda asked. She noticed Melanie's door was closed, which answered her question.

"Do you think we should put them to bed?" Lex stopped at their bedroom.

Amanda shook her head. "Not yet. They've had a pretty stressful day. Let them play for a while. There's no school tomorrow."

"Sounds good to me." Lex took Amanda's hand and led her into their bedroom. "That was nice of Lois to call after your dad's tests were complete. Although plaque in the arteries is nothing to sneeze at, I'm glad they can control it with medication. I was really worried about him today."

Carefully peeling Lex's sweatshirt off, Amanda tossed it in a nearby chair. "Turn around." She checked the bandage for any seepage, and was relieved to find it clean. "I was pretty worried about you, too," she whispered.

Lex turned and looked into her eyes. "Hey, everything turned out okay. And once we catch the horse, it'll go into the corral by the bunkhouse. Let the guys take care of it. How's that sound?"

"Too late. I called Ronnie earlier and told him to come get that monster. I don't want it anywhere near you or the kids."

"You did? When?"

Amanda sighed. "Right before dinner. I'm sorry, Lex. I know you handle the ranch, but there was no way in hell I could look at that horse again without wanting to put it out of its misery."

"That's all right. I totally understand."

"So much could have gone wrong. Teddy. You, even Lorrie." Blinking the tears from her eyes, Amanda leaned into Lex's chest.

"I know, sweetheart. But it didn't. And we were finally able to tell Lorrie the entire truth about everything. That's got to count for something, right?"

Amanda nodded. "I was terrified. What if she wanted to go back to Jeannie?"

At this, Lex laughed. "You're kidding, right? Lorrie is so much our kid, I don't think there's anything that can tear her away."

"Don't sound so smug. I saw the look on your face, too."

Lex cleared her throat. "Uh, well—" her stammering was cut short by the feel of Amanda's lips on hers. All thought left her head, as she was tugged toward the bed.

Chapter Twelve

THE SILVER-HAIRED man hummed along to the music that came from the office supply store's overhead speakers, as he dusted the display of computer paper. He seemed perfectly content at his job and nearly dropped the feather duster when he heard a throat clear behind him. He turned around and smiled at the well-endowed blonde who stood a few feet away. "Hi. Is there something I can help you with?"

"Oh, yeah," she purred with a sultry grin. She made a point of eyeing his nametag. "What time do you get off, Hubert?"

He swallowed heavily and brushed a hand down the green uniform vest he wore. "Three, but, um, well, Miss, I'm afraid—"

The blonde winked a green eye at him. "There's nothing to be afraid of, hon." She stepped closer and backed him into the shelves.

"No, really. I'm engaged. I mean, I'm flattered, but—"

She ran a finger across the buttons on his shirt. "Sssh."

Hubert ducked beneath her hand and slipped away. Something about her was vaguely familiar, but he couldn't place her face. Not to mention she was at least twenty-five years his junior. "Do I know you?"

"Maybe." She touched his close-cropped beard. "Although, I don't remember this."

"Uh—"

She laughed at his discomfort. "Meet me at the sandwich shop on the corner after you get off work, and I'll answer your question." At his panicked look, she kissed her finger and placed it on his lips. "Just to talk, I promise." Before she walked away, she turned and pointed at him. "It really would be in your best interest to meet me, Hubert Walters." She blew him a kiss and left.

Hubert watched as the woman left the store. "How did she know my last name?" He looked around to see if anyone had witnessed their encounter. "The last thing I need is for Larry to see me with another woman." Larry Buchanan was his fiancée's father, and the owner of the store.

When Hubert was released from prison two years prior, he decided to stay in Oklahoma City, since he had nothing in Texas to go back to. As a part of his parole, he was assigned to a church program that was designed to help non-violent offenders ease their way back into society, where he met Ramona Buchanan. Ten years his senior, she was a volunteer counselor at the program. Her gentle friendship slowly broke away at the chip that had always been on his shoulder.

It took over a year before Ramona would even agree to go on a date, and she had declined the first two times he asked her to marry him. "I'm not about to screw this up," he muttered. Their romance hadn't always been smooth, but he was happier now than he could ever remember being. Hubert looked at his watch, wondering if he could last the two hours until he got off work to find out what the mysterious blonde woman wanted with him.

HUBERT CLOCKED OUT and removed his vest, draping it over one arm. He was almost to the back door when he heard his boss.

"Hey, Hubert? Do you have a minute?" Larry Buchanan was pushing eighty, and time had bent his frail body. He caught up to his future son-in-law and peered over his bifocals at the taller man. "Have you heard from Ramona?"

"She called me last night, and said she hoped to be back in a few days. Would you like me to have her call you if I hear from her tonight?"

Larry shook his head. "Nah. She doesn't get a chance to see her mother that often. I'd hate to bring the wrath of the old biddy down on me, if she heard I'd asked." His ex-wife lived in Tulsa, and even the distance hadn't softened their tempestuous relationship. "I just wanted to make sure Ramona was okay."

Hubert loosened his tie and lightly patted the old man's shoulder. "She's great, but can't wait to come home."

"That sounds like my Ramona." Larry waved him off. "You'd better get on home, yourself. I'm betting that apartment you two share needs some cleaning, since she's been gone for a week."

Laughing, Hubert nodded. "You know me too well, Larry. It's going to take me a couple of days to get rid of the pizza boxes."

"Then I'll see you back here, day after tomorrow. I don't want my daughter to come home to a messy place."

"You're a lifesaver, Larry." Hubert saluted the old man as he stepped out the rear door.

He stopped at his truck to leave his vest and tie. The old Chevrolet had seen better days, but he was proud of paying cash for it. At first glance, a person would be hard-pressed to identify the original paint color. Whatever wasn't rusted, was either coated in gray primer or a different color altogether.

Unable to put off the inevitable, Hubert strolled across the parking lot to the sandwich shop. He opened the door and saw the blonde sitting in a booth at the back.

She stood and met him halfway. "I wasn't sure you'd come."

"Me, either," Hubert admitted. He stuffed his hands into his khaki slacks and tried to fight off his discomfort. "So, what did you want to talk about?"

"You really don't remember me, do you?"

He shook his head. "You look a little familiar, but no, I'm sorry. I don't."

The blonde took his arm and pulled him toward the back booth.

"Let me try to refresh your memory. My name's Dina." At his blank look, she added, "Dina Hoglund." He continued to shake his head. "Think back, about a year ago."

"A year?" He blinked in confusion when they arrived at the booth. "Wait. Uh, isn't that—"

Dina hefted an oversized bag and handed it to him. "Your son," she finished for him, gesturing to the sleeping baby in the infant seat.

"Mine? B...b...but how?" he stammered, holding the bag to his chest.

"You're a big boy. I'm sure you're familiar with the birds and bees." When he frowned she continued, "Sugar Babies? I was a dancer?"

Hubert's eyes widened as clues fit into place. After Ramona had turned down his second proposal, he had driven to the nearest place that served alcohol and proceeded to try and drink himself into oblivion. He vaguely remembered a frantic groping session in the parking lot of the club, with a faceless blonde woman who had been more than eager to accept his drunken attentions. It escalated into a weekend of booze, sex and the worst hangover he'd ever had. "But, really? Mine? Are you sure?"

"Honey, I may have been a stripper, but I wasn't easy. There was just something about you that I couldn't resist. You're the only man I was with in the past three years. He's yours, all right. I've been looking for you ever since I found out I was pregnant. It cost me a chunk of my savings, but the private detective I hired finally caught up to you." Dina picked up her purse and dug through it, before handing Hubert an envelope. "There's his birth certificate, and a notarized paper giving you all legal rights to your son. I named him Edward Lee, and you're listed as his father."

"But, I can't—"

She kissed his cheek. "Sure you can. I've got a job waiting for me a long way away from this shitty town, and a kid isn't part of my plans. Have a good life, daddy."

Hubert watched as Dina walked out the door. A quiet squeak from the baby carrier in the booth caught his attention. "Shit."

ONCE HUBERT GOT the child to his apartment, he placed the carrier in the middle of the bed he shared with Ramona. "What the hell am I gonna do with you?" he asked the baby. Blue eyes, lighter than his own, tracked to his face as the infant looked at him. "Ramona won't understand. Hell, I don't understand." He brushed his hand through his hair, which had turned completely gray while he was in prison.

The baby cooed and kicked. It waved a tiny hand in the air.

"It's nothing personal. But I'm the last person who should be raising a kid, you know?" Hubert held out a finger, which the baby immediately grasped. "Hell." He paused. "I mean, heck. I was thrilled to hook up with a woman who didn't want kids any more than I did. We're old enough to be your grandparents."

With his free hand, Hubert picked up the birth certificate and looked at it. "Edward Lee Walters. What a kick in the pants, huh?" When the baby started chewing on his finger, Hubert couldn't help but grin. "Guess that means you're hungry. Hope your mom left instructions in that bag of hers." He awkwardly lifted Edward and carried him into the living room, where he'd dropped the diaper bag.

One bottle and a nauseating diaper later, Hubert put his son back into the carrier. He glanced at the digital alarm clock on the nightstand and sighed. "It's getting late, and keeping you here isn't doing me any good. Guess I'll drop you off at the nearest fire station. I've heard that's the best thing to do."

Hubert hooked the bag's strap over one shoulder and lifted the carrier in his other hand. He picked up the plastic grocery bag that he had put the dirty diaper in, and locked the apartment door behind him. At the end of the hall, he dropped the smelly bag into a trash can. "Son, that was the nastiest thing I've ever smelled in my life," he told the baby as they headed down the stairs. "And I grew up on a ranch."

Half an hour later, Hubert cruised by the fire station–for the third time. He looked across the seat at his son, who was quietly chewing on a little fist. "I can't do it, Eddie. I can't just drop you off like that." He pulled into a vacant parking lot and turned off the truck, to contemplate his next move. "You're family, son. Even I'm not that big of an assho-, I mean, jerk. There's no way I can just dump you with strangers." He drummed his fingers on the steering wheel as he stared off into the night.

LEX SAT ON the edge of the bed and gingerly pulled on her boots. It had been a week since Thanksgiving, but she was still sore from the hit she took to her back. She tried to ignore the irritated look she got from her wife, who stood by the French doors with her arms crossed. At the sound of a heavy sigh, she fought back one of her own. "Go ahead and say it."

"What?" Amanda snapped. She turned away and looked out the doors into the hazy morning.

Slowly standing, Lex brushed her hands down her jeans to settle them over her boots. She moved to stand behind Amanda. "I wouldn't be going if it wasn't important."

Amanda felt Lex's hands on her hips and relaxed in spite of her anger. She leaned back into Lex's body, causing Lex's hands to slip around her waist and rest on her stomach. "I know. But do you understand how I feel? I've spent the last week watching you try to move around. The thought of you doing more damage to your back scares the hell out of me."

"I won't," Lex vowed. She kissed Amanda's head and closed her eyes. "Roy hired a few extra guys for the day. I'm only going to supervise. Since this is the first shipment of cattle to Houston, I really want to be there to make sure things go right."

"God, I hate when you're reasonable." Amanda turned and linked her hands behind Lex's neck. "How am I supposed to stay mad at you?"

Lex grinned. "You're not." She lowered her face and kissed Amanda, who tightened her grip. Once they separated, she kissed the tip of Amanda's nose. "The guys and truck will go directly to the loading pens off the south road. We should be finished before lunch, as long as the weather holds." The local news had predicted a winter storm for the day, but so far, the skies were only overcast.

"That's fine, love. Just remember your promise." Amanda straightened the collar on Lex's denim shirt.

"I don't think you have anything to worry about. I'll be good. Walk me downstairs?"

Amanda put her arm around Lex's waist. "Of course. Someone has to make sure you remember your coat."

As they walked slowly down the stairs, Amanda tightened her grip. "You sure you're up to this?"

"Yep. I'm mainly stiff. Once I move around a little, I'll be fine." Lex headed for the back door. She stood patiently as Amanda helped her with her coat, and placed her black cowboy hat on her head. She stopped the helpful hands from buttoning her duster. "It's okay, sweetheart."

"Sorry." Amanda looked into Lex's eyes. "Too much?"

"Never." Lex kissed her. "I've got to go."

Amanda sighed. "Be careful."

"I promise." Lex opened the back door and started down the steps. She straightened her back and walked with purpose, to prove she was feeling all right.

"Smartass," Amanda mumbled. She waited until Lex drove away before she closed the back door. With the girls in school, the house was eerily quiet. "Guess this would be a great time to get caught up on the laundry and housework." Amanda paused at the foot of the stairs. "Or my blog." She grinned and jogged upstairs to get her laptop.

THE GROCERY STORE was practically empty at such an early hour, for which Hubert was thankful. He searched the aisles, pushing a cart with one hand, while trying to comfort his crying son in the other. "Sssh. Come on, now, Eddie. Give your old man a break. I'm doing the best I can." He arrived at the baby aisle, stopped, and stared at the huge selection of products. "How in the hell am I supposed to know what to get?"

"You sound like my husband," a female voice said behind him.

Hubert turned and saw a petite woman, wearing a shirt with the store's name across one breast. "Um, yeah. Most of us guys are pretty clueless when it comes to stuff like this," he said, with a wry smile. "My, uh, girlfriend went to visit her mother, and this is the first time Eddie and I were left alone."

The younger woman nodded. "Let me guess. You lost the instructions she left for you." She stepped closer and held out her hands. "Here, let me try."

"Sure. Thanks." Hubert handed the screaming baby to the woman, and was completely amazed when the infant silenced. "How the hell did you do that?"

"It's the Mom gene. How long has your girlfriend been gone?"

"Since around four yesterday afternoon. Why?"

She patted Eddie lightly on the rear. "I'm betting this little guy is missing his mommy."

"Probably so." Hubert scratched at his beard. "Um, you wouldn't happen to know what kind of baby milk and diapers I should use with him, would you?"

The woman smiled at him. "Ran out, huh?"

"Completely." With his hands stuffed in the front pockets of his khaki slacks, Hubert tried his best to charm the woman. "I'd really appreciate any help I could get."

"No problem." She wrinkled her nose when a putrid odor assailed her senses. "Just in time, I think."

Hubert laughed. "If you'll help me figure out what diapers to buy, I'll get him changed." He watched as the woman opened the one-piece cotton jumper and looked at the front of the diaper. She pointed to a brand on the shelf, which Hubert grabbed and tossed in his cart. "What about the milk?"

"I used that one with my kids and it seemed to work well," she said, gesturing to a large display. "Follow the directions on the back, and you shouldn't have any problems."

"Thanks." He picked up several cans. "Anything else?"

She shrugged her shoulders. "Do you have enough baby wipes, diaper cream, powder?"

"Um—"

"Do you at least have a diaper bag?"

He nodded. "It's in my truck. Should I go get it?"

"I just got off work a few minutes ago. Once you get checked out, I'll follow you outside, okay?"

"Thanks. You're a lifesaver." He held out a hand. "I'm Hubert."

She propped Eddie onto her shoulder and shook his hand. "Tonya." Eddie started to fuss. "I think he's tired of wearing a smelly diaper."

"Oh. Right." Hubert took Eddie from her and headed for the front of the store.

LEX ARRIVED AT the holding pens in time to see her foreman giving last-minute instructions to a group of men. She parked her truck on the opposite side of the pens. The cold, damp wind caused Lex to shove her hat down tighter on her head and walk as quickly as she could to where the men were standing.

Roy noticed her arrival and nodded. "Hey, boss."

"Roy," Lex acknowledged. She dipped her head toward the rest of the men. "Thanks for coming out this morning, guys."

Several voices answered at once, all seemingly glad to be there. Roy tugged his western hat lower over his eyes in an attempt to block the wind. "We're missing one guy, but since he's coming from town, I figure he'll get here soon."

The rumbling of a large truck and trailer halted their conversation. Roy looked to Lex, who nodded. "Chet, you want to guide the truck to the loading chute? The rest of y'all, you know what to do."

More sounds of agreement, as each man moved to his position. Roy waited until he and Lex were alone, before speaking. "I wasn't sure you would be here this morning, Lex."

"Me either," she said quietly. "I knew you could handle things, but you know how I am."

He laughed. "Yeah. Did your boss give you much trouble?"

"Yep. But you know all about that sort of thing now, don't you?" Lex chuckled at the chagrined look on Roy's face. "Your wife is almost as bad as mine."

Roy lightly clapped Lex on one shoulder. "Uh-huh. I'm going to make sure Chet doesn't let that truck knock over the fence. Take it easy, Lex."

She flipped the collar of her duster up to block the cold air. "Damned nanny goat," she grumbled, good-naturedly. But she decided to stay right where she was, unless she was needed.

AMANDA WAS COMFORTABLY ensconced in one corner of the leather sofa, her feet stretched out across the cushions. She passionately typed on her laptop, the words flowing easily. The ringing of the doorbell caused her to look up in irritation. "Damn." She looked at the clock on the fireplace mantel and frowned. Lex had only been gone an hour.

When the doorbell rang again, she placed her laptop on the coffee table and stood. "I'm coming," she called out. Figuring it was one of the new hires, she grumbled, "I don't know why men can't follow simple instructions." She opened the front door and saw a gray-haired man with a matching beard, holding something in his arms. "I'm sorry. You need to go farther west on the highway, to the holding pens."

The man lifted his head and gave her a cautious smile. "Um, Amanda?"

Amanda blinked and tried to make sense of what she saw. The slender, quiet man was a world apart from her memories. "Hubert?"

"Uh, yeah." He held the bundle tighter to his chest. "I wouldn't blame you for saying no, but can I come in? It's colder than a well-digger's ass out here."

His gentle request caught her off guard. "Sure." She stepped back and allowed him to come inside. "Go into the den. I have a fire going." Belatedly, she noticed a denim bag slung across one of Hubert's shoulders.

"Thanks."

Amanda stared at his back as he walked into the den. "Lex, I hope you get home soon," she murmured. When she saw Hubert open the blanket he'd been holding, Amanda almost stumbled. "Is that—"

"Yeah." Hubert removed the diaper bag from his shoulder and dropped it onto a chair. "This is my son. He was a pretty big surprise to me, too." When Amanda moved closer, he held out the sleeping infant. "Do you mind if I use your bathroom? It's been a long drive."

Amanda took the baby. "Um, sure." She couldn't help but smile at the feel of the child in her arms. With one finger, she lightly brushed the small amount of dark hair. "You sure are a precious one." She carefully rocked him in her arms for several minutes, before a tiny squeak was emitted.

The baby frowned, then slowly opened his eyes. The light-blue orbs tracked to Amanda's face. He kicked his legs and smiled.

"Oh, you're definitely going to be a heartbreaker," she whispered.

Hubert returned and watched as Amanda was charmed by his son. "He's something, isn't he?"

"Yes, he is." When she made a move to hand the baby to Hubert, he shook his head.

"I think he's happy, right where he is."

Amanda didn't argue, but moved to sit on the sofa. "If you're looking for Lex, she's not here right now."

"That's okay." Hubert sat in the chair to the right of the sofa and leaned forward. "I'm sorry I just showed up unannounced, but I was afraid of the reception I'd get."

"Considering everything that's happened, could you blame us?"

He shook his head. "No, not at all. As a matter of fact, if it hadn't been for Eddie there, I'd have probably stayed out of your lives forever." Hubert looked at the floor and weighed his words carefully. "I got out of prison a couple of years ago. Then I was placed in a work program as a condition of my parole." He raised his head and met Amanda's gaze, before reaching into his back pocket and removing his wallet. "I met this woman, Ramona." He dug out a photo, stretched across and handed the picture to Amanda.

Amanda studied the photo. In it, Hubert stood with his arm around a sturdily built, older woman. "You both look very happy," she said, returning the picture.

"Yeah. She's done a lot for me." He tucked it safely away and returned the wallet to his pocket. "About a year ago, I asked her to marry me—for the second time. She told me no, and I kinda lost my mind. I went on a drinking binge for the weekend." Hubert nodded toward the baby. "He's the result of that."

"Oh." Amanda grimaced. "And Ramona?"

"She doesn't know." Hubert stood and put his hands in his front pockets. "Hell, I didn't know until yesterday afternoon."

"What about Eddie's mother?"

Hubert shook his head. "She took off."

"What?" Amanda glanced down at the baby. "How could anyone desert their child?" She struggled to keep from crying at the injustice of the situation.

He sat on the end of the sofa and turned to face Amanda. "She told me that a baby wasn't in her plans, and she'd hired a private investigator to find me." He sighed. "Ramona finally agreed to marry me about six months ago. But neither one of us wants kids."

"I don't think you have much of a choice, now."

"Well, see, that's kind of what I wanted to talk to you and Lex about."

Amanda frowned and started to shake her head. "You're not talking about—"

He quickly interrupted her. "Look. You know as well as I do, that I'm the last person who should be a father. Hell, I'm almost fifty years old." He stood and started to pace. "I was going to drop him off at the nearest fire station, but I just couldn't do it. It's not his fault that his father is a worthless piece of shit. He shouldn't suffer just because of me."

"But, maybe," Amanda got to her feet, "maybe you and Ramona would be good parents, together. She's obviously made you a better man."

"No. We've already discussed kids. Ramona's a recovering alcoholic, and well, you know what I'm capable of." Hubert pointed to his son. "Eddie deserves a much better life than what I could give him. Would you and Lex consider adopting him?"

Struck mute, Amanda could only stare at Hubert. The sound of the back door opening broke her from her trance. "Looks like you're about to find out."

AFTER SEEING THE old pickup truck in the front drive, Lex parked beside the house and hurried inside. She only had a moment to wonder why Amanda hadn't called about their unexpected guest, when she heard voices in the den. She stepped around the doorway and stopped in surprise. "What's going on here?"

Amanda turned and gave her a welcoming smile. "Hi, honey. I'm really glad you're back."

Lex took a moment to try and reconcile the friendly greeting, especially since Amanda was standing so close to Lex's estranged brother. "Um, yeah. Roy and the guys got the truck loaded with no problems, so our first shipment of cattle is on the way to Houston."

"That's great." Amanda moved around the furniture and walked toward Lex. "Believe it or not, Hubert's asked us for some help." She moved the baby toward Lex. "Meet your nephew, Eddie."

"My what?" Lex looked down at the peaceful infant. She automatically took Eddie when Amanda handed him to her. "Uh—"

Hubert joined the women near the fireplace. "Like I was telling Amanda, this little guy should have a good life."

Lex looked at the baby, who, other than the lighter eyes, was the spitting image of both Hubert's and her baby pictures. "And what does that have to do with us?"

"Look. I found out about this baby yesterday, and his mother's no longer in the picture. I'm not parenting material. I'm sure you'd be the first to agree. And I tried to give him up, but I just couldn't." Hubert cleared his throat when his emotions started to get away from him. "He's a Walters, Lex. And I know, more than I've known anything in my life, that you and Amanda could give him the kind of home he deserves. Would you please, raise my son as your own?"

Amanda watched as Lex stared at Hubert for a long moment. She couldn't read the look in her wife's eyes, and she held her breath as the only sound that could be heard was the crackling of the fire. She knew what her own answer would be, but she didn't want to influence Lex in any way.

"Let me get this straight. You got a baby dumped on you, and now you want to dump him off on us? What's to keep you from taking him back when he's older?"

"I'll sign whatever you want. Give up all rights. Hell, I'll even promise to never step foot in Texas again, if that's what you want. You name your price, and I'll do whatever I can to pay it." Hubert stared into his sister's face. "I know I'm the last person in the world who should ever ask a favor of you, Lex. And, believe it or not, I've changed." He glanced at Amanda with a quick smile. "Love can do that to a person. You of all people should know that."

Lex nodded. "Yeah, I do. But, are you really sure about this? Because, if we take Eddie, he will be our son. And we'll raise him with our values." She remembered all too well how hateful Hubert had been in the past about her sexuality.

"If he turns out half as well as you, then I think he'll grow into a good man." He grinned at her. "We both know you'll be a lot better father than me."

"True," Lex quipped. She met Amanda's gaze. "Well, sweetheart? I know this is kind of sudden, but what do you think?"

Amanda moved to stand beside Lex. She put her arm around her waist and exhaled heavily. "Hubert, if you're really serious about this, I think I'd better make a call to our lawyer."

"Whatever it takes. Um, can I hold him for a little while, Lex?" He swallowed hard as Lex placed Eddie into his hands. "Thanks."

Lex pointed toward the sofa. "Why don't you have a seat, while we go to the office and make that call? We'll be back in a few minutes." She guided Amanda out of the den, giving Hubert a chance to tell his son goodbye in private.

SLEET PELLETS HIT the roof, as Lex and Hubert stood on the front porch. Both looked out at the weather, neither knowing what to say.

"Guess this will help the drought, huh?" Hubert asked. "That's all we've heard about on the news at home."

"It's a start." Lex cleared her throat. "There's a lot of bad blood between us."

"Yeah."

"When I first saw you today, I wanted to smash your face in," Lex admitted. "You gave me such hell my entire life, and all I could think of was, 'what the hell is he up to?'"

Hubert was unable to meet her eyes. "I wouldn't have blamed you."

In a sudden fit of anger, Lex slammed her hand on the rail. "Goddamn it, Hubert! Why did you hate me so much?"

"You really don't know, do you? You were always the favorite, from the moment you were born. Do you have any idea how shitty it was, being told by our old man, 'you should be more like your sister'?" He walked to the edge of the porch and glanced toward Martha's home. "Our grandparents always liked you more, Mom thought you walked on water. Even our little brother worshipped the ground you walked on."

"I never tried—"

He spun around. "I know. And that's what made it worse. You were always so fucking perfect, Lex. You followed in the old man's footsteps, something I could never do. It wasn't my fault I was allergic to animals, was it? Hell, no!" Hubert stopped his rant and took a deep breath, releasing it slowly. "Sorry."

"At least you had a choice."

"What?"

Lex leaned against the rail and crossed her arms. "Since you couldn't take over the ranch, Dad groomed me for the role. But I never wanted it."

"You're shitting me."

Her laugh was short and bitter. "Nope. I had planned on going to college and getting away from here. But he was bound and determined to make sure this place stayed in the family. It took a few beatings, but I finally got the message."

Hubert's shock was evident. "He hit you too?"

"Yeah." Lex cocked her head and frowned. "What do you mean, too?"

"Hell, Lex. I don't think a week went by when that old bastard didn't lay into me for something. But I had no idea he worked you over." He moved closer and looked into her eyes. "Then I did, too." Tears of regret misted in his eyes. "I'm so damned sorry."

Lex swallowed heavily. "Me, too." She could sense his discomfort. "He played us against each other, Hube. And I'm tired of hating."

"So am I." Hubert took his hands out of his pockets and took a shaky breath. "I know we can't forget all the bullshit and nastiness. I won't ask you to. And what I did to you and Amanda was unforgivable. If I could take it back, or take back the pain I put you both through, I would." He nervously scratched at his beard. "I hope you believe that."

They stared at each other, the only sound was the sleet hitting the house and the ground. Lex looked into his eyes and for the first time, felt like she could see directly into his soul. "I believe you. Thanks, Hubert." She had her hands tucked under her arms, while he zipped his coat. "Are you sure you don't want to stay for dinner?" Lex asked.

"Nah. I need to get back home. Ramona will be back either today or tomorrow. Just overnight the paperwork, and I'll get it back to you as soon as I can." In a surprise move, Hubert put his arms around Lex. "Thank you, Lex. I know this wasn't easy, but it felt good to clear the air."

Lex returned the embrace. "I think we've both grown up in the last few years." She cleared her throat and stepped back. "Don't be a stranger, big brother. And be expecting a Christmas card from us this year, okay?"

He laughed, then sobered. "I don't know how to thank you and Amanda. After everything I've done, you still bailed me out."

"Well, it wasn't completely unselfish. We've talked about having another baby, so I think I should thank you. Because as much as I love my kids and my wife, I really didn't want to go through another pregnancy with Amanda."

"She have a rough time of it?"

Lex's smirk widened into a full smile. "She didn't, but I did. I was a total wreck the entire time."

Hubert chucked her on the shoulder. "Well, I'm glad I was able to help." Their eyes locked for a silent moment. "Don't let him turn out like his old man, Lex."

She nodded in understanding. "Drive safely, Hubert. You've got my number if you need anything."

"Yeah." He flicked a finger away from his forehead in salute. "Take care, little sister."

Lex watched Hubert's truck disappear before she went into the house. She shook her head as she closed the door. "Unbelievable."

Amanda, holding Eddie, met her in the hall. "Are you okay?"

"Sure. It's a lot to take in though, isn't it?" Lex lightly wiped her hand over the dark fuzz on Eddie's head. "He seems to be a good baby." She walked alongside Amanda, as they headed toward the stairs.

"I know. Do you remember how fussy Melanie was at this age? He's the complete opposite." Amanda suddenly stopped. "What are we going to tell the girls?"

Lex put her arm around Amanda's waist. "I guess it's too early to tell them Santa brought him, huh?" She grunted as a well-placed elbow hit her in the stomach. "Um, well. It's not like we have a cabbage patch to find him in."

"Lexington—"

"Okay, okay. How about the truth? We were planning on having another baby, and Eddie's natural parents were unable to take care of him, so we adopted him?" Lex rubbed her stomach as they made it up the stairs. "But I still like the idea of Santa bringing him."

"You're asking for it, Lexington Marie Walters." Amanda tried to keep the smile off her face. "And since you're so frisky, you can dig around in the storage building for the crib. But don't you dare try to bring it into the house by yourself." She crossed the threshold to their bedroom and placed the sleeping infant on their bed.

Lex kissed Eddie on the forehead, then kissed Amanda lightly on the lips. "Yes, dear. And how will the crib make it into the house?"

"I'm sure one of the guys will be more than happy to help. We'll set it up in our room for now, until we can figure out what to do." Amanda frowned. "I know we can convert the guest room across from Lorrie's, but I hate having him so far away from us."

"We'll figure something out," Lex said. "I'll be back soon."

Once Lex left, Amanda sat on the bed beside Eddie. "Your new sisters will go crazy over you, little man. Not to mention all the grandparents you're going to meet." She picked up the phone beside the bed and hit the speed dial. "Hello, Martha? Are you and Charlie very busy? No, everything's fine. But there's something we'd like to show you, if you have the time."

Chapter Thirteen

MARTHA AND CHARLIE met Chet as he was coming through the back door of the house. He tipped his baseball cap at Martha. "Afternoon, Mrs. Bristol. Charlie. Isn't it something?"

"What in the Sam-hill are you talking about, Chet?" Martha asked, as she removed the damp scarf from her head.

"Uh, nothing, ma'am." He grinned and jogged down the steps, hurrying out of the sleet to his truck.

Martha shared a glance with her husband as they stepped into the house. "I wonder what Lexie and Amanda did this time?"

"What makes you think they did anything?" Charlie took her coat and hung it on the hook, followed by his own. He peeked into the kitchen, finding it empty.

"Because, we don't usually see any of the hands here at the house, unless something's going on." She followed Charlie to the den. "Where in the world are they?"

A thump from upstairs answered her. Charlie walked calmly behind Martha, as she continued to mumble under her breath. It wasn't long before they were both upstairs, and could hear voices coming from the master bedroom. "Maybe Lex's back was giving her trouble, and they needed help getting her up here," he mused.

Martha crossed the threshold and stopped, causing Charlie to run into her back. "Amanda? What on earth is that?"

Amanda sat on the bed, cradling an infant in her arms. The baby suckled enthusiastically on the bottle she held, oblivious to the newcomers.

"After all this time, you don't know?" Lex teased from the corner of the bedroom, where she was putting the finishing touches on a crib. "For shame, Martha." She slowly stretched, fighting back a moan at the twinge in her back.

"I can always go downstairs for a spoon to tan your backside, you know," Martha said. She joined Amanda and looked at the baby. "Honey, where did this little tyke come from? I know I'm not going to get a straight answer from that one over there."

Lex stood next to them. "You probably won't believe us if we tell you." She flinched as Martha backhanded her in the stomach. "Ow!"

"Brat." Martha sat beside Amanda. "Now start talking, Lexie. And no smart aleck remarks, either."

"Yes, ma'am." Lex looked at Amanda, who shrugged. "Long story short, he's Hubert's, and we're going to adopt him."

"What?" both Charlie and Martha exclaimed, which caused Eddie to stop sucking on the bottle and let out a cry.

Amanda patted his bottom and put the nipple back in his mouth, to settle him down. "Ssh. It's okay, sweetie. Mada and Grandpa Charlie didn't mean to scare you."

Martha stood, grabbed Lex by the ear, and tugged. Hard. "You'd better start explaining everything, right now."

"Ow, ow. Okay, let go." Lex tipped her head to keep her ear from being torn off. Once Martha released her, she rubbed her earlobe. "Hubert showed up this morning. He told us that the mother basically dumped the baby with him and left. He knew he wouldn't be able to raise him, so he brought him to us."

"And you believed him?" Martha's face showed her skepticism.

Amanda saw Lex's face flush, and decided to jump in. "We both believed him, Martha. You wouldn't have recognized him. He's really settled down and become a different man."

"A snake doesn't change. And that man's always been pure evil. For all you know, he stole that baby, and is setting you up for a kidnapping charge!"

Charlie put his arm around Martha in an attempt to calm her. "Let them finish, hon."

"Thanks, Charlie." Lex sat next to Amanda and picked up an envelope that was on the nightstand. "Here's Eddie's birth certificate, showing Hubert as the father. And, if you looked at the baby, you'd see how much he favors him."

Martha accepted the envelope and removed the paper from inside, while Charlie observed over her shoulder. "Edward Lee Walters. Well, I'll be damned." She handed it to Lex, who put it in the top drawer. "And he just gave you his baby, out of the goodness of his heart? I'm sorry, Lexie. But I can't just forget everything Hubert has done to you in the past. There's got to be a catch. He's always had it in for you."

"We asked him about that." Amanda noticed Eddie had stopped sucking, and removed the bottle. When Lex took the towel from her shoulder, she smiled and handed Lex the baby to burp.

Lex lifted Eddie to her shoulder and gently patted his back. "He not only apologized, but genuinely seemed remorseful. Did you know that when I was born, Dad basically ignored Hubert? The only thing he ever did was yell at him for not doing anything right at the ranch. Hubert was not only afraid of horses, but the smell of the animals and feed made him physically ill. He found out later it was an allergic reaction. When he was twelve, Dad told him he was going to leave me in charge of the ranch as soon as I was old enough."

"My lord. What a horrible way to treat a child," Martha whispered. "No wonder he hated you so much."

"Yeah." Lex kissed Eddie's head after he released a mighty belch. "I can't imagine ever being disappointed in any of our kids, no matter what. Ranching is a hard life, and isn't for everyone. If they decided they didn't want to work here, I'd never hold it against them."

Martha caressed Lex's cheek. "I know that, honey. That's probably why Hubert knew his son would be safe with the two of you." She held out her hands. "Now hand me my grandson. I think I've been quite patient, up 'til now."

Charlie watched as his wife cooed at the baby. "I can't wait to see how you explain him to the girls."

Lex laughed. "I want to tell them he's a present from Santa, but Amanda won't let me." She dodged as Amanda tried to pinch her. "Watch it, woman."

"We've got all night and tomorrow to think of something. I called my grandparents, and they're going to pick the girls up at school and keep them tonight. With the way the sleet is coming down, I don't want them riding the bus home. And I wasn't about to let Lex drive all the way into town."

"I can drive just fine," Lex grumbled.

"Don't pay any attention to that lunkhead," Martha told the baby. She gasped when he opened his eyes and smiled at her. "Oh, you're going to charm everyone with that smile, handsome." She raised her head and grinned at Lex. "He sure favors you, Lexie."

"Yeah. For once I'm grateful that Hubert and I look so much alike." She couldn't help but smirk. "Although his hair is completely gray, and so's his beard."

Martha cradled Eddie with one hand, while she used the other to tug on Lex's hair. "Well, he does have seven years on you. At least you've got something to look forward to."

"Hey!" Lex glared at her.

Amanda patted Lex's thigh. "Don't worry, honey. I'm sure you won't be totally white-headed. Did you notice that little bald spot on the back of Hubert's head?"

"I'm not losing my hair," Lex argued, running her fingers through it. "Am I?"

"Of course not. It'll probably be nice and silver before it ever falls out," Charlie helpfully added.

Lex stood. "I'm going to see if I can find any old baby clothes in the storeroom. I think we saved some of the yellow and green one-piece sleepers, just in case." She ignored the laughter that followed her.

WELL PAST TWO in the morning, Ellie trudged up the stairs. So tired she could barely keep her eyes open, she paused at the top of the staircase and listened. "I must be tired. That sounded like a baby," she mumbled. She had to grab the banister to keep from falling back when the door to the master bedroom opened and Lex stepped out.

"Oh. Hi, Ellie. You're home late." Lex stood in her nighttime tee shirt and boxers, and she kept blinking, as if trying to awaken.

"Yeah. Working the swing shift is kicking my butt. Especially with the long commute. What are you doing up?"

Lex ran her hand through her hair in an attempt to straighten out the tangles. "Gotta grab a bottle from downstairs." She started to walk past Ellie, who grabbed her arm.

"Wait just a minute. A bottle?"

"Yep." Another cry from the bedroom caused Lex to shrug. "Go on in. Amanda will explain it to you." She trudged down the stairs.

Ellie watched her go, before her curiosity got the best of her. She tapped lightly on the doorframe to the master bedroom. "Amanda?"

"Come in," Amanda called. She was sitting in the rocking chair in the corner of the room, rocking back and forth. "Hi, Ellie. Are you just getting home?"

"Uh, yeah." Ellie stepped carefully in the room. "That's a baby."

Amanda shook her head and laughed. "Nothing gets past you. Come on over and meet the newest addition to our family."

"I hate to be dense, but when did you have time to get a baby?"

Lex returned with a bottle. "Haven't you heard? You can order just about anything online nowadays." She handed the bottle to Amanda and grinned as Eddie latched onto his meal. "You'd think we were starving the little guy, the way he was carrying on."

Ellie crossed her arms and glared at her cousin. "You did not order a baby online. Now where did it come from?"

"You're a nurse, Ellie. Don't tell me they didn't cover biology in nursing school," Lex quipped. At the glare she received, she started to laugh. "Sorry. I think I'm getting a little punchy from lack of sleep. My brother Hubert dropped by this morning, and asked us to adopt his son."

"Oh. Well, okay. I guess that makes sense." Ellie yawned. "Sorry. That drive is kicking my butt. Amanda? Would you mind helping me find a place closer to Parkdale? I can't keep this up for long."

Amanda stood and handed Eddie to Lex. "Sure." She put her arm around Ellie and gently turned her around. "Come on. Let's get you to your room. We'll talk about all this tomorrow."

"All right." Ellie allowed herself to be led down the hall. "I'm gonna kick Lex's butt tomorrow for teasing me," she said.

"Of course you are," Amanda soothed, guiding Ellie to her bed. She sat her down and took off her shoes, then pulled a blanket over her. "Goodnight."

Lex grinned as Amanda returned to the bedroom and closed the door. "Did you get her all tucked in?"

"Poor thing was asleep before her head hit the pillow. I can't believe she made it home safely." With a heavy sigh, Amanda crawled under the sheets and turned onto her side, so she could watch Lex feed Eddie. "As much as I'd miss seeing her around here, it would be better for Ellie to live closer to the hospital in Parkdale."

"The girls will be devastated, especially Melanie. She's still pouting because her 'El' had to work on Thanksgiving." The lack of noise from Eddie alerted Lex that he had fallen asleep. She removed the bottle from his mouth, wiped his chin, and burped him. "Didn't take much to put him back out." She kissed the top of his head before settling him in the crib. "Sleep well, little man."

Amanda opened the covers and beckoned Lex with a crooked finger. "Come here, Momma. It's time to tuck me in."

Lex grinned and quickly slid next to her. "You already look all nice and cozy. How can I help you?" Her hands snaked beneath Amanda's nightgown and started to trace a familiar pattern.

"I think you've figured it out," Amanda purred. She cupped the back of Lex's head and pulled her close. Right before their lips touched, she smiled as a warm hand stroked her ribcage. "Yeah."

THE FOLLOWING MORNING, Lex came out of the bathroom, towel-drying her hair. She noticed Amanda had her laptop open. "Whatcha doin'?"

"Car shopping. Come here and see what I've found."

Lex sat beside her on the bed and peered at the screen. "Nice. Does this mean you're tired of fighting the wind in yours?"

"Definitely. Not to mention, the Xterra isn't big enough for all of us to comfortably ride in."

"Ah."

Amanda pointed to something on the screen. "I emailed the dealership, told them about the Xterra, and here's the deal they'll make me."

"Really? Wow. So, what do we have to do?" Lex grinned as Amanda's attention went from the laptop screen to look her in the eyes. When Amanda didn't answer her, the grin widened. "Sweetheart?"

"Hmm?"

Lex waved a hand in front of Amanda's face. "Road trip this morning?"

"Sure." Amanda blinked and shook her head. "Let me email them back, and tell them we'll be there before lunch. Good thing it's not sleeting today." She leaned into Lex and stole a kiss. "I love you."

"Love you, too." Lex climbed off the bed and started to get dressed. "After we pick up your new ride, let's stop by Davenport's and get Eddie some more clothes."

Amanda sent off her email. "And diapers, formula, and everything else." She shut down her laptop. "Are we ready for this?"

Lex buttoned her jeans. "What? Buying a new SUV?"

"No, raising another baby."

"Hell of a time to ask that, isn't it? I thought you wanted another baby." After another trip to the closet, Lex had on a light gray button down shirt. She carried her boots and socks to the bed and sat on the edge. "Are you having second thoughts?"

With a shrug, Amanda stood and peeked into the cradle, where Eddie lay sound asleep. "No, I'm not. I did want another child, and Eddie's a blessing." She made her own trip to the closet, returning in jeans and a cotton blouse. "I guess I'm a little concerned about the girls, and how they'll take it. If I was trying to get pregnant, we'd have time to acclimate them to the idea of a sibling. But this is almost like we made a wish and it came true."

"Santa works in mysterious ways," Lex teased. She tugged her boots on and got up. "I know we're a little rusty with handling a baby, but everything's going to work out great. We can convert the spare guest room into a nursery, or maybe ask Melanie if she'd like to move down the hall to be closer to Lorrie. That way, Eddie won't disturb the girls if he cries at night. Although, I'm not sure they want to come home. They sounded way too happy at your grandparent's house last night when we called." She stood in front of Amanda and wrapped her arms loosely around her wife's waist. "We got all the perks, with none of the waiting. I can't wait to rub it in your sister's face."

Amanda smirked at that last thought. "Ooh. She's going to gain a lot of weight, and I haven't. You're right. She's going to be pissed." She kissed Lex on the chin. "I like that."

"I thought you would." Lex swatted Amanda on the rear. "Come on. I'll run down to the storage building, get Melanie's old car seat, and put it in the Xterra. We've got a road trip to head out on." Before she could get away, Lex felt Amanda tug on her belt loop.

"Deal." Amanda pulled Lex closer and gave her a kiss. "See you in a few minutes."

AMANDA PARKED THE Xterra near the front door of the dealership and exhaled. "After that drive, I'm more certain than ever that this is the right thing to do." On the drive in, a strong gust of wind, coupled with a patch of slick highway, almost sent them into the ditch. Only Amanda's good driving skills kept the three of them safe.

"Amen." Lex removed her hand from the "oh shit" handle above her head and flexed her hand. "I'm glad you were driving. I would have probably landed us in the trees." She glanced back at Eddie, who was kicking happily in the car seat. "I think our son is a daredevil."

"Great. Another one? Between you and Lorrie, my hair's already getting gray." Amanda unbuckled and tucked the folder of papers beneath her arm. "Do you want to wait here, or—"

Lex got out and opened the back door. "We'll come in with you. No telling how long it'll take." She removed Eddie from his seat and wrapped an extra blanket around him. "Settle down, son. I don't want to drop you." Once he was secure in her arms, they followed Amanda inside.

A thin, balding man, wearing a cheap, pea-green suit greeted them before the door closed behind them. "Good morning, little ladies. I bet I know exactly what you want. We've got a lovely, slightly used, two-thousand six Ford Freestar mini-van. It's only got eighty-three thousand miles, and I can even get you a good trade in for your vehicle." He spoke so quickly that it took Lex and Amanda a moment to understand everything he said.

Amanda cocked her head. "Do I look like a soccer mom?" She pointed a warning finger at Lex. "Don't answer that, if you know what's good for you."

With a shake of her head, Lex gave her wife her best "who me?" look, but wisely kept silent.

"Well, now, little lady, no need to get yourself all worked up, I was only trying—"

Amanda's upraised hand stopped him in mid-sentence. "I'm looking for Mike. We have an appointment with him."

The salesman's countenance changed immediately. "Second office on your left." He turned and walked away without another word.

As they headed for Mike's office, Lex whispered to Amanda. "Little lady? What was he, suicidal?" She pretended not to hear the profane answer, deciding instead to enjoy the view from behind Amanda, as she stalked away in a huff.

THE SOUND OF the key in the lock caused Hubert to look up from where he quietly sat on the living room sofa. He stood, took a deep breath, and exhaled slowly. The door opened, and the woman he planned on spending the rest of his life with came inside.

Ramona Buchanan closed the door and dropped her suitcase. When she saw Hubert by the sofa, her face wrinkled into a delighted smile. "Hubert! I wasn't expecting to see you home this early in the day. Is everything all right?" She set her keys on the table by the door and moved to embrace her fiancé.

"I had some things to take care of and your dad gave me a couple of days off." Hubert held onto Ramona as if his life depended on it. "When you get settled, I need to tell you something." He had a lot of time on the drive home to think about everything that happened. As much as he wanted to spare Ramona, and himself, from the consequences of what he'd done, he knew he needed to come clean.

She pulled away from him to look into his face. "What's the matter, honey?"

"I don't want to lose you." Hubert wiped a shaky hand over his beard. "Before I say anything, you've got to realize how much I love you, Ramona. And I'd never do anything to hurt you."

Ramona dropped to the sofa. "What happened?"

Hubert knelt beside her and took her hands in his. "Remember last year, when I asked you to marry me, and you turned me down?"

She nodded. "That was one hell of a fight. After you cussed and yelled, I believe I told you that I never wanted to see you again." The pain in his eyes almost broke her heart. "But everything turned out all right. We got back together the next week, and things have been wonderful ever since." When tears welled in Hubert's eyes, Ramona bit her lip. "They are, aren't they? I've never been happier."

"Me either." Hubert kissed her hands. "But that weekend, I screwed up. Really bad. To tell you the truth, I didn't remember much about it until recently."

"How did you screw up? I remember you telling me you fell off the wagon. But you've been sober since then, right?" She caressed his cheek with one hand. "Honey?"

Hubert lowered his eyes, not wanting to see her face when he told her. "I spent the weekend with a stripper I met at the bar," he whispered hoarsely.

"Oh, god." Ramona pulled her other hand away from him and covered her mouth.

"That's not all. She came into the store, day before yesterday, and asked me to meet her after work."

Ramona put her hand beneath his chin and forced Hubert to look her in the eye. "Did you—" She closed her eyes briefly. "Did you sleep with her again?"

Hubert frantically shook his head. "God, no! I love you, Ramona. I would never cheat," his voice trailed off. "No. I had been so drunk, I blacked out that weekend. I didn't even remember her when she spoke to me." He gathered his strength to finish. "I wasn't sure what she wanted, so I met with her, at the coffee shop across the street from the store."

"What did she want?"

"She had something to give me." Hubert lowered his face again in shame. "My son." The loss of Ramona's hand on his face hurt Hubert more than he ever thought it would. "She said she'd been looking for me since she found out she was pregnant, and didn't want to raise him on her own."

Ramona's voice was soft. "Where is he?"

"I—I," Hubert stuttered. "I asked my sister to raise him."

"Were you going to keep this a secret from me?" Ramona asked, as she stood and stepped away from him.

Hubert began to cry in earnest. "Yeah. But I couldn't." Still on his knees, he turned to her. "I didn't want any lies between us, Ramona. You mean everything in the world to me."

"I thought you were estranged from your sister. I can't believe she'd just happily take your son to help you." Ramona crossed her arms over her chest. "Especially after everything you'd done to her in the past." When they first started dating, it was the heartfelt confessions from Hubert about his past that prompted Ramona to take a chance on him.

"That's kind of the funny thing about it," he said. "They were planning on trying to have another baby soon, so it worked out."

"Made it easy for you, didn't it?"

Hubert shook his head. "Not at all. I'll admit, when she first gave me the baby, I had every intention of dropping him off at the nearest fire station. But then, I realized it wasn't his fault that he was born, it was mine." He sighed. "God, he was so damned cute. Looked just like my baby pictures. I couldn't pass him off to some stranger to raise." He climbed to his feet and stuck his hands in his front pockets. "And I knew damned good and well that I was the last person who should try to raise a kid. My sister and her partner are good people. It's taken me this long to come to terms with that. So I asked them to adopt him and raise him as theirs."

Ramona's eyes were cold. "I should hate you," she said, her voice so low it was hard to hear.

"Please, sweetheart. Give me another chance. I'll do whatever you want." Hubert took his hands from his pockets and held out his arms. "Please, Ramona. I'm begging you."

"You've hurt me, Hubert."

"I know. But if you let me, I'll spend the rest of my life trying to make it up to you."

With a sob, Ramona fell into his arms. "Thank you for telling me the truth. But it's going to take some time for me to trust you again."

"That's all right," he murmured, kissing her head over and over. "Take as long as you need. Just don't leave me."

"I won't. We've worked too hard to get this far." She tumbled onto the couch with him.

They sat quietly for a while, until Ramona kissed Hubert on the neck. "I think I realize what I was really upset about."

Hubert was almost afraid of the answer. "What was that?"

"It wasn't the fact that you slept with someone. After all, I'm the one who told you I didn't want to see you again. I mean, yes, that hurt, but I really couldn't blame you."

"What was it, then? I blame myself for sleeping with that woman. That was extremely stupid."

Ramona rubbed his chest. "Sounds to me like she took advantage of you while you were so drunk you couldn't even remember it happening. No, what really upset me was the way you decided on handling everything on your own, without any input from me."

"It was my mess to clean up, sweetheart."

"No, Hubert. There is no me or you. There's us. We have to make important decisions together, or we'll never be partners. I consulted you before I went to visit my mother, so it's only fair that you allow me to help you with your decisions." She unbuttoned his shirt and slipped her hand inside.

He nodded. "You're right. But I have to admit, at first I was doing it totally out of self-preservation. I panicked." A sharp tug on his chest hair caused Hubert to wince. "But I promise to never do it again." The tug turned into a caress, and he bent his head to hers.

Chapter Fourteen

AMANDA CHECKED THE clock on the dash of her new Ford Expedition. "It's only a little after one. Should we drop by my grandparent's and introduce them to Eddie?"

"Sure. Do you want me to find out if your sister will meet us over there? I want to see her face," Lex said. "You know she's going to accuse us of cheating."

"Yeah. Sounds like fun." Amanda concentrated on the road while Lex made the phone calls. She had to keep from laughing, when Lex was purposely vague as to the reason of their request.

"No, Jeannie. Nothing's wrong. Amanda's just excited over her new ride, and she wants to show it off." Lex listened for a moment. "Okay, fine. We'll pick up a couple of pizzas. Yes, I know what kind you like. No, I won't forget." Lex growled at the phone. "I am not asking them to do that to a perfectly good pizza. No way. I'll have them put the nasty things on the side. No. Have Lois bring you over."

Amanda tapped Lex on the arm and held out her hand. She put the phone to her ear. "Jeannie Louise, quit tormenting Lex. You don't like anchovies any more than she does. Now get your ass in gear and head over to Gramma's. Goodbye." She handed the phone to Lex. "You've just got to know how to handle her."

"Obviously." Lex dialed another number and placed a pizza order to be delivered to the Cauble's home. Once she was finished, she stretched her legs out. "These leather seats are nice. And I like how much more legroom this has, compared to the Xterra."

"Me, too. And it rides a lot smoother." Amanda glanced in the rearview mirror. "Eddie looks so small back there."

Lex turned to look at him. "At least there's enough room on either side of him for each girl. I'd hate to think about the fights they'd have over who would get to sit beside him."

"Don't remind me." Amanda mock shivered. "How are we going to handle it with them?"

"I was hoping you'd have an idea."

Amanda sighed. "I thought about picking them up from school and bringing them over to Gramma's, but there's going to be a house full of people. I was hoping for a little more privacy with them."

Lex nodded. "Yeah, I know what you mean. Why don't we let them ride the bus home, since they won't recognize us in this? That way, no matter what, we're already at home." When there was no answer, Lex shifted so she could look directly at Amanda. "What's wrong?"

"I'm a little worried about how the girls are going to handle this. Remember how Lorrie was, once the 'new' wore off her baby sister?"

"Yeah, but she was only four years old. I don't think she understood how we could love her anymore, since there was a new addition to the household. But it didn't take long for her to be totally on board with being a big sister." Lex put her hand, palm up, on the console between them. She was gratified when Amanda quickly covered it with her own. "They're good kids. What's really bothering you?"

Amanda didn't answer right away, but tightened the grip she had on Lex's hand. They drove along in silence for several miles before Amanda finally spoke. "What if he changes his mind? I know we sign the papers tomorrow, but what's to keep Hubert from not returning them once he gets them? It could hang over us for weeks."

"Not gonna happen," Lex vowed. "As soon as we get the papers signed, I'm taking them to Oklahoma, personally. And I'm not leaving until I get them back from him."

"Really?"

"Yep. Besides, I was hoping to meet the woman who made my brother human."

Amanda laughed at the comment. "I know what you mean. I'm still not sure what to think about the new Hubert." She turned onto her grandparents' street and shook her head at the amount of cars in their driveway. "Do you think the promise of free food caused this crowd?"

"Nah. I'm betting Martha already told Lois, and your dad wants to see how Jeannie reacts. He seems to enjoy watching you put her in her place."

"She does tend to be full of herself," Amanda said. "But I can't wait to see her face when we walk in with Eddie." She parked behind her sister's Pathfinder. "Since she always has to outdo me, I wonder if she'll try to find a used Excursion."

Lex got out and opened the back door. "She'd look funny, trying to climb into one. Probably would need a ladder." She wisely stopped while she was ahead, since Amanda wasn't much taller than Jeannie. Lex unbuckled Eddie and wrapped a blanket around him. "Are you ready to meet the rest of the family, little man?" The baby gurgled and kicked, giving Lex a smile. She followed Amanda up the steps to the front porch, not surprised when the door opened.

Anna Leigh greeted Amanda with a hug. "It's so good to see you. Now get in the house and introduce us to your new little friend." She kissed Lex on the cheek. "I was quite excited when I heard the news, Lexington. Please, come in."

They were herded into the living room, where Jacob, Lois, Michael and Jeannie were waiting. Lex held Eddie close to her chest. "Hey, guys." She turned to Amanda. "Do you want to do the honors?"

"Chicken," Amanda whispered, but she gently took Eddie from Lex and unwrapped him from the blanket. "Everyone, we'd like you to meet our son, Edward Lee Walters."

Jeannie was the first to step forward. "I knew you were good, Slim.

But how on earth did you manage this?" She poked Lex in the stomach and peered at the baby in Amanda's arms. "He looks just like Lex." She looked into her sister's eyes. "Cheater."

"I don't know what you're talking about." Amanda grinned at Jeannie. "He's definitely a gift, though."

Jacob and Michael joined the group. Jacob held out his hands and was rewarded with Eddie. "I didn't even know you were thinking of another child, girls. But he's adorable."

"I agree," Lois cooed.

"How did you keep him a secret for so long?" Michael asked.

Lex put her arm around his shoulders. "We didn't."

"Give them some air," Anna Leigh said. "Jacob, take the baby and sit on the sofa. Michael, bring the girls some coffee, please." She sat beside her husband, who immediately passed Eddie to her. "Thank you, dearest." She smiled as Eddie reached for her necklace.

"Of course." Jacob rested his arm on the back of the sofa. When Amanda parked on the other side of him, he patted her leg. "So, are you going to tell us little Edward's story? Or will we have to wait until he can talk? I'd really like to know how you managed to get a baby that is the spitting image of Lex."

Amanda laughed. "It's really very simple, Grandpa. He's actually a Walters."

Everyone turned and looked at Lex, who shook her head. "No, I was not pregnant." She pointed to her flat stomach. "Do you honestly think I could hide a baby here?" She sat on the chair nearest Amanda.

"Stranger things have happened, Slim." Jeannie dropped onto Lex's lap and put her arm around her neck. "So, if not you, who's the daddy?"

"My brother, Hubert." Lex had to wrap her arms around Jeannie when she almost fell off her lap.

Now the room's attention was on Amanda, who was confused for a moment, then grimaced. "Eww. No! Hubert found out he was a father a few days ago. A woman dumped the baby off and left. He couldn't raise him, so he asked us to adopt Eddie."

A chorus of "Oh" echoed around the room. Jeannie poked Lex. "And here I thought you were a stud."

"She is," Amanda asserted. She stood and tapped her sister on the shoulder. "Do you mind?"

"Not a bit." Jeannie snuggled closer to Lex as the rest of the room laughed.

Lex blushed, but kept her mouth shut.

Amanda tugged on Jeannie's hair. "Move it or lose it."

With a sigh, Jeannie got off of Lex, but not before lightly kissing her on the lips. "Anytime you get tired of old grumpy butt there, just let me know." She shrieked when Amanda pinched her on the rear.

WITH A DEEP, heartfelt groan, Lex dropped onto their bed, where Amanda already lay with Eddie. "I love our family, but damn, they can sure wear a person out."

Amanda propped her head on one hand and smiled at her wife. "I know what you mean. Jeannie was certainly frisky today."

"Yeah. She was pretty funny, and seemed to feel good. I hope she has another easy pregnancy." Lex mirrored Amanda's posture and looked at their sleeping son. "Eddie had a good time."

"I was worried he would be scared with all those people around. But he seemed to enjoy the attention." Amanda moaned. "Speaking of attention, it's almost time to meet the school bus." She tried to fight off a yawn, but failed. "Guess I'd better get my shoes on."

Lex sat up. "Nah. I'll do it. I think I've got more energy than you." She carefully leaned over Eddie and kissed Amanda. "I'll talk to them about our new little addition before we get here."

"Are you sure?"

"Yep." Lex pulled on her boots and stood. "I'll probably stop by the bridge to talk with them, so don't expect us back immediately, okay?"

Amanda's eyes shone with love. "You've come a long way, Lexington Walters. There was a time when I couldn't get five words in a row out of you, and here you are, volunteering to talk to our girls."

Lex tried to appear nonchalant, but the blush on her face gave her away. "Yeah, well. You're a bad influence, Amanda Walters." She winked and left the room.

THE TRUCK HAD barely come to a stop when Lex saw the yellow-orange school bus crest the hill. She waited patiently until the bus stopped and released two excited girls. Within moments, the back doors to the truck opened, and the silence was broken by non-stop chatter.

"Momma! I got to paint a Christmas orminant," Melanie said. She stood on the seat and waved a small box in Lex's face. "It's taped in the box so's it don't get messed up."

Lex took the box before it hit her nose. "That's great, sweetheart. Let's wait until we get back to the house, so your mom can see it, too, okay?"

"'kay." Melanie sat and buckled her seatbelt.

"How about you, Lorrie? Did you have a good day at school?"

"Yes, ma'am." Lorrie fastened her seatbelt as well. "I got a ninety-six on my math test, and only missed one word on the spelling list."

Lex stretched over the seat and ruffled Lorrie's hair. "I knew you'd do great, kiddo. You studied too hard not to. Do either one of you have any homework tonight?" After negative answers from both, Lex turned around and started the truck. "Good."

As the truck headed up the graded road toward the house, Lex tried to think of the best way to start the conversation she needed to have. "Girls? Do you remember when your mom and I told you we were thinking of adding to the family?"

"Like a kitty?" Melanie asked, excited. She had been asking for a kitten for the last month, after a classmate's cat had a litter.

"No, silly. Like a brother or sister," Lorrie corrected. "Right, Momma?"

Lex tried to keep a serious expression on her face. "Right."

"Are you going to have a baby?" Lorrie asked.

"Uh, no. I'm not." Lex parked the truck in the clearing by the bridge and unbuckled her seatbelt, so she could turn around and face them. "Why? Do I look pregnant?"

Melanie giggled. "No, Momma. You're not fat. Mrs. Sanders is fat." The second-grade teacher was six months pregnant with twins, which fascinated all the children at school.

Lex's eyes widened. "No, sweetheart. Mrs. Sanders has two babies growing inside." She could just imagine the teacher's reaction. "She's not fat at all. So let's not say that, okay?"

"Okay. Is Mommy going to have a baby?" Melanie asked. "She's not fat, either."

"No. Your mom isn't pregnant." Lex rubbed her face. The conversation was quickly getting out of hand. "I know we haven't talked about him, but I have an older brother, Hubert. He lives in Oklahoma. Anyway, he came to see us yesterday morning."

Lorrie frowned. "Is that why we stayed with Gramma and Grandpa? 'Cause you had company? Didn't he want to see us?"

Lex shook her head. "No, not at all. The reason your grandparents picked you up at school was because the roads were icy and we didn't want you riding the bus. Um, your Uncle Hubert asked us to do something for him, and we agreed."

"Is he going to live with us, Momma?" Lorrie asked.

"No, Uncle Hubert isn't, but his son, Eddie, is."

"How old is he? Can he stay in my room with me?" Melanie squirmed in her seat. "Does he like to play puzzles or games?"

Lex held up her hand to stop the barrage of questions from Melanie. "Hold on there. Eddie's just a baby, so he can't play just yet. Your Uncle Hubert had some, um, troubles, and he asked your mom and me to adopt Eddie. He's three months old."

Lorrie crossed her arms over her chest. "Adopt? Like you did me?"

"In a way, yes. So Eddie is our son, just like you and Melanie are our daughters. We love you girls so much, and we thought it would be nice for you to have a little brother." Lex noticed the unhappy look on Lorrie's face. "What's wrong, lil' bit?"

"Nothing."

Lex knew better than to accept her answer. "No, come on. Talk to me. You can say anything you want, and I won't get mad. I promise."

"Does this mean I can't play softball now?"

"Of course not. Why would you think that?"

Lorrie looked at her shoes. "'Cause you and Mommy will be too busy with a baby to take me to practices and games and stuff."

"Why would you think that?"

"My friend, Kayla, doesn't get to do anything, anymore. Her mommy had two babies this summer. She used to play soccer, but she's stuck at home helping all the time." Lorrie looked as if she were about to cry.

Lex got out of the truck and opened Lorrie's door. She brought her onto her right hip and held her. "You can still do whatever sports or activities you want, sweetheart. We may need you to help a little with Eddie, but not enough to take away from the things you already do. I promise you that."

"Really?" Lorrie sniffled and looked up into Lex's face.

"Yep." Lex kissed the top of Lorrie's head. "Are you girls ready to go meet your little brother?"

Melanie crawled across the seat to slip into Lex's other arm. "Where's he gonna sleep?"

"Right now, he's in a crib in our room. But we're going to probably redecorate the guest room that shares a bathroom with Lorrie."

"Oooh! Can I move there?" Melanie squealed, as she wriggled up and down. "I want to share with Lorrie."

It was a struggle to keep from falling back, but somehow Lex held firm. "Settle down, kiddo. Let's get up to the house, and we'll talk to your mom about it. How's that sound?"

Both girls cheered.

AMANDA HAD FINISHED snapping Eddie's one-piece sleeper closed after changing a particularly full diaper, when she heard the back door slam. Seconds later, the pounding of rushing feet on the stairway alerted her to the impending invasion. She picked Eddie up and kissed his tummy. "It's about to get wild in here, handsome. But you might as well get used to it."

Both girls hit the doorway at the same time. Lorrie was the first to reach Amanda. "Is that him?" she asked, excitedly. She stood on her tiptoes to try and see his face.

"Can I pet him?" Melanie added.

"He's not an animal, Mel. You don't pet babies." Lorrie elbowed her sister.

Lex stood in the doorway and grinned at the girls' exuberance. "I'm sure you'll both get a chance to see him, if you'd let your mom sit down."

"That's a good idea." Amanda moved to sit on the bed, where she was immediately surrounded by the girls.

Melanie studied him carefully. "He doesn't have much hair."

"It's dark, like mine," Lorrie marveled. She reached out to touch his hair, but paused. "Can I touch him?"

"Be gentle," Amanda said softly. She smiled as Lorrie used one finger to brush at his wispy hair.

"It's soft, too," Lorrie whispered.

Lex picked up Melanie and sat in her place. She held Melanie in her lap. "Touch his arm. It's really silky."

Melanie followed her sister's lead, and lightly stroked Eddie's arm. "He's softer than my baby doll." When Eddie's eyes tracked directly to her, she gasped. "He's looking at me!"

Eddie grinned and kicked his feet, causing both girls to giggle.

"Where's his teeth?" Melanie asked.

Lex laughed. "He's too young for teeth. He'll get them, a little at a time."

Lorrie sniffed and leaned closer to the baby. "He smells nice."

Amanda exchanged amused grins with Lex. "He didn't a few minutes ago."

"I'm sorry to have missed that," Lex teased. When Eddie started to wave a fist, she whispered in Melanie's ear. "Stick out your finger by his hand, and watch what he does."

Melanie did as she was told, and marveled when Eddie immediately grasped her finger. "He grabbed me!" She wriggled her hand until Eddie released her.

Lorrie did the same, and was just as excited when her finger was grabbed. "Cool." When Eddie pulled her finger to his mouth and started to gum it, she wrinkled her nose. "Eww. He's slobbering on me."

"That probably means he's hungry. Would you girls like to follow me down to the kitchen and watch me make his bottle?" Lex lifted Melanie off her lap and stood.

"Yay!" Melanie danced from foot to foot. "Can we have a snack, too?"

Lex winked at Amanda. "Sure thing. I think there's some apples we can slice up. How's that sound?"

Lorrie took one of Lex's hands, while Melanie captured the other. "We'll help with the bottle first, right, Mel?"

"Right." Melanie tugged on Lex's hand. "Come on, Momma. Eddie's hungry!"

AFTER EDDIE WAS fed and put in his crib for a short nap, Lex clipped the baby monitor receiver to her belt before she and Amanda took the girls downstairs for dinner. As they sat around the table, Amanda got caught up with the conversation Lex had with them in the truck. "Are you sure you want to switch rooms, Melanie?"

"Uh-huh. Momma said we had to talk to you about it." Melanie tucked several potato chips into her peanut butter and jelly sandwich and took a bite.

Amanda tried not to wince as she watched Melanie enjoy the unusual meal. "I guess we'll go pick out some paint colors this weekend."

Lorrie put her glass of milk down and pushed her empty plate away. "Mommy?"

"Yes, honey?"

"Can I paint my room, too?"

Lex stood and put her plate in the dishwasher. "Are you tired of the light green walls?"

Lorrie nodded. "I'm too old for a baby room."

"Green is a baby color?" Lex asked.

"Uh-huh."

Amanda covered her mouth with her hand to keep from laughing at the look on Lex's face.

"Okay. What's a better color, lil' bit?"

"Purple!" Melanie helpfully interjected.

Lorrie rolled her eyes. "Yuck. Black, or maybe silver," she said.

"Black?" Lex practically yelped. "I don't think so."

"But, Momma, I'm old, now. I want a grown up room."

Lex sat beside Lorrie and put her hand on her shoulder. "Sweetheart, we don't mind you changing the color of your room, but let's wait and look at some paint samples before you decide for sure."

"Okay."

Melanie bounced in her chair. "Can my new room be purple? That's my favorite color now."

"We'll see," Amanda said. "Why don't you two go upstairs and think about your rooms?"

Both girls grabbed their plates and left them in the sink. Melanie took Lorrie by the hand. "Come on, Lorrie. You can help me decide where my art wall will be."

Lorrie sighed, but dutifully followed. "Okay, but next you get to help me decide what posters to keep on my walls."

Amanda waited until she heard both sets of footsteps on the stairs, before she turned to Lex. "Are we going to survive those two?"

"Sure." Lex scooted over a chair to sit beside her wife. "We'll probably both be completely gray-headed before they're in high school, though." She shook her head as Amanda leaned into her. "Black or purple walls? Good lord."

"As long as you don't make me be the bad guy, this time. Don't let those little sad eyes sway you, honey."

Lex laughed as she looked into Amanda's eyes, which gave her the same sweet look that she could never say no to. "What can I say? I'm a sucker for any of my girls." She flinched as Amanda poked her in the stomach. "Watch it."

"Want to go upstairs and relax? I think the girls will be occupied for a while." Amanda stood and tugged Lex to her feet.

"Relax, huh?" Lex swatted Amanda's rear. "I've got an even better idea."

Amanda giggled. "I like the sound of that."

THE FOLLOWING MORNING, Amanda and Ellie sat at the kitchen table, relaxing after the whirlwind of getting two girls off to school. Lex had drawn the short straw, and was the one who ended up taking them to the bus. Amanda had Eddie in the seat that Hubert had brought, feeding him his morning bottle.

Ellie sipped at her coffee. "I appreciate you going with me this morning. There's only three places that I want to look at, so it shouldn't take too long."

"I don't mind at all. I need to stop at the hardware store at some point today, anyway."

"That's all the girls could talk about this morning, getting their 'new' rooms. You and Lex are brave."

Amanda laughed as she took the empty bottle from Eddie and lifted him into her arms. "Not really. That's why I'm only getting a few paint samples for them to choose from. Otherwise, I shudder at the thought of what they'd pick out."

"Yeah, I loved the look on your face when Lorrie kept going on and on about black or silver walls."

"I don't know where she gets some of these things from. I can understand Melanie's obsession with purple, since it's not far off from the hot pink she favored last year. But black? I'm hoping that Lorrie will settle for a nice, sedate gray, or maybe a subdued blue."

Ellie held out her hands, happy when Amanda passed Eddie to her. "Hey, handsome. Looks like you're outnumbered in this house." She grinned at Amanda. "Do you think he's going to survive being the only guy around here?"

"Please. You know how Lex is. She's more of a guy than most men. I've never seen someone so afraid of dresses and frills." Amanda refilled both their coffee cups. "And don't even get me started on how involved she gets watching football or baseball."

"Oh, yeah. She's really intense when the Cowboys are playing. I'd forgotten all about that." Ellie cradled Eddie and made faces at him, which made him smile. "You are just the cutest little guy I've ever seen."

The back door slammed and Lex came into the kitchen, rubbing her hands together. "Damn, it's chilly out there." She sat beside Amanda and gratefully accepted the warm coffee mug her wife handed her. "Thanks."

Amanda flicked a finger at Lex's denim sleeve. "Did you forget your coat?"

"Uh, no. I didn't see any sense in wearing it since I was going to stay in the truck. But Melanie dropped her folder before getting on the bus, and I had to get out and chase down her papers." Lex sipped at the hot brew and sighed happily.

"Why wasn't her folder in her backpack?"

Lex shrugged. "Hell if I know. It was in her backpack when we left the house. Guess it's a good thing I didn't wear my pajamas to take the girls to the bus."

"That would have been a sight." Ellie laughed. She looked at the clock on the stove. "Amanda? I think we'd better get ready to leave. My first appointment is at eight-thirty."

"All right." Amanda stood, took her coffee mug to the sink and rinsed it out. "Who's driving?"

Ellie handed Eddie to Lex and followed Amanda to the sink. "We can take mine, since it's parked behind you. I'll run get my coat from upstairs."

Once Ellie left the kitchen, Amanda stopped beside Lex. "What do you have planned for the day?"

"I'm going to call over to the bunkhouse and see if the guys will help move stuff out of the spare room. Maybe we can get it painted in the next couple of days, so we can get Melanie settled."

Amanda ran her fingers through Lex's hair. "You're not going to be lifting anything heavy, are you?"

"Only this little guy. He's going to help me supervise." Lex was pleasantly surprised when her answer garnered her a kiss.

"Thank you."

Lex grinned as Amanda backed away. "After a kiss like that, and you're thanking me? Wow. I must be better than I thought."

"You are such a brat." Amanda fluffed Lex's hair and placed a soft kiss on Eddie's head. "Don't let your momma get into too much trouble while I'm gone, Eddie. She needs constant supervision." She squeaked when Lex swatted her on the rear. "Watch it. Remember, paybacks."

"I'm looking forward to it."

Ellie poked her head into the kitchen. "Are you two still at it?"

"Aren't we always?" Lex quipped.

Amanda shook a finger at her wife. "Behave." She turned to Ellie, who was grinning. "I don't want to hear it out of you, either."

"I didn't say anything." Ellie waved at Lex. "See you later, cuz."

Lex waited until the back door closed before she stood. "You've got great timing, little man. Why didn't you dirty your diaper while Ellie was holding you, hmm?" She laughed as he grunted. "You don't have to fill it up all at once, you know," she said, as she carried him upstairs. "Save some for your mommy."

By the time they hit the top of the stairs, Lex was trying not to gag. "Good lord, son. What on earth did your mommy feed you this morning? Did she add something extra stinky to your formula?"

Eddie grinned at her when she placed him on the changing table. He started to kick his feet while Lex tried to unsnap the one-piece sleeper.

"Settle down, little guy. If you keep wriggling around, it's gonna get real messy around here." She got the sleeper tucked out of the way and opened the diaper. "Holy hell! That's nasty." Lex tried not to breathe too much while she removed the soiled diaper. She wrapped it up and placed it in the diaper genie with one hand, while the other held Eddie on the table.

Lex finished cleaning Eddie and was about to slip on a fresh diaper, when she was almost hit by a spray. "Whoa!" She quickly covered him with the diaper and laughed. "I never had to worry about that with the girls," she said, while he smiled. "Don't look so proud. You missed me."

In short order, Lex had him diapered and dressed in a fresh sleeper. She placed him in his crib and turned on the mobile over his head. "Give me a minute to wash my hands, and I'll be right back."

When Lex returned to the bedroom, she peeked into the crib and saw Eddie fast asleep. "I can't believe what a good baby you are, considering who your father is. Guess some genes are recessive." She turned on the baby monitor and took the satellite handset with her as she went downstairs to her office.

Chapter Fifteen

ELLLIE PARKED IN front of a faded, two-story condo and turned off the car. The grass in the front yard was sparse, with muddy patches fighting for dominance with knee-high weeds. She turned to Amanda. "Are you brave enough to get out of the car?"

"I'm game, if you are." Amanda turned her head to check out the rest of the neighborhood. The house they were in front of could be called the nicest on the block. "Listen, we still have one more place to check out, and it's in Somerville. Why don't we give this one a pass? I don't think I want to see you living in an area like this, especially alone."

"You've got a point. Besides, I think I've realized why Parkdale has such a nice, fancy hospital."

Amanda held onto the dash when Ellie wheeled away from the house. "Please, enlighten me. Why does Parkdale have such a nice hospital?"

"Because it makes a ton of money from all the knifings and gunshot wounds." She took the road that led to Somerville. "Not to mention drug overdoses."

"Is it really that bad there?"

Ellie sighed. "Not the wing I'm on, thankfully. But I had to get a patient from the ER the other night, and it was like a war zone."

"Maybe you should keep trying to get a job in Somerville. I know there are several good doctors' offices, and the hospital." When Ellie didn't say anything, Amanda tried another tactic. "We really like having you at the house. Have you talked to Rodney? Maybe he knows someone—"

"No. I don't want to take advantage of your family. And just because I'm looking for a new place to live, doesn't mean you won't see me anymore. I promise."

Amanda nodded. "Okay. Not to change the subject or anything, but I think I've got a buyer for your old house."

"Really? That's great. At this point, I was going to start renting it out so it wouldn't stay vacant."

"I don't think that'll be a problem. This family has one child and another on the way. They're living in a two-bedroom, one bath place at the moment, but they need more room."

Ellie drummed the steering wheel with her fingers. "I don't even know how much to sell it for. To tell you the truth, I don't think I care."

"That's why you have me. I can get you fair market value, and I can guarantee they'll take very good care of the house."

"Yeah? That's good. I know that Grandpa wouldn't want it to sit empty." Ellie cleared her throat and fought off the urge to cry. "I got a letter last week from Nancy. She's enjoying living with her daughter and playing with her grandkids." Her grandfather's housekeeper had promised to keep in touch, and was good about keeping her word.

Amanda touched Ellie's arm. "Travis would be very proud of you, Ellie. I know it hasn't been easy."

"Easy?" Ellie snorted. "He was the first person in my life who accepted me for exactly who I was. Even my step-dad, who's a great guy, didn't always know what to do with me." She wiped at her face, where a few tears had fallen. "Why can't I get past this?"

"Pull the car over, Ellie. Let's talk."

At the next row of mailboxes, Ellie parked the silver Corolla behind them. She left the engine running, but unbuckled her seatbelt so she could turn and face Amanda. "You and Lex seem to have moved along a lot easier. I don't think I even remember seeing Lex cry."

"Oh, Ellie." Amanda unlocked her seatbelt and turned also. "We both cried almost every night for the first few weeks. It was extremely hard, especially when the girls kept asking what happened to their grandpa."

Ellie began to cry in earnest. She covered her face with her hands and broke down into deep, racking sobs, while Amanda rubbed her back. After a few minutes, she accepted a tissue and noisily blew her nose. "Sorry."

"Don't apologize. Everyone needs to let go at one time or another. I'm just glad I was here for you." Amanda continued to rub Ellie's back in a soothing motion. "Maybe we should skip the last place today."

"No, I'm all right." Ellie wiped her eyes and mustered up a smile. "Thanks."

Amanda moved her hand from Ellie's back to her forearm. "Are you sure?"

Ellie nodded. "The last place is a condo on this side of Somerville. I'd like to at least know if it's livable."

"What? You didn't like the thought of sharing with the rats and cockroaches in the first apartment? Or maybe the drug dealers and hookers at the second place?" Amanda started to giggle. "My, you certainly are picky, Ms. Gordon."

"Yeah, well. I'm afraid the rats would eat too much, and the hookers would charge too much." Ellie flinched when Amanda lightly slapped her arm. "Do you abuse Lex like this?"

"All the time." Amanda chortled. "She likes it."

Ellie buckled her seatbelt and put the car in gear. "She would."

Amanda laughed and clicked her seatbelt. "I'll be sure and mention that to her when I get home."

"Uh, no. Don't do that. She'd kick my ass."

"Oh, come on. Lex is a pussycat."

When Ellie looked at Amanda in surprise, the car's tires hit the graveled shoulder of the road. "You've got to be kidding me. Are we talking about the same person?"

"Pay attention to the road," Amanda said. "And for your information, Lex has mellowed quite a bit."

"Uh-huh."

Amanda started to say something more, when she saw the smirk on Ellie's face. "You rat." She was glad to see Ellie's mood improve. "Okay, smartass. About a mile after we enter town, turn left onto Austin, and then a right onto," she checked the paper that was in the top of her purse, "Mountain View."

Ellie guided the car per Amanda's directions, and in no time they were parked in the driveway of a condo. The red brick exterior was complemented with tan woodwork, and the yard, while dormant, was well trimmed. Ellie peeked at the paper in Amanda's hands. "Are you sure this is the right address?"

"Yes." Amanda opened her door. "Come on. Let's go check it out."

WHILE HOLDING EDDIE in one hand, Lex opened the back door. "Come on in, guys." She stepped back and allowed Chet, Roy and a surprise guest inside. "Helen, hi. I wasn't expecting you."

"I know, but once Martha told me about your little guy, I had to come see him for myself." Helen held out her hands. "May I?"

"Sure." Lex passed Eddie to her. "Would you like to take him into the den? I'll bring you some coffee."

Helen smiled as Eddie gurgled and waved his hands. "That sounds great. Thank you."

Roy watched his wife walk down the hall. "That young'un sure takes after you, boss."

"Yeah. I got lucky there. He could have taken after my dad's side of the family." Most of the Walters' were short, with ruddy complexions and muddy brown eyes. Lex and Hubert both favored their mother, for which Lex was eternally grateful. "So, you guys want some coffee, or do you want to start moving furniture?"

Chet and Roy exchanged glances, and Chet shrugged. Roy took the lead. "Let's warm up with some coffee. It's not like we have that much to do around here today. We took care of the stock before we got here."

"All right. You guys go on into the den and I'll bring in a tray." Lex gathered coffee mugs and the carafe, and carried the tray to the den. She grinned at how close the men sat to Helen, and almost laughed at the silly things they were saying to Eddie. "Chet, stop that. You're gonna make my son grow up sounding like an idiot."

Chet looked up and blushed. "Aw, come on, Lex."

She handed him the tray. "Make yourself useful and help pour." Lex sat beside Helen and stretched her legs out. "Looks like you've made a friend."

"He's adorable, Lex. Usually babies this age are afraid of people they don't know."

"Yeah, it's weird. Mel wouldn't let anyone but us hold her until she was almost six months old. I guess Eddie's just social."

Helen shook her head. "From what Martha told me, I think it's more than that. It sounds like his mother didn't have much to do with him, so maybe he's just starved for attention."

"He'll surely get more than enough of that around here," Roy chimed in. "From the way things are going, he won't be walking until he starts school."

Helen shot him a dirty look, but didn't relinquish her hold on the baby. "Don't you have some furniture to move?"

Lex laughed. "Does this mean you want a baby, Helen?" She almost choked on her laughter when Roy turned white.

"Are you kidding? I have more than enough children at the bunkhouse." Helen kissed Eddie's head. "No, I think I'll just come by and spoil this little man."

"Sounds good to me." Lex put her mug on the coffee table. "If you don't mind hanging onto him for a few minutes, I'll show these two what needs to be moved."

"Take your time. We're doing just fine, aren't we, Eddie?"

Both men grumbled, but dutifully followed Lex out of the den.

AMANDA AND ELLIE exited the car at the same time. They started up the walk, which was shared by both sides of the condo. Ellie noticed that while the flowerbeds on the right were well-tended, the side they were looking at was bare. "Do you have a green thumb, Amanda?"

"I have more of a brown thumb. My grandmother has always said I could kill a plastic fern." Amanda unlocked the door and opened it. The musty smell of a long-empty home assailed her senses. "Ugh."

Ellie followed her inside and wrinkled her nose. "I don't care how cold it is outside, if I move in I'm opening every window for at least a week." She looked around the main room. "I like the size of the living room."

"The carpet is in good shape, too." Amanda walked to the back of the room, which opened up into an eat-in kitchen. "New appliances."

"Not like I'll be using them much."

Amanda shook her finger at Ellie. "I know damned good and well you can cook, so don't try that line of bull on me." She passed through the kitchen and down a short hallway. "Wow. Two nice-sized bedrooms and a little nook where you can put a desk. The guest bathroom is a little small, though."

"Desk? What would I want with a desk?" Ellie stepped around Amanda and looked around the master bedroom. "Ooh. Awesome size. And look, a walk-in closet." She turned in a circle. "If I put twin beds in the other room, can the girls come over and visit?"

"Sure, if you're brave enough." Amanda opened a door on the far side of the room. "Wow. The master has a nice bathroom."

Ellie peeked around her. "That's a huge shower, and a great tub on the other side of it."

"I bet you could get at least two people in the tub, or shower," Amanda teased. She laughed when her comment got the expected result, and Ellie blushed. "Oh, come on. Don't tell me you didn't see that little rainbow flag sticker on the window next door."

"Rainbow flag?"

Amanda rolled her eyes as they returned to the living room. "You can't be that naïve."

"I'm not. I just don't remember seeing any stickers."

A knock on the door caused both women to look at each other. They were surprised when the door opened and a slender red-headed man stuck his head inside.

"Hello, there. I hope I'm not disturbing you." He opened the door the rest of the way with a flourish. "Please tell me you're moving in. I'd love to have family as neighbors."

Ellie looked at Amanda in confusion. "Family?"

The man covered his chest with one hand. "Please forgive my manners. I live next door with my two roommates. My name is Richie Childress." He held out one hand to Amanda, palm down. "And you are?"

Amanda took his hand. "Amanda Walters. This is my cousin, Ellie Gordon."

"Cousin?"

"By marriage," Ellie added. "I'm the one that's thinking about living here."

"So, you two aren't a couple?"

Ellie laughed. "Not hardly. My cousin, *her* wife, would take exception to that."

Richie clapped his hands. "I love it. Would you two like to come next door for some coffee?"

"Maybe once Ellie moves in. I'd like to get back before my daughters get home from school." Amanda nudged Ellie. "You are going to take this place, aren't you?"

"I guess I'll have to, since you've already got me moved in." Ellie shook Richie's hand. "Can I have a rain check on the coffee?"

He pulled her into a hug. "Of course, darling. Just give a knock when you come back. Kyle, Tony and I will help you get settled." He waved at Amanda and left the room as quickly as he had arrived.

THE LAST THING to move out of the guest bedroom was a nine drawer, hand-made, heavy oak dresser. Roy took out the first drawer and set it to the side.

"What are you doing?" Chet asked.

"I'm taking out the drawers to make the damned thing lighter. Why?"

Chet picked up the empty drawer and stuffed it back in place. "If you do that, we'll have to make several more trips. I'll take one end and you get the other."

"Have you lost your mind? This thing weighs a ton."

Lex came into the bedroom. "What's going on?"

Roy pointed to Chet. "He thinks we can carry the dresser down without taking out the drawers."

"Have you tried lifting it?" Lex asked.

Chet picked up one end and set it down. "It's not that heavy. Come on, Roy. Piece of cake."

"Yeah, okay. But you're going to be the one walking backward." He lifted the end and groaned. "Are you sure about this?"

Lex moved closer. "Do you need help on your end, Roy?"

Roy grunted. "I think I've got it. Chet, you'd better get moving."

"Try to keep up, old man," Chet said. "Boss, you might want to go ahead of me."

"All right. But holler if either one of you need any help." She moved in front of Chet, but stayed close as they began to descend the stairs.

Chet shifted his grip when they got halfway down. "Hold on, Roy. It's starting to slip."

Unable to stand idly by, Lex stepped behind him. "Need a hand?"

"No, I don't think so." Chet started moving again, but his boot heel caught on the edge of a step. "Shit!" He tumbled backward and Roy was unable to stop the dresser from moving with him.

Lex lunged forward and leaned over Chet. She pushed at the top of the dresser to keep it off of him. "Roy, drop your end and grab hold," she yelled. She felt a sharp pain in her back, but held firm. "Chet, can you get up?"

"Yeah." Chet slid down a few steps and got back to his feet. He took off his baseball cap and scratched his head. "Damn, that was close."

"I could use some help here," Lex growled at him. "Help me turn it on its back and we'll slide it down the rest of the stairs."

Roy wrestled with his end, but was able to help flip the dresser. "Why didn't we do this to begin with?"

"Hell if I know." Lex moved out of the way while they pushed. She leaned against the banister and tried to catch her breath. "When you get to the bottom, take the drawers out. And Chet?"

"Yeah, boss?"

"You get to carry every damned one of them to the truck."

AMANDA OPENED THE back door and waved Ellie to go in front of her. "And when I told her about the house, she couldn't jump fast enough."

"It's crazy, your sister and her husband buying my grandfather's house. Are you sure about the price? I don't need that much, since the condo is roughly half the cost." Ellie took off her coat and hung it. She helped Amanda with hers.

"Thanks. Jeannie and Rodney can afford it. Besides, it's still a bargain. And, because they're living in a rental now, we don't have to wait for them to sell." Amanda took a deep breath. "Mmm. Smells like stew." She stepped into the kitchen, and was surprised to see Martha stirring a pot on the stove and Charlie at the kitchen table, feeding Eddie a bottle. "Hi. Um, what are you two doing here?"

Martha removed the wooden spoon from the pot, placed it on the counter, and put her hands on her hips. "Cooking dinner, of course. What does it look like?"

Amanda walked over and gave her a hug. "No, I didn't mean it that way. But, when we left, Lex was here alone with Eddie." She sat next to Charlie and looked at Eddie, who comfortably reclined in his portable car seat on the table. "Is Grandpa taking good care of you?"

"Of course I am," Charlie huffed. He wiped the milk off of Eddie's chin with a small cloth. "How did the house hunting go, Ellie?"

"Really well. I found the perfect place on the other side of Somerville. It's only about fifteen minutes from Parkdale Hospital." Ellie sat on the other side of Amanda and propped her elbow on the table. She rested her chin on her open hand. "I swear, that little guy looks just like Lex."

Once Charlie removed the bottle, Amanda took Eddie out of the carrier. She smiled at Charlie when he draped a towel over her shoulder. "Thanks." As she put Eddie on her shoulder and patted his diaper, Amanda looked at Ellie. "Everyone keeps saying how much Eddie favors Lex. I think it's great, because Melanie looks so much like me. And the older Lorrie gets, the more she's beginning to favor Frank."

"Did it bother Lex that neither girl was really hers?" Ellie asked.

Amanda shook her head. "Not at all. But I've always been fond of her looks, so I'm glad our son will look like her."

Martha snorted. "Hope he doesn't get the trouble-making gene from her."

"She does tend to get herself into messes," Amanda said. "Speaking of Lex, where is she?"

Charlie and Martha exchanged glances, and he shrugged. "She's upstairs, resting."

"What did she do?" Amanda stood and gave Charlie a deadly look.

"Uh, well," he looked at his wife for help.

Martha took Eddie from Amanda. "Go on upstairs and talk to her. Dinner will be ready in about an hour."

Amanda exhaled heavily. "I swear, if she was moving furniture after she promised not to, I'm going to kick her ass." She continued to mumble as she stomped from the kitchen.

Ellie looked at Charlie and then Martha. "Is there anything I can do to help with dinner? Because I'm sure as hell not going upstairs right now."

AMANDA STOOD IN the doorway of their bedroom and studied the still form on the bed. Lex was stretched out on top of the comforter, dressed but without her boots. One arm was over her face and she appeared to be asleep. "What am I going to do with you?" Amanda whispered.

"Anything you want," Lex answered, just as quietly. She moved her arm and turned her head. "How did the house hunting go?"

"Great. We found the perfect place for Ellie, and it's in Somerville." Amanda stepped into the bedroom and closed the door behind her. She sat on the bed beside Lex. "What happened to you? I thought you promised not to move any furniture."

Lex held Amanda's hand. "I didn't. Move any furniture, that is." She frowned as she thought about what to say. "I mean, not really."

"Lex."

"No, wait. Roy, Helen and Chet came over not long after you left. Helen fell in love with Eddie, by the way."

Amanda couldn't help but smile. "Glad it's not just us."

"Yeah. Anyway, the guys made pretty decent time clearing out the guest room until all that was left was the big dresser."

"Ooh. I'd forgotten about that monster." Amanda paused. "Wait a minute. You didn't help them move it, did you?"

Lex shook her head. "No. Not on purpose, anyway." She sighed. "Roy wanted to take the drawers out to make it lighter, and Chet wanted to hurry up and finish. So, they decided to try and move it all at once."

Amanda winced. "Either one of them need to go to the hospital for a hernia?"

"Thankfully, no. I went downstairs first, then Chet. Roy made him walk backward, since it was his bright idea. About halfway down, Chet stumbled or something, and Roy couldn't hang on. I was right behind Chet, so I was at least able to hold it up long enough to keep him from being crushed."

"Oh, my god. You held up one end? With your back?" Amanda ran one hand along Lex's jaw. "What happened next, honey?"

Lex closed her eyes for a moment and enjoyed Amanda's touch. "Um, let me think. Chet got up, we turned the dresser onto its back, and slid the damned thing down the stairs. I think we might have scratched it up some, but it's still in one piece."

"I don't care about a stupid piece of furniture, Lex. How's your back?"

Another heavy sigh was Lex's only answer. She opened her eyes when Amanda tugged on her hair. "I don't know. As soon as I reached out for that dresser, I felt something. Almost like someone stabbed me in the back. But since I've been lying here, it's doing better."

"Do you want me to take you to see Rodney?" Amanda knew the answer before she asked.

"Nah. Let me see how it feels tomorrow. If it's still bothering me, we'll go in, okay?"

Amanda unbuttoned Lex's shirt. "All right. But let's get you comfortable."

"Thanks." Lex grimaced as Amanda helped her sit up. "Martha got my boots off, but I really didn't want her undressing me like a child."

"I don't see why not. Up." With a tug on the jeans, Amanda waited until Lex raised her hips and then carefully slid them down her legs. "You are her child. And, no matter how old you get, you always will be." She took the clothes to the bathroom and dumped them in the dirty clothes hamper. On her way back, Amanda stopped at their dresser and took out a pair of soft, flannel boxers and a tee shirt. "Lift your arms, honey."

Lex rolled her eyes, but allowed Amanda to help dress her. "Thanks. Um, can you help me stand up?"

"Whatever it is, I'd rather do it for you. I don't think you're in any shape to do much."

"Yeah, but believe me, what I need to do, you can't help with." Lex tipped her head toward the bathroom.

Amanda laughed. "All right. But hold on a moment." She went to their closet and returned with a pair of crutches. "Here." When Lex opened her mouth to argue, Amanda held up a finger. "Hush. Do me a favor and use these, please? I don't think I can pick you up off the floor if something happens."

"You don't play fair," Lex said, but she stood and tucked the crutches under her arms.

"And I never will, where you're involved." Amanda kissed Lex on the chin. "I'm going to run downstairs. Will you be okay?"

"Sure." Lex looked longingly at the closed bedroom door. "The girls should be home soon. Can I—"

Amanda covered Lex's mouth with her hand. "I'll send them up after we get back from the bus stop. When you see her, ask Ellie about her new neighbors."

Lex raised an eyebrow and licked Amanda's hand.

"Ew, gross." Amanda wiped her hand on Lex's shirt. "I hate when you do that."

"Maybe one of these days you'll think about that before you cover my mouth." Lex kissed Amanda on the lips. "Send Ellie up in a few minutes. I'd like to hear how y'all's day went." She slowly made her way to the bathroom, grinning about how much fun it was to mess with her wife.

LEX WAS LAUGHING at Ellie's impersonation of her new neighbor, when she heard two sets of small feet racing up the stairs.

"Momma!" Melanie squealed as she ran toward the bed.

Ellie held out her hands to keep the girl from jumping on Lex. "Be careful, Mel. Your momma isn't feeling well."

Melanie stopped in her tracks, a few feet away, while Lorrie came into the room with a little more decorum. "Hi, Momma." She gave her sister a nasty look. "Mommy told us to be careful. Remember, Mel?"

"Uh huh." Melanie moved closer. "I just wanted to give Momma a hello hug."

Lex opened her arms. "You still can, sweetheart. But no jumping on the bed." She winked at Ellie as Melanie carefully climbed into her arms. "How about you, lil' bit?"

Lorrie put her hands on her hips. "It won't hurt you?"

"Not getting a hug would hurt worse," Lex said solemnly. She grinned as she was quickly covered by her children.

Ellie stood. "I think I'll let you enjoy the girls, and go see if I can help with dinner." She had mainly stayed to keep Lex company.

"Will you play a game with us later, El?" Melanie asked. "We haven't seen you in forever."

"Sure thing. How about after dinner?"

Both girls cheered, then got into an argument over which game to play. Ellie left them to decide, while she made a quick exit.

"Old Maid," Melanie started.

"Sorry," Lorrie countered.

"Old Maid!"

"Sorry!"

"Old—"

Lex covered Melanie's mouth, since she was the closest. "Enough! If you can't decide together, there will be no game playing tonight." She removed her hand. "And use your inside voice, before your mom comes upstairs and gets after all of us."

Melanie's lower lip quivered. "I'm sorry, Momma."

"Me too." Lorrie snuggled closer and put her head on Lex's shoulder. "Mommy said your back hurts. Are you going to Uncle Rodney to get better?"

"Um, well, I—"

"She is, if it isn't better tomorrow," Amanda said from the doorway. She came in and sat on the edge of the bed and put her hand on Lex's leg. "Isn't that right, Momma?"

Lex bit off a nasty retort. "Yep. I sure will." The look she gave

Amanda added a few choice thoughts to her words. "Want to join us for a little while, Mommy?"

"Oh, I don't know. Is there enough room for me?"

Both girls answered her at the same time. "Yes!"

"All right. Scoot over." Amanda joined her family, taking time to tickle each girl before settling down.

Chapter Sixteen

LEX BROUGHT HER small toiletries bag from the bathroom and tucked it into the overnight bag. She zipped the bag closed, but her hand was slapped away when she tried to take it off the bed. "Hey."

"Don't 'hey' me." Amanda flipped the strap of the bag onto her shoulder. "I'll take this downstairs." She ignored her sputtering wife as she exited the bedroom.

With a heavy sigh, Lex followed Amanda down. "I'm not an invalid," she grumbled.

"I know you're not, but it's only been three days since I came home to find you flat of your back. Are you sure you don't want to just overnight the paperwork to Hubert? Or maybe I should go instead."

At the foot of the stairs, Lex stood behind Amanda and put her arms around her. She kissed the side of Amanda's neck. "If you were to leave me here alone with three kids, I couldn't guarantee the house would be in one piece when you return. Besides, I'm flying instead of driving. That's something, isn't it?"

"I guess." Amanda turned in Lex's arms so she could look into her eyes. "Tell me the truth. How's your back this morning?"

"Not too bad. I still have a small twinge, but nothing like the other day. I'm okay, I promise." Lex kissed Amanda, only breaking off when she heard Martha clearing her throat from the kitchen doorway.

Martha laughed as the two hurriedly broke apart. "I swear, you'd think Lexie was going across the world, instead of an overnight trip to Oklahoma City."

Lex stuck her tongue out at Martha. "You're just jealous."

"Not hardly." Martha shook a finger at her. "You'd better get going if you're gonna make your plane."

"Yes, ma'am." Lex tugged Amanda along behind her, but stopped in front of Martha. "Want me to bring you anything back from Oklahoma?"

Martha straightened Lex's collar. "Just yourself." She smiled when Lex kissed her on the cheek. "Go on, now."

Lex swatted Martha lightly on the rear. "See you tomorrow." She turned to Amanda. "Walk me out to the truck?"

"As if you had to ask." Amanda set the bag down and helped Lex with her duster. She hurriedly slipped on her own coat, picked up the bag and followed Lex outside.

Once they were by the truck, Lex took the bag from Amanda. "I'll call you when I get to the airport." She grunted in surprise when Amanda moved in close and locked her in a death grip. "Hey. Are you all right?"

"Yeah." Amanda sniffled and buried her face in the front of Lex's shirt. She closed her eyes and absorbed the scent. The mixture of Obsession and Lex's own unique essence brought tears to her eyes. "I'm gonna miss you."

Lex cupped the back of Amanda's head and held her close. "Me, too."

THE CROWD NOISE bothered her, but Lex continued to fight her way through the boisterous group, her eyes focused on the nearest exit. She ignored a woman who roughly shoved by her, but took exception to the two men who blocked her path. "Excuse me."

One of the men turned and dismissed her with a roll of his eyes.

"Why don't you guys move out of the way, so the rest of us can get by?" Lex asked, louder than necessary.

The same man glared at her. "Why don't you find another way around? We're trying to have a conversation here."

Lex's eyes narrowed and she dropped her bag to the floor. She was about to say something else when someone shouldered the men out of the way.

"Oh, excuse me. I didn't see you there." Hubert grabbed the nearest man before he fell down. "Sorry about that, fella. But you shouldn't be standing in the middle of the walkway. It could be dangerous." He gave Lex a grin. "Hey, sis."

"Hubert." Both stood awkwardly, until Lex held out her hand. "Thanks for picking me up."

He ignored her hand and pulled her into a hug. "Like I'd let you take a cab." Hubert looked around and noticed the small bag by her feet. "Is that all you brought?"

"Yep. It's not like I'm staying that long." Lex reached for the bag, but Hubert beat her to it.

"Don't even bother arguing," he said, hooking the strap over one shoulder. "A little birdie called me and said you had messed up your back."

Lex frowned, but allowed him to take the bag. "I'm going to kill her."

Hubert laughed and gestured in front of him. "After you." He followed Lex out of the terminal and pointed to the right. "I'm parked right over there."

Lex shook her head when he unlocked the old truck. "Nice ride."

"It gets me where I need to go." Hubert put Lex's bag in the back and got in behind the wheel.

"You know, it kind of reminds me of that old truck that Dad used to own. Remember?"

Hubert looked at her. "Yeah. Damn, that seems like a hundred years ago, doesn't it?"

"Sure does. He sold it on one of his trips to Oklahoma." She tapped on the faded dash. "For all we know, this could be it."

"Hell, don't tell me that. Knowing my luck, the old bastard would probably haunt me." Hubert pumped the gas pedal a few times and turned the key. The truck sputtered, but came to life.

Once they were on their way out of the airport, Lex took out her cell phone. "I need to let the little birdie know I made it all right," she said.

"Sure."

"Hey. I'm with Hubert." Lex listened for a moment. "Yep. By the way, he mentioned that you called him earlier." She laughed. "Yeah, you're busted, all right. No, everything's fine. What? Um, okay." Lex held out her phone. "She wants to talk to you."

Hubert warily put the phone to his ear. "Hello? Yeah, sure." He looked at his sister. "Okay, I will. No problem. Bye." He returned the phone to Lex.

"Do I want to know what you two talked about?" Lex asked Amanda. "Nah. I'm just messing with you." She looked at Hubert, who was concentrating on the traffic in front of them. "Yeah. I love you, too. See you tomorrow." Lex closed the phone and tucked it away. She gazed out her window at the passing scenery.

They drove along in silence for a while, until Hubert cleared his throat. "You know, I used to be so damned jealous of you."

Lex turned to face him. "You did? Why?"

"Hell, lots of reasons. For one, you were the old man's favorite. I swear, when you were little, he probably thought you could walk on water."

"Yeah, right. I wasn't much more than a hired hand to him," Lex said. "I envied how you were allowed to do whatever you wanted, and not be tied down to the ranch."

He glanced at her. "Really? That's wild." His voice softened. "Then, when you told everyone you were gay, I figured he'd drop you like a hot rock."

"Nah. He didn't care enough to do that. He yelled a lot, slapped me around a little, and decided I was going to be in charge of the ranch, since you didn't want it." Lex crossed her arms over her chest and stared ahead. "He thought you were gay for a while, too."

Hubert almost swerved off the road. "What? You're shittin' me."

"Nope. Said that you must have been queer, 'cause you didn't like ranching." Lex shook her head. "He had some pretty fucked up ideas."

"No kidding."

Lex sighed. "You know, when he came back home," she had to clear her throat to continue, "to die, I almost threw him off the ranch."

"What stopped you?"

"Amanda. And, as much as I hate to admit it, I'm glad she did. We got a few things resolved before he passed. But I don't think I'll ever come to respect him, not after everything."

Hubert snorted. "That sorry old bastard doesn't deserve your respect. He sure as hell wasn't much of a father." His voice softened. "Not like I'm any better."

"At least you realized you wouldn't be able to raise Eddie and found another solution," Lex argued. "Dad left us to our own devices once Mom died." She watched Hubert's face. "You haven't changed your mind, have you? About Eddie?"

"No. I talked to Ramona and we both agree he's better off with you and Amanda. How's he doing, anyway?"

Lex smiled. "He's great. I've got a few photos that Amanda took with her digital camera and printed on the computer. Thought I'd show them to you when we got to your place."

"I'm looking forward to it. Um, Lex?"

"Yeah?"

"I can never thank you enough for taking Eddie, and for giving me another chance. I know I don't deserve it, but—"

"We've both done some pretty rotten things to each other in the past, Hubert. I think we should just leave everything there, where it belongs." Lex put her hand on his shoulder. "I'm kinda enjoying this second chance."

"Me, too." Hubert blinked the dampness from his eyes and smiled.

THE MORNING SUN burned Ellie's eyes as she left Parkdale hospital. She blinked to clear her vision and wiped an errant tear off her cheek. Once her car door was unlocked, she dropped into the driver's seat with a tired moan. "I don't want to meet with the inspector this morning."

She turned the ignition and held her breath until the car finally decided to turn over. "All I want to do is go home and sleep. The girls are in school, Lex has probably left for Oklahoma, and I'm sure Amanda will leave the house, too. Perfect time to sleep."

After a quick stop for a breakfast sandwich and coffee, Ellie continued to the condo she had contracted to buy. Her lowball offer had been immediately accepted, which made her wonder what hidden disasters she'd end up finding. So, instead of being surprised later, she decided that following the home inspector around would be in her best interest.

Although she was over an hour early, Ellie turned onto Mountain View and proceeded toward the condo. To her surprise, there was a blue, nineteen sixty-six Ford Thunderbird parked in her driveway with the hood up. She frowned and parked behind the car.

Ellie slammed her door and stomped to the front of the Thunderbird, where she stared at a pair of legs beneath the car. "Excuse me."

"Yeah?" The voice, while low, was definitely feminine. But the person didn't budge.

"Look, I don't know who you are, but you're parked in my driveway." Ellie crossed her arms to ward off the chill. Her light, denim jacket wasn't much protection from the cold wind. She tapped her foot against one of the legs. "Hey."

The sound of a dropped wrench rang out. "Can't you see that I'm busy?"

"You're trespassing is what you're doing." Ellie nudged the leg again. "Get up."

The body slowly started to slide out, and one greasy hand grabbed Ellie's leg. "Damn it, woman. What the fuck is your problem?"

Ellie shook her leg to remove the hand. She looked down at the gray scrubs and grimaced at the dark stain now present. "You're going to pay for cleaning my pants."

"Like hell I am." The woman slid the rest of the way out from under the car and sat up. "Who the hell are you?"

"I'm—" Ellie stopped when her eyes met the angry ones below her. The scowling woman had a blonde crew cut and beautiful hazel eyes. Her well-defined forearms peeked out beneath the rolled up sleeves of her khaki brown work shirt, which was liberally covered with grease. "Uh."

The woman tugged on Ellie's pants leg again. "Now what's the matter?"

Ellie shook her head to clear it. "Nothing." She wriggled her leg. "Do you have to put your grimy hands on my work clothes? And what are you doing in my driveway?"

"Sorry." But the grin on the woman's face didn't show much concern. She wiped the worst of the oil from her hands with a rag. "You must have the wrong house. A crazy Bible thumper lived here until six months ago, and you're too young to be her. Unless you're related."

The comment reminded Ellie of her mother, whose religious zeal and bigotry chased Ellie from their home. "No, I'm definitely not a Bible thumper. But I have made an offer on this house."

"Oh, shit." The woman scrambled to her feet. "You're the woman that Richie has been going on about?" She was only an inch or so taller than Ellie, but her stance made her appear taller. "I'm sorry. Can we start over?" She held out her hand. "I'm Kyle Lind."

"Ellie Gordon." Ellie automatically took the offered hand, before she realized it was still covered with grease. "Ugh." She looked at her hand and sighed. "Just great. Wait. Kyle?"

Kyle grinned. "Kylie, actually. But everyone calls me Kyle. I mean, if you were going to hire a mechanic to work on your car, you'd rather have a Kyle than a Kylie, right?"

"I dunno. I've never really thought about it before." Ellie took a crumpled tissue from her coat pocket and tried to wipe her hand clean.

"Is there a reason you're playing mechanic in my driveway instead of your own?"

"Three cars, two parking spaces. I room with two prissy guys who think they need to park in the garage, and I didn't want to have to stop what I was doing and move my car. Besides, this place has been vacant forever, and we'd never seen a for sale sign in the yard."

Ellie gave up on cleaning her hand when all she was doing was smearing the mess worse. "Do you know why it was so cheap?"

"Besides being next door to three deviants? No. As far as I know, everything's fine with the place." Kyle watched as Ellie made a mess of her greasy hand. "Why don't you come inside and wash up? And if you'll send me a bill for your cleaning, I'll take care of your clothes, too."

"Um, well, I don't know. I was supposed to meet the inspector at eight-thirty."

Kyle picked up her toolbox. "Please, I insist. I'll even brew you some fresh coffee while you wait." She gave Ellie a hopeful look. "You've got at least forty-five minutes. Might as well do it inside where it's warm."

"All right." Ellie followed Kyle into the other side of the condo, trying not to enjoy the view of the woman's taut backside as they went inside.

HUBERT PARKED THE truck in his assigned space and turned to Lex. "I realize I said I'd get you a hotel room, but I was kinda hoping you'd stay with us tonight. We have a perfectly good guest room, and I know that Ramona is looking forward to getting all the dirt on my rotten childhood."

Lex gave the thought a moment of consideration. "Are you sure I won't be any trouble? I saw a motel up the street from here."

"Do you want me to promise not to murder you in your sleep?" Hubert halfway teased. "I mean we're just getting to know one another again, but—"

"I think I can risk it." Lex tried to keep the grin off her face. "Does the guest room have a lock?"

He nodded. "I think so. If not, I can always..." Hubert trailed off when Lex started to laugh. "Aw, hell. You're still a damned smartass."

"Yep." Lex opened her door at the same time he did. She swung her right leg out and began to get out of the truck, when a sharp pain in her back caused her leg to buckle. Only her firm grip on the door kept Lex from falling. "Damn."

Hubert hurried around the truck. "Hey, are you all right?" He took one look at Lex's face and put his arm around her waist. "What happened?"

"I don't know." Lex blinked to try and clear the stars from her vision. Sharp pains shot from her back down her right leg. She gratefully leaned into Hubert's body. "Guess I'm a little stiff from sitting for so long."

"Can you make it inside to the elevators, or should I take you to the emergency room?"

Lex gave him a look. "I'll be okay in a minute. Maybe if I walk around a little it'll get better." She wrapped her arm around his shoulder. "Good thing we're getting along now, isn't it?"

"Yeah. If I'd gotten this close before, you'd have kicked my ass." Hubert chuckled nervously as they walked slowly to the parking garage's elevator.

Once inside the elevator, Lex pulled away from Hubert and carefully put weight on her leg. The shooting pains were still bad, but she hated being dependent on anyone. "I think I can make it now, thanks."

"Sure. Just let me know if you need anything."

They stood in silence as the elevator made its way to Hubert's floor. When the door opened he shouldered Lex's bag and motioned for her to go first. "It's the fourth door to the left."

Lex moved slowly and tried to hide her limp. She stood behind Hubert as he put his key in the lock.

The door opened, and a slightly-overweight woman stood smiling at the pair. Her salt and pepper hair was pulled back away from her face, and her dark brown eyes twinkled merrily. "Hi. I'm Ramona Buchanan." She opened the door wider and stepped back. "Please, come in. Hubert, why don't you take your sister's bag to the guest room?"

"Sure, sweetheart." Hubert kissed Ramona's cheek in passing.

Ramona held out her hands and tugged Lex into the apartment. "I would have known you anywhere, Lex. I can call you Lex, can't I?"

"Um, sure." Lex followed her into the living room. "It's nice to meet you." She allowed herself to be seated on the sofa next to her hostess. "Thanks for having me."

"Oh, please. You're family, Lex. You're always welcome here." Ramona leaned closer and whispered, "I know you and Hubert have had your issues in the past, but I really want to thank you for giving him a second chance. It's made a huge difference in his life."

Lex shook her head. "Honestly, you've made the biggest difference. It's great to finally get to know him as a good guy, and not," Lex paused, as she tried to think of a tactful way to continue.

"A complete horse's ass?" Hubert finished for her. He sat on the other side of Ramona in a nearby chair.

"Hubert!" Ramona scolded halfheartedly. She winked at Lex. "You'll have to excuse him. He spent all day yesterday with my father, who's a horrible influence."

Hubert's laughter echoed around the small living room. "Ramona, honey, I think Lex has heard the word before." He grinned at his sister.

"Hell, she's called me worse."

Lex shared his smile. "True. But with a houseful of kids, I've tried to curtail it, at least a little."

"That's right. You have two older children, besides the baby, don't you?" Ramona asked. "Do you have any pictures?"

"I sure do." Lex started to stand. "I've got an album in my bag."

Hubert quickly got to his feet. "If you don't mind, I'll get it for you." At Lex's nod, he left the room again. When he returned, he had the small album, as well as a large envelope. "I'm guessing these are the papers I need to sign?"

"Yes." Lex held her breath while he slowly took the legal papers out and read them over. She hoped he wouldn't change his mind.

He sat, took a pen from his pocket, and signed on the bright-yellow highlighted lines. Exhaling heavily, Hubert thumbed through the papers again to make certain he signed everywhere. "Okay. I think that's it." He tucked everything in the envelope and left it on the coffee table. "I hope you know what you're doing, Lex. I don't think I'd have the patience for three kids."

She slowly released her own breath quietly and willed her heart to slow down. "It's a labor of love. Those three keep me young."

Ramona held out her hand to Hubert, who gave her the photo album. "I think it's just wonderful. I've never wanted children of my own, but it's plain to see you love yours."

"Why don't you want kids?" Lex asked. To her, Ramona seemed very loving and kind, and she couldn't understand why she didn't want children.

"Oh, lots of reasons. Mostly, I'm too self-involved, and I believe a child deserves everything a person can give them. I love kids, as long as I can spoil them and send them back to their parents." She smiled at Hubert. "Thankfully, I found a man who feels the same."

Hubert nodded. "Yeah." He sat on the arm of the sofa beside Ramona and looked over her shoulder while she studied the photos. "That little one sure looks like Amanda."

"Acts like her, too," Lex added. "She'll get mad at something and put her hands on her hips, and I swear it's like a miniature version. I always have a hard time keeping a straight face."

"Oh, my." Ramona looked at the photo of Lex holding an infant. "Is that him?" she asked Hubert.

"Yeah," he muttered in a choked voice.

Ramona raised her head and looked into his eyes. "He looks just like you."

Hubert could only nod. He cleared his throat. "Uh, Lex? How's he doing?"

"He's doing great. And he loves being around a lot of people. That really surprised us."

"Really? Why?" Ramona asked.

Lex shrugged. "Most babies that age don't really care for anyone but their parents. At least our two girls were like that. But even from the start, he's always enjoyed being held by just about anyone."

Hubert nodded. "I noticed that, too. He took to me right away, even though he had no idea who I was." He put his arm around Ramona. "I think his mother wasn't very attached to him."

"That's a shame." Ramona leaned into him. "From the looks of these two girls, I'd say he's got a very happy life ahead of him."

"We'll do our best," Lex said, her eyes focused on Hubert's. "I hope they'll see a lot of their uncle. And aunt," she emphasized.

Ramona closed the album and handed it to Lex. "They'll probably get tired of seeing us," she said. The answering squeeze of her shoulder was all the confirmation she needed. "It's getting close to lunch time. Why don't we go to the restaurant downstairs? We can chat more over their prime rib."

"Sounds good to me. If you don't mind, I'd like to wash up, first." Lex put her hand on the arm of the couch and levered herself up.

Hubert stood as well. "Let me show you where the washroom is." He lurched forward when Lex's right leg gave out again, causing her to fall forward.

When Lex's left hand landed on the edge of the coffee table, the table flipped up, hit her in the head and caused her to fall face first on the floor. She lay there, motionless as Hubert dropped to his knees beside her.

Chapter Seventeen

COMPLETELY EXHAUSTED AFTER the home inspection, Ellie trudged up the back steps to the ranch house and opened the door. She stripped off her coat and hung it in its usual place, and was on her way up the stairs when Amanda met her in the hallway.

"Thank god you're home. Martha's got Eddie, my grandparents will be picking up the girls at school, and I've got to be in Austin by six. I was going to leave you a note, but I didn't know what to say." Amanda stopped babbling when Ellie grabbed her by the shoulders.

"Calm down and take a breath. What's going on?"

Amanda shook her head. "I don't have time to explain, you can ask Martha, Charlie or—"

"Hold it. Why are you going to Austin?"

"To catch a plane." Amanda started up the stairs. "I've still got to pack, but I don't know how long I'll be gone."

Ellie followed her. "Where are you flying?"

"To Oklahoma City. Hubert called about an hour ago. Lex's back is worse. She fell and Hubert took her to the emergency room."

"Wait, what?"

Amanda ignored her and took a suitcase out of the closet. She opened it and began tossing clothes inside, not really paying attention to what she was packing. She went into the bathroom and came back empty-handed. "Damn it. What was I doing?"

"Sit down for a minute, and I'll help." Ellie guided her to the rocker beside Eddie's crib. "You're not going to do Lex any good at all if you keep this up."

"I know, but—"

"Shhhh." Ellie waggled a finger at Amanda. "Now, calmly tell me what's going on."

Amanda exhaled slowly. "Lex reinjured her back the other day, but was too damned stubborn to go to the doctor. She was at Hubert's and her leg gave out, she fell and it scared Hubert so bad that he called an ambulance."

"Oh, wow. Have you heard anything else?"

"Not yet." Amanda stood until Ellie glared at her. She dropped back onto the rocker. "The last I heard was she was in the emergency room, and that was about an hour ago."

The phone rang, and Amanda jumped up to answer it. "Hello?" She nodded as the person on the other end of the line spoke. "Really? Okay. Uh-huh. Right. Are you sure? All right. Could you have her call me as soon as possible, please? Thank you." Amanda hung up the phone and turned to Ellie. "She's okay. Ramona said that they're releasing Lex in a little while, but she has to follow up with her own doctor when she gets back."

"Who's Ramona?"

"Oh, sorry. She's Hubert's fiancée. The emergency room doctor thinks that Lex may have a herniated disc, which would explain why she's in so much pain." Amanda sat on the edge of the bed. "Ramona also told me that she and Hubert will be flying back with Lex, in case she has any more problems."

Ellie joined Amanda. "That's nice of them. Although I'm glad I'm not there when they tell Lex. She's gonna blow a gasket."

Amanda laughed. "Probably. But that's too damned bad. They're going to help her and she's going to accept it, whether she wants to or not." She looked down and spotted the black grease on Ellie's scrub pants. "Is that oil?"

"Huh?" Ellie looked down and unsuccessfully tried not to blush. "Oh, yeah."

"Did you have car trouble? Why didn't you call?"

Ellie brushed her hands over her face. "Um, no. No car trouble. I had an appointment this morning to meet with the inspector at the new house."

"Oh." Amanda nodded. "Found a few problems?"

"No, he said the house was in very good shape. No mold, all the appliances are in great order, and the AC/furnace unit is only three years old. The garbage disposal needs to be replaced, and the carpet's worn in the master bedroom, but that's about it."

Amanda looked down at Ellie's leg again. "And?"

"Oh. The grease. When I got to the house, there was a car parked in the driveway. It belonged to Kyle, who needed a place to work on it."

"Kyle? One of the neighbors? Did he tell you why he was using your driveway to work on a car?"

Ellie blushed and looked at the floor. "She said her roommates used the garage, and she didn't want to stop and move the car every time they wanted in or out."

"She?" Amanda started to smile. "So, Kyle's a she?"

Ellie nodded.

"Is she cute?"

The blush on Ellie's face intensified and she mumbled something.

"What was that?"

With a heavy sigh, Ellie looked up. "She's kind of butch, I guess. Got really short, blonde hair and muscles."

Amanda's eyebrow rose. "Muscles? Like a weight lifter?"

"No, not all bulky or anything." Ellie moved her hands around as she tried to describe Kyle. "She's not much taller than me, but has really nice arms." Her face turned red again. "Her work pants must be tailored, the way they fit."

"Oh?"

Ellie covered her face with her hands. "Oh, god. Kill me."

"Come on, Ellie. Give me more details." Amanda tugged on Ellie's scrub top and pulled her back onto the bed. "So, this Kyle. She's hot?" She laughed when Ellie rolled over and put a pillow over her face. "Aw, what's the matter? Is Ellie in love?"

"No!"

Amanda tugged on the pillow. "Lust, maybe? You did say her pants fit well."

"Arrrgh!"

ALL EYES IN the room were on the woman in the wheelchair, as she continued to argue with the physician. "I don't need those, I have crutches at home," Lex told him.

"Ms. Walters, you don't seem to understand. You have two choices. Either use the crutches, or I will admit you."

Lex stared at him.

"Oh, for god's sake," Hubert said. He leaned over and whispered into Lex's ear. "Take the damn things so we can get out of here. It's not like he can see if you're using them once we leave."

"Okay." Lex took the crutches. "Thanks." She tried to keep her composure as Hubert wheeled her from the room. "Stupid jackass," she grumbled.

Hubert pushed her faster, while Lex wrestled with the metal crutches. At the end of the hall they met Ramona, who took the crutches from Lex.

"You poor thing. I've talked Amanda out of coming, but she wants you to call her as soon as possible."

"Thanks, Ramona. Wait. Amanda knows what happened?" Lex turned and looked at Hubert. "Did you call her?"

He tried to avoid the question as they went through the emergency room doors. "I'll run get the car."

Lex grabbed his belt before he got away. "Why did you call Amanda? I bet she's going crazy right now."

"Come on, Lex. You can't blame me for calling her. You scared us to death, and I had no idea if you had a concussion, or worse."

"I was stunned, that's all." Lex started to get out of the chair, but Ramona's hand on her shoulder held her fast. "It's my leg that's bothering me, not my head. I've had enough concussions to know what one feels like."

Ramona gently squeezed her shoulder. "Not to mention the doctor agreed with you. Since Hubert's going to get the car, why don't you sit tight for a little while longer? You can use my cell phone to call Amanda."

Hubert handed Lex a plastic bag. "I think all your stuff is in there. Be right back." He took off before Lex could harass him any more.

"I'll give you some privacy to make your call." Ramona patted Lex's arm and followed Hubert.

After finding her cell phone in the bag, Lex hit the familiar speed dial.

"Hello?" Amanda answered breathlessly.

Lex couldn't help but smile when she heard her wife's voice. "Hi, sweetheart."

"Oh, my god, Lex. Are you—"

"Yeah, I'm okay."

Amanda cleared her throat. "Hubert told me you were knocked out when your head hit the coffee table. He said—"

"No, my head's fine. Just a little bump, and I never lost consciousness. I feel kind of stupid, to tell you the truth. When I stood up, my right leg gave out. I started to fall forward, tried to break my fall with the coffee table, and caused it to flip over. I was stunned, but not really hurt. The doctors here verified that, so there's nothing to worry about. I promise I'm okay."

"I was going to fly up there, but Ramona talked me out of it. She said they would fly back with you to make sure you got home all right."

Lex rolled her eyes. "I don't need babysitters, Amanda."

"Honey, please. If you won't do it for yourself, do it for me. Otherwise I'll be out of my mind worrying about you."

"You don't play fair." Lex sighed at the futility of ever trying to win an argument with Amanda.

"Please?"

"All right. But only for you."

"Thank you." Amanda's voice was hoarse with emotion. "I love you so much."

Lex softened her tone as she fought the lump in her throat. "I love you too, sweetheart. See you tomorrow, okay?" She closed the phone and set it in her lap, wishing she was home with her wife.

AMANDA PUSHED THE off button on the phone and curled up around the receiver. She was alone in the bedroom, since she had convinced Ellie earlier to get some rest. Ellie had related the rest of her morning, and that she was planning on going back to her old house first thing tomorrow to start packing, so she agreed a nap would be a good idea.

The sound of the back door closing downstairs caused Amanda to sit up and return the handset to the base. She brushed her fingers through her hair and adjusted her clothing, just as footsteps hit the stairs.

"Amanda?" Martha called. "If you're going to the airport, you'd better get a move on." She stood at the entrance to the master bedroom and put her hands on her hips. "Did you fall asleep?"

"No. Come on in."

Martha joined her on the bed. "You look a little out of it, honey. What's going on?"

"I just heard from Lex. She's okay. Seems like Hubert panicked and scared us all." Amanda stood and started removing items from the suitcase on the bed. "Her leg gave out, caused her to fall, and he thought she had been more seriously hurt."

"Well, isn't that something." Martha stood, took the stack of clothes from Amanda's hands and placed them neatly in a dresser drawer. "I think it was easier on all of us when they weren't getting along."

Amanda chuckled. "Isn't that the truth? Anyway, he and his fiancée, Ramona, are going to fly back with Lex to make sure she doesn't have any more problems."

"I bet Lexie just loved that."

"Oh, yeah." Amanda stopped in the middle of the room and scratched her head. "Damn. Where are we going to put them? We've already cleared out the extra guest room."

Ellie piped in from the doorway. "They can have my room. I'm going to be staying at my old place until I get everything packed and moved. Since I'm paying cash for the condo and the previous owner wants to get rid of it as soon as possible, I'll sign the papers next week."

"What's wrong with the new place?" Martha asked.

"There's a trio of 'deviants' living in the adjacent condo," Ellie said, taking a seat on the rocker.

Amanda laughed at Martha's confused look. "Two gay men and a lesbian," she supplied helpfully.

"Oh, for goodness sakes! What in the Sam-hill is wrong with people nowadays? I've never heard such bull pucky." Martha looked at Amanda. "Doesn't that upset you?"

"Are you kidding? One person's bigotry saved Ellie tens of thousands of dollars on a new place to live. I think it's poetic justice." Amanda shoved the empty suitcase under the bed.

Ellie nodded. "I wish they'd be there at closing. After everything was signed, I was going to put the key on a rainbow keychain. It would have been great to see the look on their face."

"I swear, you girls," Martha said. "Well, since you're not traipsing off to Oklahoma, I suppose you'll be wanting your son and dog." She had kept Freckles at her house, so the dog wouldn't get underfoot while Amanda tried to pack.

"Yes, most definitely. And I need to call my grandparents so they'll know what's going on. It's too late to stop them from picking up the girls, but I can run into town and get them." Amanda starting ticking things off on her fingers. "Not to mention, calling Rodney to see if he can see Lex sometime tomorrow afternoon. And letting Jeannie know that everything's a go for the house."

Martha started for the door. "Why don't you let your grandparents keep the girls tonight? Things are going to be hectic enough around here tomorrow. You know they'll want to start painting their rooms as soon as they can. Give yourself a break. Charlie and I will be in town tomorrow, so we can bring them home that evening."

"I'll see what Gramma says. I'm sure if she had her way, the girls would spend the entire weekend with them." She turned to Ellie. "Why don't you try to get more sleep? You still look tired."

The comment caused Ellie to yawn. "I was going to argue with you, but," she shrugged. "Let me know if you need me for anything okay?" She gave Martha a quick hug on the way out.

"I'm really going to miss that girl when she moves back out," Martha said.

"Me, too. But I'm glad she won't have to drive so far after working all night. I hated thinking of her on those quiet, country roads." Amanda took a cleansing breath and straightened her shoulders. "Let's go get my son before your husband spoils him rotten."

Martha followed her out of the room. "Don't you know that's a grandparent's job? I think we've done an admirable job of restraining ourselves so far."

ANNA LEIGH PARKED her Cadillac near the front door of the school, arriving far too early, as usual. She picked up the magazine she had brought and mindlessly began leafing through it, her thoughts elsewhere. Amanda's second call was welcome news, but she still worried about her granddaughter's partner. Lexington Walters always chafed at any physical limitations, and from the way Amanda talked, Lex was in for enforced rest, time-consuming physical therapy, or worse.

A quick call to her grandson-in-law, Rodney, verified what everyone already suspected. Even without a physical exam, he was somewhat certain that Lex suffered from a herniated disc, which, with proper care, was something she could fully recover from. If they could get Lex to follow instructions. Anna Leigh shook her head. "Mandy's certainly going to have her hands full." She tossed the magazine on the seat next to her, instead occupying herself with her thoughts.

Her son, Michael, had come over for breakfast, looking far healthier than he had in months. He admitted to her and Jacob that he had ignored the warning signs from his body, afraid that if he slowed down, he'd lose business. It took his heart condition, plus a long talk with his wife, to make him realize what was most important in his life. He had spent the entire morning apologizing to her and Jacob for his actions.

The sound of the school bell broke Anna Leigh from her remembrance, as she watched the front doors of the school carefully for her grandchildren. In no time at all, the Walters' girls headed toward the car, huge grins on their faces.

The back door opened, and Melanie was the first to climb in. "Hi, Gramma! I was so excited when my teacher told me you were coming to get us. I love when Mommy picks us up, but I have a lot of fun at your house, and Grandpa is always letting me help him in the shop." Her constant chatter slowed as Lorrie got in beside her. "Penny got put in time out today 'cause she called Tommy a boogerhead. Is boogerhead a bad word?"

"Well, dearest, it's not a nice thing to say. And calling someone a name is never right." Anna Leigh smiled at Lorrie. "How was your day today?"

"It was okay, I guess. Are we spending the night with you?"

"You can if you'd like. Your grandfather and I thought we would go shopping tomorrow in Austin, then perhaps go see a movie. We'd love for you to join us."

Both girls cheered.

After a moment, Melanie sobered. "Momma comes home tomorrow from her trip. What if we're not there to give her a hello hug?"

"She'll understand that we're with Gramma and Grandpa," Lorrie said. "We can give her our hugs when we get home. Right, Gramma?"

"That's right. Maybe you can find her something special on our trip. How's that sound?"

"I like that a lot," Melanie said.

Lorrie nodded. "Me too."

"Then it's settled. Come on girls, your grandfather was about to make some hot chocolate when I left."

EARLY EVENING FOUND Amanda and Charlie in the kitchen playing cards, while Eddie napped in Martha's arms. When the doorbell rang, the three looked at each other in surprise.

Martha held Eddie closer to her, trying not to disturb his sleep. "Are you expecting anyone?"

"No. I wonder who it could be?" Amanda asked.

Charlie put his cards face-down on the table and stood. "We're not going to find out by sitting here talking about it, that's for sure." He headed down the hall, with Amanda and Martha hot on his heels.

Before the doorbell could ring again, Charlie opened the front door. He noticed their adopted son, who was not alone. Next to Ronnie stood a quiet redhead, her eyes taking in the three people on the other side of the doorway. "Ronnie? What are you doing here?"

"Hey, everyone. I know I should have called first, but—"

Amanda took his hand and tugged. "Of course not. You're family, so you never need to call ahead. Come on in, and bring your friend with you." She released Ronnie and held out her hand to the silent woman. "Hi, I'm Amanda."

The younger woman smiled bashfully. "I'm Nora. It's a pleasure to meet you."

"Let's go into the den, shall we?" Martha said. "We're all going to catch a chill standing in the doorway."

Once everyone was settled, Amanda brought in a carafe of coffee and passed it around. She sat next to Martha, and watched as Ronnie nervously fiddled with the cowboy hat he held. "Ronnie? Is everything all right?"

He looked up and grinned. "Oh, yeah. Everything's great, isn't it, Nora?" He realized his social error. "I'm sorry. Mom, Dad, this is Nora Haden. Nora, my folks, Charlie and Martha Bristol. And you've kinda met Amanda."

"Pleased to meet you all." Nora murmured. Her face was pink with embarrassment, and she kept her hands tucked demurely in her lap.

Ronnie placed his hat on one knee. "Where's Lex and the girls?"

"The girls are with my grandparents for the night, and Lex is, uh, in Oklahoma until tomorrow." Amanda said.

Eddie woke with a squeak and began to fuss. Martha checked his diaper and shook her head. "Nice timing, cutie." She started to get up, but Amanda took Eddie out of her arms.

"Let me. I'll just run upstairs and get him cleaned up." She looked at the young couple on the loveseat. "I'll be right back."

Ronnie watched Amanda leave the room. "Mom, what's Amanda doing with a baby?"

Charlie started laughing, at least until Martha lightly slapped him on the arm. "Son, nothing gets past you, does it?" At Ronnie's continued confusion, he elaborated, "Lex and Amanda adopted little Eddie about a week or so ago. I guess it slipped our minds to let you know about him."

"Wow. Well, that's great," Ronnie said. He started to bounce one leg, until Nora covered it with her hand.

"So, how's things at the vet's office?" Charlie asked, more to fill the silence than anything else.

Ronnie's head bobbed up and down quickly. "Good. Real good. I found a temporary home for the horse and Dr. Hernandez is going on vacation for a couple of weeks starting in January. He said he trusts me to handle anything that might come up."

"Of course you can. I've always said that about you," Martha said with pride. She looked at Ronnie's face carefully. "Did you forget to shave this morning?"

He brushed at his upper lip. "No. I'm growing a mustache. What's the matter? Don't you like it?"

Nora patted his leg. "I think it looks nice, honey."

Martha snorted, but didn't add anything. Her eyebrow rose at the term of endearment the young woman used. "How long have you known each other?"

Ronnie's face turned bright red. "Um, a while. We met at school."

"Oh?" Martha turned her attention to Nora. "Did you study veterinary science, too?"

"No, ma'am. Architecture. Well, Landscape Architecture and Urban Planning, to be exact."

"I see. That sounds quite fascinating."

Nora leaned forward as she nodded, her face animated and her deep brown eyes twinkling. "Oh, yes. I love it. I've recently joined a firm in Austin, and it seems like I'm learning more now than I ever did in school."

Amanda returned, with a happy and clean Eddie. She sat next to Martha. "Sorry about that. What did I miss?"

"We were just getting to know Nora," Martha said. "She's a landscape and urban planning architect. Right?"

Nora beamed. "That's correct, Mrs. Bristol."

"Oh, please. Just call me Martha."

"Thank you, ma'am, I mean, Martha." Nora seemed to be coming out of her shell, at least until Ronnie stood.

"I'd like to make an announcement," he said, taking a deep breath and letting it out slowly. "Last night I asked Nora to marry me, and she said yes." He pulled Nora up beside him and put his arm around her.

Charlie and Martha both stared at them, not saying a word. Amanda grinned, and Eddie kicked his legs, oblivious to everything.

Ronnie looked at his folks, his smile slowly disappearing. "Um, Mom? Dad? Aren't you going to say anything?"

Charlie looked at his wife, who still had a stunned expression on her face. "I do believe that's the first time I've ever seen Martha speechless." He stood and embraced the happy couple. "Congratulations, you two. Nora, I hope you know what you're getting into."

Finally coming out of her trance, Martha clapped her hands. "This is wonderful news!" She looked Nora up and down. "You're not having to get married, are you?"

"Mom!" Ronnie's face turned beet red. "I can't believe you asked that."

Martha patted his cheek. "That'll teach you to keep such a lovely young woman a secret from me." She took Nora's left hand and looked carefully at the ring. "Very nice. Have you two set a date?"

Nora shook her head. "No, ma'am. But I was hoping to maybe have a spring wedding?" She asked Ronnie, who smiled his consent.

"Anything you want, honey. Just tell me when and where, and I'll be there." Ronnie kissed her cheek.

Amanda smiled fondly at the display. "Lex is going to be so sorry she missed this."

Once all the hugs were over, everyone took their seats again. "When will she be home?" Ronnie asked. "We can always stop back by sometime this weekend, can't we, Nora?"

"Of course. I don't have to be in Austin until Tuesday."

"Why not come over for lunch on Sunday?" Martha asked. "I've got a lovely ham I can have ready."

Ronnie deferred to Nora, who nodded and smiled. "We'd love to. And I can't wait to meet Ronnie's big sister, Lex, who I've heard so much about." She caressed his reddened cheek. "Aw, it's okay, sweetie. Everyone idolizes their older siblings."

"I know it goes both ways," Amanda said, which only added to Ronnie's embarrassment. "Don't worry, Ronnie. We won't tell."

"Thanks," he mumbled. In order to take the attention off himself, Ronnie got up and walked over to Amanda. "Can I hold him?"

She immediately handed Eddie over. "Sure."

Ronnie studied the baby while he held him close. "What's his name?"

"Edward Lee Walters. But we call him Eddie."

"He's cute." Ronnie shifted Eddie a little until they were both more comfortable. "How come he looks just like Lex?"

Charlie, Martha and Amanda all laughed at the familiar question. Amanda watched as Ronnie sat beside Nora, and they both fussed over Eddie. "It's kind of a long story, if you're in any hurry to get anywhere."

"Go on," Ronnie said. "We're fine. Aren't we, Nora?"

"Sure. I'm interested, too."

Amanda took a deep breath and exhaled. "Okay, well, it goes like this." She slowly related the tale, leaving nothing out.

Chapter Eighteen

BY LATE SUNDAY afternoon, Lex was chafing at the enforced rest. The lunchtime visit with Ronnie and Nora had been fun, but after they left, she'd been relegated to her bedroom. Even with the girls doing their best to keep her occupied, she was ready to escape. As her "company" for the time being, Melanie was stretched out across the bed, coloring. The room was quiet, which gave Lex time to think about the previous day's events.

The visit to Rodney's office had frightened Lex, but she was too stubborn to admit it to anyone, including Amanda. Rodney took several x-rays, and wanted to send her to Parkdale for an MRI, which she adamantly refused. He told her that from her symptoms he believed she suffered from a herniated disc in her back. Rodney recommended a week of complete bed rest, and without bothering to get Lex's approval, made an appointment with an orthopedic surgeon for a second opinion, and the dreaded MRI.

When he explained that, in some cases, only surgery could repair the damage, Lex had felt like fleeing the office. The only thing that kept her in place was the terrified look on Amanda's face, and the knowledge that she was the only one who could take that look away. Then and there, Lex pledged to do whatever it took to appease Amanda.

But now, with the bedroom walls closing in on her, Lex had second thoughts. She didn't know if she could handle an entire week this way.

"Momma?" Melanie tapped Lex on the leg, "What color should I do the horse?" She held up her coloring book. "I was thinking brown, but it kinda looks like Thunder, and he's black. But black isn't a pretty color. Maybe red? Or I could do different colors, like Mommy's horse. But that's not as pretty as purple." When Lex didn't answer, Melanie grabbed the hem of Lex's tee shirt and tugged on it. "Momma? Why are your eyes closed? Is your head hurting again?"

Lex took a deep breath and opened her eyes. "A little. Would you mind going downstairs and getting me something to drink, please? I'm sure that would help."

"Okey dokey!" Melanie gave Lex a kiss on the cheek before she hopped off the bed and raced from the room.

A few minutes later, Amanda arrived with a glass of milk and a small plate of cookies. She placed the items on the nightstand and carefully eased herself next to Lex. "Hi, honey. Mel told me you had a headache." She caressed Lex's cheek. "You look a little worn out."

"It's the pain meds. And I don't know how I'm going to survive an entire week in this room. If I have to lie down the entire time, you may have to have me committed."

Amanda's face grew serious and she cupped Lex's chin with one hand. "I know this is hard for you, and I really appreciate that you're willing to do whatever it takes to get better. I know how I'd feel in your position. Why don't we compromise? How about stretching out on the sofa downstairs during the day, and only being up here at night? Would that help?"

Lex leaned forward and kissed her. "Will you be keeping me company?"

"Keep kissing me like that and you can bet on it." Amanda grinned as her lips were covered again, this time for a much longer period.

An embarrassed cough sounded from across the room. Hubert stood in the doorway, his face and ears red. "Uh, sorry to disturb you." He and Ramona had accepted Amanda's offer to stay, at least until Lex met with the specialist. They both enjoyed being a part of the large family and were thrilled to help out. "Martha sent me up to see if Lex wanted anything, but I can see she already has it." His eyes grew big. "I mean, I saw the milk and cookies. Um, I think I'll go back downstairs now. Talk to you later, sis."

Both women laughed as Hubert scurried away. Lex put her arms around Amanda. "He was right, you know."

"Oh?"

"You're all I'll ever need." Lex pulled Amanda close and kissed her again.

LATE MONDAY MORNING, Lex was propped up on the couch, television remote in one hand and her head tipped back, dozing. The pain pills Rodney prescribed tended to knock her out, which was as much for Amanda's benefit as Lex's.

At the other end of the sofa, Amanda sat with her laptop, typing away at her blog. She stopped when she heard a car come up the driveway. "Damn." She put her laptop on the coffee table and hurried to the front door before the visitor woke up Lex.

She opened the door and was almost hit by her sister, who had been prepared to knock. "Jeannie! What are you doing here?"

"Nice to see you too, Mandy. I was hoping to help keep Slim company. How's she feeling?"

Amanda held the door open and gestured for Jeannie to come inside. "Her back and right leg are really bothering her, and she hates taking the pain medication. So she's either grumpy or sleepy."

"And that's new?" Jeannie glanced into the living room and could see Lex's head. "Let me guess. Right now, she's sleepy."

"I'm afraid so. She put off taking the meds until after Hubert and Ramona left for the day." Amanda's eyes softened as she looked at Lex. "I hate seeing her like this."

Jeannie rubbed her arm. "She's going to be okay. How are you doing? I can't even imagine taking care of two active girls, an infant, and a recuperating wife. You've got my utmost respect, little sister."

"Thanks. But I've got a lot of help. Martha and Charlie usually kidnap Eddie, and I don't get to see him until lunch. Then we have lunch together, and they usually stay and visit." Amanda tugged Jeannie's arm. "Come on. Lex will be out for a while. Let's get some coffee in the kitchen."

"Sounds good to me."

Amanda prepared two mugs of coffee and set one in front of her at the table.

"This may sound crazy," Jeannie said, "but you really seem comfortable here."

"Don't you think I should? I've lived here for over twelve years." Amanda sat across from Jeannie. "What makes you think I wouldn't?"

"No, no. I didn't say that right. What I meant was, I've always seen you as someone in an office. But now, you seem perfectly content to stay at home, raise your kids, and live your life."

Amanda nodded. "Yeah, it's been a bit of an adjustment for me, that's for sure. At first, I felt almost cheated because we closed the office. But it didn't take me long to realize that I really wanted to spend more time with my family. The girls are growing so fast and I don't want to miss a moment of it. And now, with Eddie, I can actually be a stay-at-home mom full-time. Even with Mel, I worked half-days once she was six months old. And as she got older, I worked even more. And when I got home, I was so busy being some kind of super mom, I had a tendency to neglect the most important person in my life."

"I can't imagine Lex giving you a hard time about working, though," Jeannie said. "She's got such a strong work ethic."

"No, she didn't." Amanda smiled fondly. "She wouldn't. But it had gotten to the point that the only time we'd see each other was at the dinner table with the kids. Then, once we'd get the girls to bed, we'd both collapse and fall right to sleep. Even though I was lying right beside her I missed her."

Jeannie wiped away a tear. "You two should be considered illegal. I've never seen two people so much in love."

"We are. It seems like every day I fall even deeper in love with her."

A shuffling at the door caused Amanda to look up. "Lex, what are you doing?"

Lex stood in the doorway, propped on crutches. "Hey, Jeannie. How are you doing?"

"I'm fine, the baby's growing, I'm eating, and poor Rodney has to run out in the middle of the night to fetch my latest craving." Jeannie pushed a chair away from the table. "Why don't you come join us?"

"Are you sure I'm not interrupting anything?"

Jeannie patted the chair. "Not in the least. As a matter of fact, I came to visit you. Come sit by me, cutie."

Lex blushed, but worked her way into the kitchen. She lowered slowly into the chair and put the crutches on the floor beside her. "One of these days Amanda's going to think something's going on between us, if you keep that up."

"So?"

Amanda took one look at Lex before she stood and picked up a coffee cake off the counter. She gathered plates and forks, and brought everything over to the table. In no time at all, she had served all of them a decent-sized piece. She poured Lex a glass of milk and returned to her chair. "You need to get something into your stomach, honey."

"Yeah, I know. Those damned pills always make me wake up nauseous." Lex picked at the coffee cake, before finally taking a small bite.

Jeannie scooted closer and rubbed Lex's shoulder. "Maybe you stole my morning sickness. I had it for about a week, and then it disappeared."

"God, I hope not." Lex gave her a crooked grin. "I lucked out when Amanda was pregnant. Didn't get sick or the weird cravings. But I did buy a lot of strange things when I was in town, just on the off chance she'd want them later."

Amanda came close to spitting her coffee across the table. "Martha was afraid you were craving those things. I think it freaked her out a little to think of you setting foot in a grocery store without being threatened first."

"She even tried to take my temperature, the first time I came home with several grocery bags," Lex added, much to Jeannie's amusement.

"Well, Slim, you have to admit, you've always acted like you were allergic to any kind of shopping."

Lex shrugged. "I tried to be prepared."

"Want to come home with me? Rodney's been good, but I think I'd like to be spoiled."

Amanda started to choke on her coffee cake. When she was finally able to take a breath, she glared at her sister. "You've been spoiled your entire life, Jeannie Louise. So don't try and tell us any different."

Jeannie stuck her tongue out at Amanda. "Turd."

"Spoiled brat."

"Ladies, please," Lex said. "Let's not resort to name calling."

Both sisters started laughing. Their favorite pastime was teasing each other.

Jeannie flicked a piece of pecan from her cake at Lex. "Who are you calling a lady?"

Lex flinched as the nut bounced off her cheek. "Not you, obviously." But she couldn't help but smile at their silliness. "You'd better not make a mess in here. Amanda's worse than Martha when it comes to the kitchen."

"Really?" Jeannie looked at Amanda. "My sister? The girl who used to get hives at the thought of cleaning?"

Amanda dropped her fork onto the plate. "I was ten, for god's sake. What ten-year-old likes to clean?"

"Pfft." Jeannie waved her hand in a dismissive motion.

"I swear, sometimes I wish I'd been an only child," Amanda grumbled.

"Yeah, right. Then whose bed would you have invaded every time you thought you saw the boogeyman? Hmm?" Jeannie turned to Lex. "Does she stick her cold feet on your legs in the middle of the night?"

Lex nodded. "All the damned time." Another piece of cake bounced off her shirt. "Hey."

Amanda pointed her fork at Lex. "My cold feet will find somewhere else to sleep, if you're not careful."

"Oh yeah?"

"Yeah." Amanda appeared quite pleased with herself, until a rather large piece of cake hit her forehead. "Lexington!"

Ten minutes later, Martha came into the kitchen, where she saw three laughing women and chunks of coffee cake all over the kitchen. "What on earth has been going on around here?"

The room turned silent, as all three pointed to each other, laying the blame. They looked at the peeved glare on Martha's face, then at each other, and proceeded to laugh even harder.

TUESDAY EVENING, LEX lay on the sofa, while the girls were playing a game on the coffee table. Amanda had taken Eddie upstairs for a bath, and Hubert and Ramona were next door at Martha's. So, she drew the short straw and was left with two rambunctious girls.

"There!" Melanie placed her game piece on the final square. "I win."

"No, you don't." Lorrie moved Melanie's piece to its original spot. "It wasn't your turn."

Melanie took the piece and slammed it on the final square. "I won!"

Lorrie rolled her eyes. "That's cheating." She petted Freckles, who loyally sat next to her.

"Girls, behave." Lex closed her eyes and tried to ignore the pain in her back. She was long overdue for her medication, but hated to take it because it made her so sleepy.

"Lorrie, stop that!" Melanie grabbed her game piece. "I won, and you lost."

"No, you didn't. You're cheating." Lorrie's voice started to rise.

Freckles began to bark, adding to the noise.

"Am not!"

Lorrie tried to wrestle the game piece away from her sister. "Are too! Gimme!"

"Nooooo!" Melanie rolled onto the floor and started to kick at Lorrie. "Stop it! I won!"

Now Freckles was barking and dancing around the squabbling children, enjoying the game.

"Did not!"

"Did too!"

Lex had heard enough. "Damn it! You two, cut it out!" She quickly sat up and immediately regretted the action. Her hands went to her back. "Fuck!"

At Lex's raised voice, Freckles stopped barking and ran out of the room.

"Oooh, Momma. That's a bad word," Melanie said.

"I don't care," Lex yelled. "If you two can't play nice, then don't play at all. Put the game away, right now."

Melanie's lower lip began to quiver. "But I was winning."

"No, you wasn't. You were cheating," Lorrie said.

"Shut up! Both of you," Lex snapped. At the sound of both girls crying, she realized what she had done. "Damn. I'm sorry, girls."

Melanie was openly sobbing, and Lorrie kept trying to wipe her own tears away with the sleeve of her shirt.

"Come here," Lex asked, in a softer voice. When neither girl moved, she edged off the sofa and landed painfully on her knees. With a grimace, she held out her arms. "Please, come here." Her arms were filled with crying girls, and soon Lex was crying, too. "I'm so sorry, girls. Please forgive me."

Amanda came into the room and saw the three on the floor. "What's going on?"

Lorrie pulled away from Lex. "We made Momma mad and she yelled."

"I didn't mean to," Lex choked out. "I'm sorry." She held both girls tightly.

"I thought I heard something." Amanda came around the sofa and put her hand on Lex's head. "Girls, why don't you go upstairs and wash your faces? I'll be up in a few minutes, okay?"

Lex kissed each girl and whispered more apologies before she allowed them to leave. She stood on her knees with tears trailing down her face. "I can't believe I did that."

"Oh, honey." Amanda helped Lex up. "Those two would try the patience of Job. I've snapped at them a few times, myself."

"I made them cry," Lex said. "I yelled, cursed and told them to shut up." She wiped her face with her hand and leaned heavily against Amanda. "I'm a horrible parent."

Amanda shook her head and chuckled. "Honey, if we were considered bad parents every time we made one of them cry, we'd have been locked up a long time ago. Don't sweat it. I guarantee that by tomorrow, they'll have forgotten all about it." She held Lex close. "Your back's killing you, isn't it?"

"Yeah. But that's no excuse."

"Uh-huh. And when was the last time you took anything for it?" Amanda asked, as they slowly walked out of the room together.

Lex limped along beside her. "I don't remember."

"Right. And you were watching the girls without any medicinal aid? Honey, that's crazy." Amanda patted Lex on the hip. "Let's go upstairs and get you ready for bed. The girls are so rambunctious because of the pie they had earlier. I'll ask Hubert and Ramona to play with them when they come home. Might as well enjoy the built-in babysitting while we can."

"You're evil." Lex kissed the top of Amanda's head. "One of the many reasons I married you."

LORRIE STACKED SEVERAL game boxes on the kitchen table. "I really like my new room color, Uncle Hubert. Thanks for helping us paint the other day."

"Sure. It was fun, wasn't it, Ramona?"

Ramona nodded. "I enjoyed it, too."

"Uncle Hubert, how come you don't live here no more?" Melanie asked. They were gathered around the kitchen table, with several games stacked to one side.

Hubert looked at Ramona. "Uh, well, I had some business in Oklahoma, and when I met Ramona, I decided to make it my home."

"But you lived here for a long time, too, right?" Melanie asked.

"That's right. Why?"

Melanie got off her chair and proceeded to crawl into Hubert's lap. "I think you're nice. Were you sad when you moved away from home?"

"Uh—"

"I don't want to ever live away from home. I love Momma, Mommy and Lorrie. And Eddie."

Lorrie opened a game box and set out the pieces. "When you grow up and get married, you'll have to live somewhere else. That's what grownups do. Right, Uncle Hubert?"

"Usually, yes." Hubert smiled at Ramona when Melanie snuggled closer and put her arms around his neck.

"But Momma said that this is the only house she's ever lived in. Did you live here, too?" Lorrie asked.

Hubert nodded. "When I was younger, yes I did. But after I graduated from high school, I went away for college, and then moved into my own place."

"Aunt Ramona, do you live with your family?" Melanie asked.

"We're in the same city as my father, but I live with your Uncle Hubert." Ramona helped Lorrie set up the Sorry game. She accepted the green game piece and placed it on the board. "Thank you."

Lorrie grinned at her. "You said you liked the green one, right?"

"I did."

"Cool." Lorrie passed out colored game-pieces to everyone. "Uncle Hubert, how come Momma never told us about you? We didn't even know she had a brother, until Eddie came to live with us."

Hubert's smile faded, as he remembered past events. "I wasn't a very nice person, Lorrie. I'm sure your moms didn't talk about me because they're too nice to say bad things about people."

Ramona put her hand on his shoulder for support. "The important thing is that now we're all together, and happy. Right?"

"Yeah," Hubert said, his voice gruff with emotion.

Lorrie still had questions. "Do you like kids, Uncle Hubert?"

"Sure."

"Then how come you didn't want Eddie? Was he bad?"

Hubert scooted away from the table and held out his free arm to Lorrie. "Come here, sweetheart. Let's talk about this."

Lorrie quickly moved from her chair to his lap. "Okay."

"Remember when I told you I wasn't a very nice guy? Well, I'll always worry that I'll be that guy again. And I loved Eddie so much that I wanted him to have the best home he could. I knew that your parents would raise him right, giving him all the love in the world." He kissed each girl on the forehead. "Besides, he needed big sisters to take care of him. Who's better than you two?"

Lorrie turned to Ramona. "Didn't you want babies?"

"Oh, sweetie. I love children, especially the ones living in this house," Ramona said, a little sad. "But your Uncle Hubert and I are too old. It wouldn't be fair to the child to have parents who couldn't do everything with them. Don't you agree?"

"I guess. But you'll come and visit us and Eddie a lot, won't you?"

Ramona looked at Hubert, whose eyes glistened with lost opportunities. "You'll get tired of seeing us, we'll be here so often," she promised.

ELLIE YAWNED AS she walked down the quiet hallway. She had agreed to work late this Thursday morning to help out a coworker, but the slow-moving clock made her regret her kindness. She saw a solitary figure in the waiting room and thought her tired eyes were deceiving her. "Amanda?"

Amanda's head lifted, and a wan smile crossed her face. "Ellie? What are you doing here this time of morning?"

"Splitting a shift with a coworker. Why are you here? Is it Lex?"

"We got a call last night from the orthopedic surgeon. He wanted Lex to get the MRI done before coming into his office on Monday. So, here we are." Amanda lowered her head and brushed her fingers through her hair. "I managed to get Hubert and Ramona to stay home and help Martha get the girls off to school. But I'm really glad to see a friendly face."

Ellie sat next to Amanda and put her arm around her in a comforting gesture. "I'm glad I came this way for my break. How long has Lex been in there?"

"Seems like hours." Amanda checked her watch. "About forty-five minutes, though. I just hope she's not going crazy in there."

"She should be okay. This hospital has an open-bore MRI, so it's not as claustrophobic. I've talked to patients who said it's not bad at all."

Amanda sighed. "I hope so. She's really not taking this whole thing very well."

"What do you mean?"

"Have you ever known Lex to sit still for very long? She's been, as she put it, 'under house arrest,' since she returned from Oklahoma. As much as she loves the kids, they're really starting to get on her nerves."

Ellie gave her a one-armed hug. "Hang in there. It's going to get better. Has she made any progress at all?"

"Not much. Her leg and back are still causing her a lot of pain, even with lying around all the time. What if they end up having to do surgery? It scares me to death to think about that."

"Let me talk to some of the surgeons around here, and see what's involved if it comes to that. Don't start worrying about it until you have to. I know that's easier said than done, but you'll be better off." Ellie checked her watch. "I'm going to call the charge nurse and see if I can wait here with you. Be right back."

Amanda caught Ellie's arm. "You don't have to. I don't want you to get into any trouble."

"It's no trouble. Besides, I don't really care for the attitudes in this place. I plan on job hunting again as soon as I can." Ellie hurried down the hall to the nearest phone.

Before Amanda could respond, the double doors at the end of the hall swung open and Lex came out on her crutches. Amanda jumped up and met her halfway. "How did it go?"

"Okay. Can we get out of here?" Lex leaned heavily on the crutches, a defeated look on her face.

"Sure, love. Let me run tell Ellie."

Lex perked up a little. "Ellie was here?"

"Yes. She saw me waiting and was going to sit with me until you got here." Amanda noticed movement down the hall. "Here she comes."

Ellie joined them, carrying a denim jacket. "Hey, cuz. I thought you'd be in there longer." She patted Lex gently on the shoulder. "You guys up for breakfast? I got cut loose early."

"Sounds good to me. Amanda? What about you?" Lex asked, suddenly much more animated.

"Sure." Amanda picked up their coats from a waiting room chair and followed them down the hall.

Once they were outside, Ellie pointed to a far-away parking lot. "I'm over there, so I guess I'll meet you someplace. Any ideas?"

Amanda tugged on the arm of Ellie's jacket. "How about you get in and ride with us? We can take you over to your car, and discuss breakfast options on the way."

"Might as well do as she says, El. I know from experience how pointless it is to try and argue with my better half," Lex teased.

"All right. I didn't feel like a hike in this cold wind, anyway." Ellie flipped the collar up on her denim jacket and shivered.

Amanda stuck her tongue out at Lex, but led the way to where she had parked her vehicle. "Is there someplace nearby to eat? Or should we just head back to Somerville?"

Ellie quickly climbed in the back and closed her door. "Honestly, I haven't bothered looking around here for anything. I usually just go to work and back. Drop me off at my car, and I'll meet you at the diner in Somerville."

Once Lex was settled, Amanda started the vehicle. "Sounds like a plan." She followed Ellie's directions, and they were soon parked beside the silver Corolla. "Don't you have a warmer coat?"

"I've never needed one, since I'm rarely outside. I've got a blanket I keep in the car to cover my legs, so I don't freeze before the heater warms up. I'll be fine." Ellie got out of the SUV. "See you in a few." She closed the door and unlocked her car, waving once she was inside.

Lex looked at Amanda. "Are you thinking what I'm thinking?"

"Definitely. At least we know what to get little miss stubborn for Christmas." Amanda waited until Ellie drove away, then followed her. "Not like that's a surprise."

"What do you mean?"

Amanda laughed. "Stubborn runs in the family." She kept her eyes on Ellie's car and was surprised by the small pinch on the leg she received. "Hey."

"Runs in the family, huh?" Lex asked. She tapped her chin, as if in deep thought. "You know, I do believe you're right. And it started about twelve years ago."

Without taking her eyes off the road, Amanda delivered a perfect slap to Lex's arm. "Smartass."

THE BOOTH SEAT was lumpy, the coffee like mud, and her breakfast plate was chipped. Lex ignored the pain she was in and enjoyed the old diner, as well as the two women with her. She looked closely at Ellie. "Hey, El?"

Ellie looked up from her own breakfast. "Yeah?"

"Did you do something different with your hair?" Lex squinted. "A haircut, or something?"

"Um." Ellie looked embarrassed. "Yeah. I got it cut and a little color added to it yesterday. Does it look okay?"

Lex nodded. "Looks great. Doesn't it, Amanda?"

Amanda stifled a laugh. "Sure does. Is there any reason you got your hair done, Ellie?"

"No! I mean, not really. I just felt like a change." Ellie wiped her mouth with her napkin. "I need to run to the restroom. Be right back." She slid out of the booth and left in a hurry.

"What's up with her?" Lex asked.

Amanda took a sip of her coffee. "Has she talked to you about her new neighbors?"

"Only the day you two came back from finding the place. Is there something else?"

"One of the roommates is a woman. They met last week when Ellie went over for the house inspection." Amanda put her hand on Lex's. "I think Ellie likes her, but I don't want you to tease her about it, okay? I think I did that enough when I found out."

Lex's lower lip stuck out. "You're no fun."

"Promise to behave?"

"Only for a little while. Then, all promises are off." Lex watched as Ellie came from the restroom. "This isn't going to be easy."

Amanda patted her thigh. "Shhh."

Ellie sat and gave Lex a funny look. "What?"

"What, what?" Lex answered.

"You look like you're up to something," Ellie accused.

Lex shook her head. "Nope."

Ellie turned to Amanda, who had trouble looking her in the eye. "You didn't."

"What?"

"You told her."

Amanda tried her best to look innocent. "Told who, what?"

"Her. About Kyle."

Lex looked from Amanda to Ellie. "Kyle? Who's he?"

Ellie sighed. "It's okay. Kyle's the woman who lives next door. I met her last week."

"Oh." Lex shrugged. "Is she cute?"

"No, I mean, yes, I, uh." Ellie bit her lip. "She's different, but in a good kind of way." Her face turned pink. "She's really nice."

"Ah. I see." Lex speared a piece of sausage and popped it into her mouth. "What does she do?"

Ellie began to fiddle with her coffee, swirling a spoon around the half-empty mug. "She's a mechanic, who also likes to restore old cars in her spare time. She doesn't like to go out much, and her roommates are always teasing her about that."

"Sounds okay to me." Lex put her fork down. "How old is she?"

Ellie stared at her own plate. "I'm not sure, but I think she's in her early thirties. She doesn't seem that old."

Although tempted to tease Ellie, Lex decided to play it safe. "Sounds like a good thing, having a mechanic that lives next door. Especially with that old car you drive."

Relieved that the conversation was heading toward a different topic, Ellie nodded. "My car's fine. It's just temperamental, that's all."

"Uh-huh. Sure." Lex waved to the waitress, Francine, for coffee refills.

Francine immediately arrived with a full pot of coffee. "Hey, ladies. How's the kids?" she asked, as she refilled everyone's cup.

"They're doing great," Amanda said. "Growing too fast, though."

"Ain't that always the way," Francine said. "Y'all take care, you hear?"

Lex nodded. "Thanks, Francine. You, too." Once the waitress was out of range, she turned to Ellie. "Now, what were you saying?"

"I was going to ask if you two would mind coming over to the old house, and see if there's any furniture that you want. Otherwise, I thought I'd see if Jeannie and Rodney wanted it."

Amanda stirred sweetener and creamer into her coffee. "You don't want it?"

"Only a few things. My bedroom furniture, the kitchen table, and maybe one of the sofas. I want to get a few new things, too." Ellie looked at Lex. "Is that okay?"

"You're asking me? Ellie, it's your house and your stuff. Of course it's okay."

Ellie rubbed one of her eyes and took a cleansing breath. "I thought you might want some of Grandpa's furniture."

"Ellie," Lex reached across the table and covered her cousin's hand with hers, "you gave me the greatest thing in the world when you passed along that quilt. Besides, if Jeannie and Rodney have the furniture, it's still in the family, right?"

"Right." Ellie squeezed Lex's hand. "Whatever they don't want, let's donate. Are you okay with that?"

"Yep." Lex winked. "Now, tell us more about this Kyle person. I want to know if I need to go have a talk with her."

Ellie's eyes widened. "You wouldn't dare."

"It'll be good practice for when our girls get older. Gotta see what her intentions toward you are, right?"

"B, bu, but, Lex, you—"

Lex laughed. "No more secrets from me, right?"

Ellie growled and threw a piece of toast at Lex, who caught it and took a bite.

"Thanks. I was still hungry."

Amanda shook her head and covered her face, as the two women laughed loud enough to draw attention to their booth. "I can't take you two anywhere."

"Sure you can," Lex helpfully answered. "As long as you don't mind having a little fun, right, El?"

"Right." Ellie wiped her mouth and put her napkin on her plate.

Chapter Nineteen

LEX ANGRILY SLAMMED her door after she got into the SUV. "We had to pay how much to hear that shit? Hell, I could have saved us money, time and aggravation by staying at home."

It was mid-afternoon on Monday and Lex's mood was not helped by the hour and a half doctor's visit. "I tried telling that quack that my leg doesn't hurt anymore, so I don't understand why he insisted on twisting me like a demented pretzel."

"Honey, please. No one was happier than me when you woke up yesterday pain-free. But we already had the appointment and didn't have time to cancel." Amanda bit her lip to keep from smiling at Lex's pout. "Besides, wasn't it worth it to hear that you're going to be okay without surgery?"

Lex sighed, but didn't comment. She glared through the windshield, focusing on nothing in particular.

Amanda started the engine and backed out of the parking space. "I know you want to go back to work, but another couple of weeks of taking it easy won't kill you."

"Hrumph."

"Is there really that much to do around the ranch right now?"

Lex turned her head toward Amanda. "That's not the point."

Fed up with Lex's attitude, Amanda slammed her hands down on the steering wheel. "That's exactly the point! You've got well-trained men working for you, and the only problem is your damned stubborn pride." So mad she could barely think, Amanda immediately parked in the nearest lot. Once the Expedition stopped, she unbuckled her seatbelt and turned toward Lex. "I know it's been hard for you, being cooped up in the house. But do you have any idea what the alternative would have been? I've researched it, so I do. And the last thing I wanted to do was see you having surgery on your back."

"Amanda—"

"Shut up." Amanda took a deep breath. "When that horse kicked you, it could have been so much worse. Paralysis, to start with. Did you hear me?" Amanda's voice continued to rise. "Paralysis! And if that damned beast had hit you higher, it could have fucking killed you! And you're upset because you have to rest for a few weeks? Get over it."

Lex blinked a few times. It had been a long time since she'd seen Amanda so angry. "Um, sweetheart?"

"What?" Amanda yelled.

"I'm sorry."

"You, but," Amanda stammered. "Why do you do that?"

"What?"

Holding out her hand, Amanda waited until Lex took it. "Ruin a perfectly good pissed off."

Lex laughed and tugged Amanda across the console and into her lap. "Self-defense." She nibbled on her wife's neck. "We've got some time to kill before we can pick the girls up at school. You want to go park someplace secluded and fool around?"

"Probably a better idea than getting caught here in the parking lot of the Baptist Church." Amanda stole a quick kiss and moved to her side of the SUV.

LORRIE OPENED THE door for Melanie, and waited patiently while she got in. She heard Melanie exclaim happily and hurried in behind her to see what caused the outburst. "Momma! Are you not grounded no more?"

"She still has to behave herself," Amanda said. "No riding for a few more weeks and no lifting or too much bending. But Momma's going to be fine."

"That's awesome." Lorrie fastened her seatbelt and squirmed to get comfortable. "Where's Eddie?"

Lex flipped her visor down and looked in the mirror at Lorrie. "You mean he's not back there with you?"

Melanie's eyes grew large. "Did you lose him?"

"Behave," Amanda said, slapping Lex on the arm. "Your Aunt Ramona and Uncle Hubert wanted to keep him while we went to the doctor."

Lorrie put her hands on her hips in an uncanny impression of Amanda. "I don't want them to go home tomorrow. Why can't they stay?"

"They have their own home to go to, honey. But they promised to come and visit." Amanda pulled away from the curb. "Should we take pizza home tonight?"

Both girls cheered their agreement.

After a stop at the local pizza shop, the grocery store for everyone's chosen ice cream and Lex's new prescription, the family headed for the ranch.

Melanie took her favorite book out of her backpack and read quietly to herself, while Lorrie stared solemnly out the window.

Although she enjoyed the silence, Amanda couldn't help but be worried about their oldest. "Lorrie, is something wrong?"

Lorrie shrugged, but kept quiet.

"Just what we need," Amanda said softly, so only Lex could hear, "another you."

Lex shook her head, but grinned. "Lorrie?"

"Yes, ma'am?"

"What's bothering you?"

"Jerry's back in school," Lorrie said.

Lex started to turn around, but the twinge in her back stopped her. "Is he picking on you again?"

"No. He's been real quiet, but he told Joey his gramma won't tol'rate him gettin' into trouble no more." She sighed. "But I still don't like him."

Amanda glanced in the rearview mirror. "His grandmother? What about his mother?"

"I dunno. Joey said that Jerry had to live with his gramma now."

Amanda didn't want to discount her daughter's feelings, but also didn't want her harboring bad thoughts. "Lorrie, I know you've had trouble with Jerry in the past, but try and be nice, okay? Maybe he's lonely and needs a friend."

Lorrie frowned and wrinkled her nose, but wisely kept silent.

Melanie put down her book. "Can Uncle Hubert and Aunt Ramona live with us?"

The subject change caused both parents to do a double-take. Lex was the first to recover. "No, sweetheart. They live in Oklahoma."

"But, maybe they live there 'cause they don't live here."

Lex looked at Amanda, who shrugged. "Okay, what?"

Melanie rolled her eyes as if her parents were idiots. "I asked Uncle Hubert, and he said they have to live in Okleyhome 'cause that's where their house is. But if they had a house here, they could live here. Can't they stay in our house? I'll share my room with them."

Amanda bit her lip to withhold her laughter. "Go ahead, Momma."

"Thanks a lot." Lex scratched the back of her neck in a nervous gesture. "Um, okay. Do you like spending the night at your grandparents' house?"

"Uh-huh. It's a lot of fun."

"How would you feel if they wanted you to stay there all the time?" Lex asked.

Melanie frowned. "But I live with you."

Lex nodded. "Why wouldn't you want to stay with them?"

"'cause I'd miss you and Mommy." Melanie pointed to Lorrie. "And Lorrie, and Eddie and all my toys."

"Yep. At home is where all your stuff is, and everyone else who loves you, right?"

Lorrie nodded. "Aunt Ramona would miss her daddy, and Uncle Hubert has a job in Oklahoma. Right, Momma?"

"That's right. Just like you don't want to be without your family, neither does Aunt Ramona and Uncle Hubert." Lex felt proud of herself until Melanie asked one final question.

"But aren't we their family, too?"

Amanda snickered. "She's got you there."

"Shhh," Lex ordered. She turned her head so she could see Melanie, who sat in the seat behind Amanda. "Let's just say that they like where they live, and leave it at that, okay? Maybe someday they'll change their mind."

"Cheater," Amanda whispered.

"Brat," Lex said, just as quietly. She felt like cheering when Amanda turned onto the familiar graveled road. "Thank god."

"Bwawk, bwawk," Amanda teased.

Lex pointed a finger at her. "Keep it up, woman."

Amanda checked the rearview mirror, pleased to see the girls' attention elsewhere. She stuck her tongue out at Lex.

"That's so mature." But Lex was smiling. "Wait 'til we get home."

HUBBERT HUMMED A lullaby as he gently rocked a fussy Eddie in his arms. They were alone in the living room, since Hubert had convinced Ramona to spend the afternoon drinking coffee at Martha's. "Sssh, little man. Don't cry." He tried to get the baby to take his pacifier. After a moment, Eddie accepted the pacifier and settled down. "See? Daddy made it all right."

"Daddy?" Ramona asked, as she stepped into the living room and sat next to him. "Are you having second thoughts?"

"No, of course not. It was just a slip of the tongue."

Ramona edged closer and caressed the baby's head. "It's a little late, anyway. We filed the signed papers last week." She smiled when Hubert passed Eddie over to her.

"I know. Really, I'm fine with him being here." But Hubert couldn't take his eyes off his son.

"Honey, if you truly want a child—"

"No. We've discussed this, and you're right. Neither one of us is really up to the task of raising a kid. He's a lot better off here, with two loving parents and a pair of sisters who adore him."

"But you're going to miss him, aren't you?"

"Yeah. More than I ever expected." Hubert cleared his throat. "I'm going to miss those two crazy girls, too. I never thought I'd enjoy being Uncle Hubert."

Ramona leaned into him and put her head on his shoulder. "I know what you mean. All three of these kids quickly worked their way into my heart, and I didn't even like kids before."

He laughed. As tough as Ramona talked, Hubert knew she was a softy. "I wish I still had my old place here. Then we'd have somewhere to stay when we visited."

"Have you ever thought about going back to bookkeeping?"

"Nah. Who wants an ex-con as an accountant?" Hubert sighed. "But I do miss it."

The back door opened and two pairs of feet ran down the hall.

"No running in the house," Amanda yelled after them.

Ramona turned her head and saw the girls. "How was school today?"

Melanie was the first to come around the sofa. "Hi! We made Christmas trees out of tree cones," she said proudly.

"Tree cones?" Hubert asked.

Lorrie sat beside Hubert. "Pine cones."

"Ah." Hubert smiled when Melanie crawled up into his lap. "What else did you do today?"

"Me and Ray kicked the ball, but then we had to line up for cal, cala, um, jumping jacks and stuff. And when we all yelled, it was loud inside." She placed her head over Hubert's heart and relaxed. "You smell nice, Uncle Hubert."

He blushed and chuckled. "Thanks. Aunt Ramona picked out my cologne. Why were you yelling inside? Didn't you get into trouble?"

"Nope. We was in the gym, 'cause it's too cold to go outside and play. The older kids get to play basketball, but we're too small."

Lorrie sat on the arm of the sofa beside Ramona and looked at the sleeping Eddie. "And if you come over where we're playing basketball, you little kids always get hurt. I'd let you play, though."

Melanie looked at Lorrie with something akin to hero worship. "You'd help me win?"

"I'd show you how to throw the basketball right," Lorrie said. "Maybe when it gets warmer, we can put a basketball goal on the barn."

Lex came slowly into the room, relying only on a cane. "Maybe on the garage. Not the barn." She sat in the overstuffed loveseat perpendicular to the sofa. "Does this mean you're giving up softball?"

"Uh-uh. Softball's in the spring, basketball's when it's too cold to play outside."

Ramona laughed. "What do you do in the summer, Lorrie?"

"Everything," Lorrie said emphatically. "Right, Momma?"

Amanda joined the family and sat beside Lex. "That's the truth. I like the slower pace of winter, myself."

"I don't blame you in the least," Ramona said.

Lorrie's one-track mind would not be deterred. "Momma? Since it's cold outside, can we put a basketball goal in the hay barn? It's big enough."

"Where would we put the hay, lil' bit?"

"Um, upstairs in the barn?"

Lex shook her head. "You want me to go upstairs every time I need a bale of hay, just so you can play basketball inside?"

"Yes?" Lorrie gave her a hopeful look.

"Sorry, kiddo. That's not going to happen. But we'll see about pouring a concrete pad this spring beside the garage, how's that?"

Lorrie grinned and moved to sit on the arm of the loveseat next to Lex. "Awesome." She carefully put her arm around Lex's neck. "Is this okay, Momma?"

"It's perfect."

Hubert watched Lorrie snuggle as close to Lex as she could. He exchanged looks with Ramona and gave her a slight nod, acknowledging once and for all that his son was in the best hands.

"Uncle Hubert?" Melanie said, "Will you ever change your mind about living here?"

Not used to the lightning fast way a child's mind worked, Hubert was caught off-guard. "Um, what?"

"Momma said that you live in Okleyhome 'cause that's where your house is. Didn't you have a house here?"

"Uh—"

"If you had a house here, you'd live here, right? And you said the other day you had a house here before. So why did you move away?"

"Mel, that's enough. Uncle Hubert and Aunt Ramona live in Oklahoma, and that's that."

Hubert held up his hand. "It's okay, Lex." He shifted Melanie on his knee so he could see her face. "A few years ago I did some stupid things." He silently conveyed his regrets to Lex and Amanda with his eyes. "I had a house here, but because I was selfish and mean, I lost it. Then I traveled to Oklahoma. For once I was innocent, but couldn't prove it. So I spent a few years in jail to pay for someone else's mistake."

"You were in jail?" Lorrie asked, surprised.

"Yes, I was. And even though I didn't do what they said I did, I pretty much deserved it, anyway. When I got out, I met your Aunt Ramona and she helped me start my life over."

"Wow," Lorrie said. "Did you kill someone?"

"No. The police found a packet of drugs in my car. Someone had tossed them in when I wasn't looking. I've been a bad man, but I've never done drugs."

Melanie got off his lap and went to sit by Amanda. "Why were you bad?"

Hubert sighed. "I don't know. I used to believe it was because I was jealous. But I think that's just an excuse." He brushed his hand over his beard. "I thought people would respect me if I acted a certain way, but they didn't." He lowered his gaze, unable to look anyone in the eyes.

Ramona put her hand on Hubert's leg in an attempt to console him. "You've changed, sweetheart. Being here is proof of that."

Amanda stood. "Hey, girls, how about helping me set the table for dinner? We brought pizza, remember?"

"Yay!" Melanie started to follow her mother and sister, but stopped and walked over to Hubert. "I don't think you're a bad man, Uncle Hubert." She crawled onto the sofa and kissed him on the cheek. "I love you."

Hubert blinked in surprise. "Love you too, sweetheart." His voice broke on the last word, but his smile was bright.

Once Amanda and the girls left, Lex cleared her throat. "You didn't lose your house," she said quietly.

"What?" Hubert asked, his own voice still hoarse from emotion.

"I said, you didn't lose your house." Lex got up and went into the office. A moment later, she returned with an envelope, which she handed to Hubert.

He opened the envelope and stared at the papers in his hand. "I don't understand."

"When I first found out that you'd left me your house with two mortgages, I told the bank to go ahead and foreclose. But after Amanda and I talked about it, I made an arrangement with them and paid the house off." Lex lowered herself onto the loveseat again. "God, it's been a long day."

"That's right. How did the doctor's visit go?" Ramona asked.

Lex sighed. "After being poked, prodded and twisted, the brilliant," her voice dripped with sarcasm, "surgeon decided that all I needed was more rest, and my back should heal okay on its own."

Hubert put the papers back in the envelope. "That's great news, sis." He waved the envelope. "Now, about this."

"Don't argue with me, Hubert. I don't even know what kind of condition the house is in. It's been vacant since you left town. We pay a guy to go over once a month and mow the yard, but that's about it."

"But, Lex. I can't accept this. Not after everything."

Lex shook her head. "Well, I sure as hell don't want it."

"Then why did you keep it?"

She shrugged, looking a lot like one of her kids. "I honestly don't know."

When Hubert opened his mouth, Ramona patted his leg. "The proper response is 'Thank you, Lex,'" she said gently.

Hubert blushed. "Uh, yeah. Thank you, Lex." He waggled a finger at her. "You should be more careful, though. Leave us a house and we might make good use of it, someday."

"Why do you think I gave you the key?" Lex asked.

He had no answer for that. Hubert looked at Ramona. "So, do you feel like taking a little drive?"

"I'd love to," Ramona answered.

WITH THE HOUSE finally quiet for the night and Eddie tucked away in his crib across the room, Amanda curled up in bed beside Lex. "God, I love this time of night."

"Me, too." Lex raised her left arm so Amanda could snuggle closer. "Ahhh. This is perfect."

"Yeah." Amanda closed her eyes. "Do you really think Hubert could move back and start up his old business again?"

Lex was quiet for a moment as she thought about the question.

"I mean, Somerville already has an accountant. And it's not like he's going to welcome Hubert back with open arms."

"Well, old Ted's getting up there in age. The last time I talked to him, he mentioned something about wanting to retire and raise a few head of cattle."

Amanda rolled so she could prop her head on her raised arm. "Really? And when was this?"

"Oh, I don't know. Maybe six months ago." Lex's mouth slowly curled up into a smile. "Why?"

"But, didn't you buy most of Ted's land a few years ago, when he was having financial trouble?"

"Yep."

The implications all came together for Amanda. "Do you think, if the right terms presented themselves, Ted would say, consider retiring and turning his accounting business over to someone else?"

"Hmm. You know, when you put it that way it makes sense. I wish I would have thought about that." Lex grunted when Amanda pinched her arm. "Hey."

"You are so busted, Ms. Smartypants." Amanda poked Lex in the ribs for good measure.

Lex captured Amanda's hand and held it close to her chest. "You keep poking me like that, you're gonna end up regretting it."

"Oh, yeah?"

"Yep." Lex brought Amanda's hand up to her lips and began to lightly kiss her knuckles and fingers.

Amanda moaned. "Lex."

"Uh-huh?"

"You'd better not," she gasped as soft lips hit a very sensitive spot on her wrist. "Oh, god."

Lex continued her careful assault. "Hmm?"

"What about your back?"

With a growl, Lex pulled Amanda over onto her. "What back?" She started to nip a path down Amanda's throat.

"Um, oh, yeah." Amanda raised her head as Lex ripped open her pajama top, causing buttons to scatter all over the bed. "Never mind."

THE FOLLOWING MORNING, breakfast was a somber affair. Both girls picked at their plates, doing their best to stall.

Lex realized what they were doing. "Melanie, Lorrie. You need to finish your breakfast. We have to leave for the bus in about ten minutes."

"But, Momma," Melanie said, "we want to stay until Uncle Hubert and Aunt Ramona leave. I want to say goodbye."

Lorrie nodded. "I don't want them to go." She gave her aunt and uncle her most pitiful look.

"Honey, we have to go home sometime." Ramona patted Lorrie's hand.

Amanda came into the kitchen with Eddie. "Why are you girls still at the table?"

The children looked up guiltily.

"Lex?" Amanda sat beside her. "They still need to get washed up so we can leave."

"I know. But—"

Amanda handed Eddie to Ramona. "Girls, take your plates to the sink right now and run upstairs."

Melanie frowned and shook her head. "I don't wanna go."

"Me either," Lorrie said.

The first sign that they were in trouble was when Amanda put her hands on her hips. "Girls."

"Nooo," both whined at once.

"One," Amanda began to count. No movement. "Two."

Melanie and Lorrie looked at each other.

"Three."

Eyes wide, both jumped from their chairs and grabbed their plates. "Four."

Dishes clattered in the sink, and two blurs raced from the room, a frisky Freckles not far behind.

Hubert covered his mouth to keep from laughing out loud. "What happens when you get to five?"

Amanda shrugged. "I don't know. I've never gotten that far."

Lex laughed. "And that's why you're in charge." She turned to Hubert. "I hate to sound like the kids, but I'm not ready for you to go."

"Honestly, sis, I'm feeling the same way." Hubert glanced at his fiancée, who nodded. "Ramona and I have talked about it and we're thinking about coming back."

"Really?" Lex grinned. "That would be great. If you want, I'll even let you take over the book work for the ranch. I'm sure it won't be long before you get even more clients."

Hubert held up his hand. "Hold on. We're only thinking about it right now. I've got a job with Ramona's father, and I don't want to let him down."

Amanda put her hand on Lex's shoulder. "We can certainly understand that. But I hope you realize that you're always welcome here, and we hope you decide to move home."

Ramona rocked Eddie. "If everything works out, we'd love to be close to watch your children grow up. Right, honey?"

"Definitely," Hubert said.

Lorrie and Melanie rushed into the room, their faces still wet. Melanie tugged on Amanda's sweater. "We're all done, Mommy. See?"

"Yes, I see." Amanda wiped at Melanie's face. "Give your aunt and uncle big hugs, so we can get going."

"Aw, Mommy." Melanie pouted and moved to cling to Hubert. "Uncle Hubert, do you really have to go?"

Hubert allowed one girl onto each knee. "We have jobs to get back to. But I promise," he embraced each child, "that Ramona and I will be back to visit. Now, give us each a big hug that will last, and we'll see you soon."

Amanda corralled the girls and guided them toward the back door. "When I get back, we'll head for the airport."

"Take your time." Ramona shifted Eddie to her shoulder. "I'm going to try and get my fill of this little guy."

Chapter Twenty

WITH A FRUSTRATED curse, Ellie flipped her cell phone closed. "Damn it! Now what am I going to do?" She looked around the living room, which was cluttered with packed moving boxes.

Now in full panic mode, Ellie called the one other person, besides her grandfather, who had always been there for her.

"Hello?"

Ellie took a deep breathe to calm herself. "Amanda? Hi. Sorry to bother you so early."

"It's no bother. I've already gotten the girls on the school bus. What's up?"

"My movers cancelled on me. Something about their truck being repossessed." Ellie rubbed her forehead, trying to fend off the impending headache. "Oh, god. Jeannie and Rodney's stuff will be here later this afternoon. I was hoping you had contacts with some movers or something, since you used to be in the real estate business. What am I going to do?"

"First thing you're going to do is sit down," Amanda said in her best mom-voice.

Ellie could hear another voice in the background.

"Hold on. Let me tell Lex what's happening."

Ellie groaned and sat on the cleanest available space, her grandfather's old sofa. "Damn, damn, damn. I knew I should have scheduled things differently," she mumbled.

A new voice came on the line. "Hey."

"Lex? This is a disaster. There's not enough room for my stuff and theirs, even if I started moving boxes to the garage. I guess I can try to fit some things in my car, but—"

"Hold on. Everything's going to be fine. You're not moving that much stuff, are you?"

"No, not really. Well, I mean, boxes, of course. Oh, and my bedroom furniture, and the smaller couch. Jeannie was excited about all the other stuff, so not much went to charity. Why?"

"Because, I can send Roy and the boys over with one of our hay trailers. It's nothing fancy, but they'll get you moved and set up in no time."

Ellie fell back against the sofa. "Oh, my god. You are my hero."

Lex laughed. "Let's not go overboard." There was muffled speaking for a moment, then she came back on the line. "Amanda's going with them to supervise, but I'll make her leave her whip at home. Ow! Um, hold on."

The sound of two of her favorite people playing with each other brought a smile to Ellie's face. She listened as Lex whined about being abused, and could clearly hear another slap.

"Damn it, woman, stop it," Lex growled.

Suddenly Amanda was on the phone. "Ellie?"

"Uh, yeah?" Ellie couldn't contain her giggles.

"The guys and I will be over shortly. I've got to get Martha over here to babysit."

In the background, Lex could be heard quite clearly. "I can take care of Eddie."

Amanda spoke to Ellie and Lex at the same time. "Not for Eddie, but for Lex. Otherwise, who knows what kind of trouble she'll get into. Hey!" Amanda sighed. "You might want to tell your cousin goodbye, Ellie."

"Why's that?"

"Because I'm going to kill her for throwing a wet dishtowel at my head. See you soon." The phone clattered as it was hung up.

Ellie closed her cell phone and emitted a loud belly laugh, picturing in her mind the chaos at the ranch house.

LEX LAY ON the sofa, a blanket over her legs and a scowl on her face. "Did Amanda put you up to this?" she asked the smirking woman on the chair opposite her.

"No, and for the record, neither did Martha," Helen said. "When Roy and the guys left for town, I didn't feel like being alone. Naturally, I thought perhaps you'd like some company." She brushed a strand of hair away from her eyes. "Do you want me to leave?"

Although she was grumpy, Lex didn't want to be alone. The house felt emptier after her brother and Ramona left earlier in the week. "No, of course not. Thanks for putting up with me."

"Well, it's a tough job, but I think I'm up to the task."

Lex's bad humor began to evaporate. "You sound like Martha." She picked up her cell phone from the coffee table and glanced at the screen. "I wonder how Eddie's doing?"

"Probably asleep, after you called Martha and woke him ten minutes ago." Helen stood. "Would you like more coffee, or maybe something to eat?"

"No, I'm fine. As it is, if I keep eating like I have been, I'll end up fat and lazy." Lex patted her stomach. "Amanda's been stuffing me like a prize heifer."

Helen laughed at the expression on Lex's face. "If you ask me, you needed it. Maybe she's trying to keep you from blowing away."

"Yeah, right." Lex glanced at the dog bed by the fireplace, where Freckles napped. "Maybe the dog has the right idea. She sleeps all day, gets up and plays with the kids, then goes to bed with them."

"How's she handling having a baby in the house?"

"She was curious, at first. But when Eddie started to cry, she high-tailed it to Lorrie's room and hid under the bed. I nearly dropped him, I was laughing so hard." Lex grinned. "She probably thinks he's a funny-smelling noise machine. Come to think of it, she didn't care much for Mel when we brought her home, either. At least until she was able to play with her."

Helen returned to her chair and took a sip of coffee. "No matter what you say, I'm going to make lunch for you. And you'd better eat every bite."

"I'll never turn down your cooking, Helen. As a matter of fact, I think—"

The sound of the house telephone ringing stopped Lex in mid-sentence. She flipped the blanket off her legs and slowly stood. "I'd better see who that is."

"Do you want me to get it for you?"

"Nah, I needed to stretch my legs anyway." Lex went into the office and picked up the phone. "Rocking W ranch, Lex Walters speaking. Yes, I am. Really? Um, sure. No, we used to. Well, yes. I can see how that would help. Let me speak with Amanda, and we'll let you know. Thanks for calling." She hung up the phone and returned to the living room.

"Is everything all right?" Helen asked.

Lex shrugged and sat on the sofa. "That was the music teacher at school. She said that Melanie has an aptitude for music, and asked if we had a piano at home. Seems like Mel's been tinkering with the one at school." She rubbed the back of her neck. "I had no idea."

"That's wonderful, isn't it?"

"I guess. I just never thought," Lex frowned. "I played piano when I was younger, and we had one in the sitting room years ago, before the house burned down and we remodeled."

Helen patted Lex on the leg. "Maybe she got it from you."

Lex adamantly shook her head. "That's not possible. She's Amanda's and an anonymous sperm donor's. Genetically, I have nothing to do with her."

"Hmm. That is rather interesting. Maybe genetics through osmosis," Helen joked.

"Maybe so. Anyway, the music teacher offered to give Mel private lessons, if we'd like. But I don't know. I guess I'll wait and see what Amanda thinks and if Mel's even interested."

Helen checked her watch. "Why don't you join me in the kitchen, while I whip us up something to eat? I'm sure we could talk Martha, Charlie and Eddie into joining us."

"Sounds good to me. No offense, but I'm getting kind of tired of this living room. Maybe after lunch we could take a short walk to the barn? If you're with me, I probably won't get into too much trouble."

"Why do I have the feeling I'm being set up?" Helen asked, as she walked with Lex out of the room. "You'd better behave, or we'll both have to answer to your wife."

"NO, NO. IF you put that chair on top of that box, you'll crush the glasses." Amanda climbed into the trailer and pointed to the writing on the top of the box. "What's wrong, Chet? You're usually more on top of things."

He blushed slightly. "I'm sorry, ma'am." He lowered his gaze. "I just can't help but think about what happened to the boss. If I had been paying better attention, she wouldn't have had to catch that dresser."

Amanda rolled her eyes. "Is that what's bothering you? Chet, it was an accident."

"I know, ma'am. But it was still my fault." He took off his baseball cap and wiped his brow with his sleeve. "I don't know why she keeps me around. I'm always screwing things up."

With a worried glance at the threatening sky, Amanda shook her head. "That was an accident. It could happen to anyone, and no matter what happened, I'm glad Lex was there to help." She squeezed his forearm. "Chet, when it comes to the ranch, Lex only hires and keeps the best. She's told me what a great job you've done training the horses. Don't let that little accident bring you down. She's doing better every day, and it's been a blessing in disguise."

Chet raised his head. "Really? How?"

"She was able to spend a lot of quality time with her brother when he was here. That's something she needed more than anything."

Roy came out of the house carrying a large box. "Are you taking a nap back there, Chet? We've only got a few more boxes to bring out."

"Uh, sorry, Roy." Chet placed his hat on his head and tipped the bill toward Amanda. "Thanks, ma'am." He jumped off the trailer and headed for the house.

"For the last time," Amanda yelled after him, "my name's Amanda, not ma'am!"

Roy laughed as he carefully stacked his box. "At least he's talking to you now. Remember how he used to just stammer and blush whenever you'd come into the room?"

"How could I forget? Lex used to tease me about it. It's a good thing we're almost finished. I don't like the looks of those clouds."

He looked up at the sky. "Yeah, I know what you mean. The forecast was for rain and sleet later this afternoon. They said with this storm system and several more coming after it, we should be breaking the drought this month. But I hope we'll be home before it gets too nasty."

"Me, too. At least it'll be faster bringing stuff inside. Ellie gets to have all the fun unpacking."

"You're not going to stay and put everything away?" Ellie teased, handing Roy a box. "What am I paying you for?"

Amanda hopped out of the trailer and dusted off her hands. "If you want help organizing, I'll send Martha over. She's forever rearranging the kitchen, although I don't think she realizes it."

"Does that bother you?" Ellie asked.

"Are you kidding? If it wasn't for her, I'd never be able to find anything. Lex and the girls usually help put the dishes away, if that gives you any idea."

Ellie laughed at the thought. "Lex helps in the kitchen? Now that I'd like to see. Do you help your wife, Roy?"

"Uh, well." Roy ignored the women's laughter. "I'll run see if Chet or Jack needs anything."

Amanda sat on the edge of the trailer next to Ellie. "How are you doing?" Earlier, she'd noticed Ellie's melancholy mood as things were being taken out of the house.

"I'm all right. All this is actually helping me move on. Now maybe I won't be expecting to see Grandpa around every doorway." Ellie's sigh was more of relief than anguish. "Thanks for coming to the rescue."

"That's what family's for." Amanda put her arm around Ellie's shoulder. "I think Travis would be very proud of you. He once told me that you were a gift to him, coming into his life when you did."

Ellie cleared her throat before she looked into Amanda's face. "Really?"

"Yes, he did. When I first met him, I could see how much he missed his wife and how hard it was for him to get through each day. But, having you and Lex in his life brought new joy to him." When Ellie began to softly cry on her shoulder, Amanda pulled her closer. "Don't discount the effect you've had on all our lives, Ellie. Our family is much richer for having you in it."

Sniffling, Ellie exhaled heavily. "Thanks." She stood and straightened her shoulders. "I think I'll do a quick run through and make sure we got everything. I'll meet you at the new place, okay?"

Amanda nodded. "Sure." She stood and brushed the dust from her jeans. "I wonder what Lex is up to?"

"OH, MY." HELEN touched the soft nose of the stallion. "I've seen you ride up on him, but being this close, he's magnificent."

Lex grinned at the look of pure joy on Helen's face. "You a horse person, Helen?"

Helen nodded. "I was born on a farm in Arkansas. Nothing like this ranch, but we had plenty of animals running around. My mother swore I was half equine."

"Would you like to ride him?"

Helen turned to Lex, her eyes bright with excitement. "Don't tease me."

"I'm not. He can be a handful, but he's not as wild as most stallions. Any time you want to ride, go right ahead."

"Next time Roy wants to go out checking fence, I may take you up on that. I'd love to see more of the ranch, and not in a truck." Helen kissed Thunder on the nose and grinned at Lex. "I've teased Roy that I married him to live out here. Sometimes I think he believes me."

Lex sat on a bale of hay and watched how Helen interacted with the horses. "Roy told me once he dreamed of having his own spread."

"We've talked about it." Helen took a brush and ducked into Stormy's stall. "But we decided neither one of us are young enough to put that much work into a place. Being here on your ranch is the next best thing."

"Are you sure? I'd hate to hold y'all back from having what you want."

Helen stopped brushing Stormy, stepped from the stall and joined Lex on the hay bale. "Lex, you'd have to kick both of us off the ranch in order to get us to leave. We love it here." She put her hand on Lex's leg. "What's this all about, anyway?"

Embarrassed by the scrutiny, Lex stood and put her hands in the front pockets of her jeans. "I'm not sure I want to keep living way out here," she said quietly.

"What?"

"The kids are growing up, Helen. Is it fair to keep them secluded out here? Lorrie's into so many sports, we'll be spending all our time shuttling back and forth to town. And now, with Melanie maybe playing piano," her voice trailed off. "Damn."

Not certain how to handle this revelation, Helen got to her feet and took Lex by the hand. "Come here."

Lex followed her out of the barn. "Where are we going?"

"Close your eyes."

"Why?"

Helen squeezed Lex's hand harder. "Just do it."

With a heavy sigh, Lex did as she was asked. "Now what?"

"Think about spring; about how green everything gets, and slowly open your eyes." Helen had them both standing on the far side of the barn, facing an empty pasture. "If you listen closely, you can almost hear your children laughing, as they play and swing. Maybe you and Lorrie are riding. Do you remember the look on her face when she's with you?"

Lex opened her eyes and could almost see what Helen was describing. "I was being an idiot again, wasn't I?"

"No, not an idiot. You're a good mom, Lex. I know you want what's best for your family, but sometimes we tend to over think things. I nearly didn't marry Roy because I thought I wasn't good enough for him. But every day he shows me how wrong I was and I've never regretted a moment of our life together."

"I'm glad you're here, Helen. You've been good for Roy, and for the rest of us." Lex grinned as Helen hooked an arm with hers, just as a light mist began to fall. "Guess we'd better get back inside."

Helen laughed. "Let's go pester Martha and Charlie. I'm dying to get my hands on your son again."

ROY TOOK HIS time backing the trailer into the driveway. He was surprised to see the group of people standing nearby. Amanda and Ellie had been joined by two men and, he looked closer, a very sturdily-built woman. He stopped a few feet from the garage door and turned off the truck. "Looks like we've got some extra help," he told Chet and Jack.

"Cool. That means we'll get done quicker." Chet opened his door and stopped when he noticed the extra people. "Roy?" he whispered.

"Yeah?"

Chet tugged on his baseball cap. "Uh, is that a lady?"

Jack snickered, but kept his mouth shut.

Roy slammed his door. "Sure looks like it. Try to act like you've been around people before, will ya?"

"Grumpy old man," Chet grumbled, as he followed Roy and Jack to the rear of the trailer.

Amanda wanted to laugh at the look on Chet's face. "It took you long enough," she teased Roy. "I was beginning to think you were lost."

"Nope. Stopped for a cup of coffee." Roy stopped and pushed his cowboy hat back so he could see everyone better. "Hi."

Ellie moved away from Amanda. "Oops. Sorry. Roy, Chet, Jack, I'd like you to meet my new neighbors. Richie, Tony, and Kyle. These guys were nice enough to come to my rescue when my movers cancelled on me."

Jack nodded and Chet blushed.

"Nice to meet y'all," Roy tipped his hat. He nodded to Ellie. "Ready to get started?"

"Sure." Ellie watched as he opened the trailer. "Oh. Guess I'd better unlock the house." She gave Kyle a bashful grin before she hurried to the front door.

Amanda watched in amusement as a flustered Ellie stumbled before reaching the door. She turned to Kyle, who was also smiling. "She's normally not such a klutz."

Tony tugged on Richie. "Come on, let's help unload some boxes. I sense some girl talk coming."

"Girl talk? You mean, Kyle?" Richie giggled. He flinched as Kyle pinched his rear. "All right, girl. I get it."

"I'm sorry about those two," Kyle said. "They're not used to being around humans," she added loudly.

Richie huffed and waved a dismissive hand. "Paybacks."

"You have to sleep sometime," Tony muttered, as he walked by carrying a box.

Kyle waited until the men had all taken something into Ellie's condo. She stepped closer to Amanda. "Is Ellie seeing anyone?"

"No, she isn't. But there's something you should know." Amanda kept an eye on the front door, in case Ellie returned.

"Oh, god. She's not out?"

Amanda shook her head. "No, nothing like that." She paused. "As far as I know, she's not been in any serious relationship."

"You're kidding. How can someone as cute as her be alone? Wait. Is she a head case? I mean, she seemed really nice, that one day we talked, but—"

"No, no, she's not a head case. Up until this past year, she was living with her grandfather, helping him out. When he passed away she stayed home and hid in her grief." Amanda lowered her gaze. "We were all pretty torn up about it."

Kyle touched Amanda's arm in an attempt to console her. "Hey, I'm sorry. I didn't mean to bring up bad feelings. I was just thinking about, you know, maybe asking her out sometime." She grinned. "She's the first woman in a long time who I couldn't scare off with my grumpiness. I figure that has to count for something."

Richie walked by the pair and hip-checked Kyle, almost knocking her down. "Why don't you use those muscles of yours for something besides showing off? I'm going to start to glisten, at this pace."

"Glisten?" Amanda asked.

He stopped and put his hands on his hips. "Well, girlfriend, someone as lovely as I certainly wouldn't sweat." He ignored Amanda's laughter as he returned to the trailer. "Crazy little dykes. They'll never understand."

With a nod, Jack quickly moved past them and took another box off the truck.

Chet and Roy walked by Amanda. Roy grabbed Chet's arm. "Help me with the sofa."

"Uh, sure." Chet's eyes met Richie's, as they crossed paths. He blushed as Richie moved around him, carrying another box. "Um, excuse me."

Richie stopped in front of Amanda. "Does that cutie play on my team?"

"I honestly don't know," Amanda said.

"Oh, well. Could be fun finding out." Richie winked and continued into the house.

An hour later, the entire group was seated in the living room eating delivered pizza. Some were on the sofa and chairs, while others were scattered around the floor.

Ellie, on one end of the sofa, had trouble concentrating on her meal, since Kyle had seated herself on the floor beside her leg. She took a bite of pizza and almost choked as Kyle's shoulder brushed her knee.

"Are you all right?" Amanda asked as she patted Ellie on the back.

Ellie coughed and nodded. "Yeah. Guess it went down wrong." She took a swallow of bottled water to wash the pizza down.

The phone attached to Amanda's belt started to ring. She juggled her plate before Ellie took it away from her. "Thanks. Hello? Oh, hi, honey. No, we're just sitting here stuffing our faces." She laughed. "Uh, no. Pizza. Uh-huh, right. I bet you had something unhealthy, too. Liar." Amanda's face turned a lovely shade of pink. "Lex! Stop that. I'll see you in a little while, okay? I love you, too." She closed her phone and looked around the room. "Sorry about that."

Tony, who was seated on the floor nearby, smiled at her. "Don't apologize. I think it's wonderful to see someone in a loving relationship. How long?"

"Over twelve years." Amanda paused for a moment. "Wow." She couldn't keep the smile from her face. "Doesn't seem that long."

"Still in the honeymoon phase, are you?" Richie asked.

Amanda nodded. "Even with three kids."

"Three!" Kyle exclaimed. "Wow, you look great!"

"Oh, no. I didn't have all three of them," Amanda said. "Just one."

Kyle grinned and waggled her eyebrows. "You still look great."

"Um, thanks." Amanda couldn't fight back the blush.

"So, did your partner have the other two?" Richie questioned.

Roy and Chet both choked on their food at the same time. Jack sat quietly and smirked.

Richie stared at them. "What did I say?"

Roy shook his head and continued to gasp for air.

Amanda laughed. "Let's just say that Lex isn't the kind of woman to carry a baby for nine months."

"No kidding," Ellie said. She giggled at the thought of Lex pregnant.

"What are we missing?" Kyle asked.

All eyes were on Amanda as she riffled through her purse. She took out a small photo album and passed it over to Kyle. "She's on the first page, pushing our two daughters on the swings."

Kyle opened the album and looked at the first page. "Whoa." She passed it over to Tony, who whistled in appreciation.

"Nice."

"Let me see," Richie said, snapping his fingers. "Oooh, girlfriend! You hit the jackpot. Nice butch thing. But you're right. I can't imagine her pregnant."

Tony nodded. "It's a shame, though. Nice genes."

"I like how she looks in them," Amanda said.

Tony guffawed. "I was talking about genetics."

Not to be outdone, Amanda winked. "So was I." She waited until the laughter died down before adding, "But you don't have to worry. Our son definitely has her genetics."

"Impressive," Richie said, applauding.

When the rest of the room joined in, Amanda stood and took a bow. "Thank you. Now, if you'll excuse me, I think I'll head home and check on my better half."

Ellie stood as well. "I'll walk you out. Be right back, everyone."

They walked to Amanda's SUV in silence. When Amanda unlocked the doors with her remote, Ellie stopped her. "Thank you for everything."

"I had a great time," Amanda said, tugging Ellie into a hug. "I like your neighbors a lot."

"Me too." Ellie stepped back. "What do you think about Kyle?"

Amanda touched Ellie's cheek. "I think she's sweet. And I believe she likes you."

"Really?"

"Uh-huh. Do me a favor?"

Ellie nodded. "Sure. What?"

"If she asks, give her a chance? I think there's a lot more to her than what we've seen."

"You think so?" Ellie lowered her head and scuffed her toe against the Expedition's tire. "How did you know? I mean, with Lex?"

Amanda's smiled softened. "There was just something about her. It was in the middle of a horrible storm and she saved my life. But even if she hadn't, the moment I looked into her eyes, nothing else mattered to me."

"I really envy that, you know. I've seen how she looks at you and I wish someone would look at me like that, someday." Ellie raised her head. There were tears in her eyes. "You two are so lucky."

"We are." Amanda embraced her again. "Neither one of us was looking for anything, but we found everything with each other. I believe you'll find that, too."

Ellie held her tight for a long moment. "Thanks." She moved back and put her hands into the back pockets of her jeans. "Tell that cousin of mine to come visit as soon as she can."

"I sure will." Amanda opened her door. "Now go back in and visit with your company. And send the guys home after they're finished eating. Otherwise, you may never get rid of them."

MARTHA PLACED THE sleeping Eddie in his crib. "Are you sure about this, Lexie?"

"Yep." Lex stood beside Martha and put her arm around her shoulders. "He won't need another bottle until after Amanda gets home. I think I can handle anything that comes up between now and then, don't you?"

"Oh, I wasn't doubting your ability, honey. I just don't want you to hurt yourself if you have to pick him up." Martha turned and looked

Lex in the eyes. "You're moving around a lot better and I don't want anything to mess that up."

Lex shook her head and chuckled. "Don't worry. I promised Amanda that I wouldn't do anything to jeopardize my recovery. You know I take my promises seriously."

"All right. I guess I can't blame you, wanting to spend some alone time with your baby. But if you need anything, please call. There's three of us over at my place who would be more than happy to help."

"I know. And I appreciate it. But it feels like I haven't been alone in the house in a long time. The constant company is starting to get to me."

Martha patted Lex's hip. "All right. I can take a hint." She kissed Lex on the cheek. "Enjoy your quiet time."

"Thanks." Lex waited until Martha left before she dragged the rocker near the crib. "What they don't know won't hurt them, right?" She sat as close to the crib as she could and watched Eddie sleep.

"So, little man. What are you going to grow up to be?" Lex asked softly. She reached over the top of the crib and lightly rubbed his back. "Will you want to work the ranch? Or will you be like your sisters and do all sorts of things?"

Eddie kicked in his sleep, but didn't waken.

"I don't care what you do with your life, as long as you're happy. Maybe find a nice girl and settle down?" She laughed quietly. "Or boy, I guess. If you're lucky, they'll make your heart race every time you see them, just like your mommy does mine."

"I could say the same thing," Amanda said from behind Lex.

Lex spun her head around and grinned. "Hey, sweetheart."

Amanda stepped closer. "Has he been asleep long?"

"About twenty minutes." Lex held out her hand. When Amanda took it, she tugged until Amanda ended up in her lap.

"I don't want to hurt you."

Lex tightened her grip around Amanda's waist. "Then don't fight me," she whispered. "Don't worry, this doesn't hurt my back at all."

"Liar." Amanda put her arms on Lex's shoulders and linked her hands behind her wife's head. "Ellie's all moved in."

"That's good." Lex kissed her gently. "So, did the guys do okay? Nothing broken?"

Amanda laughed. "They did fine. Although I think Richie, one of the new neighbors, was interested in Chet."

"Really?"

"Uh-huh. Poor Chet got really flustered."

Lex relaxed as Amanda's head came to rest of her shoulder. "Was Chet interested?"

Amanda shrugged. "I have no idea. Is he gay?"

"I dunno. It's never came up. I mean, the guy's what, thirty? He's never talked about dating, one way or the other." Lex kissed the top of Amanda's head. "Guess if he wants us to know, we'll know."

"Mmm." Amanda played with one of the buttons on Lex's shirt. "If things go well, we may have a new family member one of these days."

"Oh?"

"Yeah. I think Kyle really likes Ellie. She was so sweet around her today."

Lex closed her eyes and moved the rocker back and forth. "How did Ellie act?"

"A lot like a certain rancher did when we first met."

"That bad, huh?"

Amanda giggled. "Worse. Ellie nearly choked when Kyle's shoulder brushed up against her."

Lex's laughter caused Eddie to squeak and stretch. "Oops." With one hand, she rubbed his back until he settled down. "Sounds like I missed a lot of fun today."

"That's okay. Maybe this weekend we can stop by and you'll be able to meet everyone. Although they're already impressed with you."

The rocking stopped. "What?"

"I took out my little photo album and showed Ellie's neighbors a picture of you."

"You did, huh? Did it scare them?"

"No, but I did get a nice round of applause." Amanda almost fell off Lex's lap when she released her in surprise. "Careful."

Lex put both arms back around Amanda. "Sorry." She was quiet for a moment. "Applause?"

"Uh-huh. They all thought you were hot."

"Oh, god." Lex buried her face in Amanda's hair. "Maybe I'll meet them at Ellie's wedding."

Amanda laughed and hugged her. "Aw. Don't worry, honey. I'll protect you from them." She laughed even harder when Lex began tickling her.

Chapter Twenty-One

ELLIE CLOSED THE door after Richie left. He and Kyle had come over and brought sandwiches for lunch. It was a welcome respite from cleaning and unpacking. She turned and looked at Kyle, who was quietly picking up the empty paper plates. "Don't worry about that. I'll clean everything up in a little while."

"I don't mind. Richie has me well-trained, or so he claims." Kyle carried the trash into the kitchen and looked around. "Uh, do you have a trash can?"

"I did before I moved." Ellie put her hands on her hips and surveyed the many boxes. "Just toss everything in the sink. I'll find a trash bag later. I was so tired last night that I barely got my bed made before I fell asleep. At least today I was able to get my bedroom and bathroom sorted out."

Kyle did as she was told and followed Ellie to the living room. "Would you like some help getting the kitchen unpacked? I mean, I don't have to work until tomorrow, and I'd be glad to give you a hand."

"You don't have to do that. I'll get to it, eventually." Ellie dropped onto the couch and stretched out her legs. "You're welcome to stay, though."

"How can I resist such a charming offer?" Kyle sat beside Ellie, who started to get up in a huff. "Wait." Kyle grabbed her arm. "I'm sorry. I was just kidding."

Ellie frowned, but kept her seat. "No, that's okay. I tend to get a little touchy. Always have."

"Why?"

With a shrug, Ellie tried not to think about how good Kyle's hand felt on her arm. "I got a lot of flack from my mom, while I was growing up. Old news."

Kyle edged closer, until their legs were almost touching. "If you need or want to talk about it, I'm a pretty good listener." She cautiously put her hand on Ellie's leg. "My parents kicked me out of the house when I was fifteen, so I won't be one to judge you."

"Fifteen? My god, why?" Ellie turned and almost gasped at the intensity coming from Kyle's hazel eyes.

"I made the mistake of telling them I liked girls." Kyle tried to grin and joke about it, but failed. "My old man slapped me across the room, and my mother held the door open. Nice family, huh?"

Ellie shook her head and covered Kyle's hand with hers. "I'm sorry. Makes my mom sound tame, by comparison."

"How?"

"She's a religious zealot and swears I'm going to burn in hell. I haven't talked to her in ten years. I suppose she's still that way." Ellie sighed. "Worst part is, I used to be the same way. When I first met my cousin, Lex, I told her how horrible I thought she was. If it hadn't been for Amanda, we'd have most likely killed each other."

Kyle cringed. "Ouch."

"Yeah."

"Well," Kyle squeezed Ellie's hand, "it seems you got everything figured out."

Ellie laughed. "Yeah. After trying to kiss Amanda."

Kyle jerked up straight. "Whoa! I didn't see that coming."

"Neither did she," Ellie said. "It was a long time ago. I had just figured out I liked women, and she was so nice to me. Needless to say, it didn't work out."

"No, I guess it wouldn't. So, did you get involved with anyone after her?"

With a shrug of her shoulders, Ellie sighed. "I've gone out a few times over the years, but never really clicked with anyone, you know? And I really hate that 'first date, getting to know you' awkward stage."

"Oh, god. Me too." Kyle leaned back against the sofa and closed her eyes. "Did you do the bar scene?"

"No, never got that desperate. Did you?"

Kyle nodded. "Yeah. Too much. A few years back I spent a month drying out, so now I just hang out at home with the guys."

"Are they partners?" Ellie asked.

Kyle started laughing. "I'm sorry. I didn't mean to laugh. It's just funny, because it would be like the Odd Couple hooking up. Tony's the ultimate slob, and Richie can't stand to see anything out of place. They bicker like an old married couple, though. Tony's been seeing a guy he works with at the restaurant, so I don't know how long he'll be living with us."

"How long have you three been together?"

"They've been roomies since college, on and off. One will move in with a boyfriend, break up, and move back. When my last long-term girlfriend kicked me out, they took me in." Kyle closed her eyes in thought. "God, that's been close to five years ago." She took a deep breath and released it slowly. "Sorry, didn't mean to go down that road."

Ellie pulled their linked hands into her lap. "That's all right. I'm a good listener, too."

MELANIE SKIPPED IN a circle, holding hands with Mallory, another girl from her class. "And then, my Momma threw the rope real far and it went over the cow's head. The cow mooed a lot but Momma made it mind her."

"My mommy bakes cookies," Mallory said. She stopped skipping and sat on the gym floor. "How come your mommy plays with cows?"

Melanie joined her. "It's not playing, it's work. Momma has to take care of the cows 'cause they're dumb animals."

"What's that mean?"

"I dunno. I heard her say it once." Melanie squirmed around. "Hey, wanna patty cake?"

"Sure!" They began clapping their hands together, until Melanie saw her cousin walking nearby. "There's Teddy!"

Mallory shrugged her shoulders. "So? He thinks he's so smart, just 'cause his daddy's a doctor."

"Well, his daddy is smart. And nice. I like Uncle Rodney a lot." She got up and followed Teddy. "Hey, Teddy!"

Teddy turned around. "What?"

"Where's your cowboy clothes?" Melanie asked. "You're not wearing your hat."

"That's 'cause I don't want to be a cowboy no more. Cowboys are dumb."

Melanie frowned. "No they're not."

"Are too!"

"Uh-uh. You're dumb!" Melanie stomped her foot for emphasis. "My Momma's a cowboy, and she's not dumb."

Teddy thought about that for a moment. "No, she's smart. But being a cowboy was a dumb idea."

"Why? 'Cause you're scared of animals?"

"I'm not scared! Horses are big and dumb," Teddy said. He stuck out his lower lip and crossed his arms. "You don't like horses neither."

Melanie shrugged. "They're okay, but they smell funny. So, if you're not gonna be a cowboy, whatcha gonna do?"

He puffed up his chest with pride. "I'm gonna be a fireman. My daddy took me to the fire station and let me meet the firemen. They're really strong."

"Cool. I'm gonna be a princess when I grow up."

"Really?"

"Uh-huh. Momma already calls me princess." Melanie twirled in a circle. "Do you want to come play with me and Mallory?"

"Sure." Teddy's bad mood evaporated as he followed her across the gym.

ON THE OTHER side of the gym, Lorrie bounced a basketball and looked around. She saw that Melanie was having fun with Teddy and Mallory, which eased her mind. Although they fought constantly, Lorrie always kept her eye on Melanie. She frowned when she saw a solitary figure sitting on the bleachers, away from the other children. Her mother's reminder from the other day rang in her head.

"Lorrie, don't just stand there," Allison yelled, "throw the ball."

With a shrug, Lorrie bounced the ball to her best friend. "I'll be right back." She ignored Ally's entreaty and walked toward the bleachers. When she got close, she put her hands in her front pockets. "Hey."

Jerry Sater looked up. "Hey."

"Whatcha doin'?" Lorrie asked as she sat next to him.

He shrugged. "Nothin'." He stared down at his dirty and scuffed sneakers.

"Um, are you okay?"

Jerry shrugged again.

"You know," Lorrie said, as she tried to think of something to say, "we've got to make teams for the next science project. Allie and I are together, but we need somebody else. Do you have a team yet?"

"No."

Lorrie rolled her eyes. "Would you like to be on our team? I bet we can come up with some good ideas."

"Really?" Jerry looked at her, his brows scrunched together in confusion.

"Yep. Hey, do you think your grandma will let you come to my house sometime? You could see my horse."

He lowered his eyes again. "I dunno. She's kinda old and doesn't drive or nothin'." He sniffled and started to cry. "I miss my mom."

"Is she coming back?"

Jerry shook his head and locked his hands behind his head, lowering his face until his elbows were on his knees. "Grandma says she's in heaven."

Unsure of what to do, Lorrie awkwardly patted his back. "Heaven's supposed to be nice. My grandpa and daddy are there."

"They are?" Jerry turned his head to look at her.

"Uh-huh. But my Gramma said they're there to watch us, like angels."

Jerry sat up and wiped his face with his hand. "My mom was sometimes bad. Do you think she's still in heaven?"

Lorrie considered the question. "Probably. Hey, do you want to play basketball with us? You can be on my team."

"Okay." Jerry sniffled and used his shirt sleeve to wipe his runny nose. "Don't tell no one I was crying, okay?"

"I won't. Come on." Lorrie jumped off the bleachers. "Let's go beat Russ's team."

WITH EDDIE AT Martha's and Lex napping in the bedroom, Amanda decided it was time to take care of a load or two of laundry. She had called Jeremy earlier and asked if he knew anything about Jerry's return to Somerville. The sheriff said he didn't, but would check it out and call her back. So, she kept her cell phone on her belt while she gathered dirty clothes out of the girls' rooms.

Melanie's room, as usual, was neat. Their youngest daughter liked keeping everything in its place, other than the finished pages from coloring books that adorned her "art wall," which was a deep purple. The other walls were a more sedate pale violet. Amanda took Melanie's laundry basket from her closet and cut through the Jack-and-Jill bathroom the girls shared.

She picked up two pink towels from where they were draped across the tub, as well as a royal blue one that had been tossed on the floor beside the toilet. "Lorrie, I swear, you're just like your Momma," Amanda grumbled. After getting two washcloths from the sink, she made her way into Lorrie's room.

It had taken Amanda time, but now she was warming up to the light gray walls that Lorrie had chosen. As she stepped across the threshold, a pungent odor assailed her senses. "Lord. What has that girl done now?"

Freckles, who was in Lorrie's room, excitedly pranced around Amanda.

"Calm down, you silly dog." Amanda started picking up dirty clothes from all over the room. She shook her head at how Lorrie had made her bed. The comforter was askew and there were several suspicious lumps beneath it.

When she bent over to pick up a shirt that was partially under the bed, Amanda almost fell back. "What the hell?" Freckles began to lick at her face. "Stop it."

Lex stood at the doorway. "What's the matter? Did you yell?"

"You'll never believe it." Amanda crooked her finger at Lex, who joined her beside the bed.

"Damn. That smells like a dead animal. Or has Lorrie been leaving dirty dishes in here?"

Amanda pointed under the bed. "I don't think this one's Lorrie's fault."

"Yeah?" Lex cautiously dropped to her knees, much to Freckles delight. "Freckles, no." She started to reach under the bed, when Amanda handed her a washcloth.

"Don't touch it with your hands."

"Why? I think it's dead." But to appease Amanda, Lex used the cloth to snare the item. As she pulled it from under the bed, Freckles tried to take it away from her. "Stop it, Freckles."

The dog barked and danced around. Lex removed the dead squirrel and held it away from her. "Ugh." She held it out to Amanda, who stepped away.

"Don't you dare," Amanda warned.

Lex waved the carcass back and forth. "It's definitely dead. Stiff as a board." She put her free hand on the mattress and levered herself up. Then she looked at the dog, who seemed proud. "Brought Lorrie a gift, did you? Good girl."

Amanda shivered. "Don't congratulate her. She brought a dead animal into the house." She wrapped her arms around herself.

"Aw, come on. It could have been worse." Lex walked out of the room, with Amanda and Freckles at her heels.

"How?"

Once down the stairs, Lex stopped by the back door. "It could have been alive. Imagine trying to catch a squirrel in the house."

"No thank you." Amanda opened the door. "Freckles, stay." The dog whined but sat next to Amanda. "What are you going to do with it?"

"If you'll bring me a trash bag from the kitchen, I'll wrap it up and have one of the guys bury it away from the house. No sense in having the trash stink."

Amanda shivered in revulsion, but quickly fetched a bag. "Throw the washcloth away with it. I'm not putting it in with our laundry."

"Why not? It'll get clean."

"No. Absolutely not. I will not wash something that touched a dead animal with our towels."

Lex shrugged, but did as she was asked. "Maybe I should turn Freckles loose in the barn. I've seen a few mice out there." Lex tied up the bag, walked to the gate, and placed it on the other side.

"Like hell you will," Amanda called after her. When Lex came back into the house, she pointed to the bathroom off the hall. "Go sanitize your hands, please." She patted Freckles on the head. "Good girl."

With a roll of her eyes, Lex went into the bathroom and washed her hands. Amanda stood at the door, watching. When she was finished, Lex held out her hands. "How's that, Mommy?"

"You are such a brat." Amanda turned and headed for the kitchen.

Lex grinned and followed, popping Amanda on the butt before she sat at the table. "Next time I'll let you remove the dead critter." She snapped her fingers and Freckles immediately came over. "You're such a good dog." She scratched the happy pooch behind the ears.

"Don't encourage her," Amanda said. "Do you think she really killed the squirrel?"

"It's hard to say. But I'm betting the thing fell out of a tree or off an electrical wire, and she just brought its carcass in to give to Lorrie."

Amanda poured each of them a cup of coffee and joined Lex at the table. "Well, whatever happened, I hope she doesn't do it again. That was disgusting."

"At least she hadn't eaten any of it."

"Gross." Amanda held up her hand. "Please don't say anything to the girls. It's bad enough that I've got to move Lorrie's bed and disinfect in there before they get home."

"Do you need my help?"

Amanda glared at her. "No. I shouldn't have let you stretch under the bed to get the squirrel, but I just couldn't bring myself to touch it. It's easy enough to push the bed around on the wood floor."

"All right. Just remember I offered."

When Amanda's cell phone rang, they both jumped. Amanda took it from her waist and flipped it open. "Hello?"

"Amanda? This is Jeremy. I hope I haven't disturbed you."

She looked at Lex and mouthed, *Jeremy*. "No, not at all. Do you mind if I put you on speakerphone so Lex can hear?"

"Sure, go ahead."

Amanda placed her phone on the table between them. "Can you hear me okay?"

"Yes. Hey, Lex. How are you doing?"

Lex grinned. "I'm great. What's up?"

"Well, I have information about Jerry Sater. He's under the guardianship of his maternal grandmother, Isabel Brooks."

Amanda nodded to Lex. "That's what Lorrie told us, that he was living with his grandmother. Did his mother lose custody of him?"

"It's worse than that. A few weeks ago, Susan Sater and her live-in boyfriend, Vincent Walsh, were killed in a one-car accident. Jerry was in the backseat, but buckled in and not injured. I don't know all the particulars, but it seems that Susan's ex-husband and Jerry's father, Marvin Sater, is out of the picture. He left her before Jerry was born and took their other two children with him. The authorities tried to track him down, but there's no sign of him."

"That's so sad." Amanda shook her head. "So, it's just him and his grandmother?"

"I'm afraid so."

Lex tapped the table in a nervous gesture. "Is there anything we can do for him?"

"I don't know," Jeremy answered. "Hopefully, his grandmother will be a stabilizing influence on him. Anyway, you folks have a great evening. Lex, take care of yourself. Amanda, try not to kill her. I hate filling out paperwork."

Both women laughed, but Amanda was the first to gain her composure. "I'll do my best, Jeremy. Thank you for your help." She closed her phone and sighed. "That poor kid."

"Yeah. I hope he makes it through this okay. I'd hate for our kids to go through something like that."

Amanda held out her hand, which Lex automatically took. "It breaks my heart. But I suppose we can't take in every child, can we?"

"Unfortunately, no. But maybe he'll be okay with his grandmother."

"Maybe so." Amanda stood and tugged on their joined hands. "Let's go to Martha's. I have this need to see our son."

Lex stood and joined her. "You took the words right out of my mouth, sweetheart." She kissed Amanda on the cheek.

ELLIE LOOKED AROUND the kitchen and sighed. The counters were clear and all of the trash had been bagged and put in the garage. "I can't believe we finished."

"Looks great," Kyle said from her perch on the bar. She swung her legs. "I don't know about you, but I'm famished."

Although she hadn't thought about it, the moment Kyle mentioned food, Ellie's stomach growled. "I guess I could eat."

Kyle laughed and jumped down. "Let's go grab a burger. I know this awesome little dive not too far away."

"I don't know. I don't think I'm exactly dressed to go out." Ellie gestured to her clothes. Worn, faded jeans and a stained sweatshirt matched her ratty sneakers.

"You look perfect," Kyle said. She brushed a strand of hair away from Ellie's eyes. "Beautiful, in fact."

Ellie blushed, but couldn't take her eyes off of Kyle's. "Kyle, I—"

Kyle put her finger over Ellie's lips. "Shhh." She leaned in and removed her finger. "I really want to kiss you right now."

"Uh." Ellie's eyes grew wider and Kyle's face moved closer. "Yes," she whispered, just as Kyle's lips lightly touched hers. Warmth settled over Ellie as the kiss deepened. Her hands went to Kyle's waist, while Kyle's hands threaded behind her head.

Kyle finally moved back to breathe. "Thank you."

Ellie turned bright red and a nervous giggle escaped. "Thank you?"

"Yeah," Kyle whispered dreamily. "I've wanted to do that since the moment you chewed me out for parking in your driveway."

"Really?"

Kyle nodded. "Really." She put her hand on Ellie's cheek and left a soft kiss on her lips. The noise from Ellie's stomach broke the intimate moment, as both women laughed. "I guess we'd better feed that monster before someone gets hurt."

"Sorry." Ellie lowered her head and silently cursed herself.

"Hey." Kyle's hand cupped Ellie's chin and forced her to look up. "I think you're adorable. And to tell you the truth, my stomach's starting to grumble, too. Let's go eat."

Ellie's grateful smile caused her eyes to sparkle. "Sounds good." Before she could stop herself, she leaned forward and gave Kyle a quick kiss. "Let's take your car. I've always wanted to ride in a classic."

"You got it, pretty lady." Kyle held out her arm playfully, grinning wide when Ellie took it.

Chapter Twenty-Two

CHRISTMAS DAY AFTERNOON, Lex stood at the corral and watched as Ronnie led Stormy around in a circle, while Nora did her best to stay on. Lex laughed as Nora desperately hung on to the saddle horn with both hands.

"Ronnie, make her slow down! I'm going to fall." Nora giggled.

Ronnie laughed but stopped the horse. "Honey, she's not very tall and it probably wouldn't hurt if you did happen to slide off."

The redhead looked over at Lex. "Save me, Lex. My fiancé's a brute." When Ronnie scoffed at her, Nora stole his cowboy hat and put it on her head. "Okay, let's try again. I think I needed to be properly attired."

"Are you sure?" Ronnie asked.

"Yes, honey. I'm sure. Let's put this horse in drive, or however you make it go."

Ronnie let the lead out and clicked his tongue, which caused Stormy to break into a trot. "How's that?"

"F, f, fi, fi, fine," Nora stammered, as she bounced.

Lex was laughing so hard that she had to hang on to the top rail of the corral to keep from falling. She felt a hand on her back and turned around to see Amanda, bundled in Lex's old leather jacket. "Hi, sweetheart."

"What's going on?" Amanda asked, huddling close to Lex.

"Ronnie's giving Nora a riding lesson."

Amanda watched as Nora bounced around the corral. "It looks more like he's trying to turn her into a milkshake." She giggled as Nora started to slide from the saddle, and Ronnie jogged to keep her upright.

Lex put her arm around Amanda. "Where are the kids?"

"Eddie's being hogged upstairs by my dad and Lois. Lorrie, Melanie and Teddy are playing board games in the dining room. Martha and Jeannie are supervising, and everyone who's left is in the den watching basketball."

"And you left all that to come out here?" Lex asked, nuzzling Amanda's neck.

Amanda moaned and wrapped her arms around Lex's waist. "Keep that up and I'll drag you into the barn."

"And that's supposed to be a deterrent?" Lex asked, as she slipped one hand beneath Amanda's jacket.

"Not really. Yeow! Your hand is cold."

Lex chuckled. "Not for long."

Amanda slapped her hand away. "Stop it."

"Come here, sweetheart. I'll just warm my hands for a minute," Lex said, wriggling her fingers.

The squeal from the corral caused them both to look that direction. Lex immediately started laughing.

"Help!" Nora had slid over to one side. The only thing keeping her on the horse was the leg she had hooked over the saddle horn.

Ronnie was on his knees in the middle of the corral, laughing hysterically.

"Damn it, Ron. Help me!" Both of Nora's hands were full of Stormy's mane. "Lex! Do something!"

Amanda grabbed Lex's arm to stop her, then crawled between the rails and hurried to where Stormy stood. Well-trained, the horse stopped the moment she felt her rider slide. "Okay," Amanda put both hands on Nora, "let go, and I'll help you slide off."

"Noooo!" Nora wailed. "I'll be trampled!"

"No, you won't. Stormy will stay still, I promise." Amanda glared at Ronnie. "Get your butt over here, Chuckles."

"Yes, ma'am." Ronnie picked up his hat. He dusted it off against his leg before putting it on. In a gallant motion, he swung Nora from the horse and set her on her feet. "Are you okay?"

Nora slapped his chest. "No thanks to you, I could have been seriously hurt."

"Aw, come on, honey. Maybe a little dirty, but I doubt—" Ronnie cut his reply short when Nora pointed a finger at him.

"Not another word." She gathered what was left of her dignity and stomped across the corral. "Thank you for your help, Amanda."

Ronnie watched as his fiancée struggled through the rails. "Honey?"

"You know, I believe cluelessness runs in this family," Amanda muttered. "Give her time to calm down before you end up eating that hat."

"Huh?"

Amanda shook her head and walked away. She patted Lex on the side when she got outside the corral. "Why don't you give him some pointers on how to understand women, while he's brushing Stormy down?"

"You think I'm an expert?" Lex asked, incredulously.

"Not really. But you're getting better." Amanda blew her a kiss and headed toward the house.

Once inside the barn, Ronnie led Stormy into her stall and removed her saddle and blanket. He placed them, along with the bridle, over the gate and ran a brush over her coat. "I wouldn't have let her get hurt," he grumbled. "I don't see why she made such a big deal out of it."

Lex sat on a nearby bale of hay and stretched out her legs. "There's something you need to know about ladies, Ron."

"What's that?"

"No matter what you know, or perceive to be the truth, it's what she thinks that matters. And the sooner you remember that, the happier you both will be."

He stopped brushing and peered over Stormy's back. "Are you trying to tell me that you always let Amanda win?"

Lex laughed. "Of course not. But I am smart enough to realize that when she's happy, we're both happy. We don't always agree on everything, but we respect each other's feelings. And when we do happen to disagree, we leave our egos out of it."

"Egos?"

"Yep. Nothing will destroy a relationship faster than always trying to one-up each other. It's pointless and hurtful."

Ronnie left the stall and joined her on the bale. "Yeah, I don't ever remember seeing you and Amanda do that."

"And you never will. When we got together, I swore to her that I would always love and respect her, and I always keep my promises."

"I hope Nora and I can have the same kind of relationship. I love her like crazy."

Lex patted him on the back. "Just remember how much you love her, and you'll never go wrong." She stood and brushed the hay off her jeans. "One more thing."

"Yeah?"

"A little groveling never hurts, either. Especially when you've put your foot in your mouth."

LEX AND RONNIE stepped into the house and hung their jackets and hats on hooks by the back door. He gave her a sheepish shrug and went in search of Nora, while Lex went into the dining room to see how the kids were doing.

"Ha! You can't catch me now," Teddy said.

Lorrie rolled her eyes. "I don't care. This is boring." She saw Lex in the doorway. "Momma. Can we go outside and play?"

"Only if you wear your coats. And don't leave the yard." When the kids cheered and started to leave, Lex stopped them by putting her hand on Melanie's head. "Not so fast. You have a mess to clean up in here."

Three bodies turned into cleaning whirlwinds, and in no time at all, the boxes of games were stacked neatly at one end of the table. "Is this okay?" Lorrie asked, anxiously.

Lex pretended to think about it. "I don't know. Are all the games in their right boxes?"

"Yes, ma'am." All three children answered at once.

"Hmm. I guess I only have one more thing to say."

Melanie danced from foot to foot. "What, Momma?"

"Why are you still in here? You should be out back, playing." Lex dodged out of the way to keep from being run over by excited children.

She laughed as they rushed to get their coats by the back door.

Jeannie came out of the den and met Lex in the hallway. "I take it you told the terrible trio they could finally go out and play?"

"Yep. It's not that cold, and I figured it was better than letting them destroy the house."

"I'm tempted to join them. Watching basketball isn't my idea of Christmas fun." Jeannie linked arms with Lex. "How's your back?"

Lex patted Jeannie's hand. "A lot better. Don't tell Amanda, but she was right. Lazing around for a few weeks has done wonders."

Jeannie laughed at her. "Don't worry. I'm not about to give her any ammunition. We've got to stick together, right?"

"We sure do." Lex felt herself being led toward the kitchen. "Got the munchies again, little mama?"

"I shouldn't, but I do. I know I'm going to regret pigging out, especially later tonight." Jeannie released Lex and headed for the refrigerator. "I love Martha's barbeque. It's the best part of Christmas here at the ranch."

Lex sat at the table and watched as Jeannie made herself a large sandwich out of leftover barbeque brisket. She grimaced when sliced jalapenos and coleslaw were added, along with a dollop of potato salad. "You're not seriously going to eat that, are you?"

"Of course. Why not?" Jeannie sat beside Lex and bit into one end of the sandwich. "Mmm." As she chewed, she looked up at Lex and held out her masterpiece. "Wan' smmm?"

"Uh, no. Thanks." Lex grinned as barbeque sauce dribbled down Jeannie's chin. She took a paper napkin from the holder on the table and dabbed at the mess. "You're as bad as the kids."

Jeannie blinked innocently, and was saved from answering when Amanda came into the kitchen.

"There you are. I was wondering if you had gotten lost." Amanda sat beside Lex. "Are you enjoying the show?" she asked, pointing toward her sister.

Lex put her arm around Amanda's shoulder. "Yep. Nothing more exciting than watching a pregnant woman put away a disgusting sandwich." She flinched when Jeannie tossed her wadded napkin at her. "Behave."

Jeannie stuck out her tongue, food and all.

"Eww, Jean Louise. That's disgusting," Amanda said. "You'd better finish pretty soon, because I think your husband is exhausted from napping on our sofa."

After swallowing, Jeannie wiped her mouth with a clean napkin. "I was going to drag him home, anyway. We still have stuff to unpack. Although I'm tempted to take up Ellie and Kyle on their offer of helping."

"It was nice of them," Amanda said.

"You don't think they offered just because Rodney asked Ellie if she wanted to come to work for him, do you?" Rodney had cornered Ellie not long after she and Kyle had arrived. He had a nurse who was leaving the practice, and he'd hoped that Ellie would take her place. After making certain he wasn't offering the job out of pity or some misplaced family loyalty, Ellie happily agreed.

Lex leaned back and stretched. "Nah. I think they offered because they're nice folks. At least Kyle is, anyway. Ellie can be a little grumpy at times."

"I wonder where she gets it?" Jeannie teased.

"I have no idea." Lex grunted when Amanda poked her in the stomach. "What?"

Amanda poked her again. "Don't 'what' me, little Miss Butter-Won't-Melt-In-My-Mouth. You can give lessons on being grumpy."

Lex leaned close and growled playfully, nipping Amanda on the neck.

Jeannie groaned. "My god, you two are so sickening."

"Jealous, much?" Amanda asked.

Jeannie shook her head and went back to her sandwich.

ON THE LOVESEAT in the den, Ellie startled when Kyle touched her hand. They were watching the basketball game with Charlie, Rodney and Martha, but neither one seemed focused on the television.

"Hey, want to get some air?" Kyle whispered.

Ellie looked at the others in the room. Rodney was dozing with his head back, Charlie and Martha were conversing quietly, and Nora and Ronnie were in a serious discussion by the hearth of the fireplace. Anna Leigh and Jacob had left earlier, having promised their presence at another gathering. "Sure." Ellie stood and followed Kyle out of the room and to the front door.

"How about the front porch? The swing looks comfortable." Kyle waited until Ellie nodded her agreement before she opened the front door. Both were wearing sweaters, so the cool December air wasn't a deterrent. Kyle sat and patted the seat beside her. When Ellie joined her she scooted closer and put her arm around her. "Is this okay?"

"Yeah." Ellie snuggled into Kyle's embrace. "I'm glad you came with me today. It's been one of the best Christmases I can remember."

"Thanks for inviting me. I wasn't sure if you wanted me to meet your family so soon."

Ellie chuckled. "You'd already met Amanda, so it was inevitable that you'd meet Lex, too. Besides, with your roommates at Tony's mother's house for the day, I didn't want you to be alone."

Kyle kissed Ellie's temple. "You're sweet. But I've been alone on holidays before."

"Before today, even when I was surrounded by family, I felt alone," Ellie said. "Especially after my grandfather died." For once, the thought of Travis didn't bring tears, only a slight ache. "He would have liked you."

"You think so?"

"Definitely."

Kyle grinned and leaned her head against Ellie's. "Cool."

LEX CLOSED THE front door after the last family member left and released a heavy sigh. "Remind me again why we do this?" She asked Amanda, who stood nearby holding Eddie.

"Because we love our family," Amanda answered. Eddie gurgled and kicked, putting in his two-cents worth. "At least that's what we say when we volunteer to have holidays here at the ranch."

Lex went over and kissed Amanda lightly on the lips. "Not to mention, we have the largest place. Can you imagine this bunch crammed into your dad and Lois's house?"

"That's a scary thought. We'd be stacked three or four deep on their sofa. Gramma offered to do it, but I hate putting that much work onto her and Grandpa." Amanda followed Lex upstairs, where they heard the combined voices of their daughters. "I wonder what they're up to?"

"Let's sneak in and find out," Lex whispered. They peeked into Melanie's room first, but found it empty. Lex shrugged and motioned for Amanda to follow her.

When they looked into Lorrie's room, both women had to struggle to keep from laughing.

Lorrie was sitting at a small table in the middle of the room, looking decidedly uncomfortable. She was wearing a scraggly blonde wig from Melanie's dress-up box, along with one of Amanda's old dresses and heels. Melanie was sitting across from her, dressed in one of her pretend outfits as well. Freckles sat beside Lorrie, hoping for a treat.

"Can we quit playing tea? I wanna do something else," Lorrie said, as she scratched her head beneath the wig.

"You promised to play tea party with me if I didn't tell on you." Melanie pretended to pour from the tiny tea pot into their cups. She picked up the cup and acted like she was sipping something hot. "You should try your tea. I made it with peanut butter and strawberry juice."

Lorrie wrinkled her nose. "Ugh."

"It's only make-believe tea," Melanie said.

Amanda looked at Lex. "I wonder what Lorrie did that Melanie blackmailed her with?" she whispered.

"No telling." Lex backed away from the door. "I'm sure we'll find out, sooner or later." She trailed Amanda to their room. They started laughing at how ridiculous Lorrie had been dressed.

In a short time, both were changed into their sleepwear and Lex joined Amanda on the bed. They stretched out together with the baby in between them. "All things considered, it was a better holiday than most," Lex admitted. She rolled onto her side and propped her head on her upraised hand, mirroring Amanda's position.

"Yes, it was." Amanda ran her finger along Lex's cheek. "No calamities, no fights. Well, unless you count Nora threatening Ronnie."

"Yeah, but they seemed pretty cozy by the time they left." Lex turned her head and kissed Amanda's palm. "He'll learn."

Amanda cupped Lex's cheek. "What sage advice did you give him? He seemed like a man on a mission when you two came in from the barn."

"I told him to respect her feelings and remember why he loved her. Everything else would work itself out."

"Pretty smart, aren't you?"

Lex smirked. "Years and years of trial and error," she said.

"You know, it doesn't seem that long ago that we were as clueless as they are," Amanda said. "I remember how nervous you were, the first time I kissed you."

"Well, yeah. I was totally gone on you, and when you fell into my arms, I thought I'd died and gone to heaven." Lex stretched across Eddie and kissed Amanda lightly. "Even now, whenever our lips touch, I feel it all the way to my toes."

Eddie raised his hand and slapped at Lex's face. She laughed and began to kiss him all over. "Are you jealous, handsome?" When Eddie tangled his fingers in Lex's hair, she gasped. "Uh, Amanda? Could you help?"

Amanda laughed while Lex tried to untangle his grasp. "I don't know. He seems like he's doing okay on his own."

"Paybacks, woman," Lex said. She finally escaped Eddie's clutches and rolled onto her back and closed her eyes. "Whew."

"Are you all right?"

Lex didn't answer.

"Honey?" Amanda got off the bed and walked around to Lex's side. She leaned over her wife and squealed when her hips were grabbed.

"Gotcha!"

Amanda fell across Lex's chest. "Faker!" She started laughing when Lex's hand slipped under her shirt. "Stop it."

"Nope. I've got you now."

Their laughter was loud enough to bring in both girls, who raced into the room and immediately climbed onto the bed. Both were careful to keep off of Eddie, but happily joined Lex in tickling Amanda.

"Stop, please!" Amanda begged, unable to breathe.

Her family had mercy and ceased their attack. Amanda fell across Lex in exhaustion. "Three against one isn't fair," she muttered.

"But it was fun, Mommy," Melanie said.

Lex gently poked Melanie in the stomach. "It was, wasn't it? Thanks for your help."

Lorrie sat at the top of the bed and petted Eddie on the head. "I think Eddie wanted to play too, Momma."

"I'm sure he did, sweetheart. And one of these days, when he's bigger, he's going to be right in the middle of things." Lex helped Amanda stand before she sat up.

"Thanks, honey." Amanda perched at the foot of the bed. "Are you girls finished playing?"

Lorrie looked at Melanie. "I hope so. Can Mel sleep with me tonight? We want to have a sleepover."

"You do?" Amanda knew as well as Lex that although Lorrie loved her little sister, she rarely initiated such things. "Why?"

Lorrie shrugged her shoulders and looked down. "Just 'cause."

"I wanted to and Lorrie said I could," Melanie said. "We're going to read with flashlights under the covers." Each of them had a flashlight in their nightstands, in case of a power outage.

Lex bit off a smile. "Why do you want to read under the covers?"

"'Cause Teddy says it's fun." Melanie climbed onto Lex's legs. "Can we Momma? Please?"

"What do you think, Mommy? Should we let them?" Lex asked Amanda.

Amanda tapped her chin. "Hmm. I don't know. How late will you be reading?"

"Not long," Lorrie promised.

"All right." Amanda grabbed Melanie before she could jump up and down on Lex. "Settle down. You two go get in your pajamas, and we'll be there in a few minutes."

Melanie hopped off Lex. "Okay!" She waved at Lorrie. "Come on, Lorrie."

With a long-suffering groan, Lorrie got off the bed and followed her. "I get to pick the book," she called after Melanie.

Eddie started to cry, so Lex picked him up. "What's the matter? Did you want to go with your sisters?" He stopped crying as soon as Lex spoke.

Amanda crawled up to sit next to her. "Poor thing. I have a feeling he'll be trailing after them both in no time."

"Probably." It only took a moment of Lex rocking Eddie in her arms to get him to relax, and he peered up at her and kicked his feet. "I wonder who he'll take after? Will he tag along after Lorrie, or will Melanie be his hero?"

"Well," Amanda put her head on Lex's shoulder and looked at him, "if he's anything like his sisters, he'll probably think his Momma is the greatest thing in the world. Not that I can blame them, since I feel the same way."

Lex's face flushed. "Amanda."

"Sorry, honey. But it's true." Amanda pulled back and ran a finger down Lex's reddened cheek. "You're such a good mom, and our kids are so lucky to have you in their lives. Even your brother realized what a special person you are."

"It's great having him in our lives in a positive way," Lex said. She kissed Eddie on the head. "And I'll never be able to thank him enough for this gift."

Amanda gently cupped Eddie's head. "If I had put in an order for a baby, he would have fit perfectly. He looks so much like you."

"Yeah, poor kid."

"Let's go check on the girls. I think Eddie's about ready to go down for the night." Amanda stood and held out her hands. "My turn."

Lex gave up Eddie. "I can carry him, you know."

"Not yet. Remember what the doctor said. 'No lifting for at least a month.' You've still got a good week or two to go." Amanda gave her the sweetest smile she could. "I promise as soon as you're allowed to, I'll gladly hand him over."

"Uh-huh." Lex got off the bed and straightened her clothes. "I'm a little worried about the girls. They're too quiet."

Amanda laughed. "That's always a warning sign with them, isn't it?" She headed down the hall and looked into Lorrie's room.

The only light in the room came from two flashlights. The red flashlight was lying on the floor beside the bed, and the blue flashlight was still in Lorrie's grip, only she was sound asleep.

"That's just too cute," Amanda whispered. "I guess all the excitement of the day finally hit them."

Lex stepped into the room and turned on the nightlight next to the bed. She picked up the red flashlight and turned it off, before carefully removing the light from Lorrie's hand. After placing both flashlights on the dresser, Lex covered up the girls and kissed each of them on the head. "Sleep well. We love you," she whispered.

Amanda watched as Lex tucked them in for the night. "See, Eddie? Every night, your Momma will kiss you goodnight and make sure you have good dreams." She smiled at Lex when she came out of the room. "All done?"

"Yep." Lex kissed Amanda on the lips. "Ready to head to our room?"

"Most definitely."

While Amanda put Eddie down for the night, Lex turned back the covers on the bed. She opened the drawer of her nightstand and took out a small, brightly wrapped box.

"What's that?" Amanda asked as she climbed onto the bed.

"Your last Christmas gift." Lex sat on the bed and held out the box.

Amanda took the box and looked at it from all angles. "What is it?"

"Open it and see."

Carefully peeling the paper away, Amanda noticed the jeweler's name on top of the box. "Lex."

"Go on."

Amanda slowly opened the box. Nestled in blue velvet was a gold ring with three stones: an opal, a diamond, and a sapphire between the two. "It's beautiful. The children's birthstones?" She held the box out to Lex. "Put it on me, please?"

Lex grinned and brought the ring out of the box. She took Amanda's right hand and kissed her ring finger, before slipping the ring on. Once it was in place, Lex kissed the ring as it rested on Amanda's finger. "It's actually from Eddie, but he was too small to give it to you."

"I love it." Amanda leaned forward and kissed Lex. "I love you." She put the box and wrapping paper on her nightstand and got under the covers. When Lex got comfortable, Amanda snuggled down beside her and put her arm over Lex's stomach.

"Love you too." Lex turned off the lamp on her nightstand and turned to put both arms around Amanda. "Sleep well, sweetheart."

Amanda closed her eyes and listened to Lex's heartbeat. "I always do," she murmured. She fell asleep to Lex's gentle stroking of her hair, and the feeling of being loved and protected for life.

Other Carrie Carr titles published by
Yellow Rose Books

LEX AND AMANDA SERIES

Destiny's Bridge - Rancher Lexington (Lex) Walters pulls young Amanda Cauble from a raging creek and the two women quickly develop a strong bond of friendship. Overcoming severe weather, cattle thieves, and their own fears, their friendship deepens into a strong and lasting love.

Faith's Crossing - Lexington Walters and Amanda Cauble withstood raging floods, cattle rustlers and other obstacles to be together...but can they handle Amanda's parents? When Amanda decides to move to Texas for good, she goes back to her parents' home in California to get the rest of her things, taking the rancher with her.

Hope's Path - Someone is determined to ruin Lex. Efforts to destroy her ranch lead to attempts on her life. Lex and Amanda desperately try to find out who hates Lex so much that they are willing to ruin the lives of everyone in their path. Can they survive long enough to find out who's responsible? And will their love survive when they find out who it is?

Love's Journey - Lex and Amanda embark on a new journey as Lexington rediscovers the love her mother's family has for her, and Amanda begins to build her relationship with her father. Meanwhile, attacks on the two young women grow more violent and deadly as someone tries to tear apart the love they share.

Strength of the Heart - Lex and Amanda are caught up in the planning of their upcoming nuptials while trying to get the ranch house rebuilt. But an arrest, a brushfire, and the death of someone close to her forces Lex to try and work through feelings of guilt and anger. Is Amanda's love strong enough to help her, or will Lex's own personal demons tear them apart?

The Way Things Should Be - In this, the sixth novel, Amanda begins to feel her own biological clock ticking while her sister prepares for the birth of her first child. Lex is busy with trying to keep her hands on some newly acquired land, as well trying to get along with a new member of her family. Everything comes to a head, and a tragedy brings pain — and hope — to them all.

To Hold Forever - Three years have passed since Lex and Amanda took over the care of Lorrie, their rambunctious niece. Amanda's sister, Jeannie, has fully recovered from her debilitating stroke and returns with her fiancé, ready to start their own family. Attempts to become pregnant have been unsuccessful for Amanda. Meanwhile, a hostile new relative who resents everything about Lex shows up. Add in Lex's brother Hubert getting paroled and an old adversary returning with more than a simple reunion in mind and Lex begins to have doubts about continuing to run the ranch she's worked so hard to build.

Something To Be Thankful For

Randi Meyers is at a crossroads in her life. She's got no girlfriend, bad knees, and her fill of loneliness. The one thing she does have in her favor is a veterinarian job in Fort Worth, Texas, but even that isn't going as well as she hoped. Her supervisor is cold-hearted and dumps long hours of work on her. Even if she did want a girlfriend, she has little time to look.

When a distant uncle dies, Randi returns to her hometown of Woodbridge, Texas, to attend the funeral. During the graveside services, she wanders away from the crowd and is beseeched by a young boy to follow him into the woods to help his injured sister. After coming upon an unconscious woman, the boy disappears. Randi brings the woman to the hospital and finds out that her name is Kay Newcombe.

Randi is intrigued by Kay. Who is this unusual woman? Where did her little brother disappear to? And why does Randi feel compelled to help her? Despite living in different cities, a tentative friendship forms, but Randi is hesitant. Can she trust her newfound friend? How much of her life and feelings can Randi reveal? And what secrets is Kay keeping from her? Together, Randi and Kay must unravel these questions, trust one another, and find the answers in order to protect themselves from outside threats — and discover what they mean to one another.

ISBN 978-1-932300-04-8

Diving Into The Turn

Diving Into the Turn is set in the fast-paced Texas rodeo world. Riding bulls in the rodeo is the only life Shelby Fisher has ever known. She thinks she's happy drifting from place to place in her tiny trailer, engaging in one night stands, and living from one rodeo paycheck to another – until the day she meets barrel racer Rebecca Starrett. Rebecca comes from a solid, middle-class background and owns her horse. She's had money and support that Shelby has never had. Shelby and Rebecca take an instant dislike to each other, but there's something about Rebecca that draws the silent and angry bull rider to her. Suddenly, Shelby's life feels emptier, and she can't figure out why. Gradually, Rebecca attempts to win Shelby over, and a shaky friendship starts to grow into something more.

Against a backdrop of mysterious accidents that happen at the rodeo grounds, their attraction to one another is tested. When Shelby is implicated as the culprit to what's been happening will Rebecca stand by her side?

ISBN 978-1-932300-54-3

Piperton

Sam Hendrickson has been traveling around the Southwest for ten years, never staying in one place long enough to call it home. Doing odd jobs to pay for her food and gas, she thinks her life is fine, until fate intervenes. On her way to Dallas to find work for the upcoming winter, her car breaks down in the small town of Piperton. Sam's never concerned herself over what other people think, but the small minds of a West Texas town may be more than she bargained for—especially when she meets Janie Clarke. Janie's always done what's expected of her. But when she becomes acquainted with Sam, she's finally got a reason to rebel.

ISBN 978-1-935053-20-0

COMING SOON

Heart's Resolve

Gibson Proctor, a Park Police Officer for the Texas Department of Parks & Wildlife, has returned after twenty years to the rural area she once called home. She's able to easily adapt to the slower pace of the farming communities that surround the town of Benton, Texas, and tries her best to handle the expectations of her family, as well. Gib's comfortable existence is set into a tailspin when she unwittingly offends Delaney Kavanagh, the fiery-tempered architect who's in charge of repairing the spillway at Lake Kichai.

Although Delaney is currently in a relationship, she can't seem to get the amiable officer out of her mind. Not used to the type of attention she receives from the chivalrous woman, Delaney keeps waiting for the "real" Gib to show up. Will she ever accept Gib's acts of kindness as truth, or will she be content to stay in a relationship where she has to fight for everything?

Available May 2012

Other Yellow Rose Titles You Might Enjoy:

The Other Mrs. Champion
by Brenda Adcock

Sarah Champion, 55, of Massachusetts, was leading the perfect life with Kelley, her partner and wife of twenty-five years. That is, until Kelley was struck down by an unexpected stroke away from home. But Sarah discovers she hadn't known her partner and lover as well as she thought.

Accompanied by Kelley's long-time friend and attorney, Sarah and her children rush to Vancouver, British Columbia to say their goodbyes, only to discover another woman, Pauline, keeping a vigil over Kelley in the hospital. Confronted by the fact that her wife also has a Canadian wife, Sarah struggles to find answers to resolve her emotional and personal turmoil.

Alone and lonely, Sarah turns to the only other person who knew Kelley as well as she did-Pauline Champion. Will the two women be able to forge a friendship despite their simmering animosity? Will their growing attraction eventually become Kelley's final gift to the women she loved?

ISBN 978-1-935053-46-0

Love Another Day
by Regina A. Hanel

Plagued by nightmares and sleepless nights after a tragic loss, Park Ranger Samantha Takoda Tyler longs for a calm day at Grand Teton National Park in Wyoming. But when she's summoned to the chief ranger's office and introduced to Halie Walker, a photojournalist working for The Wild International, her day is anything but calm. When she's assigned to look after Halie, their meeting transforms into a quarrelsome exchange. Over time, the initial chill between the women warms. They grow closer as they spend time together and gain appreciation for each other's work.

But Sam's fear of loss coupled with rising jealousy over an old lover's interest in Halie grinds their budding relationship to a halt. Halie finds that anywhere near Sam is too painful a place to be, and Sam is unable to find the key to open the door to a past that she's purposely kept locked away.

With fires raging out West and in the Targhee National Forest, Sam works overtime, helping fill the staffing shortage. She misses Halie and wants to take a chance with her. Before she gets the opportunity to explain herself, Sam learns the helicopter Halie is on has crashed. Ahead of an oncoming storm, Sam races to the rescue. Can she save the woman she loves? Or will the past replay, closing Sam off from love forever?

ISBN 978-1-935053-44-6

OTHER YELLOW ROSE PUBLICATIONS

Brenda Adcock	Soiled Dove	978-1-935053-35-4
Brenda Adcock	The Sea Hawk	978-1-935053-10-1
Brenda Adcock	The Other Mrs. Champion	978-1-935053-46-0
Janet Albert	Twenty-four Days	978-1-935053-16-3
Janet Albert	A Table for Two	978-1-935053-27-9
Georgia Beers	Thy Neighbor's Wife	1-932300-15-5
Georgia Beers	Turning the Page	978-1-932300-71-0
Carrie Brennan	Curve	978-1-932300-41-3
Carrie Carr	Destiny's Bridge	1-932300-11-2
Carrie Carr	Faith's Crossing	1-932300-12-0
Carrie Carr	Hope's Path	1-932300-40-6
Carrie Carr	Love's Journey	978-1-932300-65-9
Carrie Carr	Strength of the Heart	978-1-932300-81-9
Carrie Carr	The Way Things Should Be	978-1-932300-39-0
Carrie Carr	To Hold Forever	978-1-932300-21-5
Carrie Carr	Trust Our Tomorrows	978-1-61929-011-2
Carrie Carr	Piperton	978-1-935053-20-0
Carrie Carr	Something to Be Thankful For	1-932300-04-X
Carrie Carr	Diving Into the Turn	978-1-932300-54-3
Cronin and Foster	Blue Collar Lesbian Erotica	978-1-935053-01-9
Cronin and Foster	Women in Uniform	978-1-935053-31-6
Pat Cronin	Souls' Rescue	978-1-935053-30-9
Anna Furtado	The Heart's Desire	1-932300-32-5
Anna Furtado	The Heart's Strength	978-1-932300-93-2
Anna Furtado	The Heart's Longing	978-1-935053-26-2
Melissa Good	Eye of the Storm	1-932300-13-9
Melissa Good	Hurricane Watch	978-1-935053-00-2
Melissa Good	Red Sky At Morning	978-1-932300-80-2
Melissa Good	Storm Surge: Book One	978-1-935053-28-6
Melissa Good	Storm Surge: Book Two	978-1-935053-39-2
Melissa Good	Thicker Than Water	1-932300-24-4
Melissa Good	Terrors of the High Seas	1-932300-45-7
Melissa Good	Tropical Storm	978-1-932300-60-4
Melissa Good	Tropical Convergence	978-1-935053-18-7
Regina A. Hanel	Love Another Day	978-1-935053-44-6
Maya Indigal	Until Soon	978-1-932300-31-4
Lori L. Lake	Different Dress	1-932300-08-2
Lori L. Lake	Ricochet In Time	1-932300-17-1
Lori L. Lake	Like Lovers Do	978-1-935053-66-8
K. E. Lane	And, Playing the Role of Herself	978-1-932300-72-7
Helen Macpherson	Love's Redemption	978-1-935053-04-0
J. Y Morgan	Learning To Trust	978-1-932300-59-8
J. Y. Morgan	Download	978-1-932300-88-8
A. K. Naten	Turning Tides	978-1-932300-47-5
Lynne Norris	One Promise	978-1-932300-92-5
Linda S. North	The Dreamer, Her Angel, and the Stars	978-1-935053-45-3
Paula Offutt	Butch Girls Can Fix Anything	978-1-932300-74-1
Surtees and Dunne	True Colours	978-1-932300-529
Surtees and Dunne	Many Roads to Travel	978-1-932300-55-0

Vicki Stevenson	Family Affairs	978-1-932300-97-0
Vicki Stevenson	Family Values	978-1-932300-89-5
Vicki Stevenson	Family Ties	978-1-935053-03-3
Vicki Stevenson	Certain Personal Matters	978-1-935053-06-4
Cate Swannell	Heart's Passage	978-1-932300-09-3
Cate Swannell	No Ocean Deep	978-1-932300-36-9

About the Author

Carrie calls herself a "true Texan." She was born in the Lone Star State in the early sixties and has never lived outside of it. Currently a resident of the Dallas-Fort Worth Metroplex, she lives with her partner of 10+ years whom she legally married in Toronto in September 2003.

As a technical school graduate and a quiet introvert, publishing her fiction—lesbian-based books—was something she never expected. She says, "Living on a farm probably influenced me the most because I had to use my imagination for recreation. I made up stories for myself, and my only regret is that I didn't save the ones I had written down and hidden away when I was growing up." Her writing also brought Carrie her greatest joy—her wife, Jan, who wrote her when she posted *Destiny's Bridge* online. They've been together since 1999.

She has written eight books in the Lex & Amanda series. Carrie has also published three stand-alone romances. She has just finished the first draft of her fourth, *Heart's Resolve*, which will soon be available from Regal Crest Enterprises.

Carrie's website is: www.CarrieLCarr.com

VISIT US ONLINE AT
www.regalcrest.biz

At the Regal Crest Website You'll Find

- The latest news about forthcoming titles and new releases

- Our complete backlist of romance, mystery, thriller and adventure titles

- Information about your favorite authors

- Current bestsellers

Regal Crest print titles are available from all progressive booksellers including numerous sources online. Our distributors are Bella Distribution and Ingram.